BOSS FROM HELL

Boss from Hell

LAURIE BELL

Boss from Hell
ISBN:978-0-6455747-2-2
Cover design by Pat Naoum, Red Tally Studios
Publishing services by Mark Furness, Liquorice Light Publishing

ABOUT LAURIE BELL

Boss from Hell is Laurie Bell's sixth novel.

Laurie lives in Victoria, Australia with her partner who she adores. As a sci-fi aficionado, she maintains an active blog of science fiction, fantasy, and flash fiction pieces (found at www.solothefirst.wordpress.com) and serves as a volunteer for her local theater company. She has had several short stories published in the *Antipodean SF* e-magazine on www.antisf.com and in the *Etherea* magazine. And of course she has many new books on the go.

DEDICATION

For Janet and Margaret.
My A-Team.

Chapter 1

My left arm is tingling. Cold office air presses down on my skin like a damp wetsuit, heaviest around my chest. *I'm having a heart attack.* My best friend, Elisa, warned me to be careful this week. Her spirit guides told her something bad was going to happen and here it is—happening.

Glancing into the outer room beyond the frosted glass of Jack's office, I expect to find a slew of curious faces gawking at me. No one even looks my way.

My back aches. I *am* having a heart attack.

I'm probably not, but I *am* in shock.

"I'm sorry, what?" I repeat.

"Margaret, incorrect data is not something I can take lightly and . . ." Jack's ruddy complexion is darker than usual and sweat beads the edges of his cropped, silver-speckled hair. The stale cigarette smell that hangs in a perpetual cloud around him doesn't usually bother me, but now it turns my stomach.

"I'm . . . *fired?*"

He scrubs a hand through his hair. "Margaret, you have to understand—"

"Understand what?"

"The data entered—"

"I told you. It was on the form. I entered what was written."

"The form we cannot find?"

Fury fights with disbelief. *This is Toby's doing.* He gave me the forms. It was his understaffed team that needed help, so of course I assisted. He's the only one who knows what was on the original file. He did this. "Jack, Toby knew—"

"Margaret, it is out of my hands. Without the file to prove what you're saying, I . . . I'm sorry."

He thought I'd made a mistake—an astronomical one—and the client lost money as a result. Unforgiveable. Fireable.

I press my damp palms to the table surface. There's no response I can give that's worth articulating. *Oh my God. My new house.* My mortgage payments are astronomical. Without a job . . .

I moved in a few weeks ago. It's a small house, tiny really, but it's all mine, along with a shiny new giant-sized mortgage. And now—no job. *What am I going to do?*

I glare at Jack. My boss. Ex-boss.

"Jack, you know how I've been stressing about my house payments. I worked all those extra hours." I tilt forward, digging my elbows into the surface of Jack's black-stained wooden conference table, and grip the back of my neck. The muscles there are rock-hard.

My mind darts back to Elisa's call and her premonition something bad was coming. I'd brushed it off like I always do, despite her history of always being right, and I'd had those terrible stomach cramps last night that kept me from sleeping.

Jeez, Mig. Always listen to Elisa.

I give myself that lecture every few weeks.

Pulling air into my lungs until they're full, I rub a hand against my chest. Everything is tight. There's not a lot to look at in Jack's office but I need a distraction or I'm going to lose my shit. Austere colors. Desk, chair, computer. Nothing I can focus on, so I stare at the boat picture hanging on his wall. "Rich people like boats," I'd told him when I picked it out. He'd wanted a golf picture.

My career plays back in my head like I'm watching a streaming episode catch-up. *Last week on Margaret Solder's life . . .*

I'd started in the admin pool, got promoted to Jack Keet's personal assistant, and basically became his work wife, on-call at all hours. I'd even shopped for his wife's birthday present last week. Five years of loyal service, and for what?

I'll have to rent out my place. Move back in with Mom and Dad. Won't they be happy about that!

Jack pushes his chair out and stretches his legs beside me. I focus on his feet and his favorite shoes. White snakeskin. They look ridiculous. "Margaret—"

"I helped your son with his exams," I blurt out. Nausea hits me like a truck. *How can you do this to me?*

I need a plan. If I have a step-by-step checklist, I can hold my fear at bay for a while. Obviously, step one is to find a new job. "How long do I have? Four weeks, as stated in my contract? Will you give me time off for interviews?"

Jack lifts his cell phone to check the time. *Gee, Jack, I'm sorry my freak-out about you imploding my life is wasting your precious time.*

I still can't believe this is happening.

His gaze shifts from the phone to the table and his fingers rap against the wood. *Tap tap tap.*

Oh no. I've seen that tell before; specifically on the night he'd admitted to cheating on his wife. Firing me isn't the worst news he has. "Jack, what is it?"

"Because of your access levels to sensitive client information, we . . . uh . . . I have to escort you from the building today."

My heart sinks. "What?"

I hadn't made a mistake. I don't make those kinds of mistakes. I'm really meticulous when it comes to figures. I double-check everything before I hit submit. The missing form would prove that. This is Toby's doing. It has to be. I'm swinging from anger to sadness to shock and back like a carnival ride, unable to focus on any one thought for too long.

Mom and Dad are going to be so disappointed.

I am frozen at the meeting table as Jack saunters to his desk and plops his heavy body down in his expensive ergonomic chair. The seat squeaks in protest. Jack's habits are ingrained so I know without looking that he'll check his email first. Two fingers peck hungrily at the keyboard as if nothing has changed between us.

Fighting back tears, I stare around his office again. Framed photographs face out from his desk; he needs everyone to be impressed with his perfect family. The Hawaii photo is the most prominent, golf club in hand, giant grin on his face. Who goes to Hawaii just to play golf?

Jack's keyboard poking slows then stops. I feel his stare and look up. Cold jade eyes meet mine and hold. He looks away first. I twist my fingers together under the table where he can't see them.

I need time to process this. *This is so unfair.* I focus on that. It *is* unfair. An unfair dismissal. I can raise this . . . fight it. The thought disappears as quickly as it occurred. *Don't be silly, Mig. HR protect the company first.* Besides, if I fight this decision and, against all odds, actually win, it would be unbearable returning to work for Jack anyway. How can I work for someone who doesn't trust me? Who I can't trust to have my back?

No, I won't fight it. But I do need a plan.

"You'll have to pack your stuff." His voice is kinder than I've ever heard it. "I don't do soft shit, Margaret," he'd once told me, so it feels like an even bigger slap in the face to hear him play nice now.

I will not cry here. I straighten my back and thrust out my chin. Who cares what he thinks.

I snatch a tissue from the dispenser on the table, staring at the scented white square. He put a tissue box on his table instead of the usual candy jar.

I wipe my eyes and blow my nose with the damp tissue. "I take it you have to watch me pack?"

The next ten minutes are the most horrendous of my life. I work hard to avoid looking at my colleagues as I gather my belongings. Surely they didn't believe I could make such a horrible mistake?

I leave all my work devices on my desk. Laptop, work-issued cell phone, tablet, laptop bag, chargers. It feels like amputating a limb. I even leave my coffee mug. The one Jack gave me last Christmas. The *Best Administrator—as long as I have coffee!* message is a taunt I can't face today. As I pass Robert and Steve, it occurs to me I won't see them again. My heart clenches when people I've known for years don't look up as I pass. I've seen it all before. That awkward moment when someone in the team gets fired and is led away. I get it. I've done it too. The uncomfortable what-can-I-say? feeling, the weird sense of relief that it's not you. I just never expected it to *be* me.

I stop at Becky's desk automatically, as I always do for a gossip on my way to get coffee. "Good luck with the wedding, Bec."

"I'm so sorry, Mig," she whispers, shooting a glance at Jack like she's scared he'll catch her being nice to me.

"Watch out for Toby."

She nods. I float outside on clouds of uncertainty.

When I next glance up, I'm on the train home. The carriage is busy. The midmorning demographics are different to the peak-hour ones I'm used to. Uni students carry backpacks, parents rock prams and shift workers look exhausted. It's louder too. People in peak hour usually keep to themselves. Passengers here are talking. I don't like it.

I clutch my almost empty backpack tighter to my chest. Normally, if I manage to get a seat, I use the ride home to work on my screenplay, my secret little dream. I haven't told anyone

I'm doing it because it's far too fanciful for my pragmatic family. My love of movies has led to a desire to write one, and I have a great concept. A detective story-slash-western, set in space. It's fun getting lost in my imagination but I'd be embarrassed if anyone ever found out. It's not like it's a viable career. Just something silly for me to pass the time with on public transport. Right now, I can't stomach the idea of it. *Too frivolous.*

Reality has punched me in the stomach and it hurts. I stare, unfocused, through the grubby window at the multi-colored concrete and the vehicles and foliage that blur past in a mockery of my current mental state. Chimes break the silence, like a lone crow cawing. Only an hour ago, things had been so, so—

"Honey, I think that's your phone."

I need a plan. I snatch my notebook out of my backpack and start a list. First, I have to update my resume and business social media profile. A tap on my arm jerks me around to glare at the offender sitting beside me. "What?"

Two caramel eyes widen as a woman in nurse's scrubs and a brown overcoat flinches back, her hands flying up to prevent an attack. Her startled look becomes a glare of her own. "Your phone is ringing."

"What?" The chimes sound again. "Oh." I bite my lip. "I'm sorry. I don't . . . I'm not . . ."

The woman sniffs and twists her body away from me. Heat and ice go to war inside my body, a battle neither wins. My skin is both clammy and sweaty. I've been in a sauna and it feels much the same way. Blinking back tears that sit too close to the surface, I groan at another chime. What if it's Mom? I clear my throat and wipe a hand over my face to stay present. It's probably Elisa calling to ask what's happened. She'll know. She always knows. I don't know why I'm so skeptical of her abilities. It's just . . . come *on*. Witch ancestors? Magic, witchcraft, telling the future? Madness. I come from a family of engineers and teachers. Practical people. We don't do mystical.

Well, except my grandmothers. But they're a different bags of nuts.

When my bag stops jiggling, I suck in a breath and wrench the zipper back to grab my personal cell phone. *My only cell phone now.* Tears threaten again. I moan at the notification message: *Grandma Berry.*

I can't call my grandmother back or even listen to her message until I know my voice won't crack. She always tells me not to trust anyone. She's so right.

The plastic case creaks under the pressure of my fingers. While my phone is in my hand, I jump onto my business social media profile and click the button that says *looking for a job.* I complete the prompts and update my skills and experience. Then I jump onto the employment websites and set up alerts for admin positions. I loosen my grip on the phone and leave it sitting on top of my bag. My unfocused gaze finds the window again, and my mind puts up a vacant sign. I let myself have the moment and then shake my head. *Come on, Mig. Stop feeling so damn sorry for yourself. Get organized.* I jot down a few resume updates. I'll do a deeper search on the employment websites tonight and start applying. With luck, I'll get a job within weeks. At least a temp job to keep me going. I might only need Mom and Dad's financial help once.

I flip my phone over and it rings in my hand, an unknown number.

"Hello?" If this is a robocall to sell me insurance or someone claiming to be from the tax office, I'm going to scream—to hell with what the strangers on the train think.

"Good morning. Am I speaking to Ms. Solder?"

I close my eyes, inwardly sighing. *I'm not in the right headspace for this.* "Look, whatever you're selling—"

"Ms. Solder, I apologize if I have caught you at a bad time."

"You have." On my best days I don't react well to people cutting me off. And today is not my best day. "I'm not—"

"Ms. Solder, I spotted your updates and availability change on your profile. We are urgently searching for a personal assistant. Executive-level. As you are based in Melbourne, perhaps you might be interested in applying?" The woman speaks fast and her voice is a little too sharp. It takes me a minute to realize what she's saying.

"I'm sorry?"

"I know this call is a little out of the blue, Ms. Solder, but would you—"

"Are you offering me a job interview? Which agency are you from?"

"Fair Dinkum Recruiting. My apologies, Ms. Solder, I don't think I even introduced myself. My name is Paula Najee. I saw the recent updates to your social media and have reviewed your listed skills and experience. I believe you fit the criteria we are looking for. You mentioned you are available for immediate start, is that correct?"

"You said the role is urgent?" To my own ears, my voice is high and uneven. Have I really been lucky enough to be headhunted on the same day I was fired? I rub a hand over my breastbone. My heart is pounding like I've just run a marathon.

Ms. Najee inhales deeply. "A client has approached us looking for an experienced executive assistant to start immediately. It's an excellent package. Are you asking because you might be interested?"

I nod, but she can't see that over the phone. My gaze flies to the window and I clear my throat. "I could be interested. When would they want to interview?" She says something, but I'm too busy obsessing about my tone to hear it—do I sound too squeaky and desperate? "Could you repeat that?"

"The client would like to interview straightaway. Would this afternoon be acceptable?"

If I could have jumped in my seat, I would have. The strong sense of propriety, drilled in by Mom over the years, stops me —just. Still, I do bounce a little. Sensing a judgmental stare, I glance at the woman beside me. She's watching my twitching leg. I cover the phone's microphone and mouth. "Sorry." She turns away, but not before I catch sight of her eyeroll. Ten minutes ago, it might have bothered me. Now, it reflects off my mental shields without leaving a dent. "Just to confirm—your client is based in the city? Uh, in the Melbourne CBD?"

Her voice takes on a lighter tone and she speaks quickly. "Oh, yes. Their office is in Bellbird Tower. That's where the interview will take place."

Wow. I pass Bellbird Tower on my lunch walk every day. It's brand spanking new and reportedly has magnificent views from every window. "What can you tell me about the company?"

Ms. Najee clears her throat. "To be honest, Ms. Solder, the client only joined us today. We haven't completed our usual checks on Bacitriet Consulting. Of course, we could help each other out if you succeed in securing this role. It would certainly be a lovely client for us to have on our books."

Oh, how nice. I'm the bait to hook a whale. Well, I need a job, so I don't argue. I can research the company as soon we hang up.

"What time is the interview?"

"Can you do four p.m.?"

A grin breaks out across my face. I nod at my reflection in the train window. "Yes, I can do that."

"Reception is located on the forty-second floor. Ask for Mr. Bacitriet. Good luck, Ms. Solder. I'll send the details of the position and the interview through to the email listed on your profile."

I confirm my email and end the call. A soft *whoop* escapes my mouth. Shifting bags beside me draws my attention to the nurse. She pointedly ignores me. I don't take offense. Not now.

My luck has changed in a big way, and I can't shake the smile off my face.

The nurse stands up. Her back cracks and she winces. The train slows as it approaches the next station. *Tooronga.*

"Oh crap!" I blurt.

I'm on the wrong train.

Chapter 2

Waiting for the train back to the Richmond interchange gives me plenty of time to research Bacitriet Consulting on my phone. The company website is bright and colorful with lots of high-resolution photographs of offices and city landscapes. I can't find any staff photos, and there's only a generic reception contact. The company description states Bacitriet Consulting is a hands-on, client-focused firm. Well, that doesn't tell me a lot.

It's not even midday yet, and so much has happened. My skin is still a little clammy. I figure I'm in shock. I need chocolate and I don't have any in my bag.

Though Melbourne is heading into winter, the sky is clear, and the sun makes itself known against my face. I unzip my coat and check the platform display. The next train is expected in four minutes.

I have trouble hitting the call button on my cell but when I finally manage it, Dad answers on the second ring. "All set for tonight?"

"Hi, Dad. I have to cancel the party."

"What? Why? What happened?"

"Dad, can I . . ." Suppressing a cough, I wander along the uneven asphalt and concrete of the platform. I hate giving Dad bad news, and telling him I've just lost my job is the worst kind of news. I breathe deep and spit it all out in one go.

It's a while before I stop talking. The silence stretches interminably and the stopwatch in my head becomes a grandfather clock, each tick pounding my body like it is bread dough.

"What do you need? Money?"

Mom and Dad are happily retired. They've paid off their house but they don't exactly have a lot of cash to flash and always budget carefully. They were super excited when I moved out. I know I was at home longer than they'd expected but they're proud of what I've accomplished. I can't let them down. I'm an adult. I can sort this out.

"Actually, Dad, if you can believe it, I already have a job interview."

"Really?" His voice is suddenly a lot lighter.

"Yeah, but they want me to come in tonight."

There's another pause. "Right, so the party is off. No problems. I'll call Andy and your grandmothers. Your mom and I will pop round tomorrow instead."

I hadn't realized how hard it was to breathe until he said that. "Well, since I'm not working . . . yeah, tomorrow is perfect. I'll call Elisa." Turning thirty-four is not that big of a deal, right? My brother, Andy, won't mind the last-minute cancelation but I know my grandmothers were looking forward to seeing my new place. I hate to put them off. They'll be round on the weekend now, guaranteed. I'd better get some stuff for afternoon tea.

I sag onto a peeling dark green-painted metal bench and listen to a kookaburra laugh in the distance. I glare at the gum tree harboring the winged devil. *Rude.*

"Thanks, Dad." Hopefully the train pulling into the station hides the quaver in my voice. "I might not get the job, though. Or I might not like the boss."

"All true."

"My train's coming. I'll tell you all about it when I see you tomorrow. I need to call Elisa."

"Take care, honey. See you soon."

"Love you, Dad." I step aboard the second-last carriage. This train will return me to Richmond, where I can catch my actual train home. I glance through the scratched window and remind myself to pay attention to the stations this time.

Pressing down on my bouncing knee to still it, I watch suburb after suburb zoom by. I've always taken the train to work. The population in Victoria changes constantly; you can see it in the way the inner suburbs have influenced those further out. It takes most of the train ride home before I see larger properties and trees instead of graffiti-covered concrete. Townhouses have jammed into what were once large single blocks, and the streets grow skinnier by the year. More fences and hedges have popped up too, as neighbors close themselves off from one another. A sign of the times.

I find Elisa's number and hit call. A weird smell penetrates my mental bubble and I examine the empty fabric-lined seats around me. *Gross.*

"Hey, sweets. Are you excited?" Elisa's happy voice takes my mind off the smell.

"I have had the worst day," I moan.

"Ooo, I told you. Remember I said there were bad signs around this week?"

I suppress a sigh. "Yeah, I remember."

"You trust me, right?"

"Since preschool." And isn't that something? Somehow, Elisa and I have remained friends through years of house moves, changed schools, and now her married-with-kids life. Her new-agey premonitions are part of the package that is my best friend. *I should listen to her more.* "The party is off."

"What? No! Frank's taking the twins bowling. I have the whole night free." The horror in her voice tells me she'd planned for a boozy evening. "What happened?"

I focus on the empty train seat in front of me. Foam padding has spewed from a frayed gash.

"I have a job interview."

There's a long silence over the line. "Where are you? It sounds like you're on a train."

"I got fired."

"WHAT?" I count silently, waiting for her to continue; I get to seven. "I *knew* it. I knew something bad was going to happen this week. I've been skittish all day. It was that Toby character, wasn't it? I told you I had a bad feeling about him. Surely you can contest this? It's got to be an unfair dismissal."

"The file I used for the data entry is missing, so I've got no proof. And even if I did win, how can I work for Jack after this? And Toby is still there. I think if I ever see that smug face of his again, I'd punch it and get fired anyway."

"Argh, this is so infuriating." I smile at the tone in her voice. This is just the support I needed. "Do you want me to do a reading? I have my tarot cards here."

"Maybe later? I'm freaking out. I just wanted to tell you about tonight. None of this was in my plan, you know?"

"I know. You have everything planned out for years to come. I don't know how you do it. If it helps, I don't feel like you'll be out of work for long. And remember, my last reading didn't bring up any money issues."

"I already have a job interview. Maybe it's meant to be?"

My friend huffs out a breath. "I'm not sure how I feel about that. Tell me what happened?"

I fiddle with the strap of my fake leather handbag as I tell her about the phone call. The black plasticky-rubber peels away under my fingers. "So you think I should go?"

I can hear her shuffling cards. "I didn't say that, exactly. Something feels . . . off. How did you get an interview so fast?"

What I'd imagined was a long story didn't turn out that way. I tell Elisa all about my morning as the train pulls into

Richmond. Ignoring the new bald patch on the strap, I shoulder my bag and hike my backpack over the top of it. I tug my jacket free from bunching under my armpits and stagger off the carriage, fighting the icy wind that tries to blow me back onto the train. "Damn, it's got cold all of a sudden." The sky is now a gloomy gray and the smell of rain hangs heavy in the air.

"So, to top it all off, you caught the wrong train?"

"Yep, quite the horror show."

"Honey, these days, anything can happen." The shadow cast by the long roof panels make the platform even chillier. I edge away, searching for even a miniscule bit of warmth. The platform display screen sets me grumbling further. Eleven minutes?

"What about the interview, have you heard of the company? Who will you be working for?"

"The recruitment agent said they're a new client so she didn't have many details to give me. I did a basic search but there's not much on them."

Elisa gives a long-thinking hum. "Well, it *could* be meant to be. Still, take care, okay? I'm coming over tonight after your interview. You can tell me how it went over a drink or two. Or three. It's still your birthday. We're celebrating. We have to invite all the good vibes in for the coming year."

Elisa's gift—at least, that's the way I think of it—is a way of seeing the truth, good or bad, via feelings, energy and auras. It's all a bit mumbo-jumbo but she's my best friend and I love her. Besides she's rarely wrong. About anything.

I grin. "If you do sense something, you will tell me, won't you?"

"Of course. Text me tonight after the interview and I'll pop right over."

I love the sound of that. "Will do." I disconnect our call and breathe hot air onto my icy fingers. Twin yellow lights appear in the distance, breaking through the gloom. *Finally!*

After another endless train trip, I walk what seems like the half mile to my car and plonk down in the driver's seat. I hesitate before putting the key into the ignition. *This is crazy. Why am I sad?* I shake my head. I have to focus on the coming interview, not on Jack's betrayal.

Next steps. Go home, freshen up and travel back into the city for the interview. Then come back home and—

My handbag jiggles on the wool-covered passenger seat. Welcoming the delay, I fish out my cell phone and check the screen. Grandma Berry. Nope. I can't talk to her just yet. I'll call her back later. She's probably with Grandma Rose, and who knows what crazy shenanigans they're getting up too. Hopefully, the call isn't to complain about the missed party tonight.

I let my phone ring for a moment and glance out through the car windshield, catching sight of a fluttering piece of paper jammed beneath the wiper blade. *No, no, no!* I spring out of the car, snatch up the offending paper and curse loudly. The number on the parking ticket appears to grow larger right before my eyes. "Oh, come on!"

Chapter 3

I like predictable. I like boring.

Changes I'm not prepared for discombobulate me, leaving me wrong-footed. I've got a plan—a five-year plan. I like to know what's coming and what I'm working toward. It's how I saved enough money in the first place to get a house—all on my own—and how I've gotten so proficient as an assistant. Getting fired was not in my plan.

Buying a house was supposed to be a smart commitment. Now I'm not so sure. I hadn't realized how fleeting stability can be. My old job is suddenly gone, and I'm in debt up to my hairline. If I don't get this new job, I'll come close to a meltdown. Damn Toby. I've never hated anyone more in my entire life. Even thinking about his smarmy face makes my teeth clench. Karma will get him one day. I'm sure of it. Though, just in case karma is busy, maybe I should get Elisa to put a whammy on him instead.

I rub my chest, feeling an ache in the muscles. *Come on, Mig. Push through.* I just have to tweak my plan—extend the timeline a little and factor in more unknown risk.

Tonight, I'll drink a toast to my last day at work and raise a glass to my new job. Well, fingers crossed. If I'm offered the job, I'll take it—no matter what the new boss is like. At least that way I'll have a steady pay-check coming in. I can worry about looking for a better job once the dust settles.

I find my laptop under my discarded dressing gown. Step one: freshen my resume. I'll have to impress my potential new boss with my updated skills. I can hand over a printout at the interview. The itch under my skin lessens with a clear step forward.

A gurgle from my stomach interrupts my plan.

I pull the leftover veggie soup from the fridge, heat it in the microwave and eat while checking my email. I go over the details from Ms. Najee again. After a quick shower, I dress in my interview suit. I suck in my belly. Damn. I pop the button on the waistband and tug my shirt out to cover my slightly lumpy hips. It'll do. I update and print my resume and jump back in the car. Before driving off, I stare at myself in the rear-view mirror. *You need this job, Mig.*

As always, I glance at the creepy house next door and a shiver runs down my spine. Though the house itself looks pretty normal—a single story brick veneer—it exudes menace. It makes me avoid going anywhere near the fence on that side. The curtains are closed and the shrubbery surrounding the house and the lawn is overgrown. *Bloody fire hazard.* I bet there are rats inside. I wish someone lived there; having a vacant property beside my own is a little spooky.

I flip on the radio and back out onto the road. Katy Perry comes on. I crank up the volume and sing along.

It's been five years since my last interview, but I know they are all about confidence. Working for Jack was the longest I've ever stayed in the one job. Prior to that, I only managed a year or two before boredom set in and I moved on. Working admin can be a bit of a curse. Once you learn what you need to know about a company, the work becomes a little same old, same old. It's great for people-watching though. My screenplay has benefited greatly from the different personalities I've met over the years.

I park closer to the station this time. Twisting the key off, I let a thick silence fill the car. All of my hopes are pinned to this interview. It's an insane amount of pressure. What if I don't get it? And it's not even the job interview filling me with doubts. I thought—no, I know—I'm good at my job, but . . . Jack fired me. Maybe . . . maybe I'm not as good as I think I am. Maybe I'm just . . . *Ugh*.

Back on the train, I continue my research into Brian Bacitriet. I get the same results as before—nada. How is it possible to not have any presence online in this day and age? Especially as a consultant.

The notepad I carry in my handbag to write down my story ideas allows me to jot down a list of average interview questions and brainstorm answers. It's a plan of a sort and helps to settle my nerves.

Before I know it, the train has returned me to the city. Bellbird Tower is a short walk from Southern Cross Station—an excellent point in favor of taking the job. Crowds are starting to thicken as rush hour approaches. I cross Collins Street at the tram stop. Though it's only quarter to four, the overcast May afternoon brings evening on quickly. The air is colder too. The Antarctic wind blasts off Port Phillip Bay, whipping down Collins Street from Docklands. I wrap my scarf tighter around my neck and zip my waist-length puffer jacket higher, halting at the loud *ding ding ding* of an oncoming tram. It rushes past me with a burst of air as commuters madly scramble to get off the tracks in time.

I love working in Melbourne. I wouldn't want to work anywhere else in the world. The streetlights are popping on already and cars are quickly turning Collins Street into a parking lot. It's going to be freezing tonight.

Nerves always make me desperate for the loo. I glance into a window as I pass and sigh at my wild hair. The problem with my natural waves is that they always spring in the wrong direction. I distract myself while I walk by going over my interview checklist. A decent pay package, easy to reach via public transport, and a good vibe from my boss. Point three is the big unknown. Elisa would say it's the most important, and she's not wrong. You want to respect the person you work for—or, at least I do. Still, no job means no money, and no money means I can't make the repayments on my mortgage. I can work for someone I don't like for a little while. Probably.

At this end of Collins Street, if I peer back over my shoulder I can see the Rialto, and at a right angle from there I can see Eureka Tower's golden top across the river sending beams of light across the city. I approach Bellbird Tower with plenty of time to spare and crick my neck staring up at the purple tinted windows stretching off into the clouds. I feel a little awestruck. Will I actually get to work here?

When I enter the lobby, I'm immediately drawn to a gigantic Aboriginal painting covering the entire back wall. The plaque reminds me that the Wurundjeri people of the Kulin Nation are the traditional owners and custodians of this land. Yellow, orange and red dotted colors create a dry desert landscape. It's a glorious warmth-evoking painting, and feels out of place in such a cold foyer. I tear my gaze from the artwork to peer around the spacious waiting area. A black-suited man with a buzz cut and frameless glasses stands at a rectangular reception desk at the end, with blue and gray couch chairs forming several rows in front of the elevator banks. I glance around for a public restroom but can't find any obvious signage. There's a shadowed corridor. I head in that direction and find what I'm looking for.

I use the bathroom quickly and examine my hair in the mirror. It's wild. Wispy waves dart off in all directions like I've touched one of those science balls in high school. I brush it out but I'm not hugely successful. I wet the strands and roll my eyes in the mirror.

My presence garners a strange look from the concierge as I return to the lobby. I'm early, so rather than approach the desk, I plonk myself down in one of the chairs to review my notes again.

I remove my puffer jacket and scarf and straighten my suit jacket, brushing a hand over my sleeves to check for dandruff or stray hairs. I'm fortunate that my interview suit had been clean. My usual work outfits are a bit like a uniform—black trousers that I can match with a range of business shirts. Today's is emerald. It brings out my eyes. Elisa loves it on me and it makes me feel confident. I need all the confidence I can get today.

After reviewing my notes, I shove my notepad deep into my bag and do a last compact mirror check. My eyes look a little red—if I sneeze, maybe I can claim I have hay fever? I sigh. Can I sneeze without it coming across as gross or contagious? We're paranoid enough these days and I always carry sanitizer in my handbag. I don't want to lose out on the job just because I look sickly.

The concierge approaches me with sharp clacking footsteps. His hand rises to his ear. *An earpiece?* "Ms. Solder?"

I jerk. "Yes?"

His erect posture relaxes infinitesimally. "You're expected on the forty-second floor."

Right then. I stand and hang my puffer jacket and scarf over my arm. "Okay, thank you." He hands me a visitor's pass and directs me to swipe onto the elevator.

The slow ride up increases my fears. I step out on the forty-second floor to a buzz of noise and several people rush past me to fill the elevator. Two receptionists sit behind a wall-length desk. Their sleek headsets are practically invisible, making it appear as though they're speaking to the air. Neither one looks up at my approach.

My footsteps slow. I'm unsure if I should take a seat or give them my name. Three high-backed crimson chairs look uninviting so I just hover. The reception area is gray with bursts of red, and the receptionists both wear dark red lipstick and perfect smoky-eye makeup. The blond straightens her soft-looking heart-covered scarf as her eyes narrow in my direction. The unwelcoming jolt makes me question taking the role. I don't have to work here . . . I can afford to wait, right? Maybe it will be okay if I don't succeed today.

"Who are you here to see, darl?" The dark-haired, dark-skinned receptionist has a husky voice like she's just recovered from a cold. I glance at the blond beside her. She stares back at me without blinking.

"I'm here to see Mr. Bacitriet."

The dark-haired receptionist's judgmental gaze roves up and down my body. I'm sure she knows my outfit is not designer label. "You must be Margaret Solder. We've been looking forward to seeing you. Take a seat. I'll give him a ring."

Her perfectly painted, crisp red nails gesture to the straight-backed chairs. *Darn.* I'd hoped to avoid sitting in one. As soon as I make contact, I find I'd been right to delay for as long as possible. The cushion feels carved out of wood. I shift and wriggle but nothing can make the chair any more comfortable. I cross my legs. My nerves make a reappearance and my left knee starts bouncing. I order myself to stop fidgeting and smooth my hands along my thighs to dry the sweat on my palms. You never know who is watching.

I glance at the receptionists again. They've barely moved. They are a little like two statues made of ice. Their chin-length hair is razor-straight and both wear white, fitted sleeveless dresses. Uncharitably, I wonder if the women were purchased at the same store. Discount for bulk orders perhaps? *Don't judge on appearance. They might be perfectly lovely.* Despite the effort, I can't help but cast them as aliens freshly arrived on Earth, unaccustomed to blending in with humans, and the thought makes me smile.

Cold air brushes my nape and silence falls on the room like a weighted blanket. My head snaps up as a shadow looms in the doorway to my left.

The man who steps forward is the total opposite of my ex-boss in every way, and it raises the hairs on my skin. Where Jack was in his mid-forties, short and a little rotund, this man, in his late sixties or early seventies, is tall, skeletally thin, like a deciduous tree in winter. Reception's low lighting creates shadows across his sharp nose and jutting cheekbones. I recoil very slightly as he stretches out a hand.

"Brian Bacitriet. You must be the woman I've been looking for."

My instinct is flight. Escape. I even glance toward the elevators—they're only a few steps away. I take a deep breath and stand up.

I need a job and this man, no matter how creepy he seems, might be just what saves me from defaulting on my home loan. I lock eyes with him as his hand closes around mine, and suppress a shiver at the icy touch of his fingers. I twitch my lips into a smile I don't feel. "Margaret Solder. I'm excited to hear more about the position."

He ushers me to precede him through the door and down a long, dimly lit hallway. I hear him shuffling behind me, his shoes squeaking with every uneven step, his breathing labored. Shouldn't he be retired at his age? I suddenly wonder how permanent the job as his assistant is likely to be.

The hallway leads to an open office that stretches off into the sunset. Giant floor-to-ceiling windows allow a perfect view of the pink and orange tones kissing the sky. *Wow.* I tear my gaze away to examine the rest of the floor. If I get this job, I'll end up sitting here somewhere, and for the desk space alone I would walk into hell. I count only forty desks in an area that could easily seat eighty, in rows of four. Low partitions give the illusion of privacy while allowing a view across the floor. Along one wall are closed doors which I assume lead to offices or meeting rooms. Glass panels are covered in a film of etched city landscapes reminiscent of the city images on their website. Reception's muted grays and reds extend into this space, and the docking stations have panoramic screens. It's an administrator's dream.

Bacitriet gestures to a door on my right and we walk into a six-seat meeting room. Unlike the cold, uncomfortable reception chairs, the meeting room chair devours me and I barely stifle my groan at the comfort. The door shuts us in muffled silence. A screen fills the entire wall opposite a floor-length window that overlooks the Yarra River.

He settles into the chair across from me. It appears no one else is to join us. How odd. I've never been in a solo interview before. Not for an initial pass.

"What do you think of the office?"

"It's amazing." I work to relax my body and offer him a bright smile. *Look interested, keep eye contact, nod a lot.*

Bacitriet leans forward. He sniffs a few times and tilts his head. "I am not sure what the agent told you, Ms. Solder, but I am in dire need. My previous assistant left without providing notice and I am a busy man. I have no time to sit through another arduous recruitment process."

"I see." He sounds as desperate as I am. "What precisely are you looking for? I was told it's an executive-level assistant position."

"How rude of me. Let me tell you a bit about myself. I am the chief executive officer here. The head dog, so to speak." His voice is thin, and he gasps a little, as if he's not getting enough oxygen. "I came here with nothing more than a need to survive. No money, no family, nothing to my name but a desire to assist those like me. I started Bacitriet Consulting in the back room of a bar and you can see what has become of us. We have many clients, some of whom I still deal with directly. We perform select services and I require an executive assistant who is punctual, detail-oriented and able to operate under extreme confidentiality. No questions." Unlike his labored breathing, his stare is that of a raptor, and it is fixed upon my face. I can't maintain eye contact, and shift my gaze over his shoulder to the sky growing steadily darker outside.

I can see why he is the CEO. The fire in his eyes and the determination in his reedy voice must keep him going. *No questions?* What doesn't he want me to ask questions about? I've kept confidentiality before. At my level, it's pretty common, but this description gives me the willies. I look around the room. *If he's doing something illegal, would he do it right out in the open like this?*

"Standard benefits, of course, plus many perks such as an onsite gym, massages, café with a professional barista onsite—all free for staff—as well as discounted insurance, travel, and access to an exclusive retail membership."

Honestly, he had me at the free coffee. "So, I'll book travel, maintain calendars and phones, and assist with regular reporting—that sort of thing?"

"I assume you are proficient in most programs and systems?"

This was where I excel, and I can't help but boast a little as I nod. "Yes. I pick up systems quickly and I often end up running staff inductions and training when new programs are rolled out."

"Excellent." He sits back and his bones creak. His gaze doesn't leave my face as he sniffs again. "The salary is extremely generous as I will insist on being able to reach you at all hours. However, I welcome flexible working arrangements and, provided you are fully contactable, I will allow you to work from home when the situation warrants."

The job sounds ideal. Everything here is so posh; it's intimidating. I wonder if I will have to shell out for expensive outfits and shoes if I get the job. The package better be good if I do. I won't wear heels, though. I'm always running around for some reason or another, and as my grandmothers always say, you can't run in heels. Speaking of shoes, sitting at the corner of the table means I can see Bacitriet's shoes when I glance down. Shiny black loafers.

Bacitriet slides an A4 envelope across the table. His suit fits him as if it's been sewn around his body, and the material is so shiny I can't spot a single crease even though he's hunched over.

"Well?"

My mind goes completely blank. To stall, I open the envelope. It's a contract. *I've got the job?* The number on the first page is mind-blowing. That's an insane number of zeroes, almost triple what I usually make, and an answer to all my prayers. Again, the thought flutters across my mind that he is doing something illegal here. I push it out again. "When would you expect me to start?" I clasp my hands over the envelope, hoping he won't take it away from me.

"Monday."

So no loss in my mortgage payments at all. It'll be like I was never out of work. With this salary, I can even put money toward that screenwriting mentoring course I want to do. "When do you need my answer?"

"I'd like you to sign the contract before you leave," he says, offering me a glimpse of a smile.

"So soon? What about references?" This might be where the whole house of cards falls apart. Will Jack even give me a good reference after what happened? Maybe he will, but I can't rely on that.

"I believe you will work out nicely. I prefer to jump straight into a three-month probational period rather than talk to people I do not know about you and take their word on your proficiency. You haven't lied about your skills, have you?"

My answer is immediate. "No, sir."

"Then I am comfortable with a trial arrangement. I expect to see you first thing Monday morning."

My brain shuts down. I'm speechless. No references? Could this job be any more perfect? I tear my gaze from his magnetic stare and the tiny hairs quiver on the back of my neck as I stare out the window, thinking. Elisa's warning blooms in my mind. *Be careful.* I have no idea what I'm getting myself into, but then again, couldn't I say the same about him? Trusting my resume on spec without speaking to my references. Still, there is something that niggles at me. "I'm sorry for asking this but my research into your company was a little . . . um, your website is unclear. What exactly is it that you do?"

"We consult."

"Um, yes, but on what?"

"Anything our clients desire. We are a full service consultancy, Ms. Solder. Our clients are always left satisfied. I trust this is a core value we share."

"Of course." I open my mouth to reframe my question, but he interrupts.

"Well, Ms. Solder, what is it to be?"

I need money and a job, and this is both. Besides, if it doesn't work out, I can always resign. Elisa's warning returns. I shove it back. "I'll take it."

Bacitriet draws a gleaming gold pen from his breast pocket and clicks the end. His lips stretch in a wide smile, teeth razor sharp, and he sniffs. I take the pen from his fingers, startled at how cold the metal is, and sign each section of the contract quickly. As I turn the final page, I let out a gasp at the sting of a papercut. *Crap!* Even though I'm careful, I swipe a little blood over the last page as I sign my name, and I fold the pages closed, hoping Bacitriet didn't see.

He leans back in his chair and a sigh escapes his mouth. "Excellent. I'm looking forward to Monday, Ms. Solder."

In my head, I hear a door slam.

Chapter 4

Elisa is standing outside my front door when I pull into my driveway. "Happy birthday!" She's practically glowing under the overhead porch light, her dusky Italian skin and wild, riotous hair give her an exotic, almost otherworldly appearance. The flowing yellow skirt and oversized button-down shirt tells me she's ready to kick back and relax over a few drinks. Her giant smile brings a mirroring grin to my lips, which grows as I spy the bottles in her hands.

I glance over my pride and joy, my three-bedroom house. In the dark, all I can see of the red and brown brick façade and cream-colored tin roof is what is lit by the porch light and the streetlight at the end of my block. The shadowy shapes beside my car are the young bottlebrush bushes that run the length of the gray concrete driveway. *Mine.* And now I have a job—a really, *really* well-paying job—so I can afford to keep it! The warm feeling in my body reminds me of falling in love. I *am* in love. My little house is all mine and it's staying mine.

After the day I've had, a wave of peace washes over me the instant my foot hits the wooden floorboards. My shoulders drop and I breathe deeply. I feel . . . safe. I kick off my shoes and move inside. "Come in," I call over my shoulder. Elisa makes a beeline for the kitchen bench, and the sound of a popping cork brings a giggle to my lips.

"So how did it go?" she asks.

"Well . . . okay. I think . . . I need you to tell me I didn't just make a massive mistake."

Her gaze shifts from the bottle in her hand to my face. "What happened?"

"I got the job."

Elisa squeals and grabs my hand to squeeze but calms herself at the sight of my face. "You think it's a mistake?"

A *rat-tat-tat* sound comes from somewhere inside the house. My nerves are clearly hiding just beneath the surface because my muscles tense up in less than a heartbeat. It's a dull, wooden sound. "Do you hear that? That rattle?"

A quick investigation locates the source. My laundry has a solid wooden door leading to my miniscule backyard. I can see the door trembling inside the frame. "Is that from the wind?" Elisa asks.

"Yeah. And it's supposed to get worse tonight. My *Vic Emergency* app went off in the car on the drive home. A pretty big storm is coming. Gah, that's loud. How am I supposed to sleep through that?" I tug on the door to confirm it's locked.

"You could try jamming a blanket between the floor and the frame," Elisa suggests, swigging from her wine glass. "I did that on the twins' window when they were bubs. Every rattle woke them up and they'd scream the house down, remember?" She hands me the other glass. I gulp several mouthfuls of wine instantly, pondering the problem.

"Oh, I have a better idea." Andy put my laundry box on the floor when I'd moved in and I hadn't bothered to unpack it yet. I tug at the top flap until the scotch tape comes off and tear the cardboard. Folding it, I jam the cardboard piece between the door and the frame and tug hard. No movement. Rattle fixed. "Yay, look at me. Homeowner and now handywoman."

Elisa claps. "Bravo. Let's order pizza and while we wait you can tell me all about the new job. Oh and did you notice when you pulled in you have a neighbor at last? The lights are on in the house next door."

"What?" I race to the living room window. "Where? I didn't see . . ." My voice trails off. There *is* a light on inside the house but the curtains are drawn. "I didn't even see a sold sticker go on the FOR SALE sign out the front."

"It's been empty since you moved in, right?"

"Since before then. When I first inspected this place, it was up for sale. I've never seen anyone over there. Did you see them walk in?"

"No, just the light."

I slump down on my budget sofa and drop my head onto the armrest. "Forget the neighbor." I tell Elisa everything about my exhausting day, from Jack firing me to Bacitriet's offer. Elisa folds herself into a yoga pose on the carpet in front of the coffee table and listens without interrupting. When I finish speaking, she stretches languidly. I wait for her response in the silence, breathing in the night. The wind has picked up and it sounds like a low moan. I wonder when the rain will start. The weather app warned it could be a wild storm. I glance around, searching for candles in case I lose power.

"Well?" I prompt finally.

"I'm thinking."

Used to her ways, I stare at the grubby beige carpet. Ugh, I hate the color. It's on the list of things to replace. Pounding on the door startles me out of my contemplation. "Pizza's here. Hey, do you think I should bring the hardwood floor all the way in here?"

"That would improve things," Elisa says, smirking. I open the door to find the windblown pizza delivery guy departing with a wave, leaving our dinner sitting on the porch.

"Cheers!" I call after him and bring the pizza inside. "I have food." I change my voice to a proclamation. "One more night, we shall survive!"

"You sound drunk," Elisa laughs.

I take a huge gulp to finish my drink. "Not yet." My belly tingles as it hits me. I slip my socks off. Alcohol always makes my feet hot. "Long day."

She grabs a slice and takes a big bite, hissing at the temperature of the cheese.

"How are the kids?" I ask.

"Oh yeah, ask me to talk when the food is here." She narrows her eyes at me. I know exactly what she's thinking, so I grin sweetly. She balls up a napkin and throws it at me, then tugs the garlic bread to her side as payment. I snort. She wipes her hands and grabs her phone, showing me half a dozen photos, proud momma smile on her face as she tells me a story of mud puddles and missing rain boots.

"Total ratbags," I agree, laughing at the filthy faces.

"So, we've established Jack is an asshole, what about the new boss? Tell me more about him."

"It's weird. I'm still not all that sure what he does. A consultant of some sort."

Elisa hums and stands to refill her glass. "Top-up?"

"Sure." My gaze drifts to my unpacked DVD boxes. I need to build the bookshelves that are currently flatpacks in my garage. I'm hoping I can con Dad into putting them together for me. I'd planned to ask him tonight. I'll try tomorrow. I wiggle my toes. "Elisa?" She's taking a long time to get that wine. "Elisa?" I twist my head, and it takes me a moment to locate her. She's hidden behind the disgusting green and pink curtain. Also on the list to replace. "Elisa?" She doesn't twitch. "Elisa, what do you think of my new job?"

She pulls her head out of the curtain. "There's something about your new neighbor . . ."

"What?" I drag my tired self off the sofa. "You saw them?" Elisa ducks her head back behind the curtain. "Don't be too obvious. What are you looking at?"

"There's something . . . strange. Look." She tugs me into the curtain. I inhale dusty white filmy lace and wave my hands around like I'm trying to clear spiderwebs. "He's got a super expensive car."

Cars are not my thing and Elisa knows that. I wouldn't know one model from another. Even so, the vehicle parked in my neighbor's driveway is sleek and sporty under the glow of the streetlight. "Was that there before?"

"He must be loaded," Elisa whispers.

Would he live here if he had money?" It's not a bad little estate, but it's not exclusive by any means. "Elisa, a nice car doesn't make him strange."

My friend doesn't take her eyes off the expensive car. "You didn't see him step out of that Porsche. All shadows and purpose. He practically prowled to his front door."

If my new neighbor's already gone inside, it's doubtful I'll catch glimpse of him now. "Hmm."

"He's hot, I'm telling you, something wicked this way comes." She wiggles her eyebrows.

"How can you tell?" I press closer as she turns back to the window. Elisa's perfume is new, a kind of gingery-orange scent. I like it.

"It's the way he held himself," she whispers. "The way he moved. So confident. Sexy." She makes a growling sound.

I groan at her. She sounds like a high school girl crushing on a football star, or like the two of us when we're talking about Hugh Jackman. "And that makes him wicked?"

"Well, who knows. Wicked, bad. It can be sexy."

"Bad is never sexy," I counter. "So, do I avoid him? What vibe are you getting?"

She makes a vague, thoughtful noise, her eyes still stuck on the neighboring house.

"El?"

"I'm not sure what I'm feeling." She giggled. "Maybe I need to meet him."

"Elisa, what would Frank say?"

"That I can look and not touch. Come on, hon, it's all in good fun."

I laugh. That's what Elisa always says. She "looks" often, but I know she's too madly in love with Frank to do anything to ruin her marriage.

"He could be a car salesman," I suggest. "Whatever he is, he's gone inside now. Come on. I want another drink."

Elisa's eyes glitter under my lounge room light. "I feel . . . I don't know. Weird."

"Drunk?"

"Not hardly." She chuckles. "Come on, I want to hear more about Bacitriet." She hugs me. "A pretty full-on birthday for you, huh?"

"Yeah," I agree. "Pity we don't have any cake."

Chapter 5

I stretch beneath my duvet and groan loudly, luxuriating in not having to get up at the first hint of light. Yesterday was just so crazy, I feel the need to bunker down and process all the changes. It doesn't seem like a Friday. Losing my job on a Thursday and then getting a new one that starts on Monday means I get an unplanned long weekend.

Tugging my comfy protection higher around my neck, I roll onto my left side and bury my head into the pillow. Jack fired me. Thoughts of my cozy bed are quickly pushed aside thinking about that moment. *God damn Toby.* He'd had it in for me from the moment he started with Jack six months ago. Smug smile and nasty eyes, always watching me and Jack as we laughed and joked around, trying to get invited to lunch. I thought it was creepy at the time, but now I can see how stalkery it was. He'd been looking for a way to get rid of me and I walked right into it by offering to help his team out when they were swamped. I'd thought I was buying goodwill. How naïve.

The betrayal makes my belly ache. Though that could be from all the alcohol I'd drunk last night.

After a moment, I flop back the other way and crack my eyelids open to examine my room as the sun rises. I add a note to my mental to-do list: change the bedroom curtains to block-out ones. I screw my eyes shut and burrow deeper into my pillow. For a moment, all is silent. The trill of unfamiliar birds along with the crack and whine of large machinery breaks the peace. Another clang and a louder bang moves closer. Stressed metal wails. *Garbage day.*

The sounds should have annoyed me; instead I hear the silence between the noise. No Mom pottering around the kitchen or Dad in the study. No faint toilet flush from the room beside mine or washing machine buzzing in the background. This is my place. My home. Bliss. I'll do everything I can to keep it.

Which makes me contemplate yesterday's successful interview. Bacitriet's unsteady walk and thin, rasping voice could mean he is not well. Maybe that's why his previous assistant left. Though it doesn't explain why she left so suddenly. It's good luck for me, but it's not a good sign if the previous assistant felt the need to leave without giving notice. I should have asked. I'll do that on Monday. Twitching, I roll over again and poke my nose out of my cocoon. Ugh, there's a hint of mold in the crisp air. I'll have to see if I can find it. Or maybe it's coming from the carpet. Oh, I hope not.

Regretfully, I raise my arm out of the nest I've created and wave it around until my exercise tracker flares on. Way too early. Still, I might as well get moving. Mom and Dad will probably turn up before I've had a chance to shower. Dad loves putting flatpacks together, and after my missed birthday party last night it's only a matter of time before they arrive. The awful taste in my mouth and the hangover headache tell me I need coffee. My bare toes touch the chilly carpet for a brief second before I yank them back up hissing unhappily. Might be a lovely Autumn day outside but the lack of cloud cover means it's freezing, and the icy air claws its way into every gap in my pajamas. Of course, my robe is in the hamper and my slippers are in the kitchen. I think. Maybe I kicked them off in the living room? Teeth chattering, I snatch up my pullover from yesterday and tug it on over what is probably crazy bed hair and shuffle around, dragging open my dresser drawers in the search of fluffy socks. Warmth brings my toes back to life. Now for the kitchen and my next scavenger hunt.

"Oh, crap!" I slam a hand down on the kitchen bench and stare forlornly into the vast wasteland of my empty fridge. The carton of milk barely makes a sound as I try to slosh it around. So, no breakfast, and there's no way I'm getting dressed just to buy milk. Fleetingly, I think of my new neighbor. *Dare I introduce myself and beg for a cup of milk?* I peer through the window. Mr. Sexy-and-Probably-Rich's car is gone. My shoulders drop. I press my forehead to the glass, thinking it's probably for the best. Appearing at a stranger's door looking like a horror show is not the kind of first impression I want to make. Besides, that car is intimidating enough. I decide not to risk a pre-coffee introduction.

Swearing under my breath, I find my cell phone lurking beneath my bed. A black screen greets me when I try to switch it on. *Oh, come on!* I upend everything in my frantic search for the recharge cable. It was on the bench last night. No, I moved it when Elisa and I made that cup of tea with the last of the milk before her Uber arrived to take her home. Ugh, where is it now? TV cabinet? I spin around and my sock-covered toes connect with the unmoving edge of the coffee table. I let out a screech that rattles the windows and hobble to the TV, snatching up the white cord, muttering dark curses to the gods.

Bang, bang, bang!

I drop the charger onto my already throbbing foot and swear louder. My thoughts fly to my new neighbor. I can't answer the door looking like I just got out of bed. The knocking moves to the window beside the wooden frame.

Tap tap tap. "Hellllooooo!"

"Oh, thank God!" I smile and yank the door open to find a giant takeaway coffee cup thrust into my face. "Yay!" I grab it and gulp at the life-giving liquid. "I love you." Lowering the cup, I grin at the two elderly women standing on my doorstep. "Grandma Berry, Grandma Rose."

"Happy birthday, Margaret!"

Tight gray curls and squinted hazel eyes behind wire-frame glasses are all I see before Berry's arms come around me and squeeze. "Coffee," I yelp, holding my hand out to save the liquid gold from tipping. Rose snatches the cup from my grasp. Her brown eyes shine brightly as she pushes Berry out of the way and launches into my arms. I salvage the coffee first then wrap my arms around her ample frame and press my face into her fine white hair.

"Are you going to leave us standing out here? It's bloody freezing." Berry tugs her hot pink cardigan closed and buttons it up to her neck so that only a hint of her cream collar shows.

"Where's your coat?"

"In the car, obviously."

"Obviously," I mutter, but I can't help the grin that spreads over my face. "Welcome to my new place."

Rose shuffles us to the side and allows Berry to plow past. Eventually, Rose lets me go. In a blink, her blue-clad body disappears inside. *Favorite pantsuit?* Mom and Dad's place doesn't qualify for their "good" clothes, but I guess visiting my new house does. I think I should feel special. I flop onto the sofa and twist sideways so I can keep an eye on them while they finish their inspection, sipping my coffee and listening to their comments.

"Windows in the back room are too small."

"Backyard is a pocket of nothing."

"High ceilings are nice."

"Needs new carpets."

"Curtains too."

"Blinds maybe?"

"No blinds," I call, losing the battle to hide my amusement. God, I love them. They are the best old ladies in the whole entire world. Dad calls them the A-Team, because when they really get going, trouble and hijinks follow in their wake, and heaven help anyone who crosses them. Sometimes they don't seem like old ladies at all. They're too vibrant and energetic for that. Best friends since childhood, they moved in together after both my grandpas died.

They continue as if I haven't spoken. "No, Berry, dear. Blinds are too drafty."

"But cheaper, Rose. Must keep that in mind for poor Margaret."

I lay my head on the padded chair arm and suppress a snort.

"Poor nothing. She works, doesn't she? Best to confirm the color palette now."

"Oh, I don't like the kitchen, it's too small."

"She doesn't cook. What does she need a big kitchen for? Where's the damned heater?"

This time the snort gets out.

"Are you alright, dear?" Berry's gray head pokes out of the bedroom while Rose pops up from the kitchen.

I wait for more questions.

"Heater, honey? And what will you do in summer? I can't see an air-conditioner." That's Berry.

"Which direction is the store? Have you any cookies? There's nothing in your pantry." Rose shuffles closer. Berry swoops in, her stern face the complete opposite of Rose's red round cheeks, but very similar to that of her daughter—my mom.

"Where are you two going so early on a Friday?" I ask. My verbal skills return as the coffee kicks in. "And how did you know I'd be home?"

"Your dad called," Rose says.

"Of course he did." I thump my forehead.

"We can't stay. Rose got us a gig," Berry adds.

I swallow the last of my coffee wrong. Gasping, I cough it back up. Luckily the cup is empty, or it would have ended up all over me. "You what?"

"A job, dear. A paying gig."

"Doing what?" My chest heaves as my lungs reject the liquid I'd swallowed. My cough ends up sounding like a dog barking. A pretty big dog.

"Are you quite finished, Margaret? Really, you're such an attention-seeker."

"Berry!" Being dissed by my grandma is probably the highlight of my week.

"Supermarket testers." Rose gestures toward the kitchen. "You have no food. Did you know that?"

"I know, Rose." I glance back at Berry. "Testing what?"

"You know those old biddies who stand around supermarkets forcing people to taste new brands?"

"That's going to be us. We might even get to demonstrate how something works," Rose says.

"Oh my God." I cover my eyes with my left hand—the other still clasps my empty cup, willing it to magically refill. "Am I dreaming?" I have a sudden flash of brands not related to food at all, like condoms or adult diapers. Oh God, what if they have to sell chocolate? Rose has such a sweet tooth. It'd be a disaster. She'd eat all the samples!

Rose plonks down on the sofa beside me, and I dip toward her, catching a whiff of lavender and face cream. She pats my shoulder. "It's the supermarket closest to here. You can drop in and watch if you like. It'll be lovely to see a familiar face."

"Who would hire you two—oh, never mind. Of course, I'll come." There's no way I'd miss it. I only hope it won't end in disaster, like all the other times.

I asked them once why they wanted to work so badly when they were retired and could relax. They'd stared, unblinking, before Rose took my hand and said, "Don't waste the time you have in this life when you can be out living it."

Berry had added, "Spend your life doing something you want to do, Margaret. Use your passion. Strive to be more."

It was like being hit by a basketball at high speed. That was the day I started writing my screenplay. Working full-time means it's hard to find the energy to write some days; still, I persist because these two would want me too. I have a plot and characters and I've studied format and style online. Now I just have to sit down and write the damned thing. I'll make them proud of me one day. Just you wait.

It's a hard slog, but watching my grandmothers make the most of every moment puts me to shame. Their energy is staggering. After all their kids moved out of home, they were delivery drivers until Rose drove into the factory wall. They worked in a number of shops and cafes and were fired each time for giving patrons unwanted advice. They even volunteered at the local community theater for a time until they were asked not to come back for telling stories about ghosts living in the props' cupboards and scaring the kids. They've also joined sewing teams, knitting bees, quilters workshops and more that I've forgotten about. How they got kicked out of each one is just as entertaining—if a little mortifying.

They have no problem taking life by the horns and going for it.

"Margaret, dear, we noticed your neighbor leaving this morning when we parked. What a honey."

"Rose!" My face heats.

They also have no shame.

Berry presses in on my other side. Too close. I'm left staring at her shoulder. Her blouse shifts as she hugs me, and I spy a thin white line on the pale wrinkled skin over her collarbone. *Is that a scar?* "Have you met him yet? What's his name?" Berry asks.

"Stop it, please. You two—no more." My stomach hurts from holding back my laughter.

Rose grins from ear to ear. "Bit rude, though. I got a strange vibe off him."

"Really? From watching him drive away?"

"I would trust her feelings, Margaret. In fact, you should listen to your own gut more," Berry says. "There are strange things in this world. The more warning you get, the better off you'll be."

"I listen to Elisa," I say. *Mostly.*

"You have good judgment too, Margaret. Trust yourself. You know what's right." The way Berry is looking at me freaks me out a little.

"That sort of boy is good for only one thing," Rose adds.

"Don't you have to get to work?"

"You're right, we'd better be off."

"Thanks for the coffee. You're both angels." I shoo them toward the door. "Thanks for visiting."

Rose hands me my birthday card in an envelope. "Happy birthday, dear."

Berry spears me with a sharp look. "Heed my words, Margaret. A man like that has the devil in him. Be careful."

It's odd for Berry to have such a strong opinion about someone she's never met, but I let it pass. "I'll be careful. I probably won't ever see him." Berry refuses to budge. Her face is screwed into a rather serious expression. I wrap my arms around her, touched at how deeply she cares. "I *promise* I'll be careful. Come on, you know me. I'm always careful."

She sniffs and pulls back, giving Rose a chance to get in for a cuddle. "We'll be close by. Call us if you need us."

"Of course." I bite back a grin. Exactly how did they think they were going to rescue me? I maintain my composure until the door closes behind them, then burst out laughing at the image of my dear grandmothers racing in to save me from an overflowing bathtub, brandishing bats and knitting needles.

Chapter 6

The weekend passes in a blur of birthday catch-ups. Morning tea turned into lunch with my parents—Dad made the bookshelves—and then dinner with Andy. I spend Saturday cleaning. Living alone should not produce this much mess. It's all cleaning spray, rubber gloves and buckets of water. As I empty the dirty water bucket onto the plants in my driveway I notice the neighbor's car is back. It gleams in the midday sun. It's gotta cost a mint! No sign of the driver. I wonder again what he does for a living. At least the front yard is looking neater. A lot neater. The grass has been mowed and the shrubs are trimmed back. The house looks like a completely different place. Much more inviting.

Elisa texts on Sunday morning to invite me out for coffee. There's a local statue park she's been wanting to show me for ages. I reluctantly decline. I don't even stop my mad cleaning to watch a movie or work on my screenplay. When I plop down on the sofa Sunday night, I'm covered in dried sweat, my hair is manky and my fingers are dark with grime. I also realize I've forgotten to visit Berry and Rose at their new job. I promise myself to call them after dinner to apologize. "Pizza!" I shout. Every ache makes itself known as I reach for the phone.

The idea of dragging myself into a new office tomorrow, and undergoing the standard multiple and repeated introductions, inductions and invitations to talk about myself, fills me with despair. I'll meet people whose names I have no hope of remembering and who I will have to fake an interest in. I'm still not clear on what services Bacitriet provides and my imagination caused some pretty strange dreams. I don't know whether to picture brokers, insurance people or spies. Okay, that last one is straight out of my writing brain. It's probably not that. Probably.

When I wake on Monday, I crank my alarm music up high and dance around as I get dressed, spending more time than usual on my makeup and hair. I leave the house feeling like a million dollars.

As I open the door, I'm met with pelting rain. With the music on, and my ducted heating buzzing away, I'd not heard it at all.

Rain? It's pouring—sideways—in great sheets that blur all vision of my front yard. The horror of it freezes me solid. After a moment, I dive into my entrance hall cupboard for my umbrella, unearthing it from behind my old cricket bat. *What a great start to the day.* To make matters worse, my umbrella flips inside out and snaps under the onslaught of the icy wind. I fall into the driver's seat of my car, dripping water on everything, and realize the neighbor's car is gone again. He must be the early morning sort. I keep missing him, so my curiosity is growing about what he looks like. Elisa's behavior from the other night pops into my mind. The way she'd talked about my neighbor was so odd. I've never heard her make such a strange assessment of someone before, practically sight unseen. Thinking back, I realize she'd been strange for the rest of the night too, drifting into long silences and staring off at nothing. Weird.

It's raining even harder by the time I try to park at the insanely packed train station. I manage to find a spot toward the rear of the uncovered concrete carpark, near a line of giant gum trees. Staring through the windscreen at the sheets of horizontal water, I know I'll have to brave it eventually, but I give it a minute more in the hope it will stop. At least it's not hail. Remaining positive is a battle I'm quickly losing. Nerves squirm in my belly. *This is a bad sign.* It's as though even the weather is trying to stop me from going into work.

Cursing with the creativity of a footy player, I stagger onto the platform as the train pulls to a stop and force my bedraggled body into the closest carriage, where I find dozens of equally miserable passengers. I'd counted on getting a seat this morning to calm my nerves. I peer around, grinding my teeth. I'm early. How can it be this crowded already? The only time it's like this is when . . . oh damn. Fumbling with my dripping umbrella—*why am I still carrying it?*—my handbag and my small backpack, I dig out my phone and stare at the notifications, willing them to say something different.

No such luck.

Delays all along the line. "Shit."

"Great start to a Monday, huh?"

I grimace at the elderly woman beside me. "Awful. It's my first day in a new job."

She gives me a sympathetic smile. "You might want to fix your eyes then."

More fumbling finds my compact. Mascara paints long black streaks down my face, turning me into a zombie. And a panda. A zombie panda who's been crying. "Oh my God."

Her lips tilt in a sideways smile. "I hope your day gets better."

Me too. Stretched out as I am to reach the handrail, it's impossible to manage even basic repairs to my face. *I'm cursed.*

The delays mean that despite catching the earlier train, I barely make it into the office before the clock strikes nine a.m.

The cold travels inside with me, leaving my skin chilled. I tighten my scarf around my neck and look forward to finding my desk and warming up. The dark-haired receptionist—the one I'd met briefly last Thursday—is laughing at something as the elevator doors slide open. I search for who she's talking to until I realize she's speaking into her headset.

Her eyes pop wide when she spots me and she clamps a manicured, red nail-tipped hand over her headset microphone. "Bathrooms are that way."

I mouth "thank you" and race down the corridor, praying I won't run into anyone until I can make myself presentable. I manage some luck when I find the correct door and duck inside unseen.

Catching sight of my appearance, my chest becomes a black hole, sucking my insides into a void of no return. Upending my bag, I hunt for anything I can find to repair the damage, and hold my head up, blinking rapidly. *Why? Why me? Why today?* Eyes first, then I attempt to tame my wild, windblown hair. The damp has curled what I'd labored so long over this morning to straighten. My fringe spears into my cheeks and my neat ponytail is a snaggly mess. To save it, I pull it out completely and allow waves of long brown hair to fall around my face. I reapply my matte cherry lipstick and button my damp jacket closed over my white shirt, which is now completely transparent.

I press my body against the hand heater. The Elisa-sounding voice in my head says this is not a good omen. All the signs are shouting that I've made a big mistake. I tell myself to buck up. It's just a job. Everyone has bad days.

I picture the zeroes on my pay packet and straighten my shoulders. As I thaw, I realize I'm right. It's not that bad. "Looking up from here, kiddo," I tell my reflection.

After a quick visit to the loo, I feel a hundred times better. All I need now is coffee. Where are Rose and Berry when I need them?

Before I reach the mouth of the corridor, I hear the receptionist's voice. "The new girl's here."

I freeze. A glance around confirms I'm alone in the hall. Should I linger and risk getting caught? People say eavesdroppers never hear good things. I ignore that and creep closer.

"Poor thing looked like a drowned rat. Must have caught the worst of it."

Heat blooms in my cheeks. I swipe my fingertips over the sweat beading my upper lip.

"No, I don't think she knows."

Knows what? My watch vibrates. Nine a.m. Time to meet Bacitriet. The receptionist gives her caller a weird, strained laugh that stops me from moving forward.

"Do you think I should tell her? It's three now. I mean, it's an awful coincidence."

If someone sees me, it will spread all over the office that I'm a snoop. Huffing out a breath, I walk around the corner as if I'm completely oblivious to the tension filling the waiting area.

The receptionist abruptly ends her call and smiles at me. "Ready?"

"Thanks for that. Terrible weather, hey?" I stand next to the desk, hoping she'll elaborate on her previous comment.

She opens her mouth but closes it again and replaces her headset. "Mr. Bacitriet? Ms. Solder has arrived." She looks up at me. "Take a seat, hon. He won't be long." I shiver as cold air brushes my skin. *Jeez, it isn't any warmer in here than outside.* The blond receptionist walks down the corridor toward me carrying a coffee mug. She sees me and her steps slow.

I force my lips into a smile. "Hi." She points to the waiting area chairs without a word. I shuffle forward, remembering how uncomfortable they were and resign myself to waiting in one. My phone beeps and I grab it out of my bag to switch it to mute, checking the notification. It's Mom and Dad wishing me good luck with the job. Feeling that weird pressure against my face that tells me I'm being watched, I glance up and find both receptionists focused on me. Like two judgmental crows or cats, or some other animals that stare. My default is to ramble in awkward situations. *I am allowed personal text messages, aren't I?* "Isn't the rain awful today? The trains were terrible. Oh, I'm sorry, I forgot to ask earlier. What are your names?"

The dark-haired woman points to her own chest. "Candy." She eyes the woman at her side. The blond tightens the heart-covered scarf. "That's Bethany."

Movement draws my gaze to the doorway leading to the main floor. Bacitriet hobbles in. His pale face reminds me of a walking corpse. *Maybe he is ill.* A spark of understanding dawns. That must be what Candy is hiding. Perhaps my new job won't be so permanent after all. I jump to my feet. "Mr. Bacitriet."

"Ms. Solder, welcome. Dreadful weather outside, isn't it? It looks like it caught you in the thick of it."

How nice of you to mention it. I shoot him a wan smile and follow his gesturing arm.

"Let's head straight through."

The main office looks exactly the same as I remember. There is no one around. Is it too early, or do they all start late around here? This time, instead of the meeting rooms, Bacitriet leads me straight to a messy desk. He points a bent bony finger—*arthritis?*—to the closed office door behind the desk and sniffs. "I'm in there. You sit here as my gatekeeper and keep the hunters away. Ha ha."

I fake a laugh. I'm sure he means monsters not hunters. I eye his aged body and wonder about his mind. How old is he? Glancing around my new home, I groan inwardly. Some of my horror must show on my face because he says, "Apologies for not having everything ready for you. As I stated last week, my previous assistant left rather . . . abruptly. It shouldn't take long for you to clean up. I'm sure Cassandra's manuals will provide you with a wealth of information."

Yeah, sure. I nod and follow him into his office. When the door closes, all the hairs on my body stand on end. I twitch, covering the movement by scratching my neck. I wish the door had been left open.

Bacitriet gestures to a table large enough to seat six. His desk and chair occupy one wall of the rectangular office. So, it's an office and a meeting room in one? That's what Jack had tried to do, but his office had always felt too cramped. The size of this room makes it work. The color scheme is not as garish as the outer reception area, and the frosted glass walls give the illusion of privacy while also letting lots of light in. All in all, it should be a nice room but I feel rather like a fish in a bowl. There's a post-it note on the table with four zeroes and a hash written under "Locker 016" and an A4 folder—what I assume to be an onboarding packet. I clear my throat. "These are for me?"

"Indeed. The code is for your locker. Everything you need should be inside. Your security pass, laptop, phone and so on. Your programs, access and share drive details have already been organized. Take the folder with you and work through the forms in your own time. Get them to human resources by the end of the week. Your login details should be inside. Let me know if you have any problems or if you require any additional software."

I nod. This, at least, is familiar. "Do you want to go over your expectations?" I ask, sliding the notebook out of the pile of papers. "Or perhaps discuss your diary?"

"Let's not overwhelm you with any more information now. Go and get set up. Any stationery you require that is not in your locker, speak to Bethany. She'll sort you out."

Dismissed already? Perhaps he has a meeting to get to. "Of course." I gather everything off the table under his intense scrutiny.

His voice stops me at the door. "You'll have access to your predecessor's emails. Please use discretion with correspondence and follow up on any outstanding items. I prefer my door closed."

"Yes, sir," I answer. "Is there a particular message you would like me to give when I respond to waiting emails? If anyone enquires who I am?"

His gaze remains steady, but his eyes narrow ever so slightly. He sniffs again. "Just that Cassandra is no longer with us and that you are her replacement."

I'm happy to exit the room and make sure to close the door tightly behind me. The way he'd said "no longer with us" plays in my mind as I sit down. Why say it like that? It sounds morbid that way. Perhaps he's a glass half-empty kind of guy. It's not exactly reassuring. I survey the disaster area that is my new workstation. *People are so gross.*

Lockers line the wall in front of me. I locate locker 016 and inside it find a laptop and phone, exactly as Bacitriet had said. A white access pass on a green lanyard has been placed on top of it all. My footsteps echo in the empty office as I return to my desk. It sends a shiver up my spine. *Where is everyone?*

Before things get busy, I figure I'll clean out the desk and set everything up the way I prefer.

First things first. I move the HR packet to the floor and gather the scattered papers into a pile. I can sort through it and bin the trash later. I find cleaning wipes on a nearby desk— hopefully the owner won't mind me pinching one—and scrub everything down. Feeling comfortable at last, I switch on the laptop and I'm pleasantly surprised when my password works and the laptop lights up beneath my fingertips. I spend a while figuring out how to work the display screens and check that each of my apps open while I wait for my email to load. I don't expect much, given it's my first day. My hopes are quickly dashed as email after email cascades down the screen in a river of subject lines. It looks like I have access to Bacitriet's calendar but not his email inbox. A name catches my eye. *Cassandra Chan.* My predecessor. Curious, I click on the second inbox and scroll through her mail. Pretty standard stuff. Flight bookings, catering requests, room bookings . . . and then my gaze falls on a surprising subject line. It's an email she'd sent to herself.

Help me.

A throat clears next to my ear. I spin around and find Bacitriet standing right behind me. His neck skin looks a bit like a plucked chicken from this angle. It wobbles as he speaks. "Any questions?"

"What?" I think my heart stopped beating, or maybe my chest hurts because I've forgotten how to breathe. I hadn't heard him approach. I'm glad I didn't swear.

"Do you have any questions?"

My heart resumes beating. Had Bacitriet seen that strange email on my screen? Maybe Cassandra emailed herself a warning about the job for the next assistant? Or maybe it's an explanation as to why she left? "Uh, no. I think I'm good. Do you have a specific folder or a share drive I should save things into?" The urge to hide my screen is high but that will draw his attention to the strange subject line. I slide my chair sideways as innocently as I can and straighten my back to block his view.

He gestures for me to stand up. My palms grow damp. "I've booked an orientation for you with Shannon O'Connell. She'll take you through our files and portals. Come with me."

Leaning back, I quickly lock my computer. Bacitriet stares down at my fingers and doesn't say a word. I clutch my notebook to my chest and laugh off the uncomfortable feeling that I've done something wrong. "Habit," I say to explain my behavior. "I worked admin at an IT firm at a previous job."

Bacitriet offers a smile that barely twitches his lips. "Of course. It is a good habit to secure your workstation."

I spend the rest of the morning with Shannon going through the programs I'll need in my role. I can't stop thinking about that email from Cassandra. Shannon is forced to repeat herself several times and probably thinks I'm a simpleton. "Sorry," I say for the umpteenth time. I try to project friendly interest. "So, how long have you worked here?"

She runs a hand over her graying long red hair. Her left eye twitches. "Not long. A few months maybe."

"Really? You certainly know the systems well. Do you enjoy working here?"

"It's a job." She taps her keyboard with sharp-looking nails. "About—"

"Have you worked with Mr. Bacitriet at all?"

She shudders and won't meet my eye. "Thankfully, no."

Okay. Odd reaction. "What do you mean by that?"

"We should get back to it," she says, offering me another weak smile.

Unsettled by our conversation, I buckle down, and before I notice it's gone midday. "How about I show you the food court downstairs?" Shannon offers in her lilting Irish accent. She shoulders her handbag.

"Oh, I need to find a bank," I murmur, offering a conciliatory smile. "Thanks so much for your help today." She waves me off, probably happy to have her lunch break to herself. Back at my desk, I check around for Bacitriet. His office is dark and the door is open. The floor around me is bustling now. I debate introducing myself to some of my new colleagues. The low hum of chatter in the room is both familiar and unfamiliar. But I'm dying to read that strange email. I plop into my seat and unlock the laptop with practiced movements.

The email is probably nothing more than a reminder to check something, or for a booking to be canceled. Hell, I've used that subject line so many times myself. It should mean absolutely nothing. Still, my skin itches and I need to see what's inside it, if only to settle my mind.

My screen blinks on and I click the email icon, scrolling quickly up and down.

Cassandra's email is gone.

Chapter 7

Had I really seen it? But why would I imagine an email with such a suggestive subject line?

And if I *had* seen it, then where did it go? A glitch? I can't make sense of it. I'm sure it must be perfectly innocent, but what if it's not the only email to disappear?

I leave a message with the IT department, wanting to check I'm not going mad. They don't get back to me. That makes me a little edgy. Jack's reason for firing me plays back in my mind and I know I can't start a new job by making unintended mistakes.

My afternoon flies past in a blur of faces, company policies and standard compliance modules. I'm still entirely in the dark about what they do here. I call IT again and leave a message. Bacitriet doesn't return and thankfully doesn't call, so I head home, tired but mostly pleased with how my first day has gone. The missing email still hovers in my periphery. I brush it off as first-day jitters.

As soon as I'm on the train and heading home, I jot down a few character descriptions in my notebook based on the people I've met today.

Elisa texts when I'm halfway home. *Company tonight?*

I clench my fingers around my pen and fog the train window with the strength of my exhale. I want to tell her about the strange email, but my eyeballs have that sudden hot feeling that indicates a migraine is incoming. If Elisa comes over, I'll get to talk out my confusion but I won't get much rest. My need for some alone time wars with my need for support.

The phone vibrates again. This time, it's Mom checking in after my first day. I shoot her a quick message. *Great. Easy to get to. Nice office. People are nice too. Tired though. Call you tomorrow.*

Mom will want to hear all about this morning's Rainy First Day horror show. I snicker imagining her belly-laugh and scan the carriage to see if any of the passengers caught my noisy lapse. An unspoken law of peak-hour train travel is that those exhausted after a long day prefer to sit in silence. I'm currently surrounded by men and women buried in e-readers, books or phones. Many wear headphones as a barrier against the sounds of the carriage; coughing, beeping, scratching and sniffing. It's a brave soul on the 5.16 p.m. train who dares to speak on their cell phone. They're the ones who unwittingly invite the entire carriage to listen in on their conversation. Repeated text message notifications receive multiple glares and shaking heads. The critical stares would be too much to bear today, so fortunately, my amusement was not loud enough to trigger the avalanche of attitude.

I tap my phone case—with my finger and not the nail—unsure what to tell Elisa. I still haven't responded by the time I get off the train. At six p.m., it's dark and the carpark has gaps like the missing teeth in Isabel's mouth. Elisa's daughter's gap-toothed grin always cheers me up. The lights of the carpark create great swathes of yellow that compete with the black-ness prowling the edges. A few bulbs are dark. Clearly, the night is winning. Passengers from my train climb into vehicles around me. The *beep beep* of car locks and flashing blinkers increase as I walk to the edge of the carpark. The sudden roar of an engine turns my head as a car peels away, racing its driver home. I keep a steady lookout. Inattentive drivers might not see me in my black coat.

My thoughts drift back to Elisa as I poke my car keys between my fingers. I balance on a knife-edge of guilt and selfish desire. *Just tell her you're tired.* I press the key fob and peer down, confused. I don't remember parking on a slope.

"Oh, come on!"

Immaturity gets the better of me and I kick the flat front tire. A groan forces its way through my lips as I tug the door open and collapse on the front seat. I hit the steering wheel several times, venting my anger with as many curse words as I can fit in one breath. Through the windshield, the empty car spot in front of me is nothing but a taunt.

I suck in a deep breath, lean back and let my mind go blank. Elisa says I shouldn't fixate on the things I can't control. Over the years, she's taught me simple meditations to let go of built-up stress. I breathe for a while then dial Dad, but before I hit call, I swipe back out of my contact list. *Come on, Mig. You can do this by yourself.*

Grabbing my handbag, I hunt for the card with my car service membership number. I log the call quickly with the lady who answers the phone and while I wait for the service to arrive, I call Elisa.

"Do you want me to come over?" Elisa blurts out before I even say hello. Her intuition is working overtime today. Weirdly, her reaction instantly comforts me. *So I'm not imagining it.*

I hear feet thumping on Elisa's side of the line, then two little voices shout, "Hi Auntie Mig!"

I laugh as I hear Elisa shushing Isabel and Francesco. Well, that has made me feel better. I'm grinning like a loon. "You'll never guess the day I've had."

"What happened?"

"I'm currently sitting in my car at the train station, waiting for the service guy to come fix my flat tire."

"I guess I'm not coming over tonight then?" she says.

"Did you need to escape?"

I can hear the kids squealing in the background and Elisa snaps, "Quiet! Mom's on the phone."

Isabel and Francesco chorus, "Sorry!"

"El, I'm completely wiped from my day and I have no idea how long I'll be sitting here in the dark for."

"Want me to come and get you?"

I seriously think about it. "I should wait for the car guy." I wriggle and glare at the steering wheel. "Anyway, it must be the kids' dinnertime?"

"Isabel wants to help make the spaghetti," she says with false brightness. "I'm in hell, Mig." I imagine Isabel's holy grin, Francesco's bright brown eyes, and their two pairs of grubby hands wanting to knead the dough. "Why don't you change the tire yourself?" she suggests.

"Ha! Can you imagine me, and all my five-foot-nothing self, trying to undo tire nuts? Wanna come watch? Bring popcorn."

"Whoa, okay. You *have* had a bad day. Well, stay on the phone with me while you wait. I want to make sure you're safe." Her voice softens and I hear her groan. "No, Frankie. Stop. Go wash your hands. You too, Isa."

When I have her attention back, I tell her about the train, the rain, my broken umbrella, the standoffish receptionists, then pause before I get to the missing email, wondering if I should mention it. I'd love her thoughts on it all. I often pretend a devil and an angel sit on my shoulders. Elisa is my angel and, though he'd be annoyed about it, my dad is often the voice of my devil. "And then an email went missing. I didn't delete it. I checked the deleted files and the spam folder. The subject line said *help me.* Weird, right? I don't know where it went."

"How does it make you feel?"

I can always rely on Elisa to believe me without question. Does it encourage my wild fantasies? Maybe. But I figure my own mind puts plenty of doubt into my reasoning. "I have a weird feeling . . ."

She hums. "Why did the last assistant leave?"

"I don't know. Do you think it's connected?"

"Let me think . . . Frankie, don't hit your sister with the spoon! Ugh. Hang on, Mig. He didn't mean it, Isabel."

I can hear crying over the phone and Elisa's muffled voice soothing her kids. It's cold enough in the car that I see fog puffing from my nose. My stomach rumbles, complaining at its emptiness, and my full bladder is pressing on my last nerve. I shift in my seat, but there's no use. I can't get comfortable.

I bolt from the car, needing to be physical, and slam the door shut behind me. Dancing in place, I blow on my icy fingers. Another train pulls in and ejects more passengers, who race off as if hellhounds are chasing after them. I need to be more organized. Tomorrow, I'll leave home earlier to ensure I get a closer park.

"What do you know about her?" Elisa asks when she comes back on the phone.

"Nothing, really. It's been a long day. Maybe it means nothing."

"Hey, that's not—"

"El, I just wanna go home and have a bath and a giant glass of wine. Like, the size of the bottle." My attention is focused on the tight muscles in my neck and my sore eyes. I raise and drop my shoulders but it doesn't help.

"Yes, and now the flat tire. I'm sorry, Mig. I'm sure you saw what you saw. You know I trust you. I can still come and get you."

"Do you need to get out of the house?" I ask again. "Is Frank home yet?"

She sighs. "The kids are right at that age where they need to tell me everything and help with everything. It's exhausting. Yeah, Frank's home, so if you need me, I can dump the kids in his lap and jump in the car. He can watch their cartoons rather than the soccer replay. He watched it on the weekend, honestly, why does he need to watch it again?"

I lock the car and stomp to the footpath, laughing at Elisa's whining. The phone is a comfort as I pace back and forth, listening to my black flats slap against the concrete. A horn blares from the carpark entrance. "Oh, thank God, they're here. I have to go."

Elisa wishes me luck and hangs up. I wave to get the driver's attention. My savior is thankfully quick. He garners a bit of attention with looky-loos disembarking from yet another train, but in no time at all, he's done. As he drives off, I start my car and visions of hot, salty chips start dancing in my head. Even though I'm busting for the restroom, I race through a takeaway drive-thru and turn toward home, smelling salt and chicken and listening to my belly rumble. I'm driving perhaps a tad too fast along the street toward my house, and my gaze drifts to the houses and lights hidden behind the closed curtains of my neighborhood. Lives are going on around me. Families eating dinner and laughing with each other as they discuss their day. Couples in love hugging over a bubbly pasta sauce. Loneliness creeps over me as I glance at my takeaway bag. Elisa might be annoyed right now but I'm envious of her boisterous, crowded lifestyle.

I face the road and a small black shadow dashes in front of my car. "Shit, shit, shit!" I jerk the wheel and slam on the brakes, tires screaming in protest, and end up staring straight into the wide eyes of another driver, his car stopped scant inches from my bumper. I'd driven right past my driveway and nearly into my new neighbor. I jump from my car still swearing. "Oh my freaking God, did I hit your car? There was a cat, I think. Shit. Did I hit it?" I search the asphalt, glad the streetlight is close to my driveway. Nothing moves. No glowing eyes. No flat shape on the road either, thank goodness.

The driver unfolds his body from the other car, easily standing six foot and something and . . . *Whoa.* He's hot. Like capital H hot. My stomach flips cartwheels. Black, closely shorn hair, a piercing dark gaze and sharp cheekbones. His skin is black and his gray suit looks insanely expensive.

For a second, the strangest feeling swims over me, as if I'm in the presence of someone powerful, like staring at a superhero on his downtime. It passes, but a shiver dances down my spine and the back of my neck is cold, reminding me of that old walking over your grave saying. I shake it off. Clearly, I'm the dangerous one. I almost hit him with my car.

His voice is the deep smooth rumble of a radio DJ. I don't recognize his accent. It's not Australian, that's for sure. My heart jumps at how sexy he sounds.

"—hit me."

"What?" I hadn't heard a word over my internal admiration.

He huffs out a breath, annoyance with a hint of exasperation. "You did not hit me. But it was perilously close. Fortunately, I see rather well in the dark. Are you well?"

"Yes, fine. Sorry. There was a cat."

He's shaking his head. "There was no cat."

"There was!" Now I'm arguing with my probably rich and important neighbor after almost hitting his car. *Maybe he's a movie star?* My mind has clearly packed up shop and gone home.

I touch the bumper with a fingertip. "You're sure I didn't hit you?" Imagining the cost of the repair bill makes my stomach swirl in horror.

"You did not."

Relief floods through me, soaking every limb, and I slump, steadying my body with a hand pressed to the side of his car.

"Are you well?" His fingers curl around my wrist, hot skin almost scalding.

I instinctively snatch my arm away. I can still feel the heat of his fingers against my skin. "Ah, sure. Yes, I'm fine. I've just had a long, horrible day. First day. I started my first day, I mean new job, first day at my new job." I clamp my lips shut to stop yammering. *Mig, you are an embarrassment.*

His silence is unnerving. My face must be the kind of red tomato soup would be envious of. I hope he can't see that. He probably thinks I'm an idiot. *I need to get out of here.*

I gesture to my car. "I'm glad I didn't hit you. Were you going somewhere?" Before he can open his mouth, I continue. "Of course you were and I'm in your way. I'll move my car." My stomach, released from its nausea, lets out a rumble loud enough to shake the earth, sending new flames of fire to my overheated face. I clamp a chilled hand to my cheek. "Sorry. I'm hungry. My dinner's in the car. I'll move it. The car, not my dinner. Excuse me." Without seeing his reaction, I jump into my car and, being overly cautious now—checking all of my mirrors—I inch the car back enough to turn into my own driveway.

My new neighbor doesn't move. His imposing frame stands still as a statue in my rear-view mirror. My skin continues to tingle, the embarrassment from my stammering stinging my fiery cheeks. My neck is icy cold.

I turn off the engine and breathe in the scent of my slowly cooling dinner. Chicken, chips and gravy. My rich neighbor probably only eats in fancy restaurants, or cooks three course meals. I can't remove my soggy takeaway bag in front of him. I groan without moving my lips, even though there's no way he can see me from this distance. *Well, I guess he could hardly think any worse of me.* Pretending I can't see him, I slink from my car, grab my bags and the takeout, and race to my front door.

In my head, Berry and Rose admonish me. *Be neighborly!* I throw a wave in his direction and almost brain myself with the chip bag. "Have a great evening," I call, fumbling with the front door. Getting it open at last, I stumble into the dark and slam the door. I slide down until I land on my butt and drop my head into my hands.

Chapter 8

I step into the elevator on Tuesday morning with a hot takea-way coffee and a more positive attitude. Today—depending on Bacitriet—I'll get my desk organized and become the power-house executive assistant I know myself to be.

I nod at Bethany as I walk through reception, tightening my scarf. "Good morning." *Why is it so cold in here?* Bethany covers her earpiece, her sharp gaze fixed on my face and doesn't say a word. I don't let on how much her behavior bothers me.

My good mood survives until midmorning. My desk is clean, my files and folders are labeled and color-coded, my notes are sorted according to subject and my email folders are named. I attempt to meet more of Bacitriet's staff. People do start late here, with most rocking up a little after nine-thirty. I'll be one of the few early birds, but that doesn't bother me. I'm used to getting a lot of work done before the boss comes in. When I find the staff kitchen, I nearly trip over my feet as I gaze around in wonder. *Oh my, I'm in heaven.* Luxurious red wood and gold tinted furniture create little bubbles of calm and the chairs are as soft as they look. I join the line waiting for coffee—*an actual barista, for crying out loud*—and introduce myself to the woman behind me. "I'm Mig. I started yesterday."

"Renee. Finance." The woman's rose-colored lips barely crack a smile. She immediately turns to talk to the man behind her, platinum blond hair swishing in a wave, cutting me out. *Rude.*

Chastened, I head back to my desk, the sounds of office chatter familiar at least. Once it gets busy in here, it sure gets busy. I lean over my partition when the man at the desk behind mine ends his call. "Hi, I'm Mig."

He brushes a finger over a well-groomed mustache. His white skin is slimy with sweat. "Joshua." He doesn't hold out his hand to shake.

"I'm new," I say, hoping to start a conversation. "Bacitriet's new assistant."

"I know." He picks up his cell phone and walks away with it pressed to his ear.

A hush falls over the buzzing floor as Bacitriet jerkily strides toward me. "My office."

I bolt up, notebook in hand, and follow him in. Oddly his office is freezing, even colder than the open area. Tugging my jacket tighter, I sit and search the walls for the air-conditioning monitor. When we're done here, I'll call building maintenance to check it.

For twenty minutes, I take notes on how Bacitriet likes his calendar, his regular meetings and his catering, trying not to shudder every time he sniffs. *So gross.*

"I think I've got all of that," I tell him, keeping my voice upbeat. Of course I had it memorized, he'd repeated himself a trillion times. Perhaps the assistant before me required constant repetition. His eyes thin and he stares at me for such a long time, I suspect he's trying to get inside my head. When he says nothing more, I lean forward. "And when will I get access to your email?"

His lined face turns a shade of red I've never seen before. He bares pointed teeth. "You won't."

I work to hide my surprise. "I—I usually . . . I find it easier to track invitations and follow up on requests if I have access." His expression grows thunderous so I backtrack quickly. "Of course, I don't need access. I'm sure you receive a lot of emails.

I just thought, perhaps, I could lighten the load on your . . ." The color of his face shifts into the purple spectrum. "Or you can forward me anything you would like actioned." I press my fingers into my notebook and stare at him with the most impassive face I can manage. *Hold your ground. You did nothing wrong.*

He stares.

I stare back. *Hold.* Either he's going to fire me or demand I get out.

Honestly, I've never come across someone so intimidating in their silence. Most men are predictable, but this man is anything but, and it's messing with my organized brain.

"I believe that is all."

Oh, thank God. "Will you be here for the rest of the day?"

"I will leave shortly."

Nodding, I leap to my feet, thankful to get out of his presence. "Yes, sir." I shoot him a smile and hightail it out of there. Back in my chair, I breathe deeply and try to stop my hands from shaking. It feels as though hundreds of eyes are on me, judging my failure, but the horror movie moment is only in my head because when I look up, the employees around me are seated at their desks, staring at their screens with laser-like focus. When I unlock my own screen, I find my inbox has doubled in size. Bacitriet is forwarding what looks to be a mountain of email. Hell, this is going to take all week to review.

Movement draws my gaze up. Bacitriet steps out of his office in a long black coat and gray scarf. He grasps his laptop satchel and an umbrella in one hand, his phone in the other.

"See you tomorrow," I call but he's already gone. How can an old man move so fast? Shooting my still growing inbox a side-eye, I'm horrified to find the number of unread emails increasing with the speed of a rollercoaster.

"Hey there."

I look up to find the blond receptionist standing in front of my desk. "Hi. Bethany, right?"

"The monster's gone, huh?" She flips her green scarf over her shoulder with sharp-tipped blood-red nails. "Me and the girls are going for an early lunch. Join us?" It doesn't sound like a request.

Normally, I wouldn't. Group lunches can be total bitch-fests and hold no interest for me. Today, I need the distraction. Besides, it will give me a chance to ask the questions that are filling my head. "Sure." I grab my handbag.

The restaurant we walk to is located down a little side street and I would never have known it was there without following Bethany's statuesque figure. Traffic noises fade as the door closes behind us. Bethany walks in as if she owns the place. The cold follows us inside, or maybe it just feels that way to me. Bethany and Candy shuck their jackets as I pull mine tighter around me. *How are they not freezing?*

It's an interesting group. Of the six of us, I know Bethany, Candy and Shannon, my trainer from yesterday. I brush my fingers over the white silk tablecloth and eye the gorgeously engraved wine glasses. The main dining area is completely empty. *I can't afford a place like this.* I'm afraid to check the menu.

The other women are in their mid to late twenties, younger than my thirty-four years, which makes me feel really old. Bethany sits at the end of our six-seater table and introduces Sara and Charli. Sara could have stepped right off a runway. Not a hair is out of place and her makeup is flawless. She has a real evil queen vibe. Charli is a Japanese carbon copy of Sara. Both are from France and move in sync, which is a little disturbing. Sitting on my immediate left is Candy, the other receptionist. I smile cheerfully at her and she stares blankly back at me. Okay, awkward. Shannon is the last to sit down.

The silence quickly becomes stifling. I examine my fingernails, wondering if I should paint them, glaringly aware of my department-store clothes. I glance up to find them all staring at me. It's like being a bug on a windscreen. "Ah, hi?"

Sara raps her perfectly polished nails upon the tabletop. "Tell us about yourself." Her shark-like smile gives me the sudden feeling someone has chummed the water.

"I'm Bacitriet's assistant," I say, stalling for time. I need to figure out what they want the information for, so I know what to tell them.

"We know that." Charli leans forward and her lips purse. "Tell us about *you*."

"Ha, of course." My laugh is on the hysterical side. "I've worked in admin for what seems like forever. My last boss was great." *Until the end.* "I stayed for five years, but before that, I traveled. Worked in London. Figured it was time to settle down so I came home to save money for a house. I hated being dependent on my parents, but you know how it is, homes are just so expensive." I can't tell if I'm boring them or holding their interest.

"So you do have family?" Bethany confirms. Her mouth pinches as if she's eaten something sour.

"Oh no. No kids. No hubby either. But parents, brother, grandmothers. The lot." I fake a laugh.

"Are you close?" Bethany continues. I glance around at the others. They stare, silently waiting for my answer.

"Very close." I clear my throat and decide to get the focus off myself. "And what about you all? Tell me everything."

It doesn't take long. All have traveled, all have worked in admin of various sorts and all started at Bacitriet Consulting in the last three months.

Wait . . . That doesn't make sense. "What, all of you?" I've never heard of that happening in a well-established business. "Why?"

The women fall silent, like robots shut down at the same time. I stare blankly at the menu prices. *Cripes.* Under the stoic stare of the waiter, I order a small salad and sparkling water. Bethany orders a rare steak. The surprises continue as the other women echo Bethany's order. I cringe at the price of the steak. Nope, not changing my order. I turn to Bethany, thinking I know her slightly better than the others. About half a second better—she was the one to fetch me to join them after all. "This is going to sound really dumb, but what is it exactly that Bacitriet does?"

Bethany sighs. "Anything his clients want."

"Yes, but—"

"He makes problems go away."

That sounded ominous. "The assistant I replaced, Cassandra Chan. Why did she leave?"

I'm met with silence. If there were crickets nearby, I'd hear them chirping. I gulp my sparkling water, wishing I'd ordered wine.

Bethany moistens her lips. "People leave all the time. It is an intense business, and we have high turnover. You should stop encouraging gossip, Margaret."

Ouch. "Maybe she won the lottery and just chucked it all in," I say, forcing another laugh. "Bought the family a holiday or something?"

"No family she said," Candy speaks up. She falls silent at Bethany's head snapping sharply in her direction. Gee, I thought it'd been tense before, but now, every muscle hurts.

"We said that about the first one," Charli whispers. She earns a strong look of displeasure from Bethany.

My heart sinks. "First one?" They must be messing with me. I search each face for answers, but no one flinches. Nausea curls in my belly like a snake. Something is very, very wrong here.

When I get back to my desk, I'll stalk Cassandra Chan's social media and see what job she moved onto. If she has another job. Maybe she *did* win the lotto? It would explain why she just up and left. Then again, Bacitriet said he preferred trialing assistants without referee checks. Maybe Cassandra just didn't work out? *Her email, though, the missing one.* I need to know what it said. "Did Cassandra talk to any of you? Was she unhappy?"

Bacitriet hasn't struck me as a nasty boss, only an intimidating one. Still, high turnover is not a good sign in any workplace. I should be more careful. Bacitriet is creepy—in a movie villain sort of way—but is he really so bad that several assistants felt the need to leave without giving notice?

After a short silence, Bethany catches my eye. "Do you live close by?"

"No, I'm an hour away on the train." I mutter. "I just moved into my new house actually. Did I mention that earlier? It's nice. A bit small but I want to fix it up." I fiddle with my napkin. I'm really not that hungry anymore.

The women around the table seem uncomfortable gossiping about work in front of Bethany. I'll have to figure out how to talk to them alone. I'm stuck on Cassandra Chan. Why did she leave?

Two waitresses appear with our meals. It's not until I take a few bites that I realize no one has answered my earlier question. "How long did Cassandra work for Mr. Bacitriet?" I blame my screenplay. I'm always wanting to know peoples' stories. My curiosity will be the death of me one day.

Bethany's lips twist. "Really, Margaret. You are very nosy."

I sit back and drop my fork to the table, blinking at her in surprise. She holds my gaze and cuts off a bloody chunk of steak. She pops it into her mouth and turns toward Sara. "How much was that perfume you wanted?"

Frustration eats at me. "Did any of you apply for Bacitriet's assistant role?"

Silence greets that question too. No one looks up—they are focused wholly on their meals.

"Well." My face strains to hold my smile. "Hopefully it's not because Bacitriet is a bad boss. Getting this job really helped me out of a bind and you've all made me feel really welcome." *Come on ladies. Give me something.* Why did they invite me out if it wasn't to talk?

The walk back is quiet. I keep up with their long legs, but it's not easy. A tram dings its bell noisily as it rattles past. It doesn't block out the sound of the busker on the street corner playing a guitar. He's very good. The buzz of city life seeps into my skin as I replay the lunchtime conversation. If I'd watched it in a movie, I would have suspected the women were hiding something. But what? My curiosity is piqued.

Bethany strides forward on her sharp heels like she's on a mission, the other women trail behind her like minions. The dynamics are so odd. It's rare to find an alpha receptionist. Bethany walks me to my desk and leans forward as I sit down. "Don't worry about what we said at lunch—it's nothing. The girls . . . well. We shouldn't gossip." Her grin is all teeth.

I nod. "Sure." Bethany swans away, leaving me staring at my computer. Elisa's voice rises up in my mind. *Bad vibes.* Maybe Bethany applied for the job with Bacitriet and didn't get it. Resentment would certainly explain her waspish behavior. I shoot Elisa a text, asking her to pop around tonight. I want her opinion on it all.

In the bathroom, I run into Candy. Standing at the sink, washing my hands, I stare at her reflection in the mirror until she catches my gaze. She spins away, but I won't be deterred and stop her at the door. "What did you mean at lunch about Bacitriet's assistants? The first one? How many assistants has Bacitriet had?"

"Three." Her face relaxes like she's glad to finally tell someone.

My mouth drops open. "In how long?"

"Three months."

Tippity tap tap. The anxious sound draws my gaze to Candy's fingernails on the door handle. I lower my voice. I can't hear anyone in the stalls but that doesn't mean someone isn't there, listening into our conversation. "What aren't you telling me? Did Bacitriet fire them? Was he inappropriate?"

"No one knows." Candy's lips mash together as if she's trying to stop herself from speaking. I wait, watching her steadily. "No one knows why she left. One morning, she just didn't come in. When HR called, there was no answer. No phone, no email, nothing. She just . . . vanished."

Then Candy does a disappearing act of her own through the door before I can ask any more questions. I head to my desk more confused than ever.

Bacitriet has emailed the company brand guidelines and several reports to format. It's easy work but time-consuming. As I read through the reports, Bacitriet's job becomes clearer. He consults on strategy and company restructures, and boy, he's reached some rather bloodthirsty conclusions. Poor people. No wonder Bacitriet needs an assistant who can keep secrets. He advises companies on who to terminate.

A trilling sound catches my attention midway through the afternoon, and it takes me a moment to realize it's a desk phone—a foreign sound. My last workplace introduced headsets for outside calls to come in via the computer system. A real phone is a little like stepping back in time. I pick up the handset. "Hello, this is Margaret Solder. Can I help you?"

"Who are you?" The male caller's voice sounds strained, thick, like he's got a cold.

I clear my throat in sympathy. "I'm Mr. Bacitriet's assistant. How can I help you?"

"Where is she?"

"Where is who?"

"Bacitriet's assistant. Annie Seramoph. This is her number."

"I'm Mr. Bacitriet's assistant now. Can I help you, sir?"

There's silence, then the voice screeches, "Where's my daughter?"

Chapter 9

"I think you have the wrong number," I say tightening my grip on the handset.

His voice thickens. "Where is she?"

I peer over my shoulder. The hairs on the back of my neck quiver. I eye Bacitriet's open door. He's not in. So why does it feel like he's watching me? "Sir?"

"My daughter. She works—worked—for that man. Bacitriet."

"I'm . . ." The name on the second email inbox is Cassandra, not Annie. "I think another lady—"

"Five weeks. I've been in twice and that damned bruiser in the lobby won't let me upstairs. I want to speak to Bacitriet." The caller coughs, his emotional state getting the better of him before he wrestles back control with a swallow and continues. "My Annie disappeared five weeks ago. She was last seen leaving *that* building. No one has heard from her. That man had something to do with it. I know it."

I rise up to peer over the partitions around my desk, searching for help. Joshua's desk is empty—he must be in a meeting. I catch sight of Shannon talking to Sara and Charli at a desk near the window. I wave but they don't see me. "If your daughter left, then how—"

"I know it's him."

What do I say to that? "Sir, I . . ." My hand is trembling. I squeeze it into a fist. "I only just started here and—"

"Get out. Get out while you can."

Beeping follows the whispered warning. I stare at the hand-set in shock, and inside my head, a blank wall sets up shop. My stomach cramps. I know it's not my bad week; it's just this place. I glance again at Bacitriet's open door.

Get out while you still can.

*

Swallowing the last mouthful of pad thai, I toss my fork into the plastic tub. "It doesn't make sense."

Elisa sits cross-legged on the carpet, relaxed, head tilted, thinking intently. The coffee table between us is decorated with the empty containers of our dinner.

I muted the TV when Elisa arrived rather than turn it off, leaving it on for the weather forecast. I don't want to get caught in another downpour like Monday. Once was enough, thanks. The current story is about a condemned asylum building in the next suburb. I didn't even know there was one around here. The idea of it is rather sad. Probably a lot of history there. Not good history either.

Elisa sips from her wine glass. She doesn't say anything, so I keep talking. "According to Candy, three of Bacitriet's assistants have left over the last three months. The last one disappeared without notice and—what are you doing?" I watch the back of Elisa's head as she darts away. "I was right in the middle of—" She races back before I can finish, carrying the whiteboard I use to plot out my screenplay. "Hey, I'm putting that up on the weekend."

She plonks down beside me on the sofa, dropping the markers next to the takeout containers, and takes a photo of the whiteboard's contents with her phone. She rubs the white-board clean.

"Hey!"

"You can rewrite it. We'll use this to note down what you know, like in a police show." She uncaps a black marker and jots down what I've already told her. "It'll let us look at the problem clearly. Besides, you love lists and research. Now, what were their names?"

"The assistant before me was Cassandra Chan. I've got access to her email. And there's Annie Seramoph. I don't know the name of the other one."

"So we'll call her Miss Three for now."

I scratch my nose and lean forward to read the words as they form on the board. "I think she'd be Miss One, wouldn't she? The first to leave."

"Right, right." Elisa scrubs at the name and replaces it. "We know Cassandra left without explanation. Annie has been missing for five weeks, and they all worked for the same guy."

"A week ago, Cassandra didn't show up for work, which is how I got the job. What if she was hit by a bus?"

"What?"

"It would explain why she didn't come in, right? If she's in a coma or, oh, what if she's lost her memory?"

"How can we check? Call the hospitals? I guess I can do that after I drop the kids off at school."

"You'd do that?"

"Of course. I want to know what's going on as much as you do. You're my friend. I'm worried about you. You work for this guy. I don't want you to go missing next."

I blink at her, mouth open. "You don't—you haven't sensed anything like that have you?"

"Not exactly. Just that the bad vibes I'm getting are worse. So, you don't know when the first assistant went missing?"

"If she even *is* missing. We have no idea why they left. HR called Cassandra, but I wonder if anyone went by her house." I stare at Elisa. "Maybe we should go?" I skol what's left in my wine glass.

"What's her address?"

"I don't know. I'll try to find it at work. You know, all of this is making me feel quite sick."

Elisa shoots me a serious look. "You have to listen to those feelings. You might be getting warnings too."

"What else are you getting?"

She caps the marker and closes her eyes. "My guides aren't saying anything in particular, but they are really unsettled."

"How can you tell?"

She gives me a long look and stretches for her wine glass, folding herself into another yoga pose.

I hold up a hand. "I'm actually serious. How can you tell your guides are unsettled? In what way?"

"You know I have three? I'm sure one of them is my nonna." She smiles and sips her wine. "The others are older. I don't see them, exactly, but I do get shadows and impressions. Nothing is ever clear. It's not like I hear a voice say, 'Don't do that, Elisa.' They're usually even-tempered, but at the moment, they're really agitated. It makes my heart race."

"My grandmothers just turn up at my door to tell me what to do." I uncap a whiteboard marker. "What else do we know?"

Within half an hour, the whiteboard is full. "This is all just supposition." I sink into my chair as Elisa refills my wine glass with the last of the chardonnay. I'll have to stop drinking soon if I want to be functional tomorrow. I wave my phone around. "There's nothing on social media except for standard profile pages." I sit up. "Oh hey, nothing comes up when I search on them together, but when I look individually there's a few links. Here's one on Annie's disappearance. It's just a small police report article from a news website." I add the details to the whiteboard.

"So nothing connects the missing women except Bacitriet?"

"Nothing I can see." Cassandra Chan's social media profile picture shows a pretty Asian woman close to my age. "Great references. She's not hopeless. Maybe she got headhunted and hasn't updated her page yet?"

"I think you should quit." Elisa's lips are drawn in as she presses them together tightly. The expression on her face is as serious as I've ever seen it.

I tilt my head and frown. "I can't quit. I need this job."

"Start looking for another one then." For a second I'm sure her eyes turn white. She blinks and shakes her head as if brushing off a feeling of dread.

I nod. "I'll start looking for a new job tomorrow. But for now, I have to work there, so I need to figure out what to do. Do I just pretend I'm not worried?"

She presses back into the sofa cushions. "Play it by ear. And stay where there are a lot people."

I moan at her. "So comforting."

She glances toward the window. "Have you met the neighbor yet?" A smirk dances across her lips.

I swallow a mouthful of wine the wrong way. Coughing harshly, I gasp out, "Shit. Wait until you hear this." I quickly tell her what happened the night before.

She giggles. "So, what's his name?"

"No idea, I didn't ask. Elisa, I was mortified. I just wanted to get out of there."

Her hands cover her mouth. She parts her fingers to mutter, "Only you, Mig."

"What does that mean? Besides, you said I should keep my distance from him."

Elisa's eyes lose focus.

"Elisa?" No response. "El!"

She blinks, coming back from wherever it was she went. After a moment, she stands and creeps to the windows. "The feeling I have . . . well . . . I don't know. I don't *think* it's entirely bad."

"But you're not sure?"

She drinks the remainder of her wine. "Well, he's handsome and probably rich . . . I mean, he drives a fabulous car. It could be his ego I'm picking up on. Or pride."

"We don't know that he's rich," I argue, following her to the window. "Why would he live *here* if he's rich? It's just a regular suburb. I'd live in a private estate given half a chance. Imagine the bathroom I could have."

Elisa rolls her eyes and tilts her head, but I press on. "I have a plan. I have a house. I have a new job that is a little disturbing but with great pay and free coffee. I don't have time to devote to my neighbor." We both peer through the window at the dark house next door.

"You could use some fun," she says softly.

"Fun is not in the plan."

A voice inside my head—the evil one I hear most mornings when I'm getting dressed—laughs. *Like he'd be interested in you.* The voice has a point. I'm not the sort of woman hot rich guys are attracted too. *Thank God.* It's more likely I'd become obsessed with him and make it weirder than it already is. My disparaging inner voice roars with agreeing laughter.

"Mig?" Elisa sounds panicked.

I look around to see what has spooked her. "What?"

"Look at the TV!"

A photograph of a young woman fills the screen. The label beneath her face turns my blood cold. *Annie Seramoph.* I race toward the sofa and dive on the remote to turn the sound up.

"—lead story tonight. Annie Seramoph disappeared five weeks ago. Her parents have made this appeal to the public." The reporter's well-quaffed head disappears as the vision changes to video of a white, middle-aged balding man and a gray-haired woman standing at a podium. The woman's eyes are red and she dabs at them with a torn tissue.

The man's voice trembles. "Annie, honey, we love you so much. We want you to come home. Call us, please. If anyone has seen our daughter, please call the police and uh, the help-line. Please, please, Annie. Please . . ."

I bite my tongue, tasting blood. Goosebumps cover my skin as I recognize the voice.

"Is that . . . ?"

"The one who called me," I whisper. Dark shadows stain the skin below Mr. Seramoph's eyes; his wife cries silently at his side.

"They're so sad," Elisa says staring intently at the TV.

Sad? The whole thing is horrific. The missing girl sat in my work chair only a few weeks ago.

"I think you need to ask around your office," Elisa says softly. "Someone must know something."

*

No one will talk to me. I try the ladies from yesterday's lunch first, but it's difficult to get them alone. I stalk the bathroom and finally catch Shannon at the sinks. The instant she lays eyes on me, she snaps, "Yes?"

"Is it Bacitriet?"

"What are you talking about?" She leans close to the mirror and reapplies her glistening ruby lipstick.

"Three of his assistants left abruptly. Did they leave because of him?"

"Don't be ridiculous."

"One disappeared. It's been reported to the police."

She flinches. "Really? How do—"

"It was on the news last night. Her family are freaking out."

Shannon's sharp red eyebrows rise. "I'll ask around." She leaves me in the bathroom with a swish of hair and a heap of attitude.

I randomly approach people. From Candy the dark-haired receptionist to Joel the cleaner. No one has anything to say. Most act as though they don't know what I'm talking about.

I can't work out which would be worse: that they're hiding something, or genuinely have no idea what I'm talking about?

"Mr. Bacitriet's assistant," I'd say.

"Aren't you his assistant?"

"I am now."

"Wasn't the last one named Cassandra?"

"The one before that—"

"I only started a few weeks ago."

And that's another odd coincidence. Many people I speak with only started working here within the last month or so. My initial research into Bacitriet Consulting implied the company has been around for a while. *Why have so many employees started so recently?*

In the amazing office kitchen, I catch Charli and Sara in the coffee line. "Hi."

In eerie unison, they reply, "Hello, Margaret."

I make small talk about the morning and then start, "So, yesterday at lunch we were talking about Bacitriet. Did Cassandra ever tell you she was . . . um . . . scared?"

Sara blinks and wets her lips with a swipe of her tongue. She shares a look with Charli. "No."

"Who was the other assistant? I know there was Cassandra Chan and Annie Seramoph, but who was the third?"

The women blink in unison. "You mean Maria?"

"Maria who?" If I'm to look her up, I need her full name.

Charli glances over my head. "Hello, Bethany."

"Coffee break?" The blond moves to stand right behind me. Cold air trickles down my spine and I glance up, sure I must have stepped under an air-conditioning vent. Nothing.

I turn back to Charli, refusing to be cowed by Bethany's intimidating presence. "Were you friends with Cassandra?"

Charli doesn't look at me. "No." She takes her coffee, hands Sara the next mug, and together they stride from the room.

"Are you encouraging gossip, Margaret?" Bethany smiles down at me, exposing perfectly white teeth.

When the barista calls my name, I'm grateful for the excuse to escape. *Whoa, intense!* As I spin toward the exit, I find Bacitriet standing in the doorway watching me.

"In my office."

Sweat breaks out across my palms. Collecting my notepad, I follow him into the enclosed space and sit down at the table. His face is a mask, giving no inkling of his mood.

"You have been asking about my previous assistants." His icy voice crawls into my head, and the urge to dig a fingernail into my ear is hard to suppress.

"Yes, sir."

Crack. The bones in his fingers pop as he tilts his wrist and forms a fist. His fingers remind me of a bird—they're so thin, I'm afraid they'll snap if he holds his pen too tight. He sniffs, his head tilting to the side. "You will stop."

"Yes, sir." Do I dare ask about the missing person's report on the news? *You have to know.* "Mr. Bacitriet. About Annie . . ."

His stare burrows into me. "Yes?"

"Her family were on the news last night. She's . . . she's missing."

"Unfortunate."

"She was your assistant. Did she say anything to you at all? Was she worried about anything or anyone?"

"No, and I'd advise you to leave this alone, Ms. Solder. You are here to work, not to socialize."

"But—"

I'm captivated by his thin lips. White gunk coats the corners of his mouth as he speaks. I fight not to screw up my nose in disgust. "She left and did not return. She did not provide notice. Is that all?"

Doesn't he think that's weird? He sounds like he doesn't care and I wonder if that's what he thinks of me too? Just an assistant. Easily replaceable. "Yes, sir."

He opens his laptop. "I need you to book the meetings I have just emailed you about. I also require a flight to Sydney this afternoon. I'll forward you the times and accommodation details. You may go."

I race from the office as if my pants are on fire, and I'm too busy to think about anything not work-related for the rest of the afternoon. Bacitriet's meetings are with board members. Not a single one says more than two words to me as they enter and exit Bacitriet's office. It's only after Bacitriet has left for his flight that I'm able to breathe again. The heavy silence hanging over the office transforms instantly into a wall of noise—phones ring, chatter rises and voices fill with laughter. Bacitriet's exit is a pressure release that turns everyone giddy.

I don't feel like laughing. I drop my head into my hands as my stomach rolls. *Elisa's right.* I need to look for a new job.

"Hey."

Standing in front of my desk is a young man. His dreadlocks rattle as the beads lining them flick from side to side. Sensuous lips, surrounded by a neat goatee, widen into a broad smile.

"Hi," I blurt.

His dark eyes shine with good humor. "You logged a ticket about a missing email? I'm Timber."

My thoughts snap back online. "You're IT? Great. Yes." I point to my computer, and he gestures for me to move out of my chair.

"Lemme have a looksee."

I hover, wanting to see what he's doing. He clicks the mouse over my screen. I breathe in and his body spray burns my nasal hairs. *So he's not perfect then.* I inch backward and clear my throat. "Timber?"

He throws a smile over his shoulder. "My name. I know, I know."

"Oh, don't worry, I get it. Most people call me Mig, but my name's Margaret." I point at the screen. "It was in my inbox. The subject line was 'help me'."

"Yeah, I see what happened. It's in your spam folder."

"I didn't move it." And I'd checked the spam folder. It hadn't been in there earlier. "I knew I hadn't imagined it," I mutter.

"These things happen. We have pretty strong filters."

"Well, thank you for your help." I'm a bit embarrassed he had to come here to find it.

He gives me another sweet smile. It lights up his entire face. *Maybe this place isn't so bad after all.*

"You're very welcome. Are you familiar with all our programs? Do I need to show you anything?"

My inner sixteen-year-old giggles but I shake my head. "I haven't seen anything I haven't used before." My inner sixteen-year-old snorts. "I can see the inbox of the previous assistant Cassandra Chan, the assistant I replaced, but I understand she wasn't here that long—is there any chance I can get the mailbox of the assistant before her?"

His body stills. "Annie's? Uh, I'm not sure. Why?"

"I don't want to miss anything for Bacitriet she might have been in the process of booking."

Timber shrugs. "I'll find out for you."

I give him a broad smile. "Thanks." Perhaps I'll find something in Annie's inbox that will explain why she left.

"What about our virtual meetings and chat system? Are you all good with them?"

I lean forward. "Like video conferences and text messages on my phone?"

"Exactly. See the icon here on your tool bar? Just double-click it and the collaboration tool opens up. Enter the name of the person you want to message in the search bar here and then type your message. When the person replies, you'll see these little dots pulsing before their message appears."

"That seems easy enough."

"See the icons there, you can also video call them."

I nod. "Got it."

"Any other issues, just IM me, get it?"

That's a joke? "Instant Message. Yeah, funny." My gaze follows him to another desk. What a dork.

I open the mysterious email Cassandra sent herself. It is one word.

Run.

Chapter 10

I squint through the foggy windscreen glass, searching for any sign of the dark behemoth that is my mysterious neighbor's car, or a cat-like shape that could dart out of the shadows. No light shines from his porch or from behind the closed curtains.

Breathing a sigh, I turn my car into my driveway and switch off the engine. For a moment, I don't move, just stare out into space. I'm relieved there's no sign of my neighbor. I really don't need that after the day I've had. I'm still tense from the conversation with Bacitriet. Thinking back on it sends a shiver over my skin. Doesn't he care about his missing assistants? Releasing another heavy sigh, I drag myself from the car and peer around. I open the back door to grab my bag.

"Good evening."

I yelp and spin, brandishing my bag as a weapon. The looming figure steps back to avoid my swing.

His arms move with exaggerated slow waves as they rise, showing his hands are empty. "My apologies. I did not mean to startle you."

Nervous energy bubbles up inside my chest. Holding in my laugh, it explodes out as a cough instead. "Oh, it's you. I didn't think you were home." I eye the path to my front door, all of six steps away, and clench my fingers around the strap of my bag. After my strange day, I'm on edge more than I'd realized. From now on, I'm leaving my porch light lit. "Is there something you wanted?"

He holds out a box. "Two elderly ladies came to my door earlier today and requested I hold onto this for you."

Oh God, they didn't! "My grandmothers," I say by way of explanation. Fear burns away under my embarrassment.

He smiles. "So I gathered."

Damn his voice is smooth. Like melting chocolate rolling down an ice cream sundae. Ugh, now I want chocolate. "Thank you." I take the package and his hot fingers brush mine. *Oooo.* My heart kicks into a samba. I focus on the package. Not expecting it to be heavy from the casual way he was holding onto it, I almost drop it. "Well . . . thanks."

"You're welcome." His voice disappears into the darkness with him.

"I'm sorry they bothered you. They can be insistent when they get an idea in their head," I sputter.

He stops and twists back slightly. "It is no bother." I can see his mouth but not his eyes. "They are beautiful souls."

That's one way to describe them, sure. "Be careful. If they think you're receptive they'll take advantage. They're always looking for strong muscles to help them move things." I warn with a laugh.

"And you . . . do you also require a strong hand?"

I gulp. It's practically audible. *Is he saying . . . what I think he's saying? No, not possible.* "I don't need any help. I am more than capable of handling myself." *Oh god. Did I just slap away his flirtatious attempt? Why, Mig, why?*

His smile grows wider. He must have shifted his feet because the streetlight brightens his face. Suddenly, I can see his eyes, and they're . . . twinkling? "Well, if I need a strong woman I'll know who to call on. How did your day go today?"

"Uh, fine. Why?" What did he mean by that? Is that more flirting?

"You mentioned starting a new job. Did it go better today? With your boss? I don't think you previously mentioned what the job is."

"Admin." Does he want to know more about me? I'm stunned. Hot guys don't usually flirt with me, and counting Timber this is two in the one day.

"And your boss, what is he like?"

"A bit creepy, actually," I say then slam my mouth shut. Why did I tell him that? I mean it's true, but why would I tell my neighbor that I'm worried?

"You don't like him?" His body language is open, interested, and his voice is light in that sexy, smooth way that invites listening, but I feel weird suddenly, standing here talking to my neighbor about my boss.

"Uh, I should let you go. Thanks again for looking after this for me." I jiggle the package.

He steps back. "As I said, it is not a bother. Good evening." He walks away and I feel bereft, like he took my adrenalin with him, and I suddenly feel how tired I really am.

I shake my head to clear it as he walks down my driveway. My stare locks onto his butt. *Whoo boy.* I need to date more. Two hopeless reactions to men just because they talked to me is a bit sad. He was flirting though, right? I'm sure he was.

Once I shut the door behind me, I realize I've forgotten to ask his name again. Hefting the gift box and my heart still pounding from the encounter, I head into the kitchen for a pair of scissors. The package comes apart quickly leaving me staring at a digitalized pie maker, the sort you see display ladies at the supermarket demonstrating. I laugh and leave it on the benchtop. There's no accompanying note, but I don't need one. My grandmothers are picking up freebies and I'm to be the lucky recipient. At least this is more useful than the giant pot plant my clueless brother brought over. What am I going to do with an enormous cactus? I guess I could ask my neighbor to help me move it? I flush and I pour myself a large glass of wine, drinking half of it far too quickly. Elisa's ringtone plays inside my handbag. I grab it out. "Hey."

"What did you find out?" she asks.

With the phone tucked between my shoulder and chin, I shuck my jacket and kick off my shoes. "Nothing. It's odd. Everyone I spoke to either didn't know Annie or only started with the company a few weeks ago."

"What? Everyone?" The tone in Elisa's voice reflects the buzz in my stomach.

"I think something strange is going on."

"Yeah, me too."

"I should quit." I swallow the remaining wine and hunt through my limited pantry stock for a bag of chips. I pour another full glass.

"You should."

My instincts are telling me—screaming—that I should leave. It's too much drama. My brain fights back with logic. "It's a normal office, Elisa. Full of ordinary people who come to work miserable and go home tired at the end of the day. The work is so ordinary, it's boring. I *shouldn't* quit. I need the money."

"And yet, look at all the odd."

Oh, I'm looking. "There's nothing concrete."

"You can't just ignore it."

It's on the tip of my tongue to say yes I can, but the words don't emerge. Haven't I already started asking around? I want to know what's going on. I sigh and change the subject, telling Elisa about the pie maker.

"Your grandmothers are a riot." She pauses and then says. "Wait, so the neighbor met your grandmas?"

"Yup." Just the thought of the two old women being inappropriate with him sends me into a fit of giggles.

"And? What's his name? Did he say anything else to you?"

"Oh, oh. Listen. He—he was flirting with me."

"What?"

I tell her what he said.

"Oh my God," she breathes the words like a benediction.

"And get this, the IT guy at work is really cute too."

"You go girl!" We laugh as I refill my glass, sipping slower this time. I'm getting that mellow feeling that tells me the booze is kicking in.

"So, what are you doing on the weekend?" she asks.

"Not much, why?"

Her voice grows excited. "I'm taking you for coffee down by the river."

"The statue park?"

"That's the one."

"I'd love—" A buzzing from my handbag catches my attention. "Hang on, El. That's my phone."

"We're on your phone."

"No, my work phone. It's probably Bacitriet."

"Don't answer it." Elisa's voice wobbles. "I've got a bad feeling. My guides are really skitty all of a sudden."

"I have to answer it. It's a work call."

"Ring me right back."

I disconnect my personal phone and answer the white, work-issued one. "Mr. Bacitriet?"

"I need you to fetch something for me."

The order sends a shiver down my spine. "Sir? It's seven o'clock."

"Yes, it is. There is a small black bag under my desk. I need you to take it to an address for me. It is quite urgent." His cold tone certainly doesn't convey a sense of urgency. He sounds the same as he does every day. Coma inducing.

Surely this can be done in the morning? "Sir, I catch the train." I can't drive. I've already had that giant glass of wine. "At this time of night, I don't feel comfortable—"

"Catch a cab. Charge it to the office. I need you to do this tonight."

"Ah . . ." Damn it. "Yes, sir. The bag is under your desk?"

"A small black bag. I will text you the delivery address."

God, why me? "Oh, okay."

"Text me when the job is complete."

He hangs up. Groaning, I eye my slippers and pajama pants. So much for a relaxing evening. I shoot a quick message to my favorite Uber driver and text Elisa to let her know what's going on. I get six notifications in quick succession, ranging from *don't go* to *I'll come with you, Frank will watch the kids.*

She's such a good friend.

Gerald will take me. I've already had too much wine. I'll message you when I'm on my way home.

In my head, I swear up a storm and trip on the leg of my jeans as I pull them on. I curse Bacitriet again while shoving everything into my handbag and locking the front door.

Where the fence is lower beside my driveway, a sliver of light betrays a curtain twitch in the neighbor's window. I catch the reflection of two glowing orbs. Oh great. The neighbor has a cat. My eyes pop wide. *I knew it! That liar.* I knew I'd seen a cat the night I nearly hit him with my car. Well, there goes any sort of potential flirtation. The wisp of what-if deflates inside me like a balloon, right down to the *phawp* sound of wet rubber splatting on the pavement. Though glass separates us, my nose tickles and clogs up. Fucking cats. I shoot it a nasty glare. It turns to present me with its butt.

Well, excuse you too, you ugly critter.

As if it heard me, it turns back and hisses.

I stomp to the end of the driveway and stare at the house opposite. Bright streetlamps create circles of yellow around the suburban court. Neighboring homes run around in a wide loop, with established trees and hedges blocking the sight of front windows. A lone car drives past. It turns into a driveway at the end of the court. The garage door rolls up and the car drives straight in, the door rattling down behind it. Friendly folk around here.

The court is quiet and still. The overcast night allows no sight of the moon, but I search the sky for it anyway as I stamp my feet against the cold.

"Are you quite well?" The question, and the voice, come out of the dark and send my heart rate skyrocketing. *Again?* The red end of a cigarette flares as a shadow moves on my neighbor's front porch. Why didn't he turn his porch light on? *Dramatic much?*

I bite back another sigh. There is the other dealbreaker. A smoker. Such a shame. At least it ends the unrealistic daydream about him I have in my head. My evil inner voice laughs like a hyena. *Like you'd stand a chance.*

"Oh, hi." My voice is flat, my tiredness and sadness over the might-have-been dream infecting me down to my toes. In the distance, I make out the sound of traffic, but no headlights turn into the court.

"Waiting for someone?" His smooth tone invites me to move closer. I stomp on the urge.

"Yup." What is he doing out here? Oh, the cigarette. It's probably rude not to say anything more, but I don't know the guy well enough to explain my movements to him. For all I know, he's an axe-murderer. One who smokes and owns a cat.

He says nothing more. Neither do I. I craft a few neighborly questions for him in my head in case the silence grows too awkward. Why would a guy like him—*a rich guy*—live in this little court? Something small thunders along the fence and leaps into the tree beside the streetlight.

"Shit!" I jump back and squint at the tree. I let out a shaky breath. "Bloody possum." Moments later, Gerald arrives, pulling up to the curb in his Beetle with a screech of brakes.

"I thought you were getting those brakes fixed?" I say, pulling open the door.

Gerald, my Uber driver friend and a perpetual student, nods, sending his straight black bangs flying. "Always is money, you know?"

"I hear ya." I settle into leather that smells weirdly of strawberries.

"Teenage birthday," he explains when I query the scent. "Where are we going tonight? Is late for you."

"I know." I scrub at the burn in my eyes. *Great. All I need now is a headache.* "It's work."

He nods. "You want music? Old-time station?"

"Thanks, Gerald." I stare through the window at my neighbor's house. There is no movement on the porch. He must have gone inside.

"I like new location. Good street. Quiet." Gerald waves one hand around as he pulls away from the curb.

"Yeah, it sure is quiet," I agree.

*

The city is full of color and movement. Cars, trams and taxis fly past. Fluorescent signs urge customers into nearby restaurants and bars. I watch life race on around me and my chest tightens as a familiar feeling of loneliness sweeps over me. "You okay?" Gerald asks, picking up on my melancholy.

"Oh yeah, sure."

"Big sigh."

"Yeah." Through the window, I spy a couple holding hands. Another couple kiss while waiting for a red light. I flex my fingers.

"Are you still writing your secret movie?"

I smile, though Gerald won't see it in the dark. "Yep. Decided on a murder mystery with a female detective."

"No more sci-fi?" His gaze catches mine in the rear-view mirror.

"Everyone is doing sci-fi these days. I think I might add a few scares and turn it into a thriller."

"Sounds fun." Gerald pulls over and parks, agreeing to wait for me.

The concierge desk is empty. The entire lobby is gloomy as all get-out as I walk inside. Only a few emergency lights and the long light bar above the Aboriginal painting illuminates my path. I glance up at the cameras, hearing my shoes squeak across the floor. I keep looking around, wondering if night security are about to appear and demand to know what I'm doing here this late. The beep of my pass over the sensor and elevator doors swishing open have me sagging with relief. I hadn't been sure my pass would work after-hours.

A shiver creeps over my skin as I wait for the elevator to reach the forty-second floor. What on earth is in Bacitriet's bag that needs delivering so urgently? I'll be back in just a few hours, I'm sure it could have waited. *This is so stupid.*

I step onto the dimly lit office floor. The air seems thicker here, still and warm. A strong scent of cleaning products linger and I realize why. *No air-con.*

Every horror movie I've ever watched plays out in my mind as I head toward my desk. The overhead lights are triggered by movement and spring into bright life above my head. Creeping around the office alone certainly ramps up my anxiety. I search every corner for moving shadows, my head twisting sharply at each minute sound.

This whole thing would make a great horror story, right down to the three missing assistants and the creepy boss. I start writing the scene in my head, but despite my overactive imagination, I reach Bacitriet's office unharmed.

Scrubbing my damp palms against my jeans, I wonder if this work qualifies for hazard pay. The bag is under Bacitriet's desk, exactly where he said it would be, along with the faintest smell of something I can't determine. Better not be dog poop he's trailed in here on his shoes. It's a canvas gym bag. I crouch awkwardly and snag a finger around the handle. The material stretches but whatever is in the bag has the weight of a bowling ball and doesn't budge.

"Geez."

The smell grows stronger. Falling to my knees, I lean under the desk and use both arms to drag the bag forward, leaving a long dark mark on the carpet. "Shit." I dab my finger on the mark to see if it's dry. It's not. *Ew.* I scrub my finger against my thigh. Now I'll have to organize cleaners to come and get rid of the stain. I try to lift the bag to avoid smearing whatever it is all over the carpet further, and something inside shifts. A flicker of a thought crosses my mind, freezing my next pull. The missing assistants. What if—inside the bag—there's . . . a head? It would explain both the weight and the smell. "Oh God, oh God!"

You'll never sleep if you don't check. Forcing my hands open, I tug on the zipper and my head flies back at the smell, cracking against the underside of the desk.

"Oh!" Scarves? I rumble through them and find what looks like gym clothes and underneath . . . filthy trainers. *Ew, that's what that smell is.* There is also a makeup bag. *What the . . . ?* Is my boss a cross-dresser? No wonder he didn't want anyone to find this here. I should never have looked inside. Forcing the zipper closed, I swear loudly and stagger to my feet. *God, why does it weigh so much?* There must be more shoes inside. A lot of them.

Mind you, given the smell, if I don't move the bag soon, the whole office will reek of sweat and gym socks in the morning. Hefting the bag, I stumble back to the elevator. Gerald is going to hate me for putting this in his car. Maybe he'll have a plastic sheet I can put down first, so it doesn't stain his car floormat. I'll have words with Bacitriet about this tomorrow. I'm not getting paid for this kind of humiliation. *Oh wait, I can't say anything.* If I do then he might ask if I looked inside. He'll know I found the scarves and the makeup bag.

I glance around the silent office. *No one is here. You could look around a bit. Search for the HR files maybe?* I shake my head. The buzz from my earlier wine has well and truly worn off and my eyes ache. *Go home and go to bed.*

Gerald winds all the windows down as I text Bacitriet and receive another address in reply. Gerald and I are both confused when it turns out to be a residential address. I wonder if this is Bacitriet's home. The drop-off is easy enough: I leave the bag on the rear porch as directed and run back to the car, texting that the job is done.

"Take me home, Gerald."

"You betcha. Your new boss is odd, yes? Gym bag with urgent courier delivery?"

"Yeah." Exhaustion weighs on me. I rest my head against the seat and slouch lower. Traffic is light and we catch green lights most of the way home. Soothing voices croon on the radio as my thoughts drift inward. If my ancient boss likes dressing as a woman it's no business of mine. Was my predecessor that closed-minded? If that's why she left then that's pretty sad. I tap my fingers together and find them slightly tacky. Using the frequent flashes of light from streetlights I examine the discoloration. *It's probably leaking face make-up. Perhaps he likes the full drag queen look?* I search my handbag but come up empty. "Do you have any hand sanitizer?"

"All out."

"Never mind." I bring my fingers to my nose. The stain had been under the bag and I'd dragged it over the carpet under his desk. Maybe it's shoe polish? God forbid it actually is dog poop. I can't smell it, but that doesn't mean it's not something gross. If I can organize the cleaner to come in tomorrow hopefully the stain will be gone before Bacitriet gets back from his trip.

Is that a hint of metal?

I gag a little. "Gerald, can you switch on the light?" My voice cracks. The light snaps on allowing me to inspect the browny-red stain on my pointer finger. It flakes a little as I rub at it. My breathing stops.

Blood.

Chapter 11

I should call the police. A suspicious bag with dirty clothes *and* blood stains? *Three missing assistants, Mig! What if the scarves are not Bacitriet's? Oh God.*

"Margaret? Something is wrong?"

I can't tell Gerald. He's basically a witness, and I'm not entirely sure of his visa status. I know he's trying to bring his family over from India. He can't get mixed up in this.

"Do you go to the gym?" I ask.

"Yes, all the time. I sit all day. Not healthy for heart."

"Do you—have you ever hurt yourself? I mean have you ever gotten blood—"

"Oh yes, sure, sure. A fingernail, or a toenail rip off. Is easy to do if you are not focused."

Right, see? It could be totally legitimate blood. And *ew!* I fight hard to not picture ripping off a toenail. Gerald tries a few times to ask what's wrong, but I can't answer. Inside my head, everything is mashed potatoes.

The court is silent when we pull up outside my house. Hardly surprising given the lateness of the hour. I climb out and slam the door shut. Cold air presses against my skin and I puff out a breath, watching it appear like exhaled cigarette smoke. The image reminds me of my neighbor. I peer over but his home is dark. Nearby tree branches shudder and I spot the possum's glowing eyes staring down at me before it darts across the top of the closest fence. I stand in the middle of my driveway, staring blankly at Gerald's red brake lights in the distance.

"Are you alright?"

I spin around, hands snapping up in defense, to find my neighbor standing directly behind me. "Shit! What are you doing?" *And why are you creeping around outside?*

"You did not respond to my query. I came over to ensure you are well. You were not moving." His voice sounds soft, concerned. A little of the standoffishness from my shattered nerves melts. I want comfort, and someone to tell me I'm not imagining things. But he's my neighbor, not Elisa. I can't bring him into this; I'll sound loony.

I keep several feet between us. It has to be past eleven. "I'm fine." The cold night air steals around my collar, freezing my skin.

"Are you?" His voice deepens, surrounding me in the silence. Again, his tone draws me forward. I desperately want a hug. Would it be weird to ask for one? It would be. I force a step back.

"I'm fine. Thank you for asking." My swooning behavior and girly helplessness annoys me. I spin around and stomp toward my front door.

"I apologize if I have offended you."

I half turn, keeping the door in sight. "It's fine, really. I've just had a long day and I need—"

"Are you injured?" Somehow, he is right beside me. I startle back. Under my porch light, I see worry in his soft gaze and tilted eyebrows.

"No, why?"

His voice deepens further. "I can smell blood."

"How—?" I step back again and my ankle turns on the edge of the driveway. His hot hands brush my shoulders as he rights my stumble before he withdraws. I breath in the scent of spicy aftershave. *Damn he smells good.* I can't smell cigarettes or smoke.

"May I help you?"

I force myself to skip back. "No, really. I'm fine. It's a, uh, hangnail." His gaze doesn't leave my face as I back toward the door.

How does he know about the blood? The thought see-saws with another. If it *is* blood, then it was under Bacitriet's desk. *Who's blood?* My brain jackrabbits. *Oh my God, I have blood on me. I need a shower. In disinfectant. For like a year.* "I have to go."

"Are you sure you are well?"

"Yep." I'm being rude. If I leave it like this, he'll consider me an awful neighbor. *He's just a neighbor, Mig. Remember the cat and the smoking!* "Um, so . . . my name is Mig." I can't stop scrubbing my hand against my jeans.

"Strange name." He steps closer, and a ripple of awareness runs over my body. Heat floods my face, yet the back of my neck stays cold, like I'm standing in the path of a polar wind.

I rub my skin to bring it back to life, but drop my hand when I remember the stain on my finger. "That's what everyone calls me." *Why are you explaining?* "I have to go."

"Sam."

"What?"

The tiniest of smiles graces his lips and in a low, soft voice, he says, "You may call me Sam."

"Okay." I shift my focus from his mouth to those glorious dark eyes. "Well, Sam, I gotta go. Thanks again for checking on me." I find my keys after a moment spent fumbling around in my purse. He waits as I open the door. I glance back one more time at his tall, lean frame and slowly close and lock the door.

I press against the wood and listen to his footsteps move away. My pulse thuds a loud drumbeat in my ears. I'm breathing too fast. Whoa, his smile should be classed as a lethal weapon. I raise my fingers to my lips to smother my grin, only pulling away at the last second when I remember. *Blood.* Dropping everything, I run for the bathroom and scrub my fingers until my cuticles bleed. Then I decide I need a shower. More scrubbing is followed by lots of body lotion. Eventually, I get a hold of myself, dress and slink into the kitchen.

Golden liquid sloshes dangerously as I fill my wine glass to the very brim. The glass trembles in my hand. When I collapse onto the sofa, all I can do is stare blankly at my dark TV and wonder what the everlasting fuck just happened. *What was in that bag and why did my neighbor smell blood?*

My cell phone is in my hand, but all I can do is stare at it, afraid to put my suspicions into words. Words will make it real. Besides Elisa will be asleep. I can't wake her just because I am freaking out.

The neighbor's name is Sam. A giggle pops out of me. I slap a hand over my lips, but amusement—*or hysteria*—wells inside my chest, bubbling away like a volcano until I explode. It dies out as quickly as it started. I helped Bacitriet hide the evidence of . . . of what? What exactly have I done? Moved a bag of gym clothes, scarves and makeup. A weirdly heavy bag of stinky gym clothes, scarves and makeup. I didn't even search the whole bag. The stain it left behind on Bacitriet's office carpet is pretty damning, though.

How had Sam known about the blood? I shudder, biting back the urge to wash my hands again. Who can smell blood? *Vampires.* Well, he is mysterious, intense, and sexy. I've only seen him at night. *Oh, don't be silly, Mig!*

Launching off the sofa, I grab my screenplay notes folder and yank out my research into vampire stories. Sam's eyes don't glow and I've seen no sign of sharp teeth. His hands were warm, scalding really. Vampires are cold in all the stories, due to a lack of blood circulation. But the nighttime thing. That's a strong case for the affirmative. I pace the length of my living area, flipping through the pages. "There's no such thing as vampires anyway," I tell myself.

My thoughts springboard off Sam and onto my boss. Why did he make me move his bag? I rub my hands together, scraping my nails over my now clean finger. There's no way I'm sleeping tonight.

I try TV. For a while a movie about uploading people's brains into robots holds my interest. It's a bit creepy. Imagine being stuck inside a robot body. How would that even work? Would the brain experience tactile sensations? Emotions? What is a soul and what's just a program? Would you even be the same person? I head for my bedroom to grab my screenplay out of my work bag. I might as well write a scene or two since I'm wide awake and feeling slightly wired.

Before I turn on the light, I spy a rectangle of glowing yellow through my window and creep closer, keeping my room dark. Sam's house sits higher than mine, and I can see a bedroom window over the fence. The open curtain lets me see . . . *Oh Lordy.*

Sam is undressing.

My eyes widen. His chest is a sculptured masterpiece. *Oh.* The inside of my mouth is as dry as a desert, yet somehow I'm drooling. His trousers barely cling to his hips as he strolls across the room. If you asked me what his bedroom furnishings look like or what color his walls are, I couldn't tell you. I can't stop staring at his back. A white mark the size of my hand colors his dark skin. It starts at the base of his neck and runs down his spine. A tattoo? I can't make it out from this distance. He disappears through a doorway.

Stifling a groan, I lean against the cold glass, knowing I should move away and give him his privacy. My feet are glued to the floor. He reappears, stepping out of what is probably a bathroom with a cream towel wrapped around his waist. I duck back, pressing myself into the wall with a gasp. Fighting the urge and failing terribly, I flick at the curtain to peer through again.

Sam approaches the window. A smirk dances on his lips as his eyes find mine. My heart stops. There's no way he can see me. The room is pitch black around me; he can't know I'm here—but he does. He knows I'm standing right there, gawping at him like a creep.

I dart back into the living room and collapse on the sofa. *Oh my God.*

*

Death. I'm a member of the walking dead, a zombie going through the motions. My head is full of cotton and my mouth tastes like the aftermath of a bushfire. It was a mental battle just to drag myself into work this morning, but it's far too soon into my new job to take a sick day.

At this point, I might have welcomed a "conversation" reminding me I'm on probation. Then I could gracefully bow out of the job by suggesting it wasn't working on both sides. I've been here less than a week. I could leave it off my resume entirely. Who would know? Then I wouldn't need a reference, and I could pretend this whole nightmare had never happened.

The photograph of Annie Seramoph—the one from the TV —pops into my mind. I can still hear the desperation in her father's voice and his whispered warnings. Should I call the anonymous helpline and report Bacitriet's mysterious bag? It's a thought that's been bouncing around my head since I read the news recap this morning.

I stand in front of the elevator dithering. My finger held scant inches from the call button. I can't seem to press it.

I don't owe Annie or her family anything. I don't even know her. I should be focusing on doing my job to the best of my ability. Inside my head, I'm aghast. When did I become the kind of person who doesn't care? I press the button and step into the elevator.

Walking through the office, I feel everyone's eyes on me. Do they know what I did?

Bacitriet's door is open. I'm sure I shut it last night. I stare at it suspiciously. Bacitriet is interstate today, he won't know if I duck in and take a photo of the blood stain. Except I have no real reason to go into his office and if anyone sees me climbing under the desk, they'll wonder what I'm doing. I don't want to draw attention to myself, or to the stain. I head straight for the kitchen and give my coffee order to the barista. He nods but doesn't smile. *It's like an unspoken rule around here not to show any emotion.* I sink into one of the comfy blue chairs and watch employees come and go around me. No one stops to speak to me, not even to say good morning in passing. I release a soft sigh when I collect my coffee mug. Loneliness fills me, drawing all of my senses to the tightness of my skin. I warm my fingers around my coffee cup.

I sit down at my desk and within minutes, I'm formatting a report to send back to Bacitriet. The distraction contains my curiosity until midmorning. Returning to my desk with another mug of coffee, I eye Bacitriet's open office door as I tap my phone's display. There's a low murmur of telephone calls and a sudden burst of laughter from the kitchen. No one even glances in my direction. I could pop inside and check the floor under his desk. My silent phone lights up, displaying a missed call message. I dial my messagebank and listen. It can't be a spam call because they don't leave messages, which means it's possibly important.

"Margaret Solder?" It's a woman's voice. She sounds crisp and clear, and a little bit bossy. "My name is Detective Connie Bryce. Please call me back as soon as it is convenient." She leaves a number and the message ends.

"Shit." I glance around again to confirm no one is watching me, then head to a vacant meeting room. I dial the number, my heart racing. *Why is a detective calling me?*

"Detective Connie Bryce."

"Uh." I cough to clear my throat which has closed up on me. My mouth dries as I ponder the possible reasons a detective has for calling me. The gym bag is at the top of the list. "Detective? My name is Margaret Solder. I'm returning your call."

"Ms. Solder. Thank you for speaking to me."

"Can I help you, Detective?"

"I understand from Rose Solder that you are related."

Oh god. This is about Rose? Of course it is. "What has she done now? I mean, yes. She is my grandmother. Is she hurt?" I slump down in a chair beside the meeting table, spinning to stare out through the window at the sapphire-blue sky. All sorts of Rose related dramas play back in my head.

"I do know her. I thought you might be related. This is actually about you, Ms. Solder. I see on your business social media that you recently started working at a company called Bacitriet Consulting as an Executive Assistant to the CEO? Would that be to Brian Bacitriet?"

"Uh, yes."

"Would it be convenient for you to come down to the station to speak to me?"

"What is this about?" I ask. *You know what this is about.* I picture the gym bag again. *Shit.*

"Could we speak, perhaps over a coffee? Away from the office. I would like to ask you a few questions about your new boss."

"I only just started here. This week. I don't know any—"

"It's just an informal chat, Ms. Solder. Can you get away today? Say two p.m.?"

"Uh." I peer around the floor. No one is paying the slightest attention to me. And Bacitriet is still interstate. Will anyone notice me missing? I name a coffee shop up the street. It's tucked away down a side alley. Hopefully no one from this location knows about it.

"Excellent. I will see you shortly." She hangs up and I stare at my cell phone like it's about to come alive and attack me. *What the heck?*

I return to my desk and stare mindlessly at my computer screen. Eventually, I stir and scroll through my emails, glancing at the clock in the corner of my display screen as it draws closer to the agreed time. *What do I do?*

The floor around me has fallen silent. It appears most of the staff have gone off to a long lunch. Just a coincidence, I'm sure, but I'm feeling particularly paranoid. I flick my gaze to Bacitriet's office. No one is around. I won't be seen. Holding my notebook tightly, I head into Bacitriet's office. My heart is pounding so hard, I'm afraid it's going explode right out through my chest, like in that sci-fi movie. *Be quick.* I duck down beside Bacitriet's chair and peer beneath the desk. There's no mark on the carpet.

I drop to my knees and lean over, pressing my fingers to the gray fibers. Dry. I pull back and sniff my fingers. A chemical smell drifts up. *Oh no.*

I jump to my feet and race out of the office, swiping my handbag off my desk. I'm breathing easier by the time the elevator lets me out in the lobby. The walk to the café is over in a flash.

I can spot the shadow of tables through the frosted windows. The door slides open as I approach. This café is a lovely blend of modern function and classy elegance. It's one of my favorites in the city. Half a dozen round tables are surrounded by chairs, and a long, curved bench is lined with high-backed stools. Though sound is hushed in here, there is also the typical urgency of the waitstaff and the hiss of the coffee machine's frother. I order a latte and sit at a table against the far wall.

What could Detective Bryce want from me? It *has* to be about the missing assistants. I'm her connection to Bacitriet. Christ, I need this job and the money, but the stress is getting to be too much. If I leave this job, Mom and Dad will have to help me financially until I find a new one. They will, I'm sure, but it's *my* house. I want to prove I can afford it on my own. Besides, they don't really have the cash I'll need if I'm out of work for long and I don't want to become a burden on them.

A shadow falls over me. I peer up, expecting the waitress with my coffee, and instead find a petite ashy-blond-haired woman standing at my side. Her lips are pursed and her cold diamond-blue eyes examine me carefully. I feel poked and prodded, though she only leans forward. "Ms. Margaret Solder?" A hint of pale pink lipstick stains her teeth.

"Yes?"

She pops the button on her jacket, and I spy a gun in the holster under her arm. *Oh!* I straighten in my seat as she cracks a smile and sits down. She flashes her badge. "As I said on the phone, my name is Detective Connie Bryce. Thank you for agreeing to meet with me." She puts her elbows onto the table, hands clasped together. Several black-suited women rush to the counter and collect prepared trays of takeaway coffee. The door slides open again, admitting a customer carrying a KeepCup. Even out of the way, this cafe feels far too exposed to be having a conversation with a cop.

"You said you had some questions?"

Detective Bryce spears me with a sharp gaze. Her hair is tied tightly back from her head. It means all business, as does her crisp white shirt and gray suit. "Were you aware that the young woman who previously worked for Brian Bacitriet has gone missing? A receptionist by the name of Annie Seramoph."

"Assistant," I clarify. "She was Mr. Bacitriet's assistant."

"Was she?" The look Bryce gives me says she already knew that.

"It's what they told me."

"Bacitriet told you?" Bryce presses her hands flat against the tabletop.

We fall silent as a harried-looking waitress places my coffee down at my elbow and blows wisps of hair out of her face. "Were you waiting for anything else?" she asks, glancing at Bryce. The detective shakes her head.

"No, thanks," I tell the waitress, or at least I tell it to her back as she's already raced away. I wish she had stayed. I'm feeling rather like a bug under a glass. Bryce's stare is intense. "Reception and the other assistants told me."

"I see. And how long have you worked for Mr. Bacitriet?" Bryce examines my face as if searching for answers.

"As I said earlier, I only started on Monday." I gulp a mouthful of coffee. It's too sweet, almost sickly, and I push it away. Why did I update my profile so fast? I should have left it as it was for a bit longer, then she wouldn't have found me.

Bryce's face softens. She relaxes her shoulders. "Ms. Solder, you are not in any trouble. We're just having a chat. There's nothing to worry about. You see, someone might have said something to you, something seemingly insignificant, that could be of great help to us."

The sharp, shocking clatter of dropped dishes snap our heads in the direction of the café's kitchen. I cup my coffee with both hands to hide the shaking. Of course I'll help the police. I've got nothing to hide. *Mention the gym bag.* "What do you want to know?"

"Whatever you know. What were you told about your predecessor's circumstances?"

I shrug. "I don't think anyone really knows anything. I, uh, I didn't ask about it in my interview because I was desperate to get the job."

"And why is that?"

What does that matter? "I was let go from my previous job and I recently bought a house, so when I got the call—"

"You received a call?"

"Yes. I jumped at the chance."

Bryce leans forward, as if scenting something enticing. "Did you call an employment agent or put your name down on a website? Apply to an ad?"

"No, actually, I was still on my way home after being fired. I just updated my profile online and I got a call from a head-hunter." Something had felt off about that. I should have asked more questions. "Look, I'm sorry. You said I don't have any-thing to worry about. Should I be worried?" My brain churns through everything that has happened in the past week.

"We are just having a chat."

Argh, come on. There's nothing more annoying than some-one trying to be clever. Does she not think I watch crime shows? I bite my lip and lean forward wanting to keep my frus-tration *and fear—definitely a lot of fear—*off my face. "Why are you here, Detective Bryce?"

"Mr. Seramoph, the missing woman's father, suspects his daughter has met with foul play. We're talking to anyone who saw or spoke to Ms. Seramoph on the day she disappeared."

My tense muscles relax. "I never met her," I said.

"You have spoken to her boss though."

"Yes. But not about Annie Seramoph." *Tell her about the bag.* "What about Cassandra. The other girl."

Bryce's head lifts, her thin pencil-drawn eyebrows rise high on her forehead. "What other girl?"

"I started this week," I remind the detective. I can't tell from Bryce's face whether she already knows about Cassandra and is testing me, or if she genuinely doesn't know. "I was told . . . Reception told me Bacitriet has had a few assistants recently. I was—It's just, I thought . . . are you looking for them too? Are they missing?"

"We do want to speak to Cassandra Chan."

"So she *is* missing?"

Detective Bryce leans back. "Missing? Why would you say that?"

"Uh, I don't . . . I just assumed." My face flames and I want to flap my hand around for cool air. The door slides open again and several customers walk in, gathering in a line at the service counter. Does anyone from my new office know about this café? Hopefully no one is going to see me talking to Bryce. At least she's not in a police uniform.

"Assumed?"

I lower my voice and hunch my shoulders. "In my interview, Mr. Bacitriet said he needed to fill the position quickly because his previous assistant just up and left. She hadn't given notice. Her name was Cassandra Chan."

"Was?"

"Is." *Oh my God. I sound guilty. Short answers only, Mig!* "They said she left work one night and didn't come back."

Bryce turns her lips inward, nodding at me. "How did they know she wouldn't just show up on Monday? Perhaps she was too ill to answer the phone?"

I sit back and glance at the moving line at the register. "That's what they said." How can I explain the weird things going on at my workplace? The silences, the recent hires. *The gym bag.* "When I heard Bacitriet lost three PA's in a short space of time, I asked a few questions. It's never good to join a place like that because it implies the boss might be difficult to work with, but as I said, I was desperate . . ."

My words stutter to a halt at the expression on the detective's suddenly pale face. One blunt unpainted fingernail taps the table. "Three?"

"Yes."

She places her phone down in front of me and activates what looks like a voice recording app. "Okay. From the top. Tell me what happened on the day you were fired."

"Am I in trouble? Why do you want—"

"From the top." Her voice brooks no argument. I gulp. Her expression remains steady as I repeat my story about the phone call and the interview.

"That's all they said?"

"Yes."

"What do you think of Bacitriet?"

My gaze drifts to the glass door. "Honestly? He creeps me out. Have you ever watched that TV show, *Supernatural*?" Bryce shakes her head, so I continue. "Well, there's an actor on it who plays the character Death and, well, Bacitriet reminds me of him. Old, cold and creepy. You're not going to tell him I said that, are you?"

"Why did you agree to take the job?"

"I was desperate."

"Not really that desperate? Not even a day passed since you lost your job."

I rub my fingers in a circle on the table. "It seemed like really good luck."

"Did you ask about the previous assistant?"

I answer with a question of my own. "Do you think Bacitriet had something to do with the disappearances?" Bryce doesn't answer. "You should talk to the reception team."

"We're just having a chat, Ms. Solder," she reminds me.

"I'm sure they can explain the conversation better than I can. I wasn't even there when the women disappeared."

"Why do you think I should speak to reception?"

"Bethany and Candy, and a few of the other ladies, took me to lunch yesterday. They mentioned the missing assistants." Sort of.

"What exactly did they say?"

I can't remember it word for word. It's why I write all instructions down. I know not to rely on my memory alone. "Well, Candy said the previous assistant, not Annie but the one before me—Cassandra—didn't call HR. She just didn't come in one day. Candy was the one who mentioned the others. Three in three months."

"And not one of the assistants called HR or Bacitriet to explain why they were not coming back?"

"I don't think so. Candy thought it was weird. I asked them if any of them had applied for the assistant job. They said they hadn't."

"Why?"

"I don't know." I stare at my hands. "Look, I only just started there. I don't know anything more than that." I peer at the glass door, wondering when I can make my escape. My stomach growls.

"Just a few more questions. Have you thought about quitting?"

"Yes."

"Why?"

Are you kidding? I lock my stare to hers. "The three people who previously sat in my chair disappeared. What would you do?"

"Have you seen anything strange or odd in Bacitriet's correspondence?"

"He won't let me access his email. I find *that* odd."

She pulls a tablet from her purse and makes a few notes. I can't see the screen from where I'm sitting. "I see. What about his calendar?"

"Nothing strange. I've only had a few days to look at it, but it seems pretty normal." *Tell her about the gym bag.*

"Is there anything else you'd like to tell me?"

I return to my original question. "Do you think Bacitriet had something to do with the disappearances?"

"I can't say."

"They were his assistants. Am I in danger? Should I be worried?" I'm determined to get an answer this time.

Her head tilts. "Do you believe you might be in danger? Did someone say something to you?"

That's not an answer. "Do you think I should leave?"

"I'm going to request that you to stay. I'd like you to keep alert and let us—me—know if anything strange occurs."

Wait, what? She wants me to spy on my boss? "Is he a suspect?" *Just answer the damned question.*

"We're investigating several possible scenarios at the present time. Will you help us?"

Tell her about the bag! I open my mouth to do just that and then slam it shut. I moved the bag. Does that make me an accomplice? Oh balls, I don't want to get arrested. Maybe, if I help the police catch Bacitriet, I can get a lesser sentence? My fears bounce around in all directions and I can't get a firm grip on any of them. "Yes, sure, of course." I probably look like a crazy person I'm nodding so fast. "Um . . ."

"Ms. Solder, you can tell me anything. No matter how odd. You won't get into any trouble. You do want to tell me something, don't you?"

"There was a . . . um . . . a bag in his office yesterday. He asked me to deliver it somewhere last night. Um . . . I think . . ."

"Ms. Solder?"

I moan. "There was blood on it."

Her tongue darts out for a split second, wetting her lips. "You saw blood?"

"I . . . I got a bit on my finger when I looked into the bag, but it was just full of old gym clothes." And a woman's scarves and makeup. "I'm sorry. I didn't know what to do. Please tell me I'm not in trouble." Tears fill my eyes and I cover them with my palms. *Shit shit shit. I'm going to jail.*

"Ms. Solder?"

I sniff and wipe beneath my eyes. "Yes?"

"Do you still have the bag?"

"No. I had to drop it off."

"Did you drive?"

I don't want to get Gerald in trouble. "I caught an Uber."

"Did you wipe your hands on anything in the vehicle?"

"I don't think so. I washed them when I got home." Oh god, what if the bag left blood in Gerald's car? I think of the stain that's no longer a stain under Bacitriet's desk. Had I really seen a stain there last night? Maybe it was all in my head and I'm imagining dark dealings and sinister outcomes where there really are none. *Stop being so naïve, Mig!*

"Unfortunately, this means we only have your word for what happened last night."

Sweat breaks out across my skin. I work my mouth searching for illusive saliva. I wish I had another coffee.

"Where did you take the bag?"

I give her the address, luckily still stored in my phone. "Now what?" I ask.

"As I said earlier, Ms. Solder, perhaps we can help each other."

I lean back in my chair. "What do you want me to do?"

Chapter 12

I'm not entirely sure how I get to the end of the day. After I returned to the office. I sat at my desk and stared blankly at my display screens, my mind replaying everything Bryce said to me. Her exact wording, her expressions, my answers, searching for . . . I don't know. A clue of some kind? Did I sound guilty? Did I seem shifty? *Ugh.* How did Bryce know I was working here? Are they talking to anyone else? I bet I'm not the only employee they've had a 'casual chat' to. She said she found my corporate socials—what were they searching for? I click to the intranet and find the company page. Right there my face stares back at me with an announcement of my hire. It's a cropped photo off my socials. My eyes look red and my hair is wispy. I sigh and click off the page.

Bacitriet has emailed me a few reports to format and a proposal for a client that I collate for him. I spend the rest of my day adjusting tables and charts and ensuring consistent text styles. Who writes a report in different fonts? It's mindless work and the hours pass quickly. I soon find myself on the train heading home, staring vacantly through the window while a million thoughts circle around inside my brain.

My boss is what . . . a serial killer?

Detective Bryce didn't say anything concrete, but her final words were to ask that I observe him. I've become a snitch.

I nibble at the inside of my mouth. There's a small ulcer I keep poking at with my tongue. I gave the detective Gerald's contact details, and as soon as Bryce left the café I called him to explain. Gerald told me I'd done the right thing and promised to tell the truth about the other night. I couldn't hear any anger in his voice, but he hung up on me soon afterward and I'm left with the uncomfortable feeling I've gotten him into trouble.

Tears prickle as I stare out through the train window at the pouring rain. The last thing Bryce told me was, "Don't tell anyone about our conversation." I grab my phone and my notebook. If I'm going to do this, I need to get organized and keep a log of the day. I need to mark down the time anything happens.

In my screenplay, the first thing my detective character does is write down all of the details of the killer's victims. Elisa and I did that the other night. I need a photo of the whiteboard to send to Bryce. What else links the assistants together? Well, obviously my workplace. But is there something else? Maybe it wasn't Bacitriet. I wonder how the women traveled to work. Did they visit the same cafés? *The police will do all this.* What does Bryce really need me for? Access to the workplace, I guess. I don't have Bacitriet's email, but I do have his calendar.

I jot down a plan for tomorrow.

Step 1: Review Bacitriet's calendar from the past three months.

Step 2: Find any old files and reports that the assistants worked on. Look for common clients.

Step 3: Talk to more staff.

I step off the train straight into a bitter wind that bites hard at my skin and works its way into my clothing to freeze my bones. The weather matches my mood—unsettled and nervous. I have visions of home, and of all the wine bottles in my fridge.

As the heavens open I flick on my headlights. Water pounds down upon my car, sheeting over the windscreen in giant waves. The pavement outside is a shiny mirror of reflected streetlights. My drive home is perilous. The roads are slippery and a car slides sideways right in front of me at the lights. Several cars honk their horns at how slowly I'm driving. I let out an epic sigh when I finally pull into my driveway, unclamping my fingers from around the steering wheel and just breathe, my heart hammering away inside my chest as I try to relax.

Holding my backpack and handbag in one hand, my keys in the other, I dive into the maelstrom.

In seconds, I have the front door unlocked and tumble into the dry safety of my entrance hall, plopping my damp bags on the ground as I laugh at my wild escape. "Holy crap."

Kicking off my now sopping wet shoes, I tiptoe to the bedroom, holding my trouser legs up. I make it as far as the living room before I freeze. The house is cold and echoes with my entrance. I haven't turned any lights on yet, so the only illumination comes from the streetlight peeking through my half-drawn curtains.

Something's wrong.

Breath stills in my lungs as I search the shadows. I'm afraid to call out. What if someone answers? What if someone doesn't?

I force air into strained lungs and wait, listening intently to the silence. A crack of thunder rattles the windows, making me scream. I slap my hand on the light switch and welcome light exposes my imagination as a liar. Everything is exactly as I left it this morning. A stained coffee mug is on the table, a scarf hangs over the sofa, and my second pair of shoes are still where I kicked them off in front of the chair. A laugh bubbles from my chest. Hell, the stress and tension from speaking to Detective Bryce has clearly traveled home with me. I'm seeing evil everywhere I look. I tiptoe my rain-drenched self into my bedroom and strip out of my damp clothes before my body jerks from an explosive sneeze loud enough to compete with the thunder.

Clad in my favorite faded gray tracksuit pants and my thickest pullover, I hunt for the thermostat and sneeze again. My cold neck the other night must have been a warning sign of the flu. Damn it. I hate getting sick.

Within seconds, hot air bursts from the overhead ducts, along with a heap of dust. My aching fingers quickly thaw, and my stomach now makes its emptiness known, rumbling as I wander into the kitchen. I'm sure I've got some frozen dinners in the freezer. Cold air brushes my face and I frown, turning in a circle to search for the cause.

I sneeze again.

The icy tendrils lead me to a slightly puffing curtain. My heart kicks into high gear and I peek around the lacey material. The window is open. I didn't open it. I sneeze again.

Part of me wants to run. Another part shouts that this is my house and I won't be afraid inside my own home. I grab the cricket bat from my hall cupboard and on light feet examine each room for intruders. My laptop is still on the chair where I left it, my spare tablet is on the coffee table and a bunch of gold coins decorate the bowl on the side table. If someone broke in, it wasn't to steal anything.

So who opened the window?

I search the entire house with the cricket bat dangling from one hand and my phone in the other.

Nothing seems out of the ordinary.

No one is in the house except me.

I stop in the middle of the living room and turn another slow circle. *Do I have a ghost?* Normally, I wouldn't give that thought a second go, but I don't know how to explain the feeling that I'm not alone. *I'm going mad.*

Returning to the kitchen, I scream and jump backward, my phone pressed to my throat. "Fuck!"

Two honey-colored eyes blink at me. The monster's dark, furry head twitches to the side as it scratches its neck.

The neighbor's cat.

"Fuck." My life had flashed before my eyes. Everything from Elisa's birthday parties to me reading on my dad's knee as a child. From Jack to Bacitriet to my neighbor . . . *oh!*

The slow blink of the black cat's eyes are its only movement. My heart lands back inside my chest with a thump. "Shoo, shoo you!"

The evil feline doesn't budge.

"Shoo! Go home." I sneeze again, stumbling forward from the intensity. "Shit! Stupid cat." I move closer, intent on waving it off my—"Oh my God, you're on my bench! Your cat butt is on my bench. Gross, I put food there!" I swipe the bat in warning —I'm not going anywhere near the stupid thing—and it rises up on all fours to hiss at me.

"Hey, it's my house. You're the trespasser," I tell it. It blinks in reply.

Other than that reaction, it doesn't move—still arched— teeth bared. I stomp to the back door and fling it wide open. Rain ricochets into the house, landing on the floorboards with tiny splashes. "Crap!" There is no way that cat is going outside in this. I sneeze again, feeling the scratchiness growing in my throat. I glare at the cause and snatch a tissue from the dispenser on the coffee table, blowing my nose loudly. "Now what?"

"Meow."

The evil thing just called me something offensive. I narrow my eyes at it. In response, the cat sits and starts licking itself.

"Oh, come on. Really?"

My nemesis ignores me.

"Okay, look. It's you or me, and this is *my* house!"

Nothing.

I'm going to have to get him, aren't I? After the last few nights, my neighbor Sam will be thrilled to see me, I'm sure. Flashing light reflects off the damp floorboards, heralding the coming thunder, and the roll of noise seems to go on forever. I sigh. Leaving the door open, I try once more to coax the creature out. Rattling a chip bag lifts its head, but it blinks as if weighing the truthfulness of my expression then resumes cleaning.

Jeez Louise. I collapse on the sofa and tip my face into the arm cushion. Tiredness drags at me, and I sob out a sad laugh. *How is this my life?*

"Meow?"

"I'm not in the mood for this," I tell it without lifting my head. My voice is muffled but what do I care, it's not like the critter can understand me. I sneeze again. "God damn it!"

A yowl greets that.

"Listen, I'll be as rude as I like, it's my house. Just get out!" I slap my hands on my thighs and force myself to my feet. *Get Sam. Get rid of the cat. Then open the wine.* I drag my coat—the one with the hood—out of the closet, pull on my damp shoes and slosh over to Sam's front door. I'm soaked by the time I thump on the wood and pray he'll hurry because it's damned cold outside. "Come on!"

The door swings open. I stumble forward and grab the door-frame to stop from falling to my knees. A chill coats the back of my neck, as if a hand has gripped me tight and is about to shake me. I *am* getting sick. Standing in the rain is only going to make it worse. Then my gaze focuses. Flushed skin—so much skin—fills my vision. Droplets of water trail over toned pecs and a flat stomach.

"Um." Thin lines crisscross the muscular chest and small round marks pock the left side of his stomach. When I drag my gaze to his face, I find him scowling at me.

"What do you want?" That's a sharper voice than the honeyed tones from the other night. Had Nice Sam only been an act? Just playing friendly with the new neighbor, and now that I'm at his front door, he's suddenly concerned I'm a weirdo?

"Um."

"I'm not interested—"

He thinks I'm here to ask him out? "Whoa, no, no. God no."

His eyes widen and his tone softens. "Why are you banging upon my door in the middle of a storm? You are getting wet."

"Are you missing something?" I snap, at the end of my patience. I am *tired*. It has been a long day and, as the half-naked man pointed out, I am getting wet.

"What?" His expression becomes adorably confused.

Stay angry, Mig! "Your cat is in my house. I'm allergic. You need to come and get rid of it." I spin on a heel and stomp back to my porch.

Chapter 13

I leave the front door open and head straight into the kitchen to splash wine into a glass. All the while, I glare at the cat. After the day I've had, I collapse onto the sofa cushions, cross my legs and gulp my liquid courage. Eventually, footsteps approach my front door. The cat hasn't moved an inch from the benchtop, and I'm quietly stewing in anger and snot.

A sneeze explodes out of me again. I barely stop my drink from sloshing over the rim—okay, to be fair, I've drunk a fair portion of it so the risk isn't all that great. Still, I hold the glass out from my body in case a second eruption follows the first. My nose twitches.

Sam's shadow appears in the doorway, and I glance at him, eyes watering. He's taken the time to dress—*shame*—all in black, of course, and his jeans fit him like a glove. Doesn't he own anything with color? I hold up one finger, the others remain clutched around my glass, as I sneeze in rapid succession. Watery eyes blur my vision. "Get it out of here."

He tucks the beast beneath his arm. "I sincerely apologize. He has never done this before."

"I'm sure."

Sam heads straight for the door but stops in the hall.

"Yes?" *Go, so I can unclog and then eat!*

"No, really. He has never done this. He must like you."

"The feeling is not mutual." *Be nice to your neighbor, Mig.* That's my mom's voice inside my head. I slam my eyes shut, push out a breath and climb to my feet. "My window was open. I'm not sure how that happened, because I didn't leave it open." My voice croaks like a frog. I clear it and continue. "That must be how it got in."

"He. His name is Mephistopheles."

I knew it was evil. My head aches and I can feel another sneeze brewing. *Just go already.* I wave my hand toward the door.

"Are you well?"

He can't hear the nasal blockage flattening my words? "I'm allergic," I remind him.

"Mephistopheles is not an ordinary cat."

"Smells like one." My head snaps forward on another sneeze. *Leave me to die in peace.*

"Yes, well, of course. Let me remove him."

"Maybe lock your doors next time." The *snick-thump* of my front door announces I'm alone again and I throw myself back to lie on the sofa, sniffing and itching, my throat raw. I hunt for another tissue but the box is empty. *Guh!* Huffing out a heavy breath, I force myself to my feet and light two candles —the eucalyptus ones Elisa got me for Christmas—and grab a packet of disinfectant wipes. I scrub the benchtop clean and peer around, sniffing hard, wondering where else Mephistopheles put his furry cat butt. I don't have the strength to clean the whole house. I just want to relax. And breathe. At least the exercise has my blood pumping and my chilled neck has returned to normal temperature. I pop an antihistamine and eye my glass. Should I take it, given the alcohol I've already consumed? I figure that horse has already bolted along with my sanity and swallow it down.

At the freezer, I stare blankly at my selection of frozen dinner packs. I'm not really that hungry anymore.

Thumping on my front door pulls my head up. *Ignore it.* But curiosity gets the better of me.

Sam brandishes a bottle of wine. "An apology," he says. A soft uptick in his lips and a crinkle of his nose extends the apology.

I blush even as that horrible chill clamps my neck again. "Oh, uh . . ."

"Please."

My fingers close around the bottle and I glance at the name. I have no idea if it is a good sort or not, but it's red. I don't dare compound the embarrassment by telling him I can't drink red wine. "Thanks."

He tilts his head. "Mephistopheles was worried. He insisted I ensure that you are well."

His *cat* was worried? I wave a hand around and trudge back to the sofa. Allergic reactions exhaust me to a degree where I can barely function. My sinuses are so blocked my head aches from the force of it. "I'll be fine. I've taken a tablet and sleep will help. It's best if you keep him home from now on. I'll double-check all my windows so he can't sneak in again."

"He apologized for that. The window was his doing." Sam smiles.

My chest warms and I can't help smiling back. Then what he said registered. "Your cat opened a sliding window. A *locked* sliding window?"

Sam somehow manages to peer up at me through his lashes even though he's standing above me. I shiver at the look. "Mephistopheles is a smart cat."

"Well, you can tell him I'll be fine as long as he doesn't come back."

"He said you had a bad day."

"How would he . . . you know what, it doesn't matter. I *have* had an awful day. But I'm home now. I just need dinner, a hot bath and a good sleep."

His gaze falls to the frozen dinner on the benchtop and he straightens, fingers twitching. "Surely you are not having that?"

My eyes pop wide. I don't cook, so what? It's not really any of his business. I huff through my blocked nose. "Excuse me?"

"That will not be your dinner. I will take you out. I know a place—" He sounds like this is the obvious solution, but his eyes don't meet mine, seemingly unable to tear away from my defrosting dinner. *Oh, he's feeling guilty.*

"Listen, Sam. I have had a bad day, made worse by not being able to breathe." My words are a blurred bluntness, the consonants slurred. Not drunk, just blocked up. I cringe. "I don't want to go out or do anything. I just want to stay here and do nothing." I make sure my expression matches my tone. *Pissed off.*

"Very well. I will cook for you."

What? "I doubt I can breathe for long at your place."

"Of course not. I will bring everything here."

I nearly throw up my hands, but that's a little theatrical, even for me. "It's fine, really. You don't have—"

"I must ensure your breathing does not worsen. My pet has caused your discomfort and allergic reactions have a nasty habit of recurring if you are not careful." His smile again takes the sting out of his words. "I have a gloriously cut steak at home. It will take no time at all for me to cook it. Then I will leave you to your evening. I have no wish to outstay my welcome."

Steak? God, that does sound good. My mouth waters. Fresh steak trumps my frozen honey chicken, that's for sure. I try one last time, surreptitiously wiping drool from my mouth. "You already gave me the wine." *That I can't drink.*

His head tilts. "Let us agree to the steak and call it being neighborly. We live side by side. I do not wish for our first proper meeting to result in a medical emergency."

I nod. "Okay. Fine. You can cook the steak."

His face lights up with the strength of his smile, the lines around his eyes crinkling. I blame the wine for my all-over body flush. I turn my head and spy the bottle he's gifted me. What if he wants to open it with dinner? I bite my lips, but the words bubble up inside my chest until they pop out. "At the risk of potentially embarrassing you further or making my health incident worse, I should tell you something."

He winces. "You're vegetarian?"

"Oh, hell no. No, but I . . . uh . . . red wine gives me migraines."

"Of course it does." He eyes the bottle. "It appears I can do nothing right this evening."

I hold up my hands. "How could you have known?"

"I assumed. It is a bad habit of mine. One I am trying to overcome." He gestures to my glass. "Can you drink white?" I nod. "Then let me fetch you another bottle."

I close my eyes, chuckling around my embarrassment. "That would be nice."

The warmth of his fingers brush my shoulder. I want to press up into his strength, and get closer to his hard body. I don't move. *Coward.*

"Then I will return with dinner."

He sweeps away and the door snicks shut again, leaving me staring at the empty kitchen. I haven't had a homecooked meal since I moved out of Mom and Dad's. And Sam is certainly attractive. It isn't a hardship to be in his presence. Tonight might have started off disastrously but perhaps my luck is changing.

Dinner with a hot guy—a dinner *he* is going to cook. *Haven't I seen this date movie once or twice?*

Wait. *Date?* That's not what this is. He's just being neighborly. His cat almost sent me to the hospital and he's feeling guilty, that's all.

I press cold palms to my burning cheeks and race to the bathroom. The vision in the mirror sends me stumbling back in horror. My fire engine-red skin only makes the bloodshot and swollen eyes worse. Mortified beyond anything I've ever felt, I splash water on my face and curse myself for agreeing to this silly dinner. It's too late to do anything about my appearance now, he's already seen me looking hideous. No wonder he keeps asking if I'm okay.

In my bedroom, I throw on dry clothes that won't embarrass me. At least I'd planned to until I realize I haven't done any washing, so jeans from last night will have to do, along with my gray zip-up fleece—it's two sizes too big, but it's comfortable and at least I don't look like a drowned rat anymore. I also grab my favorite scarf. My neck has warmed up considerably but I don't want to get sick, so I wrap the soft butterfly scarf Elisa gave me for my birthday around my neck. He might think it's weird, but whatever. Releasing my ponytail, I fluff my hair and race to clean up the living room.

Sam hasn't returned. Does that mean he's doing the actual cooking at his place? If I get stuck with the dishes I won't be impressed. Of course, my kitchen is woefully understocked, and a gaping hole reminds me I have yet to get a dishwasher. *Who sells their house and takes the dishwasher?* My hopes are dashed when a knock precedes Sam into my kitchen with a frying pan and several bags.

"I hope you don't mind. I wasn't sure what you have unpacked." He glances around my living area. "I am sure you are looking forward to retrieving your belongings from storage."

"I *have* unpacked," I say. Embarrassment gathers in my chest as I examine the room through the eyes of a rich stranger. My furniture is mismatched and mostly built from flatpacks. Everything is nice, though. I look after my stuff and the colors aren't totally awful.

He glances over my outfit, focusing on my scarf. "My apologies again."

I sniff. *Judgmental ass.* Not everyone has the kind of money he obviously does. I don't reply. I'm not excusing my situation or apologizing. Not today.

He starts unloading his stuff and I watch in awe as he moves around my tiny kitchen like a pro. No movement is wasted or hesitant. A bit like the man himself. My gaze drops to his forearms, lightly dusted with hair, and the open neck of his shirt. My blood thrums. He doesn't say a word, just sets to work.

Within ten minutes, the most tantalizing aromas fill my small home. I sit on one of two bench stools and watch. "Smells amazing."

"Open the wine?"

"At the risk of sounding like a broken record, you really didn't need to." His nose twitches. I nod. "Thanks."

The one thing I do own is proper wine glasses, courtesy of my university days spent volunteering at the theater. Theater people sure know how to drink. I pull two clean glasses from the cupboard and spot his soft smile. *See, I'm not a total cheapass.* "You said you were trying to overcome bad habits earlier? Tell me more," I say as I pour.

His hands move quickly as he prepares the food. I wonder how they'd feel sliding over my forearms. Bet they're firm and experienced, so, so experienced. I gulp at my glass.

"I have become aware that I have much to learn about myself. A rude awakening, one might say. That is why I am here." He gestures to the window. "This is not my usual residence."

"I had, uh . . . wondered."

He stops puttering around the kitchen and stares at me. "What do you mean?" His eyes are dark pools sucking me under to drown in their depths.

I straighten out of my slump and clear my throat. "You appear quite, um, refined. Well, okay, rich. Too rich for this little court. I find it odd."

He rubs a hand over his face. "I have discovered that to live humbly is rather freeing."

I force myself to sip at the wine more delicately. I suspect it is super expensive and mentally shrug off his unintended insult. The wine tastes no different to the cheaper bottles I regularly buy. I figure I won't mention that.

"What an intriguing display."

My head snaps up. Sam is staring at the whiteboard Elisa and I wrote our serial killer list on. *Crap!* Now he is going to think I'm loony. "Um . . ."

He stills. "Does this have something to do with your bad day?"

There's no way I can talk to Sam about Bacitriet, the missing girls or midnight bloody bag drops. It's not exactly a conversation to have over dinner.

"It has all the appearance of a police board," he continues, moving closer to read it properly. His shoulder hitches slightly, so slightly I wouldn't have spotted it usually but I'm a bit tipsy and I'm staring at his back, ogling his strong muscles.

I gulp my wine and swallow it down the wrong way. Coughing harshly, I put the glass carefully on the bench. Why not tell him? Maybe it's the antihistamine and the alcohol, or maybe it's just that I desperately need to tell *someone*.

I lean my chin into my hands. "I think my boss is a serial killer."

Chapter 14

At first, I didn't think he heard me.

He's stirring whatever is in the pot, eyes cast down, examining the insides. Eventually, he speaks. "What makes you think that?"

I knew it. He *does* think I'm loony. *I should have passed it off as research for my screenplay.* I drain what's left in my glass and frown at him. "You can escape now, you know. I didn't ask you over and—"

"I did not say I do not believe you. I merely asked why it is you think your employer is a serial killer?"

Can skin actually burst into flames? I keep embarrassing myself in front of him. *It's the wine.* I jump from the stool and pace the length of the bench. "I sound crazy."

"Then explain your reasoning."

Not a chance. "Look, I don't even know you. You might be a . . . I don't even know what you are."

He flinches.

"What happened? Did you burn yourself." Two steps around the bench brings me to his side.

"Ah, yes." He holds up his pinkie finger and blows on it. I take his hand. His skin radiates heat that travels up my arm and lands in my stomach. I curl my fingers around his wrist. His pulse throbs as I tug him to the sink. This close to him, I inhale his intoxicating aftershave.

"You need to put it under cold water straightaway." My voice has slipped to a whisper.

He allows me to hold his hand beneath the tap and, after a length of time I deem enough, I lift it up to examine the burn. There is no blister, or any redness. His fingers curl around mine, sending a buzz right through me, and I stare up into his face. His lips part and I want to press myself against him and taste . . .

Whoa! I shiver. *Down girl.* I don't normally act on impulse but I'm afraid today I might. "It looks okay." I drop his hand. "You should take more care."

"Yes, I should," he murmurs softly and returns to the stove.

"It's why I don't cook," I say, my arms itching like my skin is too tight. "It's dangerous." I park my butt back on the stool to put the bench between us again. "What was I saying? Oh yes. What do you do? For work I mean?"

"Freelance." His eyes flick in my direction. "How do you like your steak?"

"Medium-rare." How can I keep the conversation going? "So you control your own hours? That must be nice." Sizzling soon fills the kitchen and the steam that lifts from the pan engulfs Sam's face. It gives him an otherworldly look. Ethereal. *What is in this wine?*

"I believe we have strayed off the topic." I'm lost in his intense stare as he turns his head to meet my gaze. "You were telling me why you suspect your employer is a serial killer." He sounds like he really wants to know. It's a little heady being such a focus of his attention.

Suddenly, I *do* want to talk about it. Sam, a complete stranger, might be able to see what I can't. "Cook another steak. You might as well join me." I pull the whiteboard over and start from the beginning, telling him about the missing assistants, the strange phone call and the gym bag. "So, it could be nothing, but—"

"This is why you returned home so late last night?" More sizzling punctuates his comment, and the scent of cooking meat makes my mouth water. Whatever is in that pot smells divine, creamy with a hint of garlic.

"Last night, you said you could smell blood?" This time, the shiver down my spine is not a pleasant one. I've told him a lot. *Too much.* Why is it so easy to talk to him? Perhaps it's because he's listened without judgment. Who even does that? I wonder if he realizes how sexy that is.

He places a dinner plate in front of me, and I can't tear my eyes from it. "Steak with white sauce, steamed potatoes with garlic, green onion, parsley and chives, and garden vegetables."

It's a freaking masterpiece. "Smells heavenly."

He laughs. "Anything but. Please enjoy."

"Oh, I shall." Earlier, I'd wanted to be alone to wallow in my misery. My decision to let him stay is my best in, like, forever. I slice off a sliver of steak and bite into it, not even attempting to hide my moan of ecstasy. "This tastes amazing."

"Really, it is nothing spectacular," he replies, cutting into his own perfectly cooked steak.

I grin. "You know, you might have made a mistake demonstrating how well you cook. I'll beg you to come over all the time now."

His lips press together as his eyebrows meet. "That would not be wise."

I force a laugh. *Awkward.* I thought we were flirting, both on the same page. I glare at my empty wine glass. "I'm kidding." I joke it off. "Um, so, this is really delicious." My cheeks are on fire as I offer a twisted smile and silently lecture myself to behave.

How many times can a person—me—embarrass themselves in one night? I must be batting a thousand. To change the subject, because he's still giving me that sleepy tiger stare, I blurt, "What do you think? Am I reading too much into it? My boss can't be dangerous; he looks as though he'd snap in half if he tried to lift a grocery bag."

"You should resign."

My hand freezes with my fork midway between plate and mouth. "You *do* think he is a serial killer?"

He purses his lips, his gaze drifting to the whiteboard. "What I think does not matter. You believe there is a chance he is dangerous. That does not bode well for any working relationship. You would prosper better where you feel safe."

I ponder that as we finish our meals. "You know, these potatoes are really amazing."

He continues as if I didn't just try to change the subject. "Do you wish to stay working for this man? Is the money truly that good?"

This time, I do laugh, loudly. "Yes. I couldn't say no. I was hoping you'd tell me I'm just imagining things."

"I do not believe that you are." His hand twitches, like it wants to touch me. To provide comfort, perhaps? Would it be weird to move closer? I could do with a hug.

He's quiet as he stands to collect the dishes. "I will take care of these. You wished for an early night and I have taken up much of your time."

"I'm feeling better," I offer, standing as well. I talked too much, didn't I? Monopolized the conversation. I should have asked more questions about him and taken the time to show that I'm interested. Now I just seem self-absorbed. Elisa will slap me silly when she hears about this. I excuse it by remembering his intense gaze and all his questions. It's a poor excuse. Not even my brain is convinced.

My face is hot again and I realize I haven't spoken in a while. "Uh, thank you for cooking. It was nice of you to offer and then to stay. I really do feel better." A glimmer of a smirk dances around his lips as his eyes dart to the empty wine bottle. "I mean, my allergy. I'm not feeling so stuffed up."

"I am glad to hear that. I will speak with Mephistopheles. He will not return."

I picture Sam sitting opposite the black furry demon, giving him a hearty lecture, and stifle a laugh. "Thanks."

At the door, laden down with bags of dirty dishes, he pauses and his direct eye contact gives me goosebumps. I shiver and blame the cold air, though I'm anything but cold.

"Do not go back to your workplace." He leaves without looking back.

I close the door and stare at where my hand presses into the wood. I need to call Elisa. I dial her number with a shortness of breath that I know means I really like my neighbor and a giggle escapes me. *He's totally into me.* He cooked dinner! People don't just do that.

Then I realize Sam never answered my question about smelling blood.

Making my way into the bathroom, I start the water running in the tub.

"Hey. It's a little late for you to be calling, isn't it?" she says straightaway.

"Do you mind? I really need to talk."

"Sure." I hear her settle into her couch, or maybe it's her bed. I can't hear Frank and the kids would be in bed by now. "How's work going?"

"It's weird, but listen, I have to tell you something or I'm going to lose it."

"What?"

I tell her about the dinner with Sam.

"He cooked for you?" I can hear the smile in her voice.

"Yes, and he's really good at it. Cooking, I mean." I giggle, placing the phone onto my bath tray next to my wine glass and press the speaker on. I splash a little water as I climb into the tub.

"Are you having a bath?"

"I have had a long day. Anyway, he was staring into my eyes, and when he touched my hand, I got tingles."

"Weren't you going to keep your distance from him? Remember the vibes?"

"I know. I just didn't get anything bad off him. He seems really nice."

She clears her throat. "You said he asked questions about the whiteboard?"

"Yeah but—"

"What does he do? His job, I mean."

My smile drops at her cautious tone. I thought she'd be happy for me. She'd said I needed to have more fun. "Ah, sales or something." I should have found out what exactly he does. Come to think of it, why didn't I ask? He'd diverted me off the subject by quizzing me about my possibly serial killer boss.

"Are you sure he was flirting?"

"I think I would know, El. There was chemistry." I'm overheating, but I blame the bathwater.

"I believe you. You know I do. I'm just . . . look, you said you weren't interested in him."

I glare at the phone. "Seriously?"

"Mig, come on. I don't want you to get hurt. He sounds like he could be a bit of a player. He just happened to have two steaks that he could bring over?"

"He can afford it, just because I don't shop for a whole week doesn't mean he doesn't keep a full pantry and fridge."

"I'm worried. My guides are really animated. I think you need to be careful around him."

"You said I need to have more fun."

"I did, but—"

"Maybe he just wants to have fun too? No strings, you know."

"From what you've told me, he's more likely to swan off to posh restaurants and travel the world. Sweetie, you're built for comfort and TV binges."

"How very dare you," I snark, pulling a face at the phone. Comfort and TV binges, my butt. Okay, there's a lot of truth in that, but seriously, kick me in the gut why don't you?"

"Do you really want a no-strings affair?" she asks.

"No!" A little excitement might be nice though. And being treated like a queen. Or at least listened to. He'd heard me. Didn't talk over me and didn't tell me how to feel. I mean, it was nice to be the center of attention for a change.

"Do you think a guy like that wants marriage?"

"Who's talking about marriage? Elisa, cut it out."

"I don't want you to get hurt."

"So it's all fun and games to talk about when he's across the fence and behind his curtains, but actually breathing and smiling and talking to me is dangerous?"

"You're right. I am out of line. I'm sorry."

I mumble that it's okay, but I'm still annoyed. Elisa's married with kids and what do I have? A big fat zero.

"You said something happened at work?"

I don't want to talk about it now. My stomach is swirling angrily. "It's way past my bedtime. I should go."

Her voice is suddenly a lot softer. "I'm sorry, Mig. It's not that I . . . joking around is fine when you don't actually know the guy. Now you do. He sounds nice and yeah, he sounds like he is into you. It's just . . . the thing with your boss and the missing assistants. And now Sam. He only moved in a few days ago and now he's spent half a night interrogating you about—"

"Oh, interrogation! I have to tell you something and you can't tell anyone about it."

"What?"

"Promise."

"Fine, yes. I promise."

"I was interrogated by a detective."

"What detective?"

By the time I've told her the whole story, my bath water has gone cold. "I should go. It's late."

"Mig, I'm getting scared. You're spying on Bacitriet for the police. What if he catches you?"

"I don't know. But if the police are watching out for me, that's good, right? I mean, he won't try anything if he knows they're onto him. I'm probably safer there than anyone."

I can hear her shaking her head just from the tone in her voice. "Please be careful."

"I will." I hang up the phone and sigh. I mean, she's not wrong. I can't see myself with Sam in two years, five years or even ten years. He's not long-term material. Yes, the attention is fabulous, but will it last? A guy like that? Rich, powerful, intelligent. What does he even do anyway? I have no idea. It could be finance of some sort. He sort of looks and acts like how I imagine a stockbroker would look and act. Besides, he owns a cat. An evil cat. *And smokes. Don't forget about that.* But even as I list all the negatives out in my head, my heart yearns for what could be.

I debate reheating the bath water so I can sigh dramatically and sink beneath the surface. I'd do it too if I could be bothered going through the lengthy routine drying my hair after such a move would necessitate. See, I'm just me. Boring, ordinary Margaret Solder. Not wanting to wet my hair because it would be too much of a hassle to dry and it would keep me up later than I want. I prefer sleep. I prefer coffee and movies and reading in the bath. I won't get the movie romance, the destined love of the ages. I am an assistant in a consultant firm and an unwilling spy for a detective who suspects my boss is genuinely evil. That's more than enough drama and excitement for me.

I climb out of the bath and grab my towel.

When I duck into my bedroom, I catch sight of Mephistopheles sitting in the window opposite. I shoot him a glare and slam the curtains shut on his snippy face. The wretched beastie enabled me to meet Sam properly and put that stupid fantasy into my head. Elisa's right. I don't know Sam at all. And he sure did ask a heap of questions without answering any of the ones I asked in return.

I groan. Reality is *such* a bitch.

*

Morning comes far too quickly and I haven't slept a wink. Every time I glanced at the clock, barely an hour had gone by. My alarm blares and though I watched it tick over, I still jump. Smacking my hand against the top of the alarm might stop the ear-splitting bleeping but it doesn't halt the arguing voices in my head.

I blink up at my dark ceiling. With the heart of winter creeping closer, the sun won't even crack the horizon for a while. Not that light will make my thoughts any clearer. Everything is a giant muddled mess. Pushing Sam from my mind only brings other stresses to the forefront. Somehow, I've gone from being an office-worker to spying for the police, and I can't tell if my stomach is squirming from anxiety or excitement. This is my chance to experience what my screenplay characters go through—the buzz, the thrill, the fear. It will ground my movie in reality and is the sort of research that writers dream of experiencing, right? So why am I lounging around in bed, trying to delay the start of my day?

Happily ensconced in a seat on the train, I pull my notebook from my bag and review my work plan. I'll snoop through Cassandra's email and Bacitriet's calendar first, then when people come in, I'll ask more questions. Candy opened up to me when she was alone, perhaps the others will too.

I stare into the dawning light through the grimy train window and watch the sky become pink with fairy-floss clouds as the sun rises.

Bacitriet is due back midmorning. What am I going to say to him? I suck on my teeth, not in the least bit concerned about wrecking my lipstick, Sam's voice plays back in my head. "You should resign . . . You would prosper better where you feel safe." Easy for him to say. Without this job I don't exactly have money to burn. Being a rich freelancer, he could probably disappear at the drop of a hat—or just leave if a boss unsettled him. Not that I imagine he'd ever feel freaked out by anyone.

Bzzzzz.

I snatch my phone from my handbag and blink at the message on the screen. I expected Elisa, but it's Mom. *Hope your first week is going well?*

I sigh and send back. *It's different.* The story is too long to go into now.

I send Elisa a message. *Can we talk more tonight?*

Of course.

Feeling brighter, I jot down a timeline for today.

8 a.m.: Start work (extra-large coffee)

9:30 a.m.: Bacitriet's flight lands.

10:15 a.m.: Bacitriet gets to work.

I tap my pen against my lips. What will happen then? Going by past actions, he'll call me into his office to go through his calendar. Then again, he has meetings booked so I might not actually speak to him. I'll take a lunch break around twelve and, with any luck, won't even see him until well after one. A thought occurs to me then: does Detective Bryce intend to interview Bacitriet? What if the police are at the airport right now, waiting for him to land? He might not come into the office at all.

That cheerful thought sustains me all the way into work.

Chapter 15

Sipping my coffee, I click through Bacitriet's online calendar over the past three months. A lot of internal meetings and travel to Sydney. A few trips to Brisbane. All in all, it's pretty ordinary. As I click back through the previous bookings, I find signature blocks for Cassandra, Annie and, at last, Maria Gutieriz.

With a quick look around, I jump on my phone. Maria's last social media post was back in February. She'd posted several times a day prior to that. I examine her profile picture. She's a pretty woman with dark hair and soulful eyes. Over her last few posts, the status had changed from happy to "not sleeping" to "tired" and "worried." I check both Cassandra and Annie's feeds and find similar updates. My mood swings as I see their posts. Each mirrors the other exactly. *I hate this.*

Does Bacitriet keep staff files in his office, or would they be with HR? I stand up. Joshua is walking straight toward me, a can of energy drink in his hand. I can't snoop now. I plant my butt back into my seat and check the time. Bacitriet should be on his flight back to Melbourne. I have time. Without intending to, I start a new list in my head—a witness list—and notice the instant messaging icon flashing at the bottom of my screen. Bacitriet doesn't seem the type to send instant messages. I figure it's probably Timber, the IT guy. I click on the icon and a pop-up box appears.

Help me.

The sender's name is blank. That's weird.

Hi, who is this? I type, and while I wait for an answer I check the IM settings. I can't see any way to disconnect my name from my login and wonder how they did it. The message disappears.

I pull my hand off the mouse. Did I click something by mistake? It's just like that missing email and I find that a freaky coincidence. Another light flashes in my taskbar. I bite my lip and flick my gaze around the office. No one is looking at me and I can't hear any sniggering or choked off laughter that might indicate a prank. I hunch closer to the computer. I'm being paranoid. With sweaty fingers, I grasp the mouse and click on the flashing icon.

Help me.

My skin crawls as if thousands of ants are having a party on my body. With a sharp move, I shut down the messaging program and stand up, peering around suspiciously. Who is doing this? When I glance back down, the icon is flashing again.

"Shit."

I power down the laptop. Hard reset. While it reboots, I wander around the office, sneaking a glance at each person's screens. No one has the instant messaging app open.

Shannon looks up from her phone as I move past. "What are you doing? Do you need help with something?"

I wave a hand around. "Just stretching my legs." I'm being too obvious. I return to my desk, log back in to my laptop and sit down. My screen pops to life and the messaging icon flashes again. My fingers tremble as I click on the message.

Don't go.

"Shit."

Another message appears. *Please.*

I type. *Who are you?*

Three little dots appear. Time stops. I can't breathe.

Annie Seramoph.

Chapter 16

Who are you really?

My stomach churns like the spin cycle of a washing machine. This has to be a prank. Someone thinks it's funny to pretend to be a missing person. I glance up again, staring at everyone over the top of the partitions. No one looks in my direction other than Joshua in the desk behind mine.

"What?" he snaps.

I shake my head and sit down. Another message appears.

I am Annie.

I bite my lips hard enough to draw blood. I hit the camera button to enable a video call and get an error message saying this call cannot be connected. I type out a message. *If you are Annie Seramoph . . . then where are you?*

There's a long pause before those little moving dots appear again.

I don't know.

That isn't good enough. If this is Annie, how could she not know where she is? It must be a prank. *Look, if you want me to believe you, you need to tell me where you are.*

Elisa always says, "Listen to your gut." My instincts are screaming at me and they're saying this *is* Annie. But why would she contact *me*? And why didn't she come forward in response to her parents pleas to return home?

I don't know where I am. I'm alone here. It's dark.

I type quickly. *Why are you contacting me?*

I've been calling for a long time. You're the only one who answered.

My goosebumps grow goosebumps. At war with my gut, my brain is insisting with all the logic at its command that this is someone playing a game. A bad one. My head wins. The goosebumps die, replaced by an electrical current of curiosity. I have to find Timber and get him to check my computer. Hopefully he can track the messages back to their point of origin and discover who is behind it, or at least get their location.

I type one last message. *Prove you're Annie Seramoph.*

There's no response. Of course, there isn't.

If I call Detective Bryce, what will I tell her about this? That someone is trying to scare me via my computer? I keep coming back to why. Why would someone pretend to be Annie? To confuse me? Scare me? Or does someone know I'm looking into this and are they trying to send me on a wild goose chase? Someone must have found out about my meeting with Detective Bryce. *Crap.* What if it's the person behind the disappearances trying to lure me in?

All the television shows I've ever watched would say that what I have is flimsy evidence at best. Detective Bryce won't be able to use any of it in a court of law. No, I need something concrete. Bacitriet says I have the same access as the previous assistant. But without Annie officially resigning, I wonder if the proper procedures to close out her remote access have been followed. My suspicions latch onto that. I have access to Cassandra's emails, which means her account hasn't been deleted yet. Annie *could* be hiding somewhere, using her remote access to talk to me, right? No. IT would surely have disabled her account. I need to speak to Timber. When I find out who is doing this, I'll call Detective Bryce and then this person will pay for trying to scare me.

*

Level forty-three looks identical to the main floor except that it's a lot more crowded. There are twice the number of desks here as on my floor. There's more chatter and movement too. Timber said IT is located in the back corner so that's where I head. I find him at a desk near the window. At least, I figure it's his desk. He's buried beneath hard drives, laptop chargers, cables and phones. "How do you find your keyboard?" I ask, approaching his side.

He yanks off his earpiece and grins. "I don't. I'm first-level support. I come to you."

At the sight of his gorgeous smile, I let out a nervous laugh. "Hey, can you look at something for me?"

"Sure."

I pull over an empty chair and plop down, opening my laptop and the messenger app. No history has been saved. "Damn."

"What's up?"

"I wanted to ask you about an instant message, but it's disappeared. Can I re-call message history or is there a sent log or something to read previously sent messages?"

He blinks. "A message? Who was it from? Sometimes messages don't close properly. Could that be the problem?"

I shake my head. "Can someone external to the company send an IM on our system?"

"Nope. It's a closed system. Are you testing me?" He leans back in his chair with a wide grin and clasps his hands behind his head.

"What about removing your name so you can send a message anonymously?"

He raises an eyebrow. "Why would you want to do that?"

"Oh, not me. That's what I mean. I got a message, but I don't know who sent it. So, are you saying we can't change the name in settings?"

"No, it's locked to your account. Well, I mean, you could change it, I suppose. It's editable by the user, but we don't enable that option for staff."

I stare at him steadily. "So someone in IT could do it?"

"Yep."

Well that narrows down the possibilities. "How many people work in IT?"

"Just me and Peter—my boss." He gestures at the desk behind his, which is—if possible—even messier than Timber's workstation. He points to a closed door behind Peter's desk. "He's in the server room at the moment. Why?"

I inch away, considering Timber with new eyes. Was it him? Did Timber send the anonymous message pretending to be Annie Seramoph?

"I didn't do it, if that's what you're asking," he says, sitting upright.

I continue to stare at him.

"Seriously," he repeats. "And I doubt Peter would do something like that either."

"But only the two of you have access?"

"Yeah, we're understaffed." He gestures to a spotless desk near the window. "New guy starts soon." Timber's teeth shine like those of a shark. "Really, I didn't play with your IM."

"I have access to Cassandra Chan's emails for Bacitriet. What's the procedure now that she's gone? How long do I have before you close her account?"

"Well, I'm sure Bethany already went through her email searching for anything urgent."

"Why would Beth—"

"Bacitriet trusts her."

"Why didn't she take the job then? As Bacitriet's assistant?"

He shrugs. "You'd have to ask her."

"How long do I have before you close Cassandra's account?"

He locates a keyboard buried beneath a giant tangle of cables. *Ha, he does have one!* He types something. "Oh, a while."

"Like a week? A month?"

"However long you need."

"What about the assistant before Cassandra? Can I access her email archive? Bacitriet's clients might have sent her—"

"No can do," he says, typing again. "Her account is disabled." His dark eyes lock onto my face. "Why are you asking about Annie's email?"

"Like I said, there might be a job she actioned that I need to follow up on. So, with her account closed, she couldn't send a . . . message?"

He scratches his chin. "Are you saying . . . ? Did Annie send you a message?"

"No, of course not, I'm just curious," I lie, shrugging.

"Okay, sure. Do you have any other issues? If you get the anonymous message again, just buzz me and I'll come down and have a look, okay? Maybe I can catch it next time."

I nod and return to the earlier conversation. "So, you delete old accounts?"

"We don't delete anything, only disable."

My eyes narrow. "You don't delete anything?" That's kinda disturbing. "Why?"

He tilts his head. "Company policy. I don't set it, only enforce it."

"Don't you think it's a bit creepy that private emails can be kept after a person leaves?"

"IT policies are the same all over. The company protects the company, you know? Besides, people email all sorts of shit. This is Bacitriet's business. I guess he feels more in control that way."

Bacitriet certainly strikes me as a man with control issues. "So, here is a weird question. How long have you been here?"

"Four months."

"Really? Not that long then. How are you finding it?"

"It's a job." He squints at me. "Why?"

"Where were you before?"

"Here and there."

I lower my voice. "You don't find it a bit strange? That so many people have started here so recently?"

"That's not the only funny thing going on." There's a manic sort of light in Timber's dark brown eyes now that we've moved off work and onto gossip.

I slide my chair closer. "What do you mean?"

He peers around. I follow his gaze but can't see anyone watching us. "Strange stuff. Peter and I can't figure it out."

"Strange?"

"Disappearing files. Like your weird email the other day. Things that are here one minute and gone the next. Space has been taken up in the drives, but we have no idea what's taking it. We can't find anything."

What would take up a lot of space? My thoughts drift to the person claiming to be Annie. She said she didn't know where she was, which is weird. If it really is her. I think about that movie I watched the other night. The horror about transferring a mind into the body of a robot.

What if . . .

Come on, Mig. That's ridiculous.

But I can't shake the thought. What if, instead of storing a mind inside a robot, you put it into a computer? Which is a little like a robot actually. What if Annie is *in* the computer. *This is crazy.* My mind jitters like I've drunk too much coffee.

A mind would take up a lot of space though, and Timber said space *is* being used by something. No, it's a stupid thought. The thing with the instant messages has to be a prank. Timber said they don't delete old accounts, only disable them. So someone could have hacked in and reactivated Annie's account. *But why? And why message me from that account?* My phone vibrates. I check the display. "I've gotta go. More training with Shannon.

"If you have any further problems—"

"I'll IM you. Yeah, thanks."

*

It's next to impossible to concentrate on work for the rest of the day. I don't see Bacitriet though, so thank God for small favors.

I park in my driveway that night and sit in the car for a long time, staring out through the windscreen at my house. No rain today, just cold air. Before I turn off my headlights, I notice my front lawn is getting long. I'll have to mow it soon. I'll have to buy a mower. And learn how to use it!

My phone rings as I grab my stuff out of the car—unknown number. "Hello?"

"Ms. Solder?"

"Yes, speaking."

"This is Detective Bryce. Have I caught you at a good time?"

I mentally groan. "Sure."

"I'm wondering how things are going?"

I shove my bags back into the car and plonk down in the driver's seat, pulling out my notebook. I go through what I've learned. It isn't a lot. I can't tell her about the IMs; I'll sound bonkers.

"Not anything we can use," she agrees a few minutes later.

Well, excuse me for not being a very good spy. "I'm sorry that's all I—"

"Don't be silly," she jumps in. "I appreciate anything you have. I'll look into these receptionists and, of course, if there is anything else you hear, give me a call." I debate mentioning the weird laptop messages. As if she's read my mind, she adds, "You can tell me anything at all, no matter how odd."

Not this odd. We hang up after I assure her I'll call if I learn anything else, and climb from my car, weary from the inside out.

A note taped to my front door stops my hand inches from the door handle. My stomach drops.

We're at your neighbor's house.

Have something to tell you.

B&R

Oh no! I bolt to Sam's front door. This is all I need. I pound my fist against the wooden frame, and hear what sounds like a moan coming from inside. I push the door open. "Sam? Berry? Rose?"

"Come in, honey!" Rose calls.

I walk inside. "Rose, I can't stay. Sam has a c—"

"Kitty. Oh yes, he's adorable," she calls back.

That's not the word I'd use. I peer around the dark interior of Sam's hallway, shivering at the cool temperature. *Doesn't he have a heater?*

A glass cabinet lines one wall. I glance inside, and then take a longer look. Swords hang in the top half—half a dozen of them—all shiny and very sharp-looking. There are knives and old pistols too, similar to what you'd see in history movies. Sam collects ancient weaponry? I hadn't guessed that about him. I bet they're expensive. *Everyone has a quirk, don't they?*

I head into the largest living room I've ever seen. There is no way this place has the square footage to allow for a room this size. A long sofa splits the room in half, creating a neat space with a freaking enormous wall-mounted TV. *Oh my God. Imagine watching movies on that!* Plush gray carpet underfoot gives me the feeling of walking on a cloud, and four lamps light the room in soft orange, creating what Elisa would call "atmosphere." I reckon it's too dark.

A sneeze bursts out of me, and I sniff, cursing softly. "Stupid cat." I can feel my throat growing scratchy as I move toward the sofa, eyes flitting from one piece of overpriced furniture to the next. What exactly is it Sam does, for goodness sake? Because this is *not* normal for a person living on this street.

I round the corner into the kitchen and spy a body lying on the floor. Sam is flat on his belly. Berry straddles him holding his wrist back.

"Berry! What are you doing? Let Sam go!" I run to her side and help her to get off him.

"Just showing Sam jujitsu, dear."

"Why? And when did you learn jujitsu?" I picture my grandmothers in a class, harassing the instructor to teach them more and more dangerous moves, and suppress a groan.

Rose shoots Berry a long look. "As kids, dear. We came to tell you something." She is sitting comfortably in a big armchair, petting the black monster with one hand and holding a cup of chamomile tea in the other. The scent makes its way into my nose despite allergies blocking my nostrils. I scowl at the evil feline. It blinks at me and snuggles its head further under Rose's scritching fingers, purring loudly.

"Need a hand?" I ask, crouching next to Sam.

"I might just stay here," he mumbles into the carpet.

"I am so sorry. They are a menace." I shoot each woman a warning glare. A flush paints my skin when Sam doesn't take my hand.

Berry grins. "He shouldn't have provoked me, dear."

"Why are you here?"

"You weren't home." Rose sips from her teacup. Her eyes twinkling.

"Yes but why wait *here*?"

Berry shakes out her slacks and then rolls her wrists. "He invited us in."

"After they pounded on my door," Sam adds. He hasn't moved. Perhaps he's serious about staying on the carpet. My gaze falls to his butt enclosed in tight black jeans. *Whoo boy.* I lift my gaze to find Rose grinning at me.

I spin away, moving closer to Berry. She raises an eyebrow. I shake my head and glance down at Sam, wondering if he has noticed the weird silent conversation I'm having with my grandmothers. I bend closer to her and whisper. "You'd better not be snooping."

Berry tilts her head, grins and says loudly, "What dear? I can't hear you."

I sigh the put-upon sigh emitted by parents throughout the ages. "Let's leave Sam in peace."

Mephistopheles appears all too content sitting on Rose's lap. I sneeze again and wonder how his world domination plot is going.

Sam climbs to his feet and takes the cat from Rose's arms. He lets the animal loose on the carpet. I scowl at the beast and when I look up I catch the tilt of Sam's lips as his eyes dart to mine. "Hello again."

My flush of embarrassment turns to awareness of how near he is standing.

Rose shoos me away and stands on her own. I let out a giant sneeze that shakes my body and knocks the lamp off a little side table. Rose catches it before it falls. "Great reflexes," I mumble. That lamp probably costs more than my car. Mephistopheles's ears snapped back at my loud noise. His tail whips from side to side as he stares at me.

"We had something to tell you, didn't we, Rose?" Berry says.

"We did?" Rose stares at Sam's jean-clad butt. Sam turns to look at her and she raises her gaze, smiling innocently. "Oh yes. Yes, we did."

"You didn't come see us last weekend." Berry's admonishment sends ribbons of fire along my skin. That's not fair. I'd cleaned most of the weekend, which they well know. And it was my birthday. It had genuinely slipped my mind.

"We're demonstrating a new product this week. It's a secret so we can't tell you what it is, but you must come and watch," Rose adds.

Their faces are lit with so much excitement that I can't possibly say no. "I'll see if I can come home from work early. I probably won't be able too, so don't get your hopes up. How about we book in Saturday morning?"

Rose turns her manipulative gaze on Sam. "You'll come too, won't you dear?"

I jump in before he can answer. "Rose, Sam has important stuff to do. He doesn't have time—"

He holds up a hand. "I would very much like to attend."

I widen my eyes at him over Rose's head. I'd given him an out—what is he doing? His eyes flash, and I shake my head at him. His smile takes my breath away.

"Why?" I mouth the question at him.

"You are an awful lot alike, you and your grandmothers."

I sputter. "I am nothing like these monsters."

"You are all fearless," he adds.

I snort but accept the compliment. Thinking of Bacitriet, Detective Bryce and that anonymous messenger, I only wish I was fearless. I'm actually scared to death.

His hand brushes mine and I bite back a gasp at the heat emanating from his skin. Oh, how I wish his flirting meant something. I could melt from the molten look in his eyes alone. My heart lets out a thump that reminds me I'm being watched by the most notorious gossips in the universe. I turn away.

"Terrific. You can bring Mig," Rose says.

The urge to slap my forehead is nearly irresistible. They're doing exactly what I'd feared: trying to set me up with Sam. I'm horrified, but Sam's smile only grows wider. "I'm so sorry," I whisper at him. Aloud I say, "Come on you two, Sam has been a good sport. Let's leave him in peace." I push them toward the door without another glance, and as we move past the weapons display case, Berry's gaze flies over each item. She nudges Rose.

"I saw," she mumbles. I hide a snort. Maybe it will stop them from matchmaking if they think Sam is a little cuckoo.

I get both women out of Sam's house before he can object. "My place, both of you," I grump, pointing to my door.

Rose spins around. "Now, Mig. Don't be like that. We had to make sure he is safe for you to be around."

"Enough. I have had a weird day and I need both of you to behave. Get inside before I explode."

"I don't think he's all that evil," Rose mutters taking Berry's arm.

"I'm not so sure," Berry whispers back.

A looming storm is witness to my overly dramatic moan. Or so I believe. A rumbling chuckle behind me brings a gasp to my lips and when I peer back over my shoulder, my fear is realized. Sam is standing at his front door, watching me, a smile alight on his lips.

Damn it! I stomp after my grandmothers and slam the door shut behind me.

Chapter 17

Friday brings with it a feeling of eternal suffering.

I stride into work with a piping hot, extra-large coffee in one hand and fantasies about the coming weekend in my head. I'm dying for a sleep-in. Nightmares have plagued my dreams of late. Glowing cat eyes follow me in the dark while computers burst to life and chase me through endless office corridors. A comically huge gym bag that I seem to have to carry everywhere overflows with body parts. And that's nothing compared to the dreams where I wake up just as I walk into the bedroom and find a shirtless Sam waiting for me. Little wonder I've barely slept.

There's no doubt my exhaustion is advertised clearly on my face, but if anyone thinks they can take advantage of me, they are so wrong. Moody doesn't begin to cover it. I'm ready to snap.

In the cold light of day, and after consuming my monster coffee, it's hard to believe the strange messages from yesterday were real. Nothing happens when I turn on my computer except for a single email from Bacitriet requesting a catch-up. I stare at my empty coffee cup. There is not enough caffeine in the world to prepare me for that.

The temperature in the office plummets and that can only mean one thing. As predicted, Bacitriet appears like a vampire in an old horror movie. He swoops past me and into his office. I clutch my notebook and follow.

"Close the door."

I do as ordered, my heart pounding like my dad one-finger typing on a keyboard. I stand with my back against the door, adrenalin urging me to flee. *Are you the reason your assistants left? Did you do something to them?*

His impenetrable stare locks onto me and his fingers interlace and rest on the desk. "I understand you have had an interesting week." His voice is low, raspy as he breathes, like a mobster in a crime show. God, first vampires and now mobsters. My imagination really is working overtime today. Interesting week? Yes, as in the curse: *May you live in interesting times.* Ugh, I'd much rather it be boring.

Feeling like a witness testifying, I answer simply. "Yes."

"What did they ask you?"

My stomach flips. "Who asked what?"

The smile playing at his lips does nothing to alter the cold look in his eyes. "The detective. I understand she spoke to you at length."

I try to buy time. "Detective?"

"Is that not who you were speaking with on Wednesday?"

Crap. How did he find out? "Barely anything. I didn't even know who she was."

His sharp stare doesn't falter. "What information did she require?"

Speaking to Detective Bryce hadn't felt this intense. "Just when I started and if anyone had spoken to me about the lady I replaced."

He sniffs. "I do hope this experience has not soured your enthusiasm for this position. I need you, Margaret. This is an unfortunate coincidence, but that is all it is. I must insist you focus on your work now. The police will discover nothing untoward is going on here. Do not be concerned."

The brief spark of relief at still having my job dissolves into frustration. "But the missing women did work for you? Aren't you concerned about them? They worked here." *What are you doing, Mig?!*

"Women?"

"Yes."

He leans forward, bones creaking as his head tilts to the side. He peers at me with an eagle's intensity. "There is no connection."

"There clearly is."

He sighs and sits back in his seat. "Are you giving notice?"

Oh God, I want to. Sam and Elisa said I should. I could do it right now. Say yes and then this whole drama would be over. But Detective Bryce asked me to stay. I gulp. "No."

"Very well." More creaking. "I have another task for you."

"Sir?"

He flashes his teeth, and the hairs on my arms rise. "Nothing too strenuous. I require a contract to be delivered to a client before one o'clock today. You may head home after."

I can't complain about going home early. I nod. His voice stops me before I can tug open the heavy door. "If the police call you again, of *course*, tell them the truth and answer all questions. You are not obligated to tell them anything more than that. Do you understand?"

Velma from Scooby-Doo wouldn't accept that. Nor would Veronica Mars, Nancy Drew or any of the other detectives from my favorite books and shows. I have to stop being Shaggy and be more like Velma. Besides, Bacitriet said he wants me to stay. I wonder how far I can push before he pushes back. "The bag you asked me to deliver. What was in it?"

"Why do you ask?"

Not far apparently. "I found blood."

His eyes narrow as he stands up. "Did you?"

"I . . . uh . . ."

He stalks toward me. "Did you look in the bag, Margaret?"

I think of the scarves and makeup bag hidden inside. "Yes."

"Have you never injured yourself exercising?" His smile is that of the Grim Reaper.

"Oh, um." I shouldn't have said anything. I should have just nodded and left. "Do you mean like a toenail?" He doesn't react or speak. He's a brick wall. "Why did I need to take your gym clothes to that house? Was that your home? I thought maybe it was a client's house, but why would you ask me to take it there?"

"You are full of questions, aren't you?"

I gulp remembering what he'd said at my interview about questions. I can't stop myself. "And you don't answer them."

His jaw clenches. "When I hired you, it was with the understanding I could trust you to remain confidential."

"Well, yes, but I—"

"You do not require that information."

I bite back my annoyed "come on!" and catch my tongue in the process. I force the anger out of my voice and lower my gaze to my hands. Am I trying to get him to fire me? Maybe I am. "I just want to make sure I didn't do anything illegal."

"You did not."

"And I should take your word for it?" *Whoa!* When did I become all assertive?

His nostrils flare and his back straightens with a crack. "Ms. Solder. I am your employer. If you feel unable to attend to your duties, you may resign."

Since he won't go so far as to fire me, it's my choice and I know I can't do it. Not yet. I need answers first. "My apologies, Mr. Bacitriet. I just prefer to understand the purpose behind my tasks." I hold his gaze while inwardly quaking. This new me is amazing and terrifying and perhaps a little bit—a lot—stupid. "If that will be all, sir?"

"Supposition, innuendo, gossip. The police do not need these things, yes? Not that you would indulge in that sort of behavior."

I work to hold his stare. "Of course not, sir."

I return to my desk, my breathing shallow, and feel a bit dizzy. I just questioned my boss's honesty to his face. I must be bonkers.

There are a heap of emails waiting for a response, and I spend a few hours booking meetings and confirming travel arrangements. All the while, I think nothing about this job seems quite real. It's like I'm playing a role. Here I am, working like normal, right after a tension-filled confrontation with my boss.

I find a request from Bacitriet to book three interstate trips for the following week. Oh, that I'll do, happily.

I rap my fingertips against the keyboard keys and grab my notebook from my handbag.

Step 1: call Bryce.

Step 2: web search the address where I dropped off the bag.

Step 3: buy more wine.

Detective Bryce will want to know Bacitriet is going out of town. Part of me is surprised the police would even allow Bacitriet to leave the state. Then again, it seems they don't have enough evidence to hold him, or they'd have arrested him already. And if Bacitriet isn't the killer and the police focus their investigation solely on him, the real bad guy could escape and kill again. Just because I find Bacitriet creepy doesn't mean he is evil.

I replay every second of Bacitriet's interrogation. He knows I suspect him. He also knows I have no proof. I don't understand how I haven't been fired yet. He said he needs me. Really? To book flights and arrange meetings? Anyone can do that. Including someone younger and cheaper than me. What does he need *me* for? It's the thought that gets trapped inside my head. Then again, senior managers really don't like getting their hands dirty. And I'm good at what I do. It would take time out of his schedule to advertise and go through the interview process yet again.

The layers that were in our conversation are staggering. Am I reading too much into it and projecting my suspicions onto him? Ugh, now I'm talking myself in circles. Elisa says go with your gut. Well, mine is screaming to get out of here. *And yet, here I am.*

When I close the travel portal, I find my instant message icon flashing and my breath catches. I peer around, searching for someone watching me. Nothing stands out. There is no sign of Bacitriet. I move the mouse cursor over the icon.

"Here is the contract, Ms. Solder. Please leave immediately."

I startle violently, my elbow scraping the side of the desk as I wheel my chair back and stand. I rub my bruised elbow.

How does he creep around so silently? He's standing so close, I'm honestly shocked he got there without me noticing. I haven't opened the IM yet. I release a shaky breath. "You scared me."

Without responding, he holds out an envelope.

I grab my laptop and notebook, and shove them deep inside my backpack. I'm more than glad to be getting the hell out. In my gut, I suspect the sender of today's IM is the same mysterious person who sent yesterday's message. I take the huge envelope from Bacitriet's hand, glance at the address scrawled on the front, and shoot him a half-hearted wave. "Do you want me to text when I've delivered the contract?"

"Yes." His emotionless stare follows me all the way to the elevator; I know because I glance back a few times to check. It's like I'm prey, and he's just waiting for the right opportunity.

*

Once I'm seated in the taxi and safely moving, I start shaking. I'm sweaty, and I'm sure seconds away from bursting into tears. I need to call Detective Bryce and tell her I'm out. I can't do this. There's no way I'm stepping foot in that office ever again.

I understand now why the previous assistants would quit without a word, and I'm about to do the same thing. No warning, no notice. I am not going back. I open the laptop. Though I have no network connection, the message is still blinking. I click it open.

They are watching you.

That strange spacy feeling I experienced when I dislocated my knee a few years ago washes over me. Nausea hits hard, enough that I'm forced to press my hand to my mouth. *What the fuck?*

"We're here, love." The white-haired driver peers over his shoulder at me through red-rimmed spectacles. He has a nice smile, though his face shows concern as he takes in my silent freak-out. "You okay?"

We're parked on a street bustling with people; dogwalkers, women with prams, suited business workers, tradies. Life is happening all around us. The drop-off address is all the way on the other side of the city from the office. A twenty-minute drive on a good day. "We're here already?"

"Must be pretty bad news."

"What?"

"You're awful pale. Did you get some bad news?"

The clock on the dash and the one on my computer confirm the truth. I'd totally zoned out. The message is still there, as ominous as ever. I blink at the driver. He's twisted all the way around. "Should I call someone?"

"I'm okay. Really."

"That will be twenty-three eighty."

I pay the driver and climb from the taxi, juggling my bags, laptop and the envelope. I'm still surrounded by tall buildings, but everything here is a little grayer than in the city. The building in front of me is an imposing monstrosity with no sign at the top and no banner or plaque to indicate who it belongs to. A man comes out of a café on the corner shouting loudly on his phone, takeaway coffee in hand. I shiver as I step into the overly air-conditioned lobby. *I shouldn't be here.* Once the thought has popped into my mind, I can't shake it and my gut clenches, urging me to turn back. The envelope in my hand feels heavier. When I flip it over, I find the seal has lifted in the corner. I peer around to see if anyone is watching me. The foyer is oddly empty. If I'm going to quit I should give Detective Bryce what I've learned today. This envelope included.

I edge a fingernail under the corner of the seal. Bacitriet said it's a contract, but a contract for what? My gaze rises to the ceiling and I bite back a curse, catching sight of the surveillance camera. I can't open it here, but I'll look too suspicious if I just turn around and leave without delivering it. I grab my phone and pretend it rings, feeling a bit foolish as I do. I'm not an actor. I speak into the silent phone and walk out, heading straight to the café. "Oh, hi, El. I'm glad you called me back. So I was thinking we should go dress shopping before." I pretend to listen as I order a takeaway coffee at the counter. "Oh, do you think Frank can take the kids?" I keep talking on my silent phone while waiting for my coffee, peering suspiciously around at the other customers. "Okay, great. Yes. What a terrific idea. Oh, no. Those shoes won't work. I snapped the ankle strap. So shoes too. Yes. Yes. Okay. Talk later, bye El." I slide into a booth, put the phone down and open the envelope, jerking violently at the sudden hiss of steam jets heating milk. Guilt eats my stomach raw. Still, I turn the pages over, determined to uncover Bacitriet's secrets.

It's a contract.

A pretty standard one by the look of it. I skim read each page. It's signed in a reddish-brown ink. A splotch stains the bottom of each page almost like a . . . fingerprint.

I raise the paper to my nose. There's no smell, but I'm sure it isn't ink.

"Your coffee?"

I fumble the pages. Did the waiter see me sniff the paper? I take the cup from his hands. "Thanks." His stare is that of someone who has seen everything and doesn't judge.

I turn back to the first page and read it through slowly. The legalese takes some deciphering. I think I understand it. In a previous job, I'd worked in a construction office and sat through numerous contracts meetings to take minutes. On page eight, I find it. A description of the goods being sold.

A body, also referred to as vacated physical vessel. *A vessel? For what?* I read on. Removal of soul upon receipt.

What the hell?

This isn't real. It can't be.

Putting aside the possibility that I *am* going crazy, I contemplate the reality of what I'm reading. *This is ridiculous. He's setting me up. I'll look loony if I tell anyone.* Oh. Is that what this is? He's trying to cast doubt on my sanity. I can't give this to Detective Bryce. I sit there staring blankly into the distance.

The bell above the door tinkles as someone walks in. I straighten, sip my cooling coffee and examine the contract again. I don't recognize the name. *Janquil Nyugen.* I take a photo of every page knowing I need proof that I'm not imagining it. The clock on my phone reminds me time is running out. I have to deliver this before one o'clock and text Bacitriet. I return the contract to the envelope and seal it properly this time before I head straight into the adjacent building. A woman stands at the desk, dressed in a replica of the outfits worn by Bacitriet's receptionists. Another coincidence? Perhaps Bacitriet owns this business too. It's like looking at a living mannequin and it makes my skin crawl. She says nothing as I hand her the envelope, but her stare stays on me as I exit the building.

Unsettled, I walk back to the café and call an Uber to drop me off at the closest railway station on my line. I don't breathe easy until I sit down and the train moves off. All the way home

I try to forget what I've seen, but like water going down the drain, my mind keeps circling.

A contract—signed in blood—for a soul and the removal and handing over of a vacated vessel. By giving that woman the envelope did I just seal Janquil Nyugen's fate?

I'm losing my mind. It can't possibly be real. Bacitriet must be testing my loyalty.

I don't remember the drive home from the station. I park in my driveway and let out a long, relieved sigh. Home. Safe. I lean my head against the inside of the car door and close my eyes. I need a new plan. I have to figure out how to get my work equipment back to the office because I sure as hell am not stepping foot in there again.

The car door opens and I fall sideways, my weight going with it. "What the . . ." Thankfully, I'm still wearing my seatbelt, which saves me from toppling all the way to the ground and onto Sam's shiny black shoes. "What are you doing?" I demand, straightening.

"Your grandmothers?" he says, with raised eyebrows. "I assumed that is why you have come home early?"

"What have they done now?"

"Did you not promise that you would witness their presentation?"

"On the weekend, sure." Right now, I just want to collapse on my sofa and stress about that contract, maybe jump online to find Janquil Nyugen, body seller. *You know how crazy that sounds?* Then again, I need something normal. What could be more normal than Rose and Berry. "Actually, sure, hop in." I glance at the passenger-side footwell, and my stomach clenches. I swipe old magazines, mail and takeaway containers away from the space. He climbs in and immediately pushes the seat back. His pinstripe suit fits him like its molded to his shoulders. I toss the trash in the back seat and jam the gear-shift into reverse, doing my best to ignore his presence and concentrate on my driving. I also fight the desire to apologize for the housekeeping of my car. "You didn't have to come with me," I say, shooting him a look.

He stares through the window. "I assured your grandmothers I would attend."

"Yes, but you could have been busy. They'd have understood."

"I don't break my promises, Margaret," he says, and his tone stops further comment.

When I flick my gaze his way, I find him staring right at me. I quickly face forward to watch the road, my heart pounding.

"Are you well?"

"Fine. All good here, why do you ask?" *I. Am. An. Embarrassment.* I can't seem to stop myself from making it worse. "Sorry my car is such a mess."

He doesn't respond, but I sense him smile. A quick glance confirms it. "You appear stressed. How was your day at work? Did you quit as I advised?"

I shrug.

"You have discovered something?"

It's one thing to half-believe what I'd read; it's another to tell someone about it. "I think I'm going crazy," I admit softly.

His voice is soft and warm as he replies, "Why would you think that?"

"Because I . . ." I drive into the open-air shopping center car-park and straight into a space. Beside us a woman is strapping her child into its car seat. I turn off the engine. Sam touches my arm, his gentle fingers caressing my skin. The gold flecks inside his brown eyes make them glow, and a shiver runs from my neck down my back.

"Something is concerning you. Tell me. I will believe you."

"I think my boss might be . . ."

He says nothing, just watches with a steady unjudging gaze.

". . . the devil."

Chapter 18

I expect him to laugh, or at least roll his eyes, but his only reaction is to twitch one eyebrow. "I assure you, your boss is not the devil."

It's not so much the tone of Sam's voice as the look in his eyes. He'd listened and genuinely heard my fear. He was serious—and he didn't think I was crazy. Still, I can't help but say it. "You think I'm nuts."

He leans toward me, and my skin tingles with awareness. "No."

"I found . . . Sam, I saw a contract. Well, I had to deliver it. That's why I'm home early. The real reason and well, the envelope wasn't sealed properly, so I peeked. I know I shouldn't have but . . . it looked like it was . . ." Ugh, I'm blabbering. I give myself an internal shake.

"Yes?"

"Signed in blood." There, I'd said it. I search his expression for laughter, but his face doesn't change. "That's what the devil does, right? Contracts signed in blood. All the movies show blood contracts."

"What was the contract for?"

"A soul removal and—" I swallow "—body handover." I whisper. "The devil collects souls, right?" Sam stiffens in his seat. The tension pouring from him as his gaze meets mine gives me a weird feeling, like I'm sitting next to a coiled predator preparing to strike. His jaw clenches and his lips thin and tighten.

I find myself inching closer to the driver's side window. Then he blinks, and the sensation disappears.

"Go on."

"I have photos." I stretch into the back seat for my handbag and drag it onto my lap to grab my phone.

He examines each image carefully. I should have taken the pictures again; they are too blurry to read. His pinched expression is the only hint I have that he gives any weight to my accusation. "He is not the devil."

Is he taking the piss? Sam's voice sounds serious, not jovial, almost like he knows for sure that Bacitriet is not the devil. But how could Sam know that? He hasn't met Bacitriet, hasn't spoken to him. He only has my word for what the man is like.

Sam slips from the car, and ducks back down to stare at me. "We should not keep your grandmothers waiting."

I climb from the car with much less grace and slam the door shut. It's chilly outside and I zip my coat closed. "You think I'm crazy, don't you?"

"I do not."

I stop and frown at his back as he walks away. *Really? Why not?*

The afterschool shoppers part before Sam and close in behind him so fast I'm hit twice, bouncing off people as I race after him. He has a presence that screams, "I'm important." It isn't the first time I've thought it. It could be the tailored suit or the strut, or those intense eyes staring forward as if on a mission. Who goes grocery shopping looking that good? I peer down at my own disheveled outfit. Yeah, I fit in here more than he does. I'm hard-pressed to keep up with his long strides. As we walk along the chocolate aisle, my stomach rumbles, reminding me I still haven't had lunch. I hope Sam can't hear it.

Above my head, Kylie Minogue sings about the devil you know, and I snicker, bopping along with the jaunty tune. Sam strides forward like he owns the place or has somewhere to be.

A woman in tight gym clothes, pushing a fully laden trolley with a bubbly infant in the front seat, eyes Sam up and down and smiles. He completely ignores her. I shrug at her sour expression as I race to catch up.

I hear my grandmothers long before I catch sight of them. Rose invites people to come closer while Berry berates the ones who don't.

Rounding the corner I find them spruiking crackers on silver trays. Rose has a glittery tutu wrapped around the middle of her pink pantsuit and . . . *OH MY GOD*. Sprouting from her head are devil horns. Berry is wearing her good slacks and a white business shirt, but like Rose, she also has a tutu around her waist—this one emerald green—and a headband with a halo attached. On top of each cracker is a pale meat mixture. Rose stands next to a buzzing microwave as something spins on the turntable inside and flashes.

"Mig, dear, you made it!" Rose waves as she catches sight of me.

I raise my hand and dance my fingers. Berry spins toward me holding her tray aloft. "What are you offering?" I ask, plucking one overloaded cracker from the tray.

"It's a new mushroom and chicken mix," Berry announces loudly. "The brand is Angel Foods and it's simply divine. The quickest, simplest mix for hors d'oeuvres you'll find any-where."

I could have swung my handbag around and not hit anyone. "Quiet day?"

"Oh, it's quiet now, but earlier it was hopping," Rose says, bouncing a little on her orthopedics. "Hello, Sam, dear. We're happy you made it."

Sam nods. I pop the sample into my mouth and a second later clap my hand over my lips to stifle an explosive cough. Tears spring to my eyes. Berry pounds my back with her fist and Sam holds a plastic cup of water he's retrieved from . .

. somewhere. I gulp at it gratefully, clearing my throat. "It's a little salty." I cough again and drain the cup.

Rose nods. "Yes, it was a little bland, so I fixed it."

"Oh, so did I." Berry pokes Rose's forearm, jiggling the tray. I leap forward to catch it, but Berry recovers with a sense of balance that would make a circus performer jealous. The two ladies squabble until a sharp squeal snaps my horrified gaze to the microwave. Light is sparking and there are popping sounds coming from inside.

"Uh, Rose? What's in the microwave?"

"The mix takes too long to heat outside of the can." She shakes Berry's hand away as the squealing from the microwave grows impossibly higher.

"Get down!" I dive on top of Berry and knock her to the ground. She rolls and cushions my fall. The laden tray crashes to the ground beside my head, shattering my eardrums, and the world rocks as the microwave door explodes off its hinges.

I lift my head, ears ringing, to survey the damage. "Is anyone hurt?" I can barely hear my own voice. The smell of burned chicken and something metallic fills the air, along with a lot of smoke. A loud pop announces the store sprinklers kicking on. The fire alarm screeches angrily. Rose is on top of Sam. Splotches of gray and brown matter cover every surface, slowly soaking in with the dousing from above. I help Berry to her feet. "Are you okay?"

"Of course."

I lean over to help Rose, but she waves me away. "I'm quite comfortable." I glare at her until she rolls nimbly to her feet and shakes the food off her clothing. I swear, they must have been dancers in another life. I had been sure her hip had been bothering her. Doesn't seem to be holding her back now.

Sam grunts. I kneel beside him. "Thank you for catching my grandma," I shout over the alarm.

"I think she caught me," he replies. Somehow, he has managed to remain food-free, but I'm not so lucky. Moving my head sends damp mushroom gunk flying everywhere. Water continues to pour down over us. Sam touches my hand. My gaze darts to his face as his eyes trail over my body. Heat follows where his eyes land. "Are you well?"

Gosh he speaks so formally! I love it. "I'm fine. I should be used to it with these two menaces." I grumble. Of all the times for him to be looking me over, it's now, when I'm a freaking mess. I take a moment to check him out too. His hair and clothes are damp but that's the only damage. *So unfair.*

"What a hero," Rose yells at Sam. "This one's a keeper, Mig. Very agile. Strong muscles." I snort. Sam's hand is still touching mine. I can almost imagine my clothes drying instantly given the inferno inside of me.

Behind us, a commotion is brewing. A balding man with a Santa-like visage huffs and puffs toward us. His damp shirt is plastered to his giant belly, soaked by the deluge from above, and is completely transparent.

"We're all fine," Berry says loudly, catching sight of the man's approach.

"Good. You're fired." Water drips off his nose.

"Well, Berry. It was rather short this time."

"Rose, this chicken and mushroom mix is awful stuff."

"I wouldn't buy it," Rose agrees decisively.

The manager's face is as red as a tomato. "Out! Out, all of you!"

Sam is glaring at the man. As the manager realizes, he falls silent, paling at the expression on Sam's face. He waves at us to go away. Sam turns and bestows a soft smile on me, gesturing for me to precede him. I force my problematic grandmothers to go ahead of us.

"Step carefully," I remind them. Given how wet the floor is, I don't want them to slip. Rose takes Berry's arm and they walk together down the aisle like queens and not the mischievous demons I know they truly are. I sense Sam close behind me. I can't believe how this afternoon has turned out.

We take off, not wanting to suffer further abuse—or possibly get sued. "Do you need a lift home?" I ask my grandmothers. "Sam needs the front seat with his height, but we can squeeze you both in the back."

Rose nods, sending a splatter of gray mush and water across the aisle. "We took the bus, so yes, that will be lovely."

I hold up my hands. "I'll drop Sam home first."

"See your grandmothers home, Margaret. I have some business to tend to," he says, gesturing toward the parking lot. A black car idles at the curb, driver at the ready. "Ladies." He takes my hand and for a brief second, I think he's going to kiss my fingers. He squeezes gently and nods at me.

"I'm so sorry about today," I tell him.

"Do not concern yourself. I can handle a little water. You were very brave."

I'm sure my eyes are wide—maybe my mouth is open. He is so hot and I must look like a fish pulled from a river, gasping for air. I wish I was more—well, more. "They're my grandmothers," I say instead.

He smiles at me, nods to Berry and Rose and stalks away. I sigh and watch him stride toward the sleek, purring vehicle. Even with a damp shirt and his hair dripping, he cuts a fine figure. Maybe he *is* a spy or an international man of mystery.

Rose hands me her halo. "That man is yummy."

"Rose!" Fortunately, she kept her voice low. My neck is warming up at last, but we're all damp from the sprinklers and need to dry out. I don't want my grandmothers getting ill.

Berry chuckles and removes her devil horns. "Was he softer than he looks, Rose?"

Rose smirks. "Oh, not at all, dear."

Chapter 19

"You and Sam seem to be getting along," Rose comments once seatbelts are on and I've backed the car out of the parking space.

"Did you deliberately wait until I was driving to say that?" It wouldn't surprise me. She's a stealth conversation starter, like my dad. I narrow my eyes at her in the mirror, and she smiles sweetly. Berry, in the passenger seat, snorts.

"What do you think of him?" I ask. They might be a little batty around the edges, but they are excellent judges of character.

"I think you should keep your distance—"

"Nonsense, Berry. The boy has money and manners. He'd be a great catch—"

"Rose, he'll hurt her. You can tell he's the cold sort. Hides a lot."

"What?" I interrupt, flicking a look at Berry. "Hiding what? I thought he was quite sweet actually."

Her wrinkled hand briefly touches mine on the steering wheel. Her touch is gentle and familiar. "I don't know, but it's something important, Margaret."

"How can you tell?" I ask.

"A man gives off a certain . . . something. And that one gives it off in waves."

Why must she be so cryptic? I pull over to the curb and turn to stare at them. "What are you talking about?"

Rose stretches forward, pressing her hand against Berry's arm. "Don't."

Berry shrugs her off and twists in her seat to glare at the older—by one year and two weeks—woman. "No, Rose. She shouldn't get involved."

This is insane. "What aren't you telling me? Did he say something?"

Rose sits back and stares out the window. "Nothing, dear. Just crazy old ladies talking nonsense. Don't listen to us. We're not saying anything sensible. Might be dementia."

I roll my eyes. "Dementia, my butt. You're both more clear-headed than I am. Do you think Sam's dangerous?"

"Yes." The pronouncement comes from the seat beside me.

"Berry!" Rose snaps.

I'd found Berry sitting on Sam only a day ago. "Dangerous to *me*?" Berry doesn't answer. "I'm not moving until you tell me something."

"You wouldn't believe us, dear," Rose mumbles.

I debate saying, "Well, my boss is buying or maybe selling people's bodies or souls, so yeah try me." They remain quiet, even under my most withering glare. Feeling hot under the collar, I puff out a heavy breath and restart the car. They have almost forty years on me; I'm not going to break them without help.

After I've parked outside their little unit, I jump out and open the back door for Rose, then help Berry out of the front seat. In summer, their little garden is chock-full of colors that tickle my nose. Right now, it's as somber as my mood and the overcast sky.

Rose takes my hand. "Trust your gut, dear." They give me a wave and head inside.

I wait until they have the front door open before I drive away. I'm struggling to get Rose's voice out of my head. The look on Berry's face stays with me too. There's no way Sam is the only one keeping secrets.

It's odd. They have never been like that before, hinting at things and then clamming up. My mind dwells on their words, twisting them around and examining my memories of their expressions.

When I get home, all is quiet. There's no sign of Sam. With a sigh, I plod to my front door. The air is crisp, and the temperature is dropping fast. The skin on my fingertips is tingling, so I scrub them against my trousers and search for my house key. Creaking wood snaps my head toward my front door.

. . . the hell? The door is open. Just a touch, but it's definitely not shut like I'd left it this morning. *Bloody cat.* I storm inside and my heart stutters to a stop before my feet do.

The glass of the back door glistens like diamonds where it is scattered all over the floorboards. My sofa is upside down, the cushions torn open and the stuffing spread across the carpet like a macabre murder. My DVDs and books have been dumped on the floor, and the tray I put my loose change in by the front door is empty. My heart lurches out of its frozen state and pounds a frenzied drum solo. Dizziness hits hard, leaving me clutching the door frame in shock. No cat did this.

I yank my cricket bat out of the cupboard. I'd only played one season as a kid, some dumb attempt at trying to find a sport, but now the thing is proving its worth.

Tilting my head, I make out the sounds of the ticking kitchen wall clock and the fridge motor. My breathing disguises any other sound. With a shaking hand, I rummage through my handbag for my cell phone and back up a step. *Eleven paces to the car. Lock yourself in and call the cops.* My feet take me forward instead. Elisa's voice pops into my head, ordering me to predial the phone if I'm going to be such a brave idiot. Despite the trembling, I manage to type triple zero and hold my finger over the green call button as I creep through the house. The light in the living area illuminates most rooms. I can't hear anyone, but that doesn't mean someone isn't here, waiting for me.

Get out. Call for help. It's Dad's voice. But Dad isn't here.

At each doorway, I slam my hand against the light switch, ready to run at the slightest movement. I find only empty rooms. The perpetrators are long gone. It doesn't stop me from searching the entire house, including the closets and hall cupboards. I find nothing and return to the kitchen to stare blankly at the shattered back door. The force required to break the toughened glass must have been immense. I delete the emergency number and call Dad.

He answers on the fourth ring.

"I can't stay here." My voice cracks.

"What happened?"

"I got broken into."

There's a pause and then Dad blurts, "Are you okay? Were you home?"

"No, I just got home." *Thank God.*

He becomes all business. "Come over and stay with your mother. I'll look at the door. Did you call the police?"

"Not yet. I . . . I wanted to hear your voice." I feel like a little girl again. I don't know what to do and I just want him to tell me I'll be okay.

"Was anything taken?"

Not that I'd noticed. With Dad on the phone, I walk through each room again. "The spare coins on the counter are gone."

"TV? Laptop?"

"Still here," I say, spying my laptop on the armchair. "They trashed the sofa though."

"No great loss."

I glance at the pile of books and DVDs. "All my movies are still here."

"Why would they take those?"

I huff. "Dad, they're important to me."

"I know, hon, sorry. Get your stuff into a bag. Call the police. I'll be over in twenty."

"Thanks." I hang up and stare at the phone, lost for what to do first. The back of my neck grows suddenly chilled.

"What has happened here?"

I scream and spin, dropping the phone to brandish the bat in both hands. Sam stands in the doorway, his expression the wildest I've ever seen it, all wide eyes and flared nostrils, and there's a light sheen to his skin. I've never seen him look so frantic. I imagine I look just as panicked. He strides toward me but stops just shy of touching me, though his hands clench like he wants to take my hands or maybe take me into his arms. I flash back to his hand squeezing mine at the grocery store. "Are you well?" he asks.

"I wasn't here when it happened." My hands are still trembling, so I put down the bat. "I've been robbed."

"Yes, I see." His gaze locks onto the giant hole that is now my back door. "Police?" His voice is harsh. I'm sure it's just the residual panic, but I jerk back feeling suddenly attacked.

"I haven't called them yet."

"Do it now."

"My dad is coming over."

"Still, call the police and report it. There might be fingerprints. Don't touch anything." He sounds annoyed with me or perhaps just with the situation. I wonder where he went earlier. Had he just got home? How did he know I was over here panicking?

"I turned the lights on," I admit. My voice is shaky. "I opened the cupboards too."

He nods. "Too late for fingerprints, then. Call them anyway."

I dial triple zero. "Please don't leave?" I whisper. I'm glad he's here. There's just something about Sam that makes me feel safe. He seems so confident, so capable. I feel like I'm falling apart. I wonder if he'd let me hug him. I feel so cold. My heart is still racing.

"Of course," he says, as if it is only natural that he would stay.

The phone dials in my ear as Sam prowls through the house. It's comforting to see his large frame fill each room. My call is not considered an emergency, so they bounce me through to my local station where I report the break-in. The duty officer informs me they'll send a car in the morning. "In the morning?" I repeat.

"We're understaffed, and you said there was no one in the house."

"My door is broken," I stutter, incredulous. *No one's coming?*

"Can you seal it?"

"I—"

"Is there somewhere you can stay for tonight?"

"My parents."

"Good. Lock up as best you can and don't touch anything. A car will come first thing in the morning."

Anger burns away the last of my fear. I disconnect the call and swear loudly. Sam's head pops out of my bedroom. "What?"

"They're not coming."

His lips tighten. "We need to seal the door."

"Yup." I don't move. My brain is full of noise. *Why me?* It's the question at the top of my list, followed by, *Why my new house? I don't feel safe.* Then *I can't stay here.* "Dad's coming," I say again.

His furrowed brow digs deeper. "Was anything taken?"

I shake my head. "Some coins. But they left my laptop. It's still on the chair." I point to the valuable tech. My tablet is in my work bag where I'd dropped it at the front door. My phone is in my hand and the TV hasn't been touched. "All my DVDs are here."

His lips quirk. Thinking about his tasteful décor and weapons collection, I snap, "Well, they're important to me. Why did you come over, anyway? How did you know what happened?"

"I was unaware of your distress," he says. There's a look on his face that makes me wonder if that's true. He'd seemed so upset when he came in the front door. "I wanted to give you something." He moves to stand in front of me and holds out a small black bag, the kind you get jewelry in. My breath catches. *What the hell?* This day has been one extreme emotion after another, and I'm getting whiplash.

"Sam, I . . ." With trembling fingers, I open the bag. A silver chain falls into my palm. Two charms dangle from it—a silver cross and angel wings, each is the size of my thumbnail. "Sam—"

"Promise me you will not remove it." He takes the bracelet and secures it to my wrist. His fingers scald my chilled skin. Pointing to the cross, he presses the top and a tiny blade pops out at the bottom.

"Whoa!"

"Promise me you will not remove it," he repeats. An alarm is sounding inside my head. The bracelet is pretty, but a knife?

I think back to the weapons in the locked case in his house. Maybe he thinks having weapons around is perfectly normal? "I can't accept this."

"Consider it a gift. For your protection."

It's gorgeous and unbelievably generous of him, but it's also super weird. "The wings are pretty."

"They'll keep you safe," he says.

"Really?"

"You must believe."

I haven't received many gifts from men, besides my Dad or my brother Andy. I can recall a pack of bubblegum from Billy Smith, a boy I went out with in second grade for two weeks until he kicked a soccer ball into my stomach. And there was a ring from Steve Fuller, which was actually a ring pull from a can of soda. So, in a way, who am I to judge this gift from Sam? "I don't know how to tell you this, but I'm not a religious person. I don't believe in God."

"Then believe in me. Please. Do not take it off." His stare holds me still.

I do believe in him. I nod. "Okay. Thank you." It's a thoughtful gift, even if there's no way a tiny cross with a hidden blade will be able to protect me. "Whoever broke in is clearly long gone. I'm fine and didn't lose anything of value. Thanks for your concern."

"The whiteboard is gone." His voice has gone tight again, emotion fighting to escape his frozen frame.

"What?" I spin around, my body on high alert. There is nothing but bare space where I'd leaned it against the wall. I race from room to room, but there's no sign of it. "Why would he take a whiteboard?"

He hums. "Perhaps it was what they were after?"

That certainly makes my skin crawl, especially after the day I've had. "How do you know *he* was a *they*?"

"I know."

I believe him. "I don't get—" The thrum of a car engine outside catches my attention. I run to the door, hoping the police have come after all, but it's just Dad. Has it been twenty minutes already?

I launch myself at him before he reaches the doorway. He holds on tight, and the scent of his familiar aftershave fills me with comfort. I cling to him, blinking back tears. Eventually, he pulls away. "How are you doing?"

I burst into tears. "I was robbed."

His big strong hand rests on my shoulder. "I know, honey."

"The police said I can't touch anything until they get here tomorrow."

"Let's look at the door then," Dad says and jerks, pulling me slightly behind him. I follow his gaze to Sam. Dad's right hand twitches into a fist. My mouth drops open. I've never seen my dad get violent before, and even the suggestion of it is shocking.

I grab his arm. "Dad, this is Sam, my neighbor. He's a friend. Sam, this is my dad."

"Not the most pleasant of circumstances, but it is, however, a pleasure to meet you," Sam says extending his hand. The rest of his body is held still, shoulders down, free hand relaxed, arm dangling at his side like he's trying not to look menacing.

Dad's squint overflows with suspicion, and his fist doesn't relax. If anything, his shoulders tense further.

I want to hug him again. "Come look at the door, Dad. I can't believe what they did."

Though his stare remains locked on Sam, Dad lets me tug him through the house. I'm so glad he's here. His hair is more gray now than black, but he's still a fit man due to his regular gym visits. He says that just because he's retired it doesn't mean he should get flabby. But standing next to Sam, I'm glaringly aware of how small he is.

Dad whistles when he sees the remains of the back door. "I brought some wood. Sam, help me get it? Mig, did you pack a bag with everything you need?"

I shake my head and race off to my bedroom. Once safely behind a closed door, I let my tears fall. This is all so shit. After a moment, I scrub my eyes and straighten my shoulders. *Come on, Mig.* You're safe and the house is okay. Things can be replaced. I grab pajamas, a change of clothes and my toiletries, and shove them into my spare backpack. I wrap my butterfly scarf around my neck and tighten it until I can barely breathe. The banging of a hammer brings me back out to the kitchen. Sam holds a large plank of wood against the missing door while Dad nails it to the wall. "This will hold for tonight."

"The police said they'll come in the morning." I know I've said it a few times, but I can't seem to get my mind out of the loop it's stuck in.

"Are you okay to drive?" Dad asks.

No. I nod. "I'll follow you home."

"Your house will be safe for the night. I will keep an eye on it," Sam says softly. He touches my arm and again I have to fight the urge to hug him. I see Dad's eyes narrow at Sam.

"Thank you," I whisper.

Sam's face holds none of the emotion from earlier, but there's a look in his eyes that makes me thankful I'm not one of the burglars.

What truly concerns me, and what I fear Sam suspects too, is what the break-in means. Whoever took the whiteboard must know what it is and why the information on it has been collated.

Whoever caused the disappearance of the other PAs has moved on to their next target.

Me.

Chapter 20

Mom's standing at the door waiting for me, a concerned squint in her eyes and her hands on her hips. "Are you okay?" Her hair still holds some of the same brown as mine. It falls over my head as she embraces me like I've been away for a year. God, I'm such a failure. First scare and I run straight back to my parents' house like a child, wanting them to fix everything. I press my nose to her neck and breathe in the scent of her skin cream.

"I've run you a hot bath. Dinner can be reheated, I saved you a plate."

"Thanks, Mom."

I'm shivering when I sink into the bathwater. The tears I'd fought since losing it at my house explode out of me, and I stifle my sobs into a small hand towel. The silver wings of Sam's bracelet catch in the towel's fabric but I don't take it off. Instead, I untangle it gently and wipe away my tears.

I don't know how long I stay in the bath for, but the water is cool when I finally emerge. Standing inside the doorway of my old bedroom, my gaze darts over the changes my parents have made. Mom has turned it into a guest room and study. Family photos dot the walls, giving it some color. When we'd deconstructed my bed and dragged the sofa bed in a few weeks ago, I'd had the first real sense of change. It wasn't *my* room anymore. The cream walls still need to be repainted. Mom's picked the new color and Dad's even bought the cans.

I scuff my feet over the worn carpet and my chest tightens.

Later, lying on the pull-out sofa bed, I stare up at the dark ceiling of my old room and replay everything that has happened, fiddling with the chain around my wrist. Being at home feels normal. Safe. A world away from missing women and burglars. I'm encased in an overwhelming feeling of protection, like I can stay in here forever and be perfectly okay.

I rub my watering eyes. Mom and Dad haven't said anything, but they don't need to. I'm letting them down. I'd thought I was growing up, becoming a new me—confident and daring. Now? Zip, zilch, nada. 'Fraidy cat little girl wants her Mom and Dad solve her problems and tell her everything is going to be fine.

The streetlight outside creeps between the blinds, giving the room an eerie glow. I can just make out the faint sounds of music from a house further down the street, the heavy bass creating a *thump thump thump* in my head.

They took the whiteboard. I roll over and grab my phone. Elisa answers on the first ring. My voice wobbles as I tell her about the break-in.

"Oh my gosh! Are you okay? Are you at home? I'll come get you."

"I'm okay, Elisa. I'm at Mom and Dad's." I taste salt and wipe a hand over my wet cheeks.

"I'm so sorry, Mig. That's awful."

"They took the whiteboard."

I count to five before Elisa screeches, "What?!"

"Whoever broke in stole the whiteboard with our list on it."

"Shizzlesticks." Her cute mom swear brings a smile to my lips. "Did you mention the whiteboard to anyone?"

"No! No, I . . . well . . ."

"What? Who knew about the whiteboard?"

There's one person, but . . . "Sam."

"You don't think—"

"I don't. I mean, well, *he* was the one who told me it was missing. I didn't even notice."

She inhales sharply. "Sam was there?"

I roll onto my other side and stare at the photo frame beside the bed. Andy is seven years old in that picture. I'm nine. Both of us are grinning like loons at the camera, wearing birthday hats with giant sevens on them. It's a lifetime ago now, another universe. I can't imagine feeling that happy again.

"Mig? Your neighbor was there?"

"Yeah. Well, not at first. Sam must have got home after. Elisa, why would someone take my whiteboard? How did they even know about it?"

"Maybe they didn't know. A crime of convenience?" she muses.

"They took a plate filled with coins but left my laptop. Nothing else is missing."

Elisa hmms. My stomach aches, not from hunger—I hadn't been able to eat the dinner Mom put aside for me—but from worry. I nibble at my bottom lip. "Do you think it was my boss?"

"Mig, come on. How would Bacitriet know about the whiteboard?"

Oh hell, so much has happened since the last time we spoke. I tell Elisa about Bacitriet calling me out.

"So, he might have done it? Or organized someone to steal it . . . oh but that's nuts, right? Why would a burglar take it? It's just a whiteboard."

My sinuses ache from my crying spells. I drag my handbag onto my lap and, by touch alone, locate and swallow a migraine tablet. The pain in my eyes predict a doozy.

"That's super creepy about Bacitriet. What did Sam say?"

"Didn't you say I shouldn't trust my neighbor?"

"Well, yeah, but he can't be all bad. He cooked, Mig."

"So he's okay because he cooks?"

"Exactly."

I laugh. "I'm hoping you can vibe the house for me. I trust your feelings, and I need to know if I'm in danger." Sam said I was in danger, and I'm sure he didn't mean from regular burglars. I pinch my new bracelet charms between my fingers.

For protection, he'd said.

"I'll come around tomorrow. Text me before the police arrive. It will be better if I can look around before it's been contaminated by too many people."

"You can't touch anything."

"I won't."

I tap my fingers on the mattress. "Something else weird has happened. I don't know what to make of it, and after everything else, I think I might be going crazy."

"You know I'd never think you're crazy."

"I think my work computer is . . . uh . . ." Possession is a magical thing, so maybe Elisa will have a better understanding of it. "Haunted. I think my computer is possessed by Annie, the girl who went missing. I know it sounds crazy. It is crazy, right? It's just that I got a strange message on my work laptop. From . . . well, they said they were Annie, but . . . that's nuts. Someone's got to be pranking me. An awful person. That's what this is. Right?"

Elisa is silent. I hold my breath, waiting for her to tell me I'm reading too much into it, but Elisa would never do that. "I believe you."

"Without even hearing my evidence?"

She laughs down the phone. "I'm not the sort to doubt anyone, Mig. Ordinarily, you're a very rational person and you wouldn't say something like that without having information to back you up." She's silent for a moment. "You know I got my nonna's diaries when her estate passed to us. I've been reading through them, and . . . well, some of the things she says . . . if she wasn't my nonna, I'd think it was fiction. My nonna wasn't senile, and she wasn't barmy. You know that."

I do. I'd loved Elisa's nonna as deeply as I love Rose and Berry. "What did she write about?"

"You first. I'm dying to hear why you think your computer is possessed."

I press my head into the pillows as my body relaxes. "Annie, or someone pretending to be her, sent an instant message to my work laptop. I spoke to IT and apparently only someone with an internal account and attached to the same network can send a message like that." My left nostril clears. I roll over again and stare at the window. The thumping music has grown fainter. Hopefully that means the party is breaking up and I'll be able to sleep.

My mind laughs at my naïveté.

"What did Annie say?"

"*If* it was her." I'm still wary of sounding bonkers.

"What did she say?"

"To be careful. And she asked for my help."

"Okay, so, putting my mom hat on for a minute, why would someone in your office pretend to be a missing girl? Do they think you're in danger? Are they trying to warn you? Warning someone doesn't sound like a prank."

"That's all they said."

"You need to find out who sent the message."

I huff. "How?"

"I don't know. Mig, if this person knows something, you need to find out who they are and what they know. If it is possession, you realize what that means, don't you? Annie would have to be dead for her soul to be able to communicate with you."

I rub at the skin of my nose. *Dead.* "I want you to tell me not to look into this."

"Liar."

I gasp. "What?"

"You say you want me to tell you to run, but I'm not going to. Mig, you want answers. I can hear it in your voice."

She's right. After Detective Bryce's request, the contract and now the break-in at my house, no matter how scared I am, I want to know the truth. What happened to those assistants? I have to know, and I'm possibly the only one in the position to find out. "So, I stay and ignore the danger to myself and investigate a possessed laptop? How do I even go about doing that?"

"You need to contact her."

"Who?"

"Annie, or the person who's masquerading as her."

"I ask again: how?"

"I'm going to suggest something. Don't dismiss it out of hand. It might be a way to prove whether this person is Annie or not."

"Tell me."

"We hold a séance."

I should laugh but the idea doesn't feel as preposterous as it should. "You think she *is* dead? Is that based on a feeling? How does a dead person type on a computer?"

"Mig, if it *is* her contacting you through the laptop, maybe you've already had validation? My guides are telling me it's her. Besides, it might not be a ghostly presence in your computer. She might just be hiding somewhere."

"With her *work* computer?"

"You never know."

"I'm not sure that makes sense."

"Ghosts, possession or someone taking a work computer?" she says. "None of this makes sense. We need to believe it makes sense and go from there. She asked for your help."

I jump up to flip on the light and grab my notebook, quickly writing down the pros and cons of doing the séance with Elisa.

In the pros column, I write: *can't hurt, save a life, learn something*, and in the cons; *doesn't work, learn nothing.* The last thing I write down is *doing something* opposite *do nothing.* I underline it twice. I suppose I could stay in the job a few more days and snoop around at work. Hold onto my laptop and do the séance. What would it hurt? If nothing happens, then great. I have no idea what I'll do if something *does* happen.

I want answers. "Let's do it."

"I'll be over first thing tomorrow."

"Thanks, Elisa."

I end the call and close my eyes. I'm positive sleep will be impossible after my adrenalin-filled night, but exhaustion and my migraine medication quickly suck me under.

*

I bolt upright, breathing hard. Dull morning light creeps in through the blinds and the shadowed wall is at once familiar and unfamiliar. Home. My old home. Mom and Dad's place. It's Saturday and I have nowhere to be.

No, wait. The police are coming. I have to get moving. Sickness churns inside my belly as a fleeting thought I'd had before falling asleep comes back to me: I should tell Detective Bryce about the break-in. I call her number. It goes straight to voicemail. Before I can change my mind, I leave a brief message and my contact number.

I climb out of bed and drag myself into the shower. Twenty minutes later, I haul myself into my car. Mom and Dad come out to see me off. "I'll pick up a coffee on the way," I tell Mom. I stare out over their perfectly tended front yard.

"Will Sam be there?"

Ah. Dad told mom about my neighbor. "I don't know."

Dad's lips twist sideways, as if he's debating whether or not to speak. I wait him out. Finally, he opens his mouth. "So. Sam. What do you know about him?"

"Dad, come on. He's my neighbor. He's nice and he helped me out yesterday."

"And you trust him?"

At the same time, Mom asks, "Is he *nice* nice or just nice?"

"Mom!" I rub a hand over my face. "I need to go. I'll tell you about Sam later, okay? I'll call after the police leave. I promise."

My parents eye each other. Mom nudges Dad's shoulder.

"Do you want us to come with you?" Dad asks.

Yes. "Nah, Elisa's coming over."

Chocolate brown eyes stare into my soul. When his lips tilt into a half smile, his whole face lights up. The tears from last night threaten to return. "I'll call you when the police are finished and let you know what they say." I wave and wind the car window up. The early morning sun blinds me and I turn my head, blinking rapidly at the faded gray-painted driveway. Spots dance across my view. I peer at the brown brick four-bedroom house that was once my home. Andy moved out a few years ago and now that I've moved out too, Mom and Dad are empty nesters. I wonder if they feel lonely.

I wave again as I drive away. The view of them in my rear-view mirror makes me smile. Dad is holding Mom's hand, and her head is on his shoulder. When they are out of sight, my breathing hitches, and I clench the steering wheel, pressing my lips together tightly and blinking back the tears bubbling under the surface. Sitting idle at the traffic lights a street away from my home, they finally break free. Fear ricochets around inside my head, compounding my headache. My lovely new home is tainted now. I don't feel safe there anymore. I dread the cost of the glass door repair. And I'll probably have to purchase a security system. Another expense. I wonder if my insurance will cover it.

Thoughts from last night crystalize: the whiteboard was the only thing in my house connected to my workplace. It must be the reason for the break-in. I glance at my mirrors, and wonder if anyone is following me. I don't see anything suspicious. Still, my blood pressure rises every time a car turns the same way I do.

My new bracelet clinks against the steering wheel. Sam was so protective last night, more than just concern for a neighbor. *He likes you.* My lips curl into a smile. I like him too.

Elisa's shiny red compact is parked on the street in front of my house. She's standing outside, leaning against the front panel, waiting for me. Foggy morning air smokes from her mouth. There's no sign of the police yet. I park in the driveway and jump out to give her a big hug, fingering the silky green scarf wrapped around her neck. She has the right idea. I blow on my icy fingers.

"I've got something for you," she says, popping her head into her car. When she straightens, she's holding two takeaway coffees.

"I love you," I breathe, taking the closest hot cup with shaking fingers.

"Me or the coffee?"

"Both."

In the distance, a kookaburra laughs. I try not to take it personally.

"The kids were upset they couldn't come see you. I promised them you'll visit next weekend. I hope that's okay?"

"Of course. We'll go to the chocolate place in Yarra Glen."

"You are the best worst aunt." She laughs and tugs open the rear door. "Sit. Talk."

I slurp loudly at the cup of life and let my fingers soak in the warmth. Steam swirls around my nose. I wave for her to shut the car door. "Let's go into the house before the cops arrive. I want to see if you can sense anything about the burglars." I hold the coffee in front of my mouth but don't drink anymore. I'm suddenly nauseated thinking about someone creeping around inside the house. *My* house. We move slowly toward the front door.

Examining Elisa's pale face, I realize I'm being a really awful friend. "Are you okay to do this? I shouldn't have asked you to put yourself through—"

"I'm okay, Mig." Elisa breathes deeply and steels herself. Guilt scratches at my insides. I owe her more than a drink, more than dinner.

I unlock the front door and try not to touch the wooden frame or the glass. Elisa goes inside. I stand back, waiting for her to do her thing. In less than ten minutes, she returns, the little lines between her eyes etched deep into her skin. We sit in the back seat of her car and I force myself to not say anything, though I'm busting to know what she experienced.

She shakes out her hands. A chill dances down my spine. "Well?" I spit, unable to hold back any longer.

"I . . . I'm not sure. It's such a strange feeling. I get a couple of different impressions. A mingling of energy. You and your shock are clear, so I can dismiss that, but . . ."

"But what?"

"Not hatred or anger, more . . . hunger. And amusement. All in the main rooms—the living room and the kitchen. Particularly around the wall where we left the whiteboard. An old presence filled with anticipation and some annoyance. There's a younger one too, fast-paced and anxious. I—"

The screech of a car's brakes draws me out of our conversation. I look up and find a police car parked in the driveway.

Elisa blinks slowly. She doesn't seem to have noticed the arrival. "Elisa, I have to—"

"Go. I'll stay here."

"Is there more?" I'm anxious to know everything.

"Give me your notebook."

Yanking a yellow spiral-bound notebook from my handbag along with a pen, I push them into her hands and climb out to greet the officers.

The man—boy—is younger than me. Lanky, with a buzz cut and crooked teeth. His partner—obviously his superior—is an older lady with kind eyes and an open smile. "Are you the homeowner who reported the break-in?" she asks, stopping in front of me. The name badge on her chest informs me this is Officer Barbara Trent.

"Yes. I'm Margaret Solder. I called last night."

"Tell me what you found, but first, is there anyone currently inside the house?" She glances at Elisa's car.

"No, but I did unlock the door."

She nods to her partner, and he heads inside.

There's a physical reaction that horror movies attempt to inspire by using music and long, wide camera shots to focus on shadows and walls or trees to create a sense of isolation and fear in an audience. I'm bombarded with these same sensations and wonder if this is a little of what Elisa gets. Colors are too bright, too crisp, and there is a feeling of wrongness I can't shake. Around me is an ordinary suburban street full of the normal sounds of cars, the buzz of a lawnmower and the beeping of a delivery truck. I can smell roses and cut grass. But my skin is cold and my breathing is too heavy.

"Who has been in the house since the break-in?" Officer Trent asks.

"Myself, my dad, Elisa and my neighbor."

"Is this your neighbor?" the officer's gaze falls on Elisa's car again.

"No, that's my friend Elisa. My neighbor, Sam, lives there." I point to his house. "I'm sure you can speak to him if he's home."

"Sam what?" she asks, making a note on her tablet.

"I don't know actually. He moved in last week. And I only moved into this place a month ago."

She nods. "Okay. So, tell me about last night."

I repeat the story I'd given over the phone, explaining that Dad and Sam had nailed a board over the broken door so I could lock up.

"Is there anything missing?"

"Only a handful of coins that were in a plate near the front door. All of my electronics were out in the open. Nothing was moved." I can't mention the whiteboard, right? I mean, it's weird. Maybe I should mention it? I don't. She'll ask what's on it and I'll sound loony to be so worried about a whiteboard. But would it help them find who did it? I should tell Detective Bryce.

My eye twitches. I pray Officer Trent won't notice and I fight to hold eye contact.

"Hmm. Sounds like a prank, or perhaps a gang initiation. We see it a bit in the area. Tagging, dares and the like. Let's do a check for prints. Please remain here. I'll collect you shortly."

"No problem."

Officer Trent heads inside without looking back. I poke my head into Elisa's car. She is scribbling furiously in the notebook. Not wanting to interrupt, I stay outside.

Gang initiation? It's possible, I suppose, if the officer has seen it before. I have seen a lot of tagged street signs and graffiti, especially on the train line.

I sip my coffee and play with my phone. It rings in my hand. Unknown number. "Hello?"

"Ms. Solder. This is Detective Bryce. I got your message. What's happened?"

I explain about the break-in and how the police are currently examining my house.

"Was anything taken?"

I pause. Well, she had said to tell her anything strange. "I didn't tell the police this, but . . ."

"What?"

"My kitchen whiteboard is missing."

"You believe that is significant?"

I pace outside the car. "I'd written down all of the things I knew about the missing girls on it."

Bryce is silent for a long moment. I stare at the house and then over at Sam's place. "Okay. Tell me the officer's name so I can get the report?"

I do, and I also tell her which station is local to me. "Do you think it's Bacitriet?"

"Why would you say that?"

"Bacitriet knows I spoke to you. He's onto you."

I can hear the smile in her voice. "Great. He's getting nervous. This is really good, Margaret. You're doing great work."

My nostrils flare. I imagine dragon smoke puffing out of my nose. "They smashed the back door!"

"Okay, calm down. I understand how it looks and I'm sorry for your inconvenience. Let me talk to my superiors. I'll call you back." She hangs up on me.

I stare at my cell and snort. *So very helpful.*

Dad texts, and I message back that the police are here. Peering inside the car to check on Elisa, I find her frozen, eyes wide and vacant. "El?"

She blinks and turns her head. Her eyes are bloodshot and a little wet. "Hey."

"Elisa?"

"I need another coffee. And about a hundred years of sleep," she says with a wan smile. "Doing a mental scan is exhausting." Her skin holds a waxy sheen that doesn't look natural.

I'm worried. I've never seen her like this before. What's wrong with my friend? "We'll go get—" The front door opens and Officer Trent beckons me inside. "You go." I tell her. "I'll meet you after? Or do you want to wait for me?"

Elisa nods and closes her eyes. She leans back against the seat.

I trudge to the front door, my thoughts on Elisa and on the sensations she's reported. *Who exactly has been in my house?*

Chapter 21

I find Officer Trent beside her crouched partner in the laundry room. "It looks like this is the first attempted entry point," he says.

My eyes widen. "I didn't even think to check the laundry door."

He holds open the door and dusts the handle. "There are scratch marks and a chunk of wood has been jimmied out. Looks like they were unable to get it open."

"We found your high-tech locking device." Officer Trent points to the folded-up piece of cardboard now on the floor.

Oh. That's the cardboard I'd jammed between the door and the frame on that windy night last week. "Ah, yeah. The door rattles."

"It's been windy, hasn't it? I had problems too," the male officer says offering a small smile. I can't see his name badge, so in my head, he becomes Officer Nice Guy.

"When they couldn't get in, they chose a more direct method." Officer Trent points to the boarded-up back door.

"No prints," the younger officer says.

Shattered glass still lies all over the kitchen floor. I gesture to the hallway. "The empty plate is on the dresser. They stole my spare coins."

"How much do you estimate was in there?" Officer Trent moves briskly to the entrance hall, leaving her partner in the laundry.

"No more than twenty dollars," I say, trailing her. I keep my hands clasped behind my back to make sure I don't inadvertently touch something.

"And nothing else was taken?"

I shake my head.

"Alright. We'll file the report and send you a copy. I have to warn you, it's unlikely we'll find the culprits. I surmise it's a group of adolescents on a prank or dare. It's doubtful they even know how to fence your belongings, therefore only took the easy cash. There's no CCTV out this way. We'll chat with your neighbors and determine if anyone saw anything or has home a security camera pointed this way. You might want to invest in a more modern security system. I'm afraid that without anything else to go on, that's all I can offer."

Peering over my shoulder at the living room, I imagine masked men touching all my things and my nausea increases. "I understand."

"If you discover anything else is missing, give me a call." She hands me a small pamphlet pack about increasing home security with a business card stapled to the front. *Super helpful.*

They each shake my hand. Officer Nice Guy—whose name badge says Officer Anthony Letty—clasps my hand with a sweaty palm and I suppress a cringe. After he turns away, I examine my fingers and find streaks of light gray on my skin. Fingerprint dust.

I'm scrubbing my hands in the bathroom when Elisa appears in a waft of rose perfume. "They're done?"

"Yeah."

"And?"

"Since nothing was taken, they have nothing to search for. No fingerprints at all and there are no street cameras."

"Bugger."

"Yeah. You still want coffee?" My skin is crawling, and not just from the fingerprint dust. Strangers have invaded my home. Maybe a gang of them. *Oh God, my underwear drawer!* "Hang on, I need to check . . ." I race to my bedroom and throw open my walk-in robe and dresser drawers. Everything appears untouched. My passport is still tucked beneath my unused sleeping bag. *Phew!* I slump onto my bed.

"Scary, huh?" Elisa sits down beside me. The mattress tilts us together and my shoulder presses against hers.

"I'm so creeped out. I don't know what else they touched. Why me, El? Why my house? I don't feel safe here anymore. They shattered the damned door!" I'm breathing hard. My skin is damp from the sweat that covers my skin. I force my breathing to steady.

"Yeah, hon. I know."

"I'm sorry. It's just, ugh, let's get out of here."

Elisa shoots me a soft smile. "I know just where to go."

*

"It's pretty."

I knew the Yarra River traveled through this area, but I hadn't had the chance to explore it yet. The park is full of mist and towering manna gums. I love that even in the heart of winter, these trees keep their leaves.

"Yeah, I come here whenever I need a place to think," Elisa says. "My guides like it, and I figured you could do with the sense of peace today." She points to the kiosk at the edge of the carpark. "And that."

I sigh happily. "Yay! Coffee."

The kiosk looks pretty new, still shiny in parts, though the birds have had their way with the tin roof and the baseboards.

"Welcome to Angels Park." The guy behind the counter beams at us. Nearly bald, his skin holds a tinge of sunburn.

"Why is it called Angels Park?" I ask.

"It's the angels, mate. Park is full of them. Sculpture competition a few years back. Park was renamed then. Go for a walk and check 'em out. Some are pretty spectacular."

"No wonder it feels peaceful here," I say. Weak sunlight presses upon my skin, melting the chill that has gripped me since this morning.

Elisa nods. "I come here when I need help making a difficult decision, or to cleanse my energy. I'll show you the best angels later. Each one is unique, and so like their namesakes."

"You believe in angels?"

"Of course. Don't you?"

I think of my computer and of the missing assistants. "I don't think angels exist."

Elisa sighs and shakes her head. "They guide us. Help us."

"Like your guides? Are they angels?"

"Oh no, my guides are different. They are energies that communicate with me. I think they're my ancestors' spirits."

"The witches?"

"Maybe."

Taking our coffee, we wander along the river's edge. She points out two of the angels. She's right. They are beautiful. The first one is made of burnished metal. The angel has glorious wings and stares up into the sky. The second one is marble and looks like it's in pain. Tear drops rest on its cheeks. Both angels evoke sadness. I can see more statues in the distance but I don't need more feelings of despair or yearning for unrealized hope. I point to a paint-chipped bench and we sit down. I lean forward, holding my hot cup in both hands to warm them. "What else did you pick up from my house?"

She tugs my notebook from her bag and consults her scribbles.

"It's what I didn't find, I guess," she says finally.

"What do you mean?"

"I should have felt your energy all over the place, and traces of mine, your parents, grandmas, and your neighbor, but they've been . . . scoured, right out of the air. All I got was your panic and your dad's reasoned energy."

Scoured? "Like . . . bleach on a kitchen floor?"

"Exactly. Someone knew what they were doing, on a psychic level. I think you might be right about your computer being possessed, Mig. Someone powerful, magically powerful, is involved in this, and it goes way deeper than we think," Elisa said seriously. "So, let's do it. A séance. Let's try to contact your computer."

I tilt my head and chew on a thumbnail, tugging on and biting off a hangnail. The sound of birds calling to each other draws my gaze to the river's edge. Brightly colored feathers of rosellas and the white of cockatoos flutter as they swoop and perch in nearby branches. Ducks sail serenely along the glassy river surface. I can make out their tiny splashes and quacking. "Just the two of us?"

"It would be better with more. Do you think Annie's parents would come?" Elisa asks.

I pinch the bridge of my nose. No way am I contacting Annie's parents to ask them to attend a séance to talk to their probably dead daughter who I suspect currently possesses my computer. I'd sound completely loony. *Perhaps I am.* "We don't know if it will work. We don't even know what happened to Annie, and I don't want to believe she's dead. Let's not ask them until we know for sure." The mysterious ghostly messenger might not even show up.

"What about your neighbor?"

"Sam?" I cringe. "I don't know, Elisa." Sam already knows I suspect my boss is up to something, but is he into spiritual stuff? He *had* given me the angel wings as a protection charm. And he'd seemed absolutely certain Bacitriet is not the devil. Maybe he's a believer? "I'll ask."

We linger at the river's edge longer than intended. I don't want to move and it seems Elisa doesn't either. We return home late in the afternoon. Thank goodness it's the weekend. I wave goodbye to my friend and watch until I can no longer see her brake lights before I turn and stare at my front door. I swallow—or try to. My mouth is as dry as the outback. *Don't go inside.*

No. It's time to reclaim what's mine.

I grit my teeth and stomp toward the door. No monster is going to make me afraid of my own house. I'm organized and determined, and I will not be cowed.

I make it into the kitchen before my resolve shrivels up like a dried apricot. I force my gaze from the wooden board that is now my back door. My home doesn't feel like it's mine anymore. Someone or someones have invaded my space. Elisa would say I need to replace my energy to make the house feel like my home again. Like she did when I first moved in. I replicate that and put my favorite music on through my streaming service and squeeze the up arrows until it's loud enough to wake the dead. I light Elisa's lavender emotive candles and dig under the sink for my pink rubber gloves and antiseptic spray. *Clean the bad juju away.*

Feeling manic, I scrub everything down, and the eucalyptus-scented spray soon coats every surface. I reinstall my cardboard security system, poking it between the laundry door and the frame—it worked well enough before—and vow to buy a chain lock. With clear steps laid out in my head, I find my Zen and restore the sofa, throwing a blanket over the torn cushions for now. *I've got money, I can buy new ones, nicer ones later. Though if I leave my job, I won't have the cash. Ugh, maybe I should wait before going on a spending spree.*

I call my insurer and log a claim. I then email the door company to request a quote for a security screen for both the front and back doors, and ask them to call as soon as they open on Monday. I also email the glaziers about a quote for a replacement sliding door. The insurer will probably want them. A few more minutes online gets me an easy-to-install security kit to be delivered the following week—I only hope their marketing is honest about the easy-to-install part.

With everything on my list ticked off, I find myself at a loss. My skin itches and not just from the cleaning products. I keep looking at the board over the shattered back door. I can't settle. *Keep busy. Don't think about it.* Thinking will lead me back to the fact that someone broke into my house when I should have been here. Bacitriet sent me home early. I would have been here if Sam hadn't reminded me to go see Rose and Berry.

That gives me reason to pause, and I decide to nip out to the hardware store before it closes and get those extra locks right now. When I reach my car, I glance over at Sam's place, wondering if the police have spoken to him yet. His presence was so comforting last night. I'd been lost in my panic but he'd known just what to do. Ever since he moved in, I've caused him nothing but trouble. He's such a good neighbor. Such a good man.

I'm walking toward his house to check in when an unfamiliar black SUV pulls into his driveway. I freeze. If Sam is expecting visitors, I don't want to interrupt. Spinning on a heel, I head back to my car.

"Hello there."

The unfamiliar male voice but similar sexy accent to Sam turns me around, and my gaze widens as a giant emerges from the car. A very, very attractive giant, with deep-set eyes, full lips and a wide smile. His designer suit looks totally out of place in the suburbs. He should have been in a law court, or walking down the street in the financial district. The skin on the back of my neck grows icy cold, sending a shiver down my spine. *Why does that keeps happening?*

"Hi," I manage. Just my luck Sam has such a good-looking friend. "I was just heading out . . ." I point to my car.

"You're Sam's neighbor?" The smile falls off his lips. Some-one must be standing behind me, because it can't be me that changed his mood so dramatically.

"Yes." What has Sam been saying about me? I turn away, and I know without looking that he's followed me. Still freaked out about the break-in, I spin around. No way is he coming any closer. "Hey!"

He stops mid-stride, eyebrows drawn together, lips pursed. I've had enough of feeling like a cork bobbing on the ocean during a thunderstorm. Ever since Jack fired me, I've been out of control, responding to events, and not controlling them. I'm done with it, and this guy, whoever he is, becomes the first target of the new me. "Look, mate, stop following me. Who are you and what do you want?"

"You are more intense than Sam implied."

"Fuck off." I stand my ground and school my face into a glare fit for an Amazon or a Valkyrie. *Or the Hulk.*

His expression slips. "My apologies. I should not have in-timidated you."

"You didn't," I snap. *Stay angry. Don't back down.*

The crease between his eyes disappears and his teeth re-appear. Damn, he's hot. "I am looking for Sam. Have you seen him?" This guy's domineering frame is more hitman than work partner. Regardless, I'm not telling him anything.

"Nope." I squint, staring at his face. They kinda look alike. Definitely family. A brother? He steps back, and I breathe freely. "And who are you?"

"I am his brother. Mike."

That explains the otherworldly accent. I wonder where in Europe they come from. "He didn't mention a brother." I exam-ine him suspiciously.

"There are a few of us. We are not close."

"Then why are you looking for him?"

"Family business."

In other words, none of *my* business. "I haven't seen him, but I'll tell him you stopped by."

Mike lifts the sunglasses from the top of his head and puts them on his face. "I'll wait."

"Knock yourself out. Watch out for the cat." I don't hang around for a reply. A few steps take me to the porch and I shut the door, hesitating a full minute before racing to the window. I don't want to go out now. What if he's not Sam's brother but is instead casing my house, waiting for me to leave so he can go through my stuff? Ugh. I hate feeling this paranoid. Mike is standing beside his car, staring at Sam's house. I creep back to the front door and double-check I've locked it.

I was quite forceful with him! And I didn't care what he thought of me. It's a rather empowering feeling.

Deciding the new me would be a decision-maker, I grab my phone and text Elisa.

Let's do the séance tonight.

*

"What's with the guy sitting in the car in Sam's driveway?" Elisa asks as soon as I open the door. Dusk is falling rapidly but Elisa is like a sunbeam lighting my porch and my soul. I give her a big hug, struggling to let go until she makes me. She's wearing her fabulous, flowy ankle-length butterfly-print dress, and her long silk scarf makes her look like a fairy princess. Even her hair kind of floats around her shoulders.

"Love the dress. He's still there?" I peer over her shoulder. "That's kinda creepy. He's been there since late afternoon."

"Who is he?"

"Sam's brother. At least, he says he is." I shut the door, making sure to lock it again securely.

"Really?"

"He mentioned the family aren't close."

"Creeper?"

"I don't know. It's not any of our business. Come on, we have things to do."

"Right. So, I have to tell you, while I was coming up your drive tonight, I got chills. That only happens when my guides are restless. I take it Sam's not joining us?" She dumps her string bag on my blanket-covered sofa. It flops over and out pours her purse, a box of kids' sticking plasters, wipes and a pink ballet shoe, Isabel-sized.

"Oh that's where it is. I've been looking all day for that!"

I snort. "Bet you picked it up for safekeeping after Isabel's class," I tell her. She shakes her head and folds herself onto the floor, cross-legged and relaxed.

"So . . . Sam?"

"I haven't seen him since last night."

Elisa puts her hands on her knees. "We really should have more people here for this to work."

"It can't be just us?"

"My nonna's book is pretty clear that the more people, the better. I guess we can try and see."

"What do you need? I haven't done anything like this before."

"I don't even know if it *will* work." She shrugs. "Contacting a computer spirit? I mean, I believe in a lot of things, but are we crazy?"

"Are you losing faith? You can do this, Elisa. I believe in you," I tell her. It's funny. She's feeling dejected just as I'm feeling pumped. Usually it's the other way around. It discombobulates me to be the super positive one for a change. She pulls an old book out of her bag. "Is that your grandma's diary?" The gorgeous brown leather has gold stamping on the spine.

"Yep."

"A real witch book?"

She sighs. "Mig, really? Come on, grab your laptop and log in."

"My laptop?"

"That's how the spirit . . . hacker . . . person contacted you before. We need that connection. Besides, if we're right, it will be easy to connect with her . . . um, it?"

Okay, that seems reasonable—sort of.

A voice inside my head, the one that sounds suspiciously like my dad, tells me to save any messages via screen captures as evidence, and hey, if it *is* someone pranking me, they aren't likely to be online after-hours, are they? So, if nothing happens, it indicates actual human interaction, right?

I log on and position the screen so we can both see it. Elisa lights several aromatherapy candles and places them on the coffee table in front of us. Hints of lavender, rose and patchouli drift by in gentle waves. It doesn't do a thing to lessen the tension that has knotted my muscles into concrete. Even my jaw hurts.

Elisa consults her book and then closes it, releasing a slow breath. "What happened last time?"

I point to the screen. "I didn't do anything. An instant message just popped up." We stare at the screen. Nothing happens. "Now what?"

She shrugs. "I don't know."

"What would you do in a real séance?" I prompt.

She holds out her hands. I clasp her fingers, opening my mouth to apologize for my cold skin but she shakes her head and closes her eyes. *Should I close mine as well?* I don't. She hums and rocks a little. I glance at the computer screen. Still no blinking icons.

"We are here to call upon Annie Seramoph. We ask that Annie Seramoph contact us." I can't tear my gaze from the computer screen. Elisa's voice becomes a whisper. "Annie, we are here."

Nothing happens.

"Annie?" I call. *What on earth am I doing?* I press my chin into my chest and sigh heavily.

Thump thump.

I startle upright, dropping Elisa's hands as if they're on fire. "Shit."

Elisa's eyes spring open and fix on the front door.

Thump thump thump.

Chapter 22

Elisa's wide stare darts from the door to me, her hand pressed tightly to her chest. "Are you expecting someone?"

"No." My heart thuds as loud as each bang.

"Do burglars knock?" Her voice is a hissing whisper.

"I don't think so." They probably don't psychically scrub a place of energy either. Would a supernatural being knock? My breathing is as rapid as my heartbeat. I don't want to open the door. "Maybe it's that guy? Sam's brother?"

"Why would he come here?" she asks.

"I don't know."

I had dropped to the floor beside Elisa at the first sound, both of us making our bodies small, as if to hide from whoever was out there. I straighten. What happened to the dynamic, angry Mig I'd sworn to be? I stand up and blow out a long breath. "Who is it?"

"Yoohoo, Margaret! I can see shadows moving, let us in."

A wave of relief loosens every muscle. "It's Grandma Rose." I jump to my feet and race to tug the door open. "What are you doing here?"

"Hello, dear. Glad you're home." Berry pushes me aside to make room for Rose. They are both dressed in their casual clothes, what they call their bingo outfits: slacks, boat shoes and cardigans, bubblegum pink for Berry, baby blue for Rose. I smell sugar and butter, and peer around, hunting for the container of baked goods they must be holding.

"You seem upset, Margaret." Berry spies Elisa on the floor beside the coffee table. "Oh hello, Elisa, dear. Lovely to see you."

"Elisa, how are you, love?" Rose asks.

My friend wiggles her fingers. "Hi, you two. Been up to trouble?"

Before they can respond, I speak. "It's late. Why are you here?"

The old ladies shoot each other a look before Rose answers. "Would you believe we have another job?"

I groan, taking their handbags from them to put on the table. "What is it this time?"

Another long look crosses between them. "Catering," Berry says.

"Catering?" I echo incredulously. "How . . . you know what, I'm not even going to ask. What are you doing here then?"

"We dropped a birthday cake off up the road and thought we'd pop in and say hello."

I stretch my neck to peer through the window. It's pitch black outside. "How did you get here?"

"We had an Uber drop us at the delivery address and we walked down."

I pinch the skin on the bridge of my nose. *Uber?* Dear Lord, who taught them how to do that? I'll have to drop them home and come back to start the séance.

Rose points at Elisa's candles. "What's going on here? What are you two up to?" They stride to the table, eyeballing the open computer.

No way am I going to tell them.

"We're holding a séance," Elisa blurts.

"Oh, I'm up for that." Rose plonks herself down in my favorite armchair and kicks off her shoes. "I love a good séance. What about you, Berry?" Her left sock has a tiny hole beneath her little toe.

"Lot of claptrap." Berry huffs. "But if you're staying, then I guess I am too."

"Lovely. I want to talk to Ronald."

"Nonsense," I tell them. "I'll take you home and—"

"Don't you move. I'm staying." Rose smiles broadly. Her upper false teeth slip, and she sucks them back in. Berry tsks softly but sits down on the sofa closest to Rose's armchair.

"More people will be better, Mig," Elisa says softly. I glare at her, but it doesn't carry a lot of weight.

"What's the computer for?" Rose asks. From out of nowhere, she pulls her crochet needle and some wool, and starts a small round center.

Elisa leans in, her face flushed, teeth shining. She focuses on Rose. "We're going to use the laptop to communicate with a restless spirit."

"Never done that before. Sounds a bit fancy. How does it work?"

"We're not sure it *will* work," I tell Rose.

"Who are you trying to speak to?" Berry asks. Her nose crinkles and she pushes her glasses up with her index finger.

"Anyone who will come through," I say before Elisa can answer. "Bit of a laugh, you know?" I don't want to scare them. The little knitbag buttoned to Berry's belt contains her heart medication.

"Well, I hope it's Ronald. It's been ages since we've spoken." Rose's hand drifts to her neck chain where she keeps grandpa's ring.

"Then you tell him to go spend time with Eddie," Berry says, pressing a hand to Rose's arm. Rose smiles, though her lips wobble and her watery eyes grow a little redder.

I don't remember much about Grandpa Ronald other than that time we visited him in the hospital. I'd been terrified of the taciturn man in the bed. We'd just read *The Billy Goat's Gruff* in school and he'd reminded me of the old father goat—

and a little bit of the troll. It's a shame we aren't trying to talk to him. I can see Elisa is ready to offer, but Berry shakes her head, as if she knows what we're thinking. I bite my lips and plonk down on the other end of the sofa.

"Shall we begin?" Elisa says instead. "Mig, can you fetch us some water?"

I do as asked and join Berry on the sofa, tugging the coffee table closer to our legs. Elisa sits cross-legged on the coffee table beside my laptop. Lit by the flickering candles, Berry's gaze looks intense, her eyes are hooded and mysterious. Elisa's face takes on an orange hue as reflected flames dance in her pupils. She sucks in a deep breath and breathes out slowly. When she breathes in again, she closes her eyes. "Take my hands and don't let go. No matter what happens."

"Yes, yes, we've done it before," Berry says, taking my right hand.

"When?" I ask.

Elisa's eyes pop open to glare at me. "Shh."

I mouth "sorry" and clasp her hand. Rose drops her crochet to her lap and takes Elisa's fingers, leaving Elisa stretched a little awkwardly across the coffee table.

"To the entity trying to communicate with Margaret Solder. We are here. We are listening. Please speak to us," Elisa says. Her voice is low, melodic and I find myself focusing on her more intently as a result. I have to tear my gaze away to watch the computer screen.

Nothing happens.

"We should have a wooden board. How can the spirit communicate with us this way?" Rose hisses, her voice shatters the silence fallen over us.

"Be quiet, Rose." Berry's harsh tone snaps my head to the side. She leans forward, her glasses shining the candlelight back at me. Given how negative she'd been earlier, I'm surprised to see her stare glued on my computer, her lips parted waiting for an answer.

Elisa remains silent, rocking in place and breathing deeply. My eyes flick from my friend to the computer and back. As the silence stretches, my nausea increases. How embarrassing. Someone at work *had* been pranking me. I'm a fool to have fallen for such a mean-spirited trick.

"Come on, love. Talk to us," Rose implores.

I'm an idiot. "Let's pack this up." My stomach twists with guilt. Rose thought she might get to talk to Grandpa. We'll have to do this again someday so she can.

"Did Elisa say this ghost has contacted you before, Margaret?"

I can't hold Berry's quizzical stare. "At work. I thought . . . well, I don't know what I thought." I search the shadows in the dark room for an answer. *This is silly. Take your grandmas home, Mig.*

"Is it supposed to be doing that?" Rose asks.

I stare at the computer. The instant messenger icon is flashing.

Oh my God.

Elisa's eyes are still closed.

"What's going on?" Rose lifts her and Berry's hands and points with their joined fist.

"Uh, a message. I guess."

"Don't let go," Elisa warns.

"Watch your scarf near the candle flame," I say pulling her further over the coffee table to reach the keyboard with our clasped hands. Using my little finger, I click the message open.

"What's it say? I can't read that, it's too small," Berry grumbles.

My pounding heart makes my fingers shake. Elisa squeezes my hand as I read the message aloud. *Help me.*

Elisa grunts to stop my grandmothers from speaking again and in the ensuing silence asks, "Who is speaking?"

Dots appear as the person—ghost—writes again. *Annie Seramoph.*

My skin quivers. Considering the company, I bite back my curse.

Elisa speaks again. "Do you have a message for Margaret Solder?"

Help me.

How would the prankster know we're even doing this?

Elisa's voice is soft but steady. "Are you alone?"

Yes.

This time I can't help myself. "Shit."

"Margaret," Rose scolds.

"Quiet, please." Elisa's face is a serene mask, but her eyes open to spear a warning in Rose's direction. "Annie, how can Margaret help you?"

The flashing goes on for what seems like ages, though it's probably only two minutes or so. I lean forward as more text appears. *Cold. Water. Dark. Help. Wings. I'm so tired. Help me.*

A hundred questions flood through me, but not one of them finds my mouth. Berry's hand is hot in my grip, like a live flame. I crave the warmth because my body aches with cold.

"Annie, who took you?" Elisa asks.

Death. My voice breaks reading the single word. Berry's fingers tighten. "Ouch, Berry!" I pull my hand away, examining the half-moons dug into my skin.

"No!" Elisa shouts but the damage is done. I glance at the screen. The message window is gone.

I swear again.

"Margaret!" Rose gestures for me to help her stand. "I'm not sure what's going on, but that certainly didn't sound like Ronald."

"Lot of codswallop." Berry stands, knocking her knees against the coffee table. The center candle extinguishes.

Rose ignores her, looking at me. "Who is Annie Seramoph?"

"That missing girl from the news, remember, Rose? Her parents were on last week." Berry takes Rose's arm as she wobbles on her feet.

"Oh, my dratted hip." Rose's sharp stare falls on my face. "I remember now. Oh yes, how sad. But why was she asking you for help?"

Berry glares in my direction. My skin prickles like her anger is physical. "It's just silly nonsense. Margaret, you and Elisa need to stop these childish games. It demeans the memory of that poor girl. Leave it alone."

"But Grandma Berry, she keeps contacting Mig," Elisa tries, quickly wilting under my grandmother's stare.

"Take us home, Margaret." Berry's voice is an order.

"I think it would have been nice to speak to Ronald. Here, take my arm, Margaret," Rose says. Her skin is dry and loose, and I want to bury myself in her embrace, breathing in the smell of cake until the end of time.

"Elisa?"

She shakes her head. "I'm just going to write down what happened before I forget it. I'll lock up before I head home. Call me tomorrow, yeah?"

"Sure." I usher my grandmothers out of the house and lock the door. When I turn around, I catch sight of the SUV still parked in Sam's driveway. A shadow moves inside the dark cabin. I get chills.

The brother is still waiting.

Chapter 23

That night, I'm plagued by nightmares and I barely get any sleep. Sunday morning arrives sooner than I'd like and I drag myself through my usual morning routine bleary-eyed. Sitting at my kitchen bench, I stare mindlessly into my coffee. In my hand, I hold the page of notes Elisa wrote after the séance. I have no idea how she did it but, she'd managed to remember each message.

I run the words around inside my mouth. "Cold. Water. Dark. Help. Wings." I can't begin to guess what they mean. The message window had closed when Annie stopped communicating. When I reopened the app all the messages were gone. I'd left the computer on overnight, but no other messages appeared. If it is real—a big if—then Annie is dead. With such nebulous clues, how the heck am I supposed to help her?

Wings? What does that mean? I finger the bracelet Sam gifted me and examine the wing charm. Does Annie mean me? On the bench next to my coffee mug is Detective Bryce's business card. She hasn't called back and that worries me.

Sunlight pours in through my kitchen window, lending a sense of unreality to my dark thoughts. I tap the card. What will I tell her if I do call? That I suspect one of the missing women has contacted me via my computer during a séance?

I tuck the business card into my bag and grab my laptop. I'm heading to the hardware store for those locks. I'm sure I'll find a coffee shop to stop at along the way where I can ponder what to do.

I tug open the front door and freeze at the sight of Mike—the creepy brother—still parked in Sam's driveway. What if he lied and he isn't Sam's brother at all? He could be parked out there watching *me* for all I know.

Enough of this! Leaving my bags in the car, I storm over and bang on the driver's side window. The guy startles upright. His shirt is creased and dark bags under his eyes take the handsome out of his features.

"What?" he grumps as he winds down the window. Though it's crisp outside, the bright morning sun is already sending a glare right into his window.

"You can't stay here, mate. Sam's not home. Come back another time if you have to speak to him."

Mike clears his throat. "You are quite protective, aren't you?"

The way he says it suggests a small, yappy dog, and I bristle. "Go home or I'll call the cops."

"I'm his brother." His gaze falls to my wrist, and to the bracelet Sam gave me. He jerks as if he's been electrocuted. "Where did you get that?"

I don't answer. Maybe it's a family heirloom Sam shouldn't have given away? I drop my hand from the car door and away from Mike's assessing stare.

He huffs out a breath and appears to accept the inevitable, which is good because I'm trembling inside and I don't think I can hide it much longer. "Maybe call him next time," I suggest as the engine purrs to life. Damn, it's a nice car. Bet it costs more than my house. I don't move as he reverses down the driveway. Rolling to a stop, he beckons at me through the open driver's window. I stand my ground.

He audibly sighs and raises his voice. "Tell Sam something is coming. He needs to be careful." Mike plants his foot and the car roars as it takes off down the street.

"What's coming?" I shout after him. The car disappears around the corner. "What the actual fuck?" No one is around to hear me swear, but I still check over my shoulder, expecting Rose to pop up out of the bushes and start lecturing me.

I slide into my car and clutch the steering wheel tight to steady my hands. My skin crawls with what feels like a thousand little bugs. Who threatens their brother like that? I'm intensely glad my family get along. For the most part.

The confrontation with Mike continues to play on my mind as I drive. Braking at a red light, I tap the steering wheel and glance in each direction. Bright sunlight makes my vision strobe. The Sunday radio announcer is interviewing some sports star and cracks a crude joke, so I flip the radio off and let silence descend. With nothing to distract me, Mike's golden eyes and judgmental eyebrows appear in my mind. *Is he really Sam's brother?* If he is, then he's an asshole, and if not, what the hell was he doing in my front yard? And that strange warning. "Tell Sam something's coming." What was that all about? I tap my fingers. Wings, water. Ugh, my mind is jumping everywhere. I need coffee.

I brake at another intersection, one close to Angels Park. Caffeine is a drumbeat in my head, and my stomach yowls in agreement. *Sod it.* The park is closer than the hardware store. I can think there too.

I flip the blinker back the other way and take advantage of the light traffic to swing onto River Park Drive and pull into the Angels Park carpark. The coffee kiosk is open. I park and jump out, eager to place my order. While I wait, I check my social media accounts and wander down to the river. Andy has posted a picture of his dog, and Rose is sharing cat videos. *Who taught Rose how to use the internet?* I hear my name and grab my coffee, sighing in bliss at the first gulp that slides down my throat.

"Like your coffee, huh, mate?" The barista grins.

"Lucky for you," I say and laugh. "You'll probably see a lot more of me. This is great."

I find the lack of customers an abomination and say so. He laughs wildly, throwing his head back with explosive force. "Have you seen the statues?"

"Two. I didn't go far yesterday," I admit.

"You should take a gander now, while it's quiet. We have some fabulous local artists."

I nod and head toward the river, slurping my coffee loudly. I force my mind off Mike and Sam and back to last night. Rose seemed to have fun, though I really should stop thinking of a séance as fun. Berry was totally put out. When Rose disappeared to the bathroom, Berry had lectured me on believing in nonsense and for getting Rose's hopes up.

Cold. Water. Dark. Help. Wings.

The messages had been horrid, but they didn't make any sense.

Help. Wings. Tired.

What has wings? Birds. But what could birds have to do with Annie? I stare out at the slow, muddy water, inhale deeply and revel in the bitter scent of coffee. I suppose it would be dark if she was inside the computer. Still, I don't know how that is even possible. How can a person end up inside a computer?

I turn left and head up the walkway opposite to where Elisa and I sat yesterday, listening to the gravel path crunch underneath my shoes. Water? There's no water in my computer. Or at the office. Though the office does overlook the Yarra River. Could that be what Annie meant?

A duck squawks loudly and flaps its wings, snapping my gaze to the river's edge. Wings. I glance back over my shoulder at the entrance sign. Angels Park.

Wings. Angels have wings, don't they?

I muse on Annie's messages as I walk. My heeled boots are not the greatest footwear for this kind of trek. A splash turns my head back to that attention-seeking duck.

"What?" I ask. "I don't have food for you."

Five minutes into my hike, I nearly twist my ankle and berate myself for my chosen footwear before my gaze falls on something shiny. *Oh wow.* My feet carry me straight to the base of a statue. Blank eyes stare down at the water's edge. They belong to a bronzed female dressed in flaming robes. Magnificent wings stretch out behind her.

Following the angel's pointed finger, I discover the wings of another statue in the distance. Beyond that, further along the riverbank, another. Lost in wonder, I make my way down the path, marveling at each extraordinary art piece. Some are no bigger than my hand while others tower over my head. All are wrought in exquisite detail. Bronze, metal, marble and everything in between. *Extraordinary.* But the blank-eyed stares make my skin crawl. Everything else about the statues is so life-like, why not the eyes? The plain orbs seem to stare inward, searching for life, or maybe a soul. It is the only feature on every statue where there is no detail.

I stop in front of one glorious angel, holding aloft a great sword on fire. The exquisite carving and fiery effect have me stepping back to view it in full. The flames seem almost real. My fingers creep out to touch the sword—cold as steel. Remarkable, given the sun blaring down.

I glance into the angel's face and stumble back at the familiarity. It takes me a moment to figure it out. "Hilarious," I mumble. The angel is the spitting image of Sam's brother. Mike's rude and acerbic behavior springs to mind—he's certainly no angel. I'll have to mention it to Sam. He'll probably find it amusing.

Wings. An alarm bell starts clanging inside my brain.

Water. And wings.

The river and the angels. It can't be a coincidence.

All peaceful tranquility now lost, I speed up. The duck continues to follow me downstream and quacks, demanding food. I scuff my shoes in the mud and watch it swim in widening circles. This duck seems quite the prankster and keeps splashing water in my direction.

Ripples roll away from the riverbed to my right. I step closer. A white face becomes visible as the water calms, staring back at me from the shallows. How amazing. The artist managed to get the statue so life-like, and how clever to put it in the river. One pale hand reaches up, as if calling for forgiveness and . . .

"Shit!"

That's no statue.

Sightless blue eyes stare right through me. The outstretched hand begs for help. Help I can no longer give. I recognize her face and let out a scream.

It is Annie Seramoph.

Chapter 24

I stare at the body until what I'm looking at really sinks in and it sends me stumbling back in horror.

Dead body.

I drop my coffee and clamp a hand over my mouth, puffing shallow breaths into my fingers.

Dead body.

Somehow, I end up at the foot of the angel statue that looks like Sam's brother. I don't remember sitting down, but I'm bent over with my head between my knees. My fingers are freezing where I press them against my lips.

Where did my coffee go?

I glance at the river. Cold, dead eyes stare back at me in accusation. Shivers wrack my body.

Where did my coffee go?

I peer up. The statue's wings arch over me, putting me in perpetual shadow. *What do I do now?* I fumble in my handbag for Detective Bryce's phone number and listen to the rings, counting them as I wait. *Cold. Water. Dark. Help. Wings.* The words repeat in my mind.

"Detective Bryce." Her crisp voice shatters the band constricting my throat.

"De–detective. This is Margaret Solder. I–I . . ."

Her words shoot back like bullets. "What is it, Ms. Solder?"

"I found, I found . . ." Why can't I speak? My chest hurts, and the cold air is caught in my throat. "I found Annie Seramoph. I found her . . . her . . . body." There is silence on the other end of the phone. "Detective?"

"Where are you? Don't leave and don't touch anything."

"Angels Park. Just out of Warrandyte, I don't know . . . a twenty-minute walk from the carpark off River Park Drive."

"Are you safe?"

I stand and turn in a wide circle, searching for signs of life. Only the blank stare of the angel and the dead eyes of the half-sunken body greet me. "No one is here. I'm near the angel statue, I mean the, uh, the fifth one. The one holding the sword."

"The Archangel Michael?"

"I don't know what it's called. Maybe?"

"Ms. Solder?"

"Can you come? Quickly?"

"Officers are ten minutes away. Ms. Solder, do not hang up."

My hand tightens around the phone case. "Okay." Dizziness swarms my senses and I bend over again. "Whoa."

"I want you to take several deep breaths. Can you do that?" says the voice in my ear.

No. "Sure."

"Close your eyes and focus on your breathing. In and out."

I do as she tells me and my head starts to clear. My stomach is swirling angrily and my mouth has dried up. The cold, spacey feeling in my neck and temples begins to fade as I count my breath in and out, over and over. *One, two, three, four . . .* The nausea abates and after a while I can make out other sounds. Bird calls, that loud duck quacking, water lapping at the riverbank and, at long last, voices. I remain seated as dozens of police uniforms appear in front of me.

"Miss, your name?" Their weapons are drawn and point directly at me. I thrust my hands up, the phone with them. "Your name?"

"Margaret Solder. I called you. I mean, I called Detective Bryce." I wave the hand holding the cell phone. The closest officer snatches it from me and speaks into it.

A different voice calls from the riverbank. "Found the body."

Rapid movement greets that statement. Another officer shouts for me to raise my hands, but they're already up so I don't move. Bedlam and chaos make a wall of noise around me that I can't penetrate. I have no idea how long I sit there for but the police won't let me leave. My eyes fill with tears. I blink them away only for more to appear.

A few weeks ago, everything had been so perfect, so normal. Now I'm being held at gun point and suspected of murder. Eventually, the one voice I want to hear calls my name. "Ms. Solder?"

"Detective Bryce." Relief fills me at her appearance. She is dressed in another crisp suit, her blond hair pulled tightly away from her face. She waves away my cordon of officers and gestures for me to stand. *Is she going to arrest me?* I avoid looking at the commotion by the river's edge and follow her back to the path. "I should, um . . . I don't know." My voice is as subdued as I feel. Tremors wrack my body. "I'm a bit cold."

"Can you tell me what you were doing here?"

I rub my arms. *Shit.* I can't tell her the sudden hunch I had was triggered by a séance held because I'm sure my work computer is haunted.

"I–I stopped for coffee. The coffee guy said I should look at the angels. I wandered down this way a bit lost in thought and when I looked down, I saw . . ."

Her expression gives no clue to her true feelings. "I'll need you to come in and give a statement. We'll need your prints—"

"What? Why?"

"To rule you out as a suspect." She points at the ground. "I take it that's your takeaway cup?"

It's got a plastic police evidence number near it.

I gulp. "Yes."

Her fierce scowl renews the ache in my chest. "You seem to be making quite a habit of being in the wrong place, Ms. Solder."

I sigh. This week has surely been the week from hell.

*

I'm totally dead on my feet when I stumble through my front door that night. My head weighs a ton and I just want to close my eyes. Well, I want to collapse on my bed first, then close my eyes because once I lay down, I'm not getting up again.

At least I'm home. Detective Bryce didn't hold me pending further investigation or arrest me.

I stare at the closed door. I found a dead body today. Annie Seramoph's dead body. *I should have told Detective Bryce about the séance.* I flop onto my blanket-covered sofa and massage the skin above my nose. It does little to alleviate my pounding headache. *Call Elisa.* My skin grows cold and I groan, scrubbing the back of my neck. When the thumping starts against my door, I'm not surprised.

Even my exhaustion is exhausted. I just want to be alone. Once panic sets in that I was interrogated in a police station, I'm going to fall to pieces and I don't want to do that in front of Sam. I have no energy to stand, yet I manage to find the strength to shout.

"Go away, Sam!"

"Margaret?" Worry colors his tone. How does he know? Or does he just assume I've had a bad day, given what he knows of me? I should be offended by that, but to be fair, he's not wrong.

I sigh. I didn't think my answer through. Now I can't pretend I'm not home.

Tripping on the flat floor, I fall into the door and yank it open, plastering a false expression of interest on my face. "Yes?"

"You have had another hard day?" Okay, I said it was false, not convincing.

"You don't know the half of it," I say, leaving the door open and wave him inside. I return to the blanket-covered sofa and collapse, laying my head back and closing my eyes. His concern brings my bubbling emotions to the surface. Hot tears well in my eyes. I dash them away with my hands.

"I am sorry to interrupt."

"Why are you? Sorry. That's rude." I force my head upright. "What's up?"

He hesitates. I see it in his stance and head tilt. Why is he preparing an answer? "I wanted to see if you were recovered from the other night's scare. If this job is truly so bad, you must leave it." His brows knit together, and I close my eyes to block out his worried expression.

"I'm not sure I'm going back."

"That is good."

"I found a body."

"I don't understand."

Unable to just lie there, I jump to my feet and pace back and forth in front of the sofa. "The PA from my work who went missing. I found her in Angels Park. Funny thing is— though none of this is funny, more weird I guess—and this is what I can't tell the detective, but last night, my friend Elisa and I held a . . . okay, don't judge me because I know it sounds crazy. We held a séance and it worked. I think. Anyway, the message was 'Cold. Water. Dark. Help. Wings' and when I was in the park looking at all the angel statues, I had this sudden feeling."

I can't look him in the eye. *Why are you even telling him this?* I flop back onto the sofa.

The cushion beside me depresses, tipping me toward him. I make myself straighten through sheer force of will. He doesn't touch me, and I'm thankful for that because I'll burst into tears if he tries to comfort me.

"Tell me," he urges.

I peer into his gorgeous, concerned eyes and nod. In a voice more tired than upset, I recount the day in detail and end with, "I think I answered the same question about a hundred times, but Detective Bryce didn't seem to believe me."

"Were you telling her the truth?"

It slips out before I can clamp my mouth shut. "No."

Idiot.

I launch off the sofa again. "I mean, of course I told Bryce the truth. I didn't kill her." I say it to the wall, because I can't bear to look at him. "That is the truth, but maybe I didn't tell the detective everything I know. Well, suspect." His silence gets to me in a way Detective Bryce's steady stare failed to. I look up at last, hoping not to see disbelief on his face or, heaven help him, a look that says he thinks I'm nuts.

His hot gaze traps me for a moment, and all I can think is, *Damn he's hot.* I become aware that he is staring at me as if he fully believes everything I'm saying. I almost blurt out, "I love you." Thankfully, I don't. Can you imagine? He'd probably run for the hills. Why would I even think that? It's not like I do. Do I?

Shit.

I don't love him. Of course I don't. I'm just tired. And super stressed.

"What do you suspect?" he says at last.

He has no idea of the madness going on inside my head. I can see him pondering what I've told him. I have to think back on what I was talking about before my insane epiphany. Oh, my possessed laptop. But I don't want to tell him that I think it's possessed and see that warm regard dissolve into panic or disgust. I go for distraction instead. "Your brother was looking for you last night."

"What?" In all the time I've known Sam, this is the first time I've seen his eyes widen in surprise. Angry, grumpy, annoyed, yes. Surprised, not once. And boy, I've managed to surprise him. "Which one?"

"How many do you have?"

"A few."

I squint at his answer. *Why does he never answer a question simply?* A question about his family shouldn't evoke a feeling of investigation. I suddenly realize Sam never really tells me anything important. He asks me questions all the time, digging deeper and deeper into my feelings and what I think, but I know next to nothing about him. Does he not want me to get to know him, to get close?

Oh bugger. Have I read this all wrong?

"He said his name is Mike," I say when I realize I've been silent for too long.

"Oh, him." Now, there's the face I've grown accustomed to.

"I take it he's not your favorite brother?"

"He is, actually."

Oh. "Well, he stayed all afternoon and through the night. Why didn't he just call you and leave a message?"

"He knows I won't listen to it."

"I told him to leave. I hope that's okay?" The pleased look Sam bestows on me makes me giddy. I flush, positive my face is bright red. "Well, good. Great. Uh, he did leave a message."

The glow in Sam's face fades. "Go on."

"He said, 'Something is coming.'"

"That's it?" Sam rises and stalks to the window, peering through the curtain at his house. He rubs his right shoulder.

"It was something like that. I can't remember exactly. As I said, I've had a bad day and my mind is spinach."

"I am sincerely sorry you had to deal with Mike. I was un-avoidably detained."

I shrug. Honestly, I'd almost forgotten the odd encounter.

Sam leans against the kitchen bench, still within my line of sight, and his brow furrows. I don't know if I should ask. Family relations can be hard to explain to an outsider. Part of me wants to go to bed and pretend the world doesn't exist, but strangely, Sam's presence brings a sense of calm to my scattered mind. I relax into the sofa cushions. I won't mention the angel statue that looks like his brother. I don't think he'd find it funny.

After what might have been an hour or only five minutes, he stirs. "A séance, you said?"

"Yes, séance. Which implies we were talking to a dead person, doesn't it? Which makes sense, because she's dead." I suck in a breath, suddenly light-headed. "Oh God, she's dead, and we were talking to her. How is it even possible to talk to a dead person? Séances aren't real." I press my trembling hands to my hot cheeks and glance toward the front door. Would it be rude to just get up and walk out? My bedroom at Mom and Dad's beckons. They'll fix everything and tell me all will be okay.

No. You can't run forever, and you can't put them in danger.

His silence jangles my nerves. "I don't know what to do," I whisper.

Sam shakes his head. Frustration fills his tone. "This is getting out of hand. Annie was left as a warning."

Goosebumps break out across my skin. *Getting out of hand.* That sounds . . . like he knew, like he . . .

I move to grab my cell phone. Sam's hand comes down on my wrist, stilling me. "Don't."

I jerk away. Ice water fills my veins. "What do you know about this, Sam?" I stare up at him. He'd said, "Annie." I hadn't told Sam it was Annie's body I'd found. A pit opens up in my chest, sucking my heart inside and sealing shut over the top of it. *The only way he could know . . .*

I launch off the sofa and stumble back until I stand on the opposite side of the room. "Are you involved? Did . . . did *you* kill her?"

Chapter 25

His dark eyes widen. "Of course not."

I don't believe him. He moved in here immediately after I agreed to work for Bacitriet. He asks endless questions. He never answers anything and he knew about the whiteboard. Did he break into my house to steal it? Did I let a killer into my home? I thrust out a hand. "You need to leave."

He doesn't move. "Margaret. I did nothing to that young woman."

"Then how did you know it was Annie I found?" My breath comes in short bursts. He steps forward. "Don't come any closer!"

He stops, eyeing me like I'm the one capable of violence. Maybe I am.

I edge toward the kitchen and find a knife. It's a butter knife, so not exactly a weapon. Still, I feel better with something in my hand. "You need to explain everything. Right now."

"Very well. You will need a drink. Have you eaten?"

"No, and now." I'm doing my best to stay calm, but my heart is pounding. My palms are damp. How is Sam involved in all this?

He opens his mouth, those gorgeous full lips parting, and I expect him to tell me, "No." Well, if he doesn't want me to stab him in the eye, he'll start talking.

His shoulders lower and he nods, backing up further. He doesn't try to intimidate me with his greater height or superior strength. Weirdly, I appreciate that. I relax a fraction. He sits down on the sofa. It puts him at a disadvantage and will give me precious seconds before he can come after me if I need to run. I shift my weight and edge slightly closer to the front door. I don't lower the knife.

He clasps his hands together and stares at his fingers. "I'm not sure how you are connected to all of this, and you must swear to me that you will not reveal what I am about to tell you."

I don't speak.

He nods and continues. "For you to contact Annie's spirit, she must be dead. You have suspicions that a supernatural element is connected to this case and you are correct. I am hunting the beast that killed your young woman."

My jaw drops. "What?"

"The beast," he repeats. "Or, to be fully transparent, the demon."

"Demon?" My head hurts. I grip the knife tighter. *This is not real.*

"Yes."

He waits, as if expecting scorn. I blink and roll my hand around—the one without the knife—for him to continue. "Explain."

"Demons exist," he says gently, as if he's afraid I'll spook.

"Explain better."

"This demon extracted the young woman's soul," Sam says flatly. "An excruciating experience. The loss would have killed her immediately."

Oh.

For a moment, I can't speak. That would explain how her spirit got into my computer. It was extracted . . . no, wait; it doesn't explain anything. How did she get away from the demon and into my computer? I realize Sam is waiting for me to say something. "A demon stole her soul? How do you know that?"

"I have been tasked with finding the demon and forcing it back to hell."

My mind jumps straight to Detective Bryce and the way she'd stared at me so intently when she insisted I could tell her anything. The way she'd stressed, "No matter how odd." Like she *knew*. "You're with the police?"

His lips twitch. "Not exactly. I am, however, in a unique position to undertake this mission."

My liar radar goes critical. "Why you?"

He hesitates. "It is . . . an atonement. I must hunt these monsters and return them to hell."

Atonement? "A punishment?" I ask. "What did you do?"

The words come as if dragged out of his throat. "I let them out."

This is ridiculous.

He sits still, his head bowed, and I feel in my gut that he's telling the truth, but I have so many questions. Why are the demons taking human souls? How many demons are there? How long has he been hunting them? Why did he let the demons out? Was it by accident or premeditated?

I feel as though I'm in a paranormal mystery movie. Or a supernatural horror. This can't be real. And yet . . . human monsters are real, aren't they? Murderers, child killers, worse. Is it harder to believe in monsters than it is to suspect my boss might be a serial killer? Or that Elisa can talk to spirits? Or that a soul is haunting my computer? If I believe Annie *is* communicating with me, is it so hard to believe Sam is a demon hunter?

I examine his slumped body. "Why did you let them out?"

"Please don't ask me that." His strained voice is an emotional wreck.

I want to fold myself along his side and comfort him. "If you're hunting this demon . . . is . . . is that why you're here?"

"It is my job to aton—"

"No. *Here* here. As in my neighbor. Is Bacitriet the demon? How did you know I was working for him?" Oh hell. All those questions about my work, about my boss, about me. He's hunting this demon the way Detective Bryce is investigating a murder. I'm just a witness he's interrogating. Or . . . or I'm bait for the bigger fish. He's using me as an informant.

Nausea swirls dangerously in the pit of my stomach. He never liked me at all, did he? He was just playing nice to get information. He's hunting my boss. Walls rise inside my mind and around my heart. *I'm such a fool.* I inch back further, using space as a barrier to create distance between us, telling my mind to do the same. "Are the other women alive?"

"I believe so, though they are in mortal danger."

"How do you know that?"

"This particular demon does not have a human form. In order to hide among people, it needs a . . . shell, for want of a better word. A body without a soul."

"Why does he need three?"

"I am not certain. I need more information."

"Am I in danger?"

He doesn't hesitate. "Yes."

From who, the demon serial killer or the man in front of me? I've seen his weapons collection. If he's been tasked with hunting the demons down, then he must be dangerous too. But Elisa said to trust my gut. I'm still not afraid of Sam and I believe he is telling the truth to me now. His face, his body, his presence . . . these all say I can trust him.

To stop myself from completely freaking out, I focus on the missing PAs. "Do you know where the other women are? Can you save them?"

As always, he answers my question by asking another one. "You mentioned a séance? Can you contact Annie again?"

I rub my hands together. The room is freezing. I explain about my work computer, and his face scrunches as he listens. Computer possession is clearly not something he has come across before. "I'm finding it hard to process all of this, but say for a moment that I believe you, and that ghosts and demons are real. If Annie is dead, how did she get into my computer? I've never heard of that happening—like ever. Have you heard of it? Spirits can possess people, right? And talk to mediums. I've seen that in movies. Annie seemed so real and scared. What would a ghost be afraid of? And why contact me via my computer? I mean, how is that even possible?" I break off, sucking in air. All through my questioning, I've paced the length of the living room. I stop now and stare at the silent man sitting on my sofa. "What do we do about it? Annie asked for my help. I didn't do anything and now she's dead. There are still two women missing. Am I going to be next?"

"You will not be next."

So many questions flood my mind. *How long have you been a demon hunter? Who taught you? What demons have you hunted?* I swallow hard though my mouth is bone-dry. "Did you use me to get to Bacitriet?"

His eyes widen. "What do you mean?"

"Were you only pretending to be nice to me to get close to Bacitriet? How did you know about me?"

He looks away. *Oh, oh no. None of that, mate.* I step into his field of vision and duck my head until I force his gaze onto my face. "How did you know about me? You moved in on the same day I got the job."

At last he looks at me. His mouth twists in bitterness. "I was watching the building. I didn't yet have a target, just a general location where the demon was hiding. There's a smell—it's not important. I did not use you, Margaret."

"Really?"

"Yes. Initially, I came here in the hope that you would assist me, but you . . . intrigued me, Margaret. You are brave and you have a good heart. You fight to do what is right. How could I not be drawn in by that? I find myself wanting to impress you. To make you smile."

My body flushes. I have to ask it. "Is that . . . is that something you don't want to feel?"

"It has not been something I have wanted before. I don't exactly know."

"Oh." I mean, what am I supposed to say to that? No one has ever said anything like that to me before. Should I tell him what I realized? That I care for him too? "I—"

He stops my fumbling for a response by speaking. "I need to speak with some people, find out if it is possible for technology to be possessed and what it means."

Who do you possibly go to for advice on haunted computers? I'm curious. I grab my handbag, fishing around for my keys. "I'll come with you."

"No."

I glare at him. "Excuse me?"

"My apologies. I did not mean to sound harsh. It is best that I go alone. The person I need to speak with is not comfortable around . . . uh . . . people he doesn't know. I do request that you set up another séance. For tomorrow night if possible. The same people must be in attendance and . . . what?"

I'm holding up my hand. "Uh . . . does it have to be the exact same people?"

"It would be best."

"My grandmothers were here."

He mutters something that I'm certain is, "Of course they were."

I scowl at him.

"Very well." He stands.

"Wait. You're going now?" He's leaving me alone after telling me that . . . that . . . I still don't comprehend it all. I end with the fact that I am in danger. "Should I go somewhere for tonight?" I peer around, my anxiety peaking.

"Margaret, I assure you that you will be safe here tonight."

"How do you know that?" I feel like there's death and destruction in the shadows all around me.

"Your home is under my protection. You will be perfectly safe."

What does that mean? Who is Sam really? I stare at him, wondering how he can be so certain. Has he fought off soul-sucking demons before? He's just a man. A really knowledge-able and hot man. So I say the only thing I can say: "Thank you, Sam."

His right eye twitches and his lips slightly part. I've surprised him again. *Huh, what do you know? I'm beginning to recognize his moods.* "What for?"

"For telling me the truth." I want to say more but I can't find the words. I touch his arm and squeeze, hoping he will understand. He stares at my hand, eyes wide. It's funny. It's like he's never been thanked before.

"You have given me your trust. With no proof or demand to see evidence. I could do nothing less than give it in return," he says softly. "You are an extraordinary woman, Margaret Solder."

My face flushes. Hell, my whole body warms up like I've just climbed into a hot bath. I hold his gaze. No one has ever looked at me like that before. Seen me like that. "Thank you."

"You are most welcome."

He disappears into the night, and I shut the door softly behind him. I'm exhausted but a question still burns in my mind: *why did you let them out?*

Chapter 26

In the cold light of Monday morning, last night's conversation with Sam feels like a dream, wispy and unreal. Like memories from childhood where you can recall feelings and impressions, but no exact words or deeds. Sam is hunting the demon who killed Annie Seramoph and probably kidnapped two other assistants. Four things stay with me.

Annie is dead.

Demons are real.

Demon hunters are a thing—and apparently Sam is one.

A demon has killed at least one of the assistants from my work, and I'm expected to go into the office today.

Well, I don't have to. I can stay home. Call in sick. What will they do? Fire me? That might not be a bad result, all things considered. It will get me out of Bryce's sights and those of the demon. If the break-in is connected to the missing women then the psychic scrubbing Elisa picked up on makes more sense now. And that means the demon knows where I live. How did he find my house anyway? Oh, employee files. I'm suddenly super glad Sam reminded me to visit Rose and Berry at the supermarket. If he hadn't, then I'd have been home. Would I be missing now, just like those other women? Was that the reason the demon was at my house, and the whiteboard was only a consolation prize?

It knows where I live. Will I ever be safe? If I go to Mom and Dad's, it could follow me, and I refuse to make my parents a target. Perhaps I could go overseas? I flop onto my other side and stare at the murky morning light just beginning to lighten my bedroom window. I'm under Sam's protection and weirdly I do feel safer.

Bacitriet. Is he the demon Sam is hunting? Sam hadn't said if I should go into work, and I don't have his cell number so I can't text him and ask. I wonder if he has returned from seeing his demon tech-support guy yet. Annie's face appears in my mind, her hand reaching out for me, and I shudder and open my eyes. Time to get up.

After I shower and dress, I go next door to see if Sam is back.

No one answers the door.

I knock louder and wait, stamping my feet and blowing on my fingers. The curtain in the window beside the door shifts and Mephistopheles peers up at me, mouth moving in a silent meow.

Sam is a demon hunter. Maybe he *can* talk to his cat. I squat in front of the glass, and feel a bit silly when I ask, "Is Sam home?"

The black cat blinks up at me. *See, stupid? Cats can't under-stand.* Then the black furry head shakes from side to side in a very human-like no.

Um.

What?

I ask again. "Is Sam home?"

Mephistopheles shakes his head again.

Coincidence? "Do you know when he's coming home?" Again, the cat shakes his head. Maybe he's just itchy? To test it, I ask, "Can you understand me?"

He nods.

I wobble and fall out of my crouch, catching myself with one hand against the cold concrete. "Should I go into work today?"

Wide honey-colored eyes blink at me. *I'm talking to a cat.* I snort and stand up.

Returning home, I eye my cell phone on the kitchen benchtop and flip it over to dial reception.

Candy answers after one ring. "Wow, you're in early," I tell her.

"The phones are diverted after-hours. What do you want? Can it wait?"

I slump down on the sofa. "Bethany said I should call if . . ."

"You're quitting?" Candy's sudden concern sounds genuine.

"I—um, no. But I'm not coming in today." Saying it out loud takes a weight off my mind.

"You have to," she urges.

I sit up. Candy had known Annie. I should tell her. "I found Annie's body yesterday. I—"

"You what?" There's a long silence. "Are you okay?" Her voice becomes a whisper.

"Not really, but—"

Beeping draws my attention to the display screen on my cell. Unknown number. I put the phone back to my ear. "Candy, I have to go. I'll call you back." I hang up on her and press connect on the incoming call. "This is Margaret Solder."

"Ms. Solder, this is Detective Bryce. Have I caught you at a bad time?"

"Uh no, it's okay."

She picks up on my hesitation. "Are you getting ready for work?"

"Actually, no. I'm—"

"I'd like to request that you go in," she says hurriedly.

"What? Why?" I move from astonished to annoyed. "I'm . . . I'm not well." I don't want to go in. That matters, doesn't it?

"Ms. Solder—"

I grit my teeth, annoyance washing over me. "I found a dead person yesterday. The person who worked in my chair. I'm not going back there, and—"

"We haven't yet connected her death to Bacitriet. Ms. Solder, we need you to go in and listen to the gossip about Annie. We're releasing the news to media outlets in a few hours and I need you on the inside."

My stomach rolls. I cover my mouth because inside I'm screaming. Should I tell her what Sam said? That Annie was killed by a demon? She'd never believe me. I bite back a moan and double over as my stomach cramps. "I really don't—"

"Ms. Solder. Margaret. I need your help. And of course, it will count toward your case."

"My case?"

"You found a body, Ms. Solder, and you aided Brian Bacitriet by removing potential evidence at his request. Your help in this matter would be greatly appreciated, and will go a long way to—"

Tears well in my eyes, and I press a palm hard into my forehead. Could she be any more obvious? Actually, that's a good question. Why isn't she trying to be more subtle? I guess she doesn't care if I know what she's doing.

"Fine. I'll go in." A sob bursts out of me.

Bryce ignores it. "Excellent. Call me when you leave the office tonight."

I hang up. Big fat tears roll down my face and plop into the blanket. "Shit."

*

The floor is buzzing when I step from the elevator. My head twists sharply as I search every shadow, every corner, every face. Do they suspect I know? What if they are . . . crap, can you tell if someone is a demon just by looking at them? I curse Sam for not telling me anything more useful.

I have to make a new list of potential suspects and note down any odd behavior. *Everyone is odd around here, idiot.* Still, making a list might help calm me down. I'm trembling like I've drunk too much coffee, feeling hot and itchy and cold all at once.

"You came in? But you said—" I jump as Candy appears at my elbow. "Are you okay?"

I force a smile. "It turns out being by myself is worse, you know?"

She peers around as if searching for someone. Probably Bethany. I know she's against gossiping in the workplace. She scares me a little. I'd hate to be Candy, who has to work beside her all day, every day.

"What happened? You said you found Annie?" The last part is whispered. Candy is paler than I've ever seen her, her eyes darting to and fro.

"Is Bacitriet here?" I ask.

Candy wraps an arm around my shoulders. I shiver. Candy's fingers are freezing. "Didn't you say he's in Sydney?"

Oh, that's right. I'd booked his trip last week. Feels like a lifetime ago now. "Right, yes."

"Let's go into the kitchen. You can tell me everything there." The unspoken "away from Bethany" is impossible to miss.

"Right." I follow Candy into the luxurious staff kitchen. Though the floor is rarely full, the kitchen is bursting with people, many I haven't met before.

"Tell me about Annie," Candy says. Her voice carries to the coffee line.

"Annie?" Timber asks.

"She found Annie's body," Candy says in a hushed voice. Instantly, I'm a gladiator walking into the Colosseum. People surround me, ravenous to know what's going on. I have a feeling the lion is going to win this battle. I just wish I knew who the lion was.

It's worse than Detective Bryce's interrogation. I'm supposed to be watching for reactions, but there are too many to note. I speak until I'm hoarse, leaving out everything Sam told me. I stick to finding the body and the police questioning. Eventually, the crowd moves off, leaving me sitting with Candy and the other ladies from the lunch—which seems like a year ago now—and Timber.

"That sounds nuts," Timber says. He's migrated closer as people drifted away. I stare at him, remembering IT are the only ones with access to the network and the backend of the Instant Messaging program. Maybe it's not Bacitriet at all . . . but Timber doesn't look like a demon. *You don't know what a demon looks like, Mig.*

"It was horrible," I say.

A man I have never seen before enters the kitchen. He goes straight to the filtered drip to refill his mug. *Why, when the barista is right there?* His head swivels and his gaze locks onto me. His vacant stare gives me the creeps and I fall silent. The women around me pick up on my mood swing. No one speaks until the man walks away.

"Who was that?" I ask. My skin is crawling and I want to scratch hard at the itch.

"Janquil Nyugen." Candy says. "He's in accounting."

My eyes pop wide recognizing the name from that bloody contract. I nearly bite my tongue in shock. He's real. He's a real person.

"Did the police actually say they thought you did it?" Candy presses closer, bringing me back to the topic at hand.

Sara and Charli stand at the same time. It's eerie how in sync they are. "Such a shame," Sara says.

"She was nice," Charli adds.

They walk away. I blink after them. Oh, I should add them to my list. The one that now also has Janquil Nyugen on it.

Their weird silent synchronizing is certainly creepy. "Are they always like that?"

Timber and Shannon laugh. I jerk a little in my seat; everyone here might be a suspect. I examine Shannon closely. She seems pretty normal.

Candy touches my arm, her nails scraping against my wrist. "Are you really okay? It must have been dreadful. Was she . . . uh . . . ?"

"Whoever did this is a horrible person." Out of the corner of my eye, I spy Timber's lips pursing. "Truly evil," I add. The expression on his face darkens.

"Oh, indeed. Yes, just awful," Candy says.

"They haven't caught the guy. Who knows why he did it?" Timber says. His mouth grows tight, and he stands abruptly. "I have to get back. Glad you're okay, Mig."

"That was weird," Shannon says, staring after him.

Yeah. Weird. I pop Timber onto my list of suspects.

Candy licks her lips and slaps her hands against her thighs. "I'd better get back too. Bethany will kill me if . . . oh, sorry, Margaret. That was in rather bad taste."

I nod but my mind is stuck on Timber's reaction. Detective Bryce was right; I do have something to report. The IT guy who was friendly to me is now acting all weird and he talked about the killer being misunderstood. Janquil Nyugen's behavior gave me the willies too.

Left alone in the kitchen, I grab my phone and start texting the detective. I jump a mile when Timber's voice interrupts. "Hey."

I drop the phone into my lap. "What?"

He steps back, eyes wide. "Sorry, I just . . . sorry."

"Sorry," I say. "I'm still a bit freaked out."

He nods but doesn't approach, his gaze darting to my phone as he clears his throat. "I forgot to ask if you had any further trouble with your laptop?"

"No." I regard him suspiciously. "Why?"

"Like I said the other day, we've had a few issues with speed and the like. We've run some tests. Peter is going to purge the system on the weekend, so that should clear up any lingering bugs. Let me know if you have any issues after then, yeah?"

Lingering . . . Turning my laptop off didn't stop Annie from communicating with me. She came back when I turned the computer on. My laptop connects remotely to the work servers, and Timber said something was taking up a lot of space. A soul would take up a heap of room.

Purge the system.

Oh.

"Yup sure, thanks for telling me." I watch Timber leave, my heart pounding. I back out of the text message to Bryce and call Elisa instead.

She picks up immediately. "Hey."

"We need another séance. Tonight."

*

I open the door to Elisa's worried face.

"Did you see the news? They found her, the missing assistant. She's dead, Mig." Elisa embraces me in a tight hug. Oh god, everything has happened so fast. I haven't told her yet. She's wearing flowers, bright yellow chrysanthemums, and her scarf is covered in colorful butterflies. I brush my hands down my ironed gray shirt and black jeans. She eyes my outfit. "Why are you dressed up?"

"I'm not, and I know all about Annie Seramoph." I usher her inside. "I have to tell you something before my grandmas get here."

"They're coming too?" Elisa can't hide her surprise. "Why?"

"Sam said all the original participants need to be here."

"Sam? Honey, what's going on?"

"I need to tell you something. Several somethings." I drag her to the sofa. Elisa's wild hair is already slipping loose from her ponytail, giving her a slightly witchy vibe. "I was the one that found Annie's body. At Angels Park, near the river."

Elisa's hands—her nails bitten, the purple nail polish chipped—cover her mouth in shock. When she pulls them away, she says softly, "Exactly as Annie told us."

"Yep."

Her nostrils flare. "And the others?"

I sigh. "I don't know." I fill her in on Bryce pressuring me to go back to the office, and Timber saying the servers would be wiped on the weekend.

"We have to speak to her again," Elisa declares immediately. "I'll set up now. When are your grandmothers getting here?"

"That's not all. Sam is . . ." It's too ridiculous to put into words. Staring into Elisa's cheery, open expression, I can't figure out what I ever did to deserve such a good friend. "This is going to sound ridiculous, but Sam said . . ." I drop my voice to a whisper " . . . demons are real and he's a demon hunter."

Her face loses color. "What?"

"Well, he didn't actually *say* he's a demon hunter, but he said whatever killed Annie is a demon and it's his job to hunt it down."

Elisa nibbles on her bottom lip. Her squinched expression sets my teeth grinding. She looks nervous. And that makes me nervous. Does she not want to do this and doesn't know how to tell me? She must know she can tell me anything.

"I . . . I never told you . . ."

Wait, Elisa has secrets now? What next? "What is it?"

"Remember I said I've been reading my grandmother's diaries? Mig, she writes about monsters. *Real* monsters, and about fighting them and I . . . it's crazy but I think she was a monster hunter too. Or at least she helped monster hunters. There are spells about binding, and casting demons out of human forms. It freaked me out to read about it." She's staring at me with terror in her eyes. "Mig, I'm afraid. I have kids. I can't put them in danger, and Frank—" she sighs "—he says he believes me and he knows about my family history but . . ."

I worry at my lips with my teeth. "You're not sure?"

"I can't lose him, Mig."

"He wouldn't leave you, El. He loves you."

"I know. I mean, I'm sure he wouldn't, but—oh, Mig. Sometimes I think he just indulges me and my odd feelings. I've heard him joke to his mates when they're all drinking and I . . ."

I don't know what to say about all of this. I've seen the way Frank looks at El when she's not looking, like she hung the moon. He would be furious if he found out she'd put herself in danger. At me too, for putting her there. And he'd be right.

I put a comforting arm around her shoulders. "I'm scared too. Bryce is blackmailing me to help her. And someone at my work is a demon. And my neighbor fights demons, apparently. This wasn't my life two weeks ago."

Elisa straightens her shoulders. "Why do you think Sam told you?"

"He wants to help."

"And you trust him?"

I stare her straight in the eye. "Yes. I know I shouldn't. I mean, it sounds . . . I know how it sounds but . . ."

Her eyes narrow. "What do you feel?"

I'm drawn to him. I lo–like him. I trust him. I want to tell her all about the other night. The way he'd touched me, and the way I'd responded. In ordinary times, I'd talk that moment to death with her over a whole bottle of wine. I long for this to be over so we can do that again. From the look on El's face, she recognizes what I'm thinking. Her lips soften into a smile. "Oh, Mig."

"He said I'm under his protection. Look, I don't know how he knows about all this, but I believe him."

Elisa nods slowly. "Good enough for me," she said. "He wants to catch whoever killed Annie."

"Yes." *And drag them back to hell apparently.*

"How do you know he wants to help the others?"

I jump off the sofa and pace to the window. "What do you mean? That's what he said." Well, technically it wasn't, but he meant that . . . right?

"He's a monster hunter, Mig. Not the demon police, or whatever it is they have."

Police are supposed to keep people safe. Monster hunters hunt monsters. "He said I'm under his protection." I remind her. I narrow my eyes as I ponder her point. "He didn't actually say he wanted to help them. He just said it is his duty to hunt the demon." I knot my fingers together. "Annie asked for *my* help." The answer is obvious. "If Sam won't help, then *I* have to."

Elisa stands up. "You're talking about possibly confronting a demon."

"Who Sam will deal with. We—*I*—need to help Maria and Cassandra."

Elisa releases a shaky breath. "I don't want you to get hurt."

I grab both her hands and hold tight. "Well, neither do I. El, no matter what Sam's actual motivations are, we have to remember those women—they could be me. Annie asked for my help, and I failed her because I didn't take her communication seriously enough." I want a glass of wine so bad, but Rose and Berry are on their way over and I don't want to drink in front of them. "So, let's do this."

By the time my grandmothers arrive, Elisa and I have recreated everything from the night of the first séance, and Elisa is reading over her ancestor's book. "Mig, I found—" She closes the book with a snap as her eyes dart to the old ladies behind me. "I'll tell you later."

"I'm not sure why we're here, Margaret. What's going on?" Berry says, peering over her glasses. I feel all of three feet tall. My grandmas might be growing older, shrinking and, in Berry's case, losing her sight, but they can still freeze me solid with a single look. Rose plonks her body into my armchair and opens her bag, removing her crochet needles and a ball of wool.

"Berry, the . . . spirit, for want of a better word, told me where to find Annie's body. The water? The wings? I found her at the park with the angel statues. She was in the river." A flash of Annie's dead face appears in my mind. "We need more information so we can find the other missing women."

"But, Margaret, a spirit can only tell you what she has experienced. How can she tell you where the others are?" Rose asks. Her fingers and crochet needle move so fast, the pale blue crochet square forms right before my eyes.

"Maybe Annie can give us a clue about who did this. Or something about where she is. Anything can help now that we have a way to communicate with her."

"Why didn't you and Elisa do this without us?" Berry asks, staring down her nose at me.

"I was told to recreate everything as it was when we spoke to her before. I don't know what I'm doing, but I know we're running out of time. What if we're the only ones that can help the others?"

Berry's nose twitches. "This is dangerous. You should leave well enough alone."

I scowl at my grandmother. "I have to do this, Berry. They need my help. Annie begged me for help. How can I ignore that? She's dead. I can't just leave her spirit in the computer. And what about the others?"

Berry flinches as Rose's finger pokes into her side. "One must choose one's own path, Berry." Rose smiles at me. "Very altruistic of you, honey. Of course we'll help." Her gaze falls to Elisa's book and her eyes widen. "Oh, what a lovely book. Look, Berry."

Berry stares. "I see it." She harrumphs and plonks herself down on the sofa. "Let's get on with it then."

"Um . . . we have to wait for Sam," I say. I'm sure he's on his way over as my skin has just turned icy. I wrap my butterfly scarf tighter around my neck. Elisa eyes the soft fabric. I tilt my head at her and she returns her attention to the candles.

Rose leans forward. "Sam's coming?"

Before I can answer, the man in question strides in without knocking. I stand up. "Did you—" He freezes by the door, as if needing permission to come closer. "Sam?"

Rose waves a hand. "Come in, dear. It's drafty out there and you standing in the doorway is making it worse."

"Uh." Elisa's eyes pop wide, and I realize with a start it's the first time she's actually met him. When he steps forward, she stretches out a trembling hand. He shakes it and her mouth twitches.

I frown at my friend's odd behavior. Then again, nothing about this night is normal. I peer up at Sam. "Did your friend—"

"Shall we begin?" he asks, cutting me off. I follow his gaze to my grandmothers. Okay, fine, he doesn't want to discuss it in front of them. I frown. We *will* have this conversation later. I want to know what his friend found out, and if he has any new details about the demon. I can see in Sam's pressed lips and in the tightness of his shoulders that he knows I want the information and that I will demand it later.

"Sure," I mutter instead. I turn on my laptop and take Elisa's hand. Sam drags a chair over to squeeze between me and Elisa. I shoot him a questioning look, but he waves it away.

Berry grunts. "I thought we had to recreate what happened the other night. *He* wasn't here."

It's a fair point. I ignore her and take Sam's hand. "Go ahead, Elisa." Sam's fingers are scalding, like he's just been holding a hot coffee, and they curl around my hand, sending warmth up my arm even as my neck remains an ice block. I glance at Elisa, wondering if she's noticed, and she meets my stare with a raised eyebrow.

"My guides are being really *vocal* at the moment." Elisa takes Sam's hand with only her fingers, shooting me a narrow look as she does so. The hairs rise all over my body. I've seen her react like this before, with that dodgy tradie who broke more than he repaired. What is she sensing about Sam? I raise my eyebrows. She tilts her head. *Later.*

The candles on the table dance shadows across all of our faces.

Elisa clears her throat. "To the entity trying to communicate with Margaret Solder. We are here. We are listening."

My gaze locks onto my computer. Will Annie speak to us again? My breath freezes as the candle flickers. For a moment, nothing happens. Sam squeezes my hand.

The app icon flashes.

Chapter 27

The blinking light is mesmerizing. It takes a nudge from Sam for me to lean over with our clasped hands and click the message open.

"What does it say?" Rose's whisper is loud enough to startle the birds in a rainforest into flight.

I read the message out loud. "I am here."

Elisa holds up her hand still clasped to Sam's, her fingers splayed. The gesture stops me from speaking further. "We need clarification," Elisa says. "Who is speaking?"

"It's a computer. It's not talking at all," Berry says.

Rose shakes Berry's hand. "Oh, hush, I want to hear."

I close my eyes and sigh.

"Not possible," Sam mutters.

I open my eyes. His gaze is glued to the computer screen. Candle flames flicker in his eyes. "What do you mean?" I ask him.

His stare darts to me then back to the laptop. "It *is* her. In your computer. My friend confirmed it might be possible, but I didn't believe it." I wait for Sam to continue. He shakes his head. "Her soul was removed. We think the transfer failed. An accident, perhaps. Somehow, her soul got into your work network," Sam says.

"How do you know that? What else did your friend say? Transfer her soul to what?" I'm overflowing with questions.

Sam glares at me as if to reiterate we'll talk about it later, but I want to talk about it *now*. "How can you transfer a soul?" I think about the contract I'd delivered for Bacitriet and of Janquil Nyugen's dead eyes.

Berry's intense stare is fixed on Sam's face. Rose hums softly. I'm shocked they haven't bombarded him with questions yet.

"There are several ways. But not in the way you are thinking. A soul contract is not always immediate; it may be a promise to collect at a later time. This was fast, brutal. Inelegant. Her soul was ripped from her without consent. A spell, more than likely."

My gaze flies to Elisa. She shrugs. "It's possible, I guess. You'd need a lot of power, the right ingredients and the right words."

"Why would the killer need her soul?" Berry asks. I knew her silence wouldn't last.

Sam doesn't answer.

"Why?" I repeat. I catch Berry glancing at Rose from the corner of my eye.

"There are different purposes, different needs." His stare locks on me as if trying to tell me something. But I can't read his mind. I have no idea what he is trying to tell me. "There are contradictory elements in this case. I still don't fully understand it. It's like there are two separate—" He shakes his head. "There is the contract and then there are the missing women."

"Contract?" Berry's voice is clipped. I widen my eyes at Sam. I don't want him to tell my grandmothers about that. He nods.

Sam continues. "In this case, I believe the spell is to enable the demon to stay here," he says at last. "The . . . demon . . . would require a disguise. The empty vessels may be a part of that disguise. Or it is a different spell entirely. One with another purpose." I shudder. Sam squeezes my hand. "You need to focus."

"So, the extraction failed, and this poor girl got sucked into Margaret's computer?" Berry questions. Her body is held tight, posture perfect. She's angry. I can see it in her every sharp move.

"Yes, though I'm not certain how," Sam replies, frowning. "And I am not sure how to help her."

"This is all very odd," Rose mutters. She and Berry are staring at each other, slight twitches and ticks tell me they are discussing something. I wish I knew what it was.

The app flashes again. I read out the next response. *You know who I am.*

I jump in with a question of my own. "I found your body. I'm so sorry we—I—was too late. How are you communicating with us?"

Another message appears.

I don't know.

Sam squeezes my fingers. "Ask her what she remembers. The last thing."

I repeat the question. The typing dots pulse, and I bite my tongue so hard I taste blood. We all lean forward as the answer appears. *Dark. Electric. Chanting. Fire. Pain.*

"Female chanting or male?" Sam spits, twitching my hand until I repeat his question.

The answer comes quickly. *Both. Neither. I don't know. A monster.*

My eyes pop wide, and I stare at Sam. The demon?

"Were the other women there? Did you see them?" I ask.

Yes.

"Where are you now? Can you . . . feel? Hear anything?" My voice drops to a whisper. I can't imagine what Annie is going through. It's the stuff of nightmares.

Trapped. Tight. Too small. Everything hurts. Help me.

"I want to help, but I don't know how." Tears press against my eyes. I blink them back, but one escapes and slides down my nose. I can't wipe it away without letting go of someone's hand. I sniff and scrub my face against my shoulder. Annie's suffering, and I desperately want to help her.

Elisa is quiet. Last time she'd been so engaged, but now she won't meet my gaze and I can't gauge her mood.

"Annie, what do you remember?" I ask. How can we help a spirit trapped in a computer?

Work. Coffee. Bag. Pain. Voices. Darkness.

"Her last day?" I wonder. Voices. So, more than one person?

Tired.

"I promise we'll help you, Annie," I say, hoping she'll hear the determination in my voice.

Rose sits up higher, almost disconnecting her hand from Berry. "Ask her what the voices said?"

I repeat the question. The ensuing wait seems interminable. When the message pops up, I gasp, then read, *Upon possession of three souls, the burning fires of hell will remain sealed to your true form forever. All will tremble in your name.*

Sam straightens with a snap. I get the feeling he's worked it out at last. "What is the name?" he demands.

I repeat his question, my hands shaking.

There's no answer. The message window shuts down and my computer turns black.

"That's all rather ominous," Rose says.

I suppress a swear and drop my hands, leaning back against the cushions.

Berry's eyes lock onto Sam. "I don't believe you told us why you're here? You seem to know an awful lot about what is going on."

Sam stands, and Berry does the same, blocking his path.

Under different circumstances I'd laugh over Berry's tiny body stopping Sam from moving. Now, I'm just shocked.

"Berry!" I jump up and pull her back.

"Sam." Berry's voice reminds me of Dad's the time I *borrowed* his car.

Sam ignores my grandmother and reaches for my hand. "This is dangerous," he says seriously. "You need to back away before you fall. Keep your friends and family safe. I will take care of this." His concern for my family and friends melts a little of the ice in my chest. "Trust me," he implores.

Annie's dead face reappears in my mind. I made a promise to her and I intend to keep it. But reminding me that I could put my family in danger sends a ribbon of fear through my soul. "Okay." I have to warn him about the time limit and the system purge, but before I can speak, he sweeps from the room like some eighteenth-century vampire.

"That boy certainly knows how to make an exit," Rose comments.

Berry takes my empty hand. Her callused fingers clasp mine tightly. "What about the girl in your computer?"

I swallow back my nausea. "I don't know. What can we do?"

"If she is stuck in limbo, then what we need is a . . . Rose?"

"Exorcism." Rose waves at Elisa from her armchair. "Could you do that, dear?"

I spin around as Elisa sucks at her teeth. I widen my eyes and give her the tiniest head shake.

"It's not a good idea. Too dangerous, as Sam said." Elisa offers a faint smile.

"But dear—" Rose pushes against the chair arms and forces her body to her feet.

"Rose, it's a computer. How can we do an exorcism on a computer?" I don't want my grandmas to be a part of this. However, the idea is not a bad one. We could do it. Elisa and me, alone. "Come on. I should take you both home. Elisa, you're staying for a cup of tea, right?" Again, I stare at her intently. I don't want Rose and Berry hurt if we get caught. I wiggle my eyebrows, willing Elisa to hear the hidden meaning behind my words.

"Of course. I'll turn the kettle on."

I leave Elisa with the tea and assist my grandmothers into my car. Rose talks a mile a minute. "That poor girl, we simply cannot leave her to haunt wires and cables forever. How can—"

"Rose, it was just a . . . a game." Beside me, Berry stares through the window. Her lips pressed tightly together.

"But dear, you can't leave her in there," Rose repeats.

"Sam said he'd take care of it."

"Pfft!" Berry crosses her arms. "That boy has enough going on."

I assume she's talking about his intention to find the killer. I wish he'd told me what information he got from his friend before he'd left. Did he know how to find the demon? I wonder if perhaps his friend is like the librarian to Sam's slayer? When this is all over, I'm determined to get answers. For now, I have to take my grandmothers home, where they'll be safe.

Because Elisa and I are going to free Annie's spirit from my work computer. And we're doing it tonight.

Chapter 28

It takes half an hour to convince Elisa we have to do it straightaway.

"I'm not ready," she insists. "I don't have my stuff, Mig. Let's be sensible."

I pace away from the sofa. Elisa remains seated, watching me with wide eyes. "I can't wait. It has to be now. They're going to purge her. We don't know what will happen to her if they do and—"

"I don't—"

"Elisa, *please.*" I should step back and calm down, think it through with a clearer head, but urgency pulses in my veins. Sam is out there hunting the demon. It will be distracted. Now is the perfect time. "We have to save Annie."

"Where do we go? We don't even know where—"

"My work."

Elisa blanches. "Why there?"

How can I explain my thinking when I don't fully understand it myself? "A brain is like a computer. But a whole person? How can that fit into one little laptop? Timber, the IT guy, said something is taking up all the memory storage at work. They can't figure out what it is. I'm pretty sure that's Annie."

Elisa's lips firm. She slaps her thighs and stands. "Instinct, Mig. You have to trust it. If you're sure we have to go now, then we go now. We'll swing by my place and get my bag—and uh, maybe some burgers? I'm starving."

"What did you think of Sam?" I ask, locking the front door behind us. "You were acting a little strange when you met him." We head for Elisa's car.

"I know I said the opposite, but my guides were completely silent."

"Is that bad?"

"I don't know. It's never happened before." She climbs into the driver's seat. "But I can tell you this, he's not who he says he is."

"What did they, uh . . . you sense?" I ask, opening the passenger side door. I slide inside.

She scrunches her nose in thought for a moment before she says so softly I can barely hear her, "I don't know." She starts the engine.

I play with my new bracelet and recall Sam's words. Protection. To keep me safe. In my heart, I know I can trust Sam, but am I just deluding myself? "El, maybe you shouldn't do this with me. You can give me the book. I'll work it out."

"Don't be silly," she replies, buckling her seatbelt. "Of course I'm helping you."

"Elisa, you have kids. You shouldn't be taking this risk."

"It's not just about you, Mig. This is my nonna's book, my nonna's power." She releases a long sigh. "I've been running from this for too long. In my family, we don't talk about our abilities, not out loud, but we're all sensitive to the flow. I need to do this. To help you and . . . I think to help myself. And . . . well, what if my kids manifest something? What do I tell them? Yep, I knew all about it but when the moment came to use it, I chickened out? Can I live with myself knowing I could have helped save a life, and didn't? What message does that send to them?" She glances at me quickly before returning to the road. She sounds so matter of fact about it all now, her fear gone. She's clearly decided on her course of action the way I decided on mine.

Once more my emotions swing in the opposite direction to hers. "I should be freaking out. Why aren't I freaking out?"

Her gaze flicks toward me before she focuses on backing out of my driveway and onto the road. "Because you're doing the right thing."

"Sneaking into work, smuggling you in—out of hours—and breaking into the server room is the right thing?"

"Okay, so we're not exactly doing the *right* thing. But after dealing with so much uncertainty, you're resolved in your action. *That* is a good thing." She smiles. "Besides, no one will be there, right? We can go in, do our thing, and get out with no one the wiser."

"Right," I agree. "But yeah, let's get burgers first."

*

We stop at Elisa's house for what she needs. Her husband and children are probably asleep, so I stay in the car while she creeps inside.

What are you doing, Mig. Elisa has kids. I breathe deeply and close my eyes, offering a silent apology to Elisa's guides. I ask them to keep her safe. They don't respond.

She returns to the car with a small bag and we drive away without looking back. Elisa's fingers are white where she grips the steering wheel, the only indication she gives that she might be second-guessing her decision. We hit the drive-thru and, with nothing left to stall over, we head into the city. As it had on the night I'd come in for the gym bag, my pass gets us inside and the elevator takes us straight to my floor.

"Nice office," Elisa comments. "Security?"

"No one stopped me on the night I fetched Bacitriet's bag. During the day, the desk is manned, but it was dark when we came in. I've got my laptop, so if we get caught, we say I need to get my charger."

She glances around and whistles. "What a great view. Where's the server room?"

I hit my forehead. "Ugh, I'm stupid! It's on the IT floor. We have to go up again."

The elevator ride is silent. I can't speak and I don't know what Elisa is thinking. Is she worried? I am. My palms are sweaty and my heart is racing. As we step out, I wave at the rear wall. "Timber's desk is this way." The empty floor hums around us. Boxes stacked against desk partitions have spewed packing foam and plastic wrapping everywhere. Cables hang like snakes off desks and are piled on the floor. There is a large door at the end of the room. I tug on the handle. "It's locked."

Elisa points to the security card reader beside the door. I grimace and swipe my pass.

Nothing happens.

"Shit." I swipe again and turn my horrified stare on Elisa. "I don't have access."

Elisa hisses out a breath. "What do we do now?"

I stare at the messy desks, hunting for inspiration. "Look for something that can get us inside."

We search under every scrap on Timber's desk—nothing. "He'd have his pass with him," I say. I can't believe I didn't think of this earlier.

"What about a different desk?"

I look at the clean one beside Timber's. "He said that's for the new starter." I click my fingers. "Look for a code or cheat sheet."

"Bingo." Elisa holds up a paper folder. Inside is a post-it. "Four digits—but the door needs a pass. Sorry. This is not helpful."

"New starter stuff is stored in their locker," I say, thinking of my first day. "Mine was, and my pass was locked inside."

We race to the locker number written on the post-it and punch in the code. Inside, we find a laptop, stationery, several IT manuals . . . and on top of it all, a door pass.

I grab the pass and we return to the locked server room. I swipe and the door lets out a beep. It's insanely heavy, and I have to use extra force to push it open. As soon as the seal around the door pops, a loud hum fills the empty office. "We're in."

Light pours in from behind us exposing the server room as a long, shadowy space. Metallic shelving covers every wall and creates a barrier through the middle of the room. Black computer hard drives are stacked on every shelf—the source of the noise. Tiny green and red LED lights flash—some in unison, some slightly off, creating a strange Christmassy affect. "Should I turn on a light?"

"I've got candles," she says.

Neither of us move. "Come on," I say. "Prop the door open and don't touch anything we don't need."

"It's icy in here." Elisa rubs her arms.

"Yeah." I stop in the middle of the room. "Now what?"

"I'm not sure the candles will stay lit," Elisa says. Her brows knit together as she peers around the room. "That air-con is crazy strong." She pulls her nonna's book from her bag.

"It's probably because of all the IT hard drives in here. Listen to the fans. This room is probably kept on a separate system and that's why it's cold."

"Huh, make's sense. So, listen. When I was at your place, I found . . . well, I guess it's a spell we can try. Mig, I haven't done anything like this before. I have no idea if it will work."

"We'd better be quick then." I creep around the central shelf, where it is a fraction warmer and out of direct line of the air-conditioning vents and the fire alarm.

Elisa pulls a car blanket from her bottomless bag. A little toy car falls out of the blanket. Elisa sighs and scoops it up, shoving it back into her bag. "Floor's cold," she explains flapping out the blanket and laying it on the floor. She lights the candles and sits on the blanket. The candles flicker wildly. I

hold my breath, but they don't go out. *I guess we're doing this.*
I kneel beside her. She drags a piece of white chalk across the
floor around us and removes a soft squishy bag and a plastic
container that looks like a kid's lunchbox. She reaches back
inside the bag for a bowl, a bottle of water and a feather. She
fills the bowl with the water and pulls the lid off the dirt-filled
container.

I open the laptop and log on. Staring into the wild, gyrating
candle flame, Annie's dead face appears in my mind again, her
blank eyes begging for help. I blink the memory away. Maybe
it's just the air-conditioning, but shivers race each other down
my spine.

"We have to be quick." I position the laptop next to my knee
so we can both see the screen.

"Trust me, I don't want to be in here any longer than neces-
sary." Elisa takes hold of my hands. Her voice deepens into the
low, sleep-filled sound I've come to associate with her doing
her thing. I sniff hard, my nose dripping in the chilly air. I can't
free a hand to wipe it, so I sniff harder.

As Elisa starts her spiel, calling for Annie's presence, I close
my eyes. I picture Annie's face, fighting to recall the smiling
image I'd seen flashed all over social media. What I manage is
blurry at best, but it's better than the image of her dead face
in the river.

I crack open my eyes. There is no flashing light and no
message on the screen.

Elisa calls for Annie again.

"Come on," I mutter. Elisa's fingers squeeze mine. She pins
me with one open eye and mouths *"focus."*

Right. "Annie?" I call. "We're here to help you." The icon
flashes and relief floods through me. Using my fingertip—
making sure not to let go of Elisa's hand—I open the message.

Help me.

I release a breath.

"Tell her to keep talking for as long as she can. Ignore me. Just talk to her," Elisa says softly.

I repeat the message and ask Annie if she is okay.

Tired. Cold.

"Annie, we're trying to help. You have to hang on a little longer."

Elisa shakes my right hand. More flashing.

Others?

"We are trying to help the others," I tell her. "Can you tell us where they are?"

I don't know.

Elisa is whispering, reading from her ancestor's book. I can't make out her words and focusing on her lips doesn't help. My gaze returns to the computer.

I'm scared.

Elisa shoves the book toward me with her foot—*Ugh, so flexible*—and shakes my hand. "Read," she mouths.

I lick my lips and then clear my throat. The words blur beneath my gaze. I don't recognize any of them. It's in another language? *How am I supposed to read this?* I widen my eyes at Elisa.

"Try," she whispers. "Just sound it out."

The blinking on the screen stops. "Annie?"

Here.

Focusing on the page beneath my hands, I start reading. The words are a jagged mix of sounds and I quickly mangle them. The last section blurs and then becomes clear, " . . . she whose soul is trapped, unwilling captive. Let go your bindings to this earth. Your physical form is found. Your captors hunted. We see you. We hear you. It is time to go. Be free, Annie Seramoph."

I fall silent, expecting a flash or one of the candles to putter out or a howling wind to rise up out of nowhere.

I've watched too many movies.

My laptop screen goes dark. I glance at Elisa. She shrugs. "Read it again?"

I must've said something wrong. I clear my throat. Beneath my butt, the floor starts to vibrate, growing steadily stronger, while red and green LED lights in the banks of black boxes flash faster. The walls shake. "What's going on?"

A charcoal-like smell fills the air. My laptop screen springs to life, blinking on and off as if the laptop is trying to connect to external screens, disconnecting and reconnecting rapidly. The candles extinguish, plunging us into darkness.

"Mig?"

"Elisa?" I still have hold of her hand. I squeeze her fingers. "What happened? Is it working?"

A roar, like the one I'd heard on the train once from that man high-on-ice, comes out of nowhere and echoes around the enclosed room, reverberating in my gut. A whisper breaks through the noise, a woman's voice. "Thank you."

And then . . . silence.

I can hear Elisa's shuddering breaths. My palms are sweaty, but there's no way I'm letting go of her hands. Cold air presses against my skin in waves. I tremble violently but I'm unable to get that pain-filled roar out of my mind.

"Mig?" Bands of steel tighten around my fingers, yanking me forward. I blink, but the darkness doesn't lift. "Mig?"

"Sorry. I'm good. Did it work?" I ask.

"It must have."

"Why is it so dark?" My heart feels like it has climbed into my throat and is choking the life out of me. I peer around. "I think the door slammed shut."

Oh God. We're trapped. I fumble for my phone and activate the screen, letting the white-blue light brighten the server room. Elisa's eyes bulge, making her look more like an anime character than a human. Sweat glues my shirt to my back. We climb to our feet and pick our way to the door, careful not to knock anything over. I press against the door. Nothing happens. "Help me."

"The pass," says Elisa.

I swipe the card against the wall. A beep signals our freedom. We both push and the door unseals with a sucking sound and creaks open. "Oh, thank heavens!"

Elisa pushes on my shoulder. "Why aren't you moving?"

"We have to clean up."

"Okay, you hold the door." Elisa flicks on her cell phone flashlight and disappears back into the dark room. What feels like hours pass before she reappears at my side. "Done. Let's get out of here."

Happily, I release the door and it shuts with a clang. I wave the magical pass in the air. "I have to put this back."

"Hurry."

I replace the card in the new guy's locker, relock it and jog back to where Elisa is standing at the mouth of the corridor leading to the elevators. A giggle pops out of me. Elisa stares blankly before her lips quirk and she chuckles. *Oh God! What's wrong with us?* The tension bunching my shoulders drops away and I feel lighter than a cloud. I bend over and gasp, laughing and sobbing in the same breath.

We did it. Saved Annie. Freed her soul.

I let a grin spread across my face. "We did it." Giggles sporadically bubble out of me as I wipe sweat from my face and press the call button for the elevator. "I wish we had a way to help the others."

"It feels like unfinished business. Maybe Sam will find them? What are you going to do tomorrow? You can't come back here," Elisa says, buttoning her coat closed over her dress.

"I don't know. I shouldn't, but I—"

The elevator doors slide open, revealing Brian Bacitriet. He doesn't look surprised to see us. His head tilts as he sniffs, gaze roving over both of us. "What are you doing here, Ms. Solder?"

"Ah." I shoot Elisa a panicked look. Her face is pale and her eyes widen with shock, probably a mirror of mine. She shakes her head. I hold up my laptop and stammer, "Forgot my charger."

Bacitriet's stare burns two holes through my forehead and into my brain. "I see." He gestures with an open palm. "Come along, then." I give Elisa an encouraging look and step into the elevator beside my boss. Elisa follows. My heart thuds painfully fast. No one speaks. My palms are sweaty and I can't look at Elisa. *Shit shit shit.* The light on the small display screen shows the elevator dropping past the ground floor and into the basement. "Shall I take you both home?" His voice curls around my spine and squeezes.

Elisa pokes my side and I nervously laugh. "Oh, no sir. We drove in together. This is my friend, Elisa. We were out to dinner and I thought, while we were close, I'd just pop in and grab my charger. I was hoping to work from home tomorrow, and I didn't think anyone would be here." Bacitriet lets me prattle on. I suck in a deep breath. "Thanks for the offer though and—" The doors slide open. I grab Elisa's hand and tug her out with me.

His hand snaps out to stop the doors closing. "There is no pedestrian exit down here. You will require the elevator to return to the lobby."

I glance at the gray concrete surroundings and listen to my voice echo. "Uh, sure. Woops." I tug Elisa's hand, but she doesn't move. Her lips are white where they're pressed together. "El?" I turn back to find out what's wrong.

A cold hand clamps down on my neck and nails dig into my skin. I cry out in shock as Elisa screams.

Chapter 29

I force my eyes open only to slam them shut against the bright light around me.

"Ugh!" Spears of pain stab my eyeballs, and I moan at the heavy thickness pressing against my skull. My stomach churns and sweat coats my skin like cold slime.

Squinting my left eye open again, I hope the dizziness will subside. For a worrying moment, my stomach lurches and bile rises into my throat. I bend forward—or at least try to—but I can't shift more than a few inches. Afraid I'll hurl on myself, I force my breathing to slow, in and out through my nose, and wait for the urge to fade.

Why can't I move? With glacially slow movements, I tilt my head and peer down. My wrists are tied to plastic chair arms. I groan. *Why am I tied to a chair?* No answer springs to mind.

Where am I? Why can't I remember? Something itches at the back of my mind, but I can't pin it down. I rock back and forth but don't gain even an inch of space around the white plastic.

"Hello?" My question is more of a frog croak than an actual word. I work my mouth, searching for saliva, and crack open the other eye. My nausea returns with a kick, and I moan, dropping my head to my chest. My fingers are cold. So is my nose. My breathing is way too fast and shallow. I'm sweating and gross and trapped. I'm trapped. I rock my chair prison. "Shit." Sucking in a gulp of air, I hold it until my lungs feel about to burst then let it hiss out between my teeth. *Come on,*

Mig. Get it together. Right now, I need to figure out what the hell is going on. I can lose my shit later.

Forcing my eyes open, I examine the room. I'm alone. Exposed wooden struts line the ceiling. The walls have peeling paintwork—green on white—and fist-sized holes punched through the drywall. There are no windows. It's a little room—no bigger than my bedroom at home. *Home.* I remember home, and voices—my grandmothers and—who else? Elisa.

Oh my God. *Elisa!*

Memories spiral back in a flash. I remember it all. My heart beats a staccato rhythm as I realize Bacitriet *is* the murderer. And now he's got us.

No one will know we are missing, not for a while, anyway. It will be days before Rose and Berry or Mom and Dad come looking for me. Wait. Elisa. Her husband knows. Frank will report her missing.

I'm afraid we're going to end up like Annie.

No. We saved Annie. Elisa and me. My memory of Annie's whispered "thank you" gives me chills of a good kind.

Who's going to save us?

I twist my hand—try to—but there's no give in the . . . the . . . I examine the binding that secures my wrist to the chair, a silk scarf covered in little hearts. My legs are equally bound with silk. Slumping back, exhausted, I stare around my prison. The paint reminds me of a hospital or aged-care facility, but the disuse is clear. An icky mold smell permeates the air. Even the walls are dying.

My chest hurts. I can't see my handbag or my phone, so there's nothing for the police to track. Tears spring to my eyes as I think about Mom and Dad worrying themselves sick when they don't hear from me. I picture them crying, and searching the streets for me, talking on TV like Annie's parents. Hot tears pour down my face. The worry might kill my grandmothers. I can't die.

I have to get out of here.

The scarves are tight, the knots unyielding. I fight wildly, pushing and pulling, jerking my arms up and down, moving the whole chair with the force of my struggles. The chair legs bash the floor with every movement. *Breathe.* I've researched this, written this. The hero tied to a chair in a locked room. Examining my wrists again, I notice that my wild actions have only tightened the knots. *Think, Mig. How do you get out?*

I listen to the silence and pray Bacitriet hasn't heard my attempts to free myself. What if he comes back right now to kill me? The fear he might return transforms into another— what if he *doesn't* come back? I could be left in here to die of dehydration, or starvation. I blow out a cold breath and watch it appear in front of my eyes—or freeze to death.

Elisa. It's my fault she's been captured. I'd asked her for help, snuck her into my workplace, and Bacitriet has caught us both. He wouldn't have taken just me and let Elisa go, so she must be in another room just like this one.

Fear for my best friend strengthens something inside me and pushes everything else aside. *Save Elisa.*

I twist my wrist again, this time with more care, and follow the scarf knots with my gaze. I use the fingers I can move to stretch for the closest knot—if I can get a finger beneath it, maybe I can pull it loose? I pick at the silk.

How long have we been gone? Have Frank or Sam noticed yet and reported us missing to the police? I didn't call Detective Bryce back. I'm sure she'll come looking for me. Bacitriet knows the cops are onto him. If I go missing too—another one of Bacitriet's assistants—he'll be the prime suspect. That has to be why I'm still alive. Hopefully it means Elisa, Maria and Cassandra are too. There is still a chance I can save them. I just have to save myself first.

"Oh, Sam. You were right," I whisper. "I wish I'd listened."

Tears crawl down my cheeks. Sam told me to believe in him. I do but I also know I can't wait for someone else to save me. I sniff up snot. The tear trailing down my nose plops onto my shirt. I twist my hand again. This time, I don't reach for the scarf but underneath it for my bracelet. I find the little silver cross on the first try. I clutch it and pray—not to God, but to any power that might be listening—and as my fingers brush the length of the cross, I remember.

Oh.

"Yes!" Flicking my fingernail against the tiny button, I release the blade and saw at the scarf. It parts beneath the razor edge.

Red lines streak the silk, creating odd, swirling patterns. I hadn't felt the blade's bite. "Sharp," I mutter, and force myself to slow down.

With a final slice, the scarf gives way. For a moment, I breathe in my success. I've done it, got myself free.

"Don't get ahead of yourself!" I whisper, working to cut through the silk around my left arm and around my legs. I can't take the time to celebrate. I'm still trapped in this windowless room. *I'm a PA. I work with computers, emails and calendars, I'm not an escape artist.* Kidnappings and murder are not my specialty. I've watched a lot of shows though, and researched plenty of real-life wild escapes for my screenplay. I can figure this out.

I tug on the door, not expecting it to move. It doesn't.

Pressing close, I listen for any movement outside. Is Bacitriet standing just beyond the door, waiting for me to escape? My pulse races. I can feel it where my fingertips press against the wall.

"Ouch!" I yank back my hand. "What the . . ." Examining the tips of my fingers I find several thin red lines, like papercuts. I check the wall. At first, I think it's only paint chips, but no, it's the plasterboard itself, flaking away as it rots. I chip at it

with a fingernail. The cardboard covering peels back, exposing chalky insides which crumble into white dust beneath my
fingers. Digging in with both hands, I watch the chunks of dis-
integrating plaster cascade to the floor around my feet and see
freedom at last. *I might actually be able to do this.*

A thump from somewhere inside the building stills my
hands. When nothing further happens, I pick at the wall again,
peeling the cardboard away in giant swathes. I move slowly,
even though the clock in my head begs for greater speed.

Soon I've managed to tear a torso-sized hole. Light from the
naked bulb above my head exposes the inner wall frame. Made
of wood, it looks as solid as it feels, but the braces are spaced
far enough apart that I can squeeze through, if I can knock
out the plasterboard on the other side. The possibility of being
seen will increase the moment I break through, so I work on
making a me-sized hole on my side first. It takes longer than
I expect and by the time I finish, my arms ache, I'm breathing
hard and every new scrape and pull sends fire through my
fingers.

Squeezing my body through the gap, I press against the
plasterboard on the other side. My pulse thuds as I count
the seconds. Now is the moment of reckoning. If Bacitriet is
standing outside, or if there is a camera, the second I poke my
fingers through, they'll be on me. I'll be recaptured—or worse.
Thoughts of Elisa keep me focused.

I rip the cardboard and jam my hands into the crumbling
insides, clawing and scraping. Chalky plaster comes away like
sand, billowing around me, making it hard to breathe. *Go go go.*
I keep pushing, my hands on fire . . . and then I'm through. I
crouch on the floor on the other side, panting softly. *I did it.*

Though I want to run, I creep along the corridor instead.
Dim tube lights and naked bulbs hang from the high ceiling.
Some dangle, unlit and fallen from cords, poking out of the
plaster. Still, it's enough to see by. If Elisa is here, she'll be in

a similar room. The corridor is wide and almost twice my arm span. Doors to either side stand open or are missing altogether. Stumbling along the endless corridor, I eye the paint-peeled walls pockmarked with more holes and I'm overcome with a sense of madness let loose. It's like all of the patients broke out at the same time and ran riot. I'm in an abandoned hospital, probably condemned. Something about it rings a bell but I can't think from where. My chest seizes. *Where the hell am I?* It's like a horror version of a modern hospital that's rotting from the inside out—and might take me with it.

The corridor opens into a wide room filled with box-like machines torn apart and left for dead. I race to the window, desperate to get out. Gripping the bars with my sweaty, bleeding fingers, I expect to find the view outside equally dismal, like an overgrown forest or endless concrete wall. The grounds fall away beneath me; I must be about three stories up. Dusk casts long shadows across the overgrown lawns. If it's becoming dark outside, then I've been here at least eighteen hours.

I turn around. Every step fills my heart with dread. I need to get out and call the police. They can rescue Elisa and arrest Bacitriet. *Why am I trying to be a hero?* Any minute now, I'm going to get caught, and all hope of rescue will be lost.

At the end of the wide room is a door that leads to a windowless office. Everything has been stripped from it. Pinned to the wall is a faded floor map, the hospital name long since worn away. The labyrinth of corridors leads to patient rooms, and a double set of doors to the surgery area. On the other side of the doors is a staircase. At least that's what I assume the multiple straight lines mean. I need to go down to get out. *What about Elisa?*

Indecision tears at me. "Elisa, where are you?" I beg beneath my breath. "What do I do?" I think of Sam and wrap my hand around my bracelet charms. "Sam, I need you."

Nothing happens. *Idiot.* Of course nothing happens. I'm on my own. *Make a plan.* I need to escape, but along the way, I'll search for Elisa.

I head for the surgical wing—the fastest way to the staircase—twitching at the crunch of broken plaster and the crackle of aged linoleum under my shoes. I expect at any moment to see Bacitriet bearing down on me. The scent of bleach saturates everything, along with a heavy mildew smell—time and rot. Something else too—urine? *Ew.* Up ahead, the corridor diverts. I choose right and walk past several operating theaters. Beds, still intact, are surrounded by the empty shells of machines with broken arms, frozen in a monstrous robotic dance. Dread and anguish soaks these rooms, and it sends shivers across my skin. The next room is pristine, with gleaming silver medical equipment and a new bed with fresh sheets. "Oh my god."

Overhead bulbs emit a light that glints off a tray of medical instruments, each item more deadly looking than the last. I creep in, peering over my shoulder for anyone hiding in the shadows, and snatch up a pipe-like object with a round, heavy head, thinking it will make a formidable weapon. Whether it's the vibration of my footsteps or that the tray is badly balanced, gravity takes over and, before my horrified gaze, the tray falls off the trolley. The crash echoes through the room and down the corridor.

"Hell!" I bolt for the stairs taking them down two at a time, reaching the ground floor in seconds. I clutch the ornately carved handrail and jerk myself to a halt. Images of Elisa strapped to a chair as I had been, her face twisted in pain, with tear tracks painting her cheeks, won't leave my mind. It's my fault she's here. I spin on a foot and run back up the stairs, cursing myself with every step. Whatever Bacitriet is doing here, I can't leave Elisa in his hands.

Another damned corridor is lit by dim bulbs. I must have searched the entire second floor by now and there's no sign of

Elisa. No sign of Bacitriet either. Elisa might not even be here. Am I wasting my time searching for her when the police could already be storming the place?

A squeak from somewhere up ahead makes me flinch, and I dally for a moment before creeping toward the sound. A louder creak—a door opening, somewhere close. At the end of the corridor, one door is conspicuously closed. I dart into the room next to it and press my ear to the wall. There's a murmur from the other side. A female voice.

Someone screams.

Elisa!

I race from the empty room and shove the next door open, brandishing my makeshift weapon. "Stop hurting her!" I bellow. The skin on my neck freezes the instant I catch sight of the blond woman poised over Elisa.

That's not Bacitriet.

Elisa is tied to a plastic chair and she struggles against her bonds. Her eyes widen as she recognizes me. "Mig! Run!"

I raise my pipe higher. "Back away."

The blond turns and I drop my arm. My mouth falls open. "Bethany?" I run to her side. "Oh, thank God you found us. Have you called the police? Where's your phone?"

Bethany stands stock-still, only her strangely red eyes flick to me. She isn't wearing a scarf. A thick pucker of red skin mars her neck.

The scarf tied around the chair in my prison cell flashes into my mind. That's where I'd seen that heart pattern before. Around Bethany's neck.

Bethany grips Elisa's wrist so tightly Elisa's hand has turned white. My friend's face is wet with tears. I back away, lifting my weapon again.

"You are trying my patience." Bethany's voice is claggy, vibrating with a depth and fury I've not heard from her before. I'm standing too close. She flings out a hand. Pain explodes in the back of my head as I smash against the wall. "How did you escape your room?" The cold metal of my makeshift weapon is ripped from my fingers. Air explodes from my lungs and pain slaps my back as I hit the wall again. Dust falls over my head from the cracked wall.

The woman—creature—snarls. Spittle flies from her mouth, teeth now pin-sharp canines. Blood seeps down her face, dripping long red lines onto her white shirt.

My horrified gaze drops to arms that are longer than they should be. *Jesus, what is she?* Fingers once tipped with red nail polish are now long, bony protrusions ending in vicious claws. As the Bethany-creature approaches, I catch a whiff of her perfume and, beneath that, the scent of something putrid and evil.

I scream.

Chapter 30

My scream does nothing to stop her approach, nor does it make me feel better, so I stop.

Bethany's acidic breath wafts up my nostrils. I twist my head, mashing my face into the wall, but she continues to puff rancid air in my face. The smell fills my brain with images of blood and raw meat, and I clamp my lips shut a second too late. Nausea swirls and I vomit all over the floor.

Bethany jumps back with a squeal and examines her shoes, swearing loudly. At least I can't smell her anymore.

"Why?" I gasp.

She shakes her head and prowls toward Elisa. "I was so close. You ruined everything."

Tears dampen my eyes, blurring the sight of her. It doesn't make her any more attractive. I scrub them away, thinking of everything Sam has told me. "You want to stay on Earth, don't you? You don't want to go back to hell. You need souls to keep your human disguise working. Annie, Maria, Cassandra . . . how many more do you need?"

She hisses. "How can you possibly know that?" She prowls closer and sniffs my skin. "You are human. How do you know of my plans?"

Sam was right. *If only I could tell him.*

Bethany grabs Elisa's hair and pulls my friend's head up to snarl into her face. Elisa's eyes roll back in her head and Bethany lets go. "No matter. I need three. And now I have you.

Go to your room." Her nails dig into my shoulder and she flings me toward the door.

I'm forced to walk in front of her, and curse my need to find my friend. My whole body trembles with fear. *I'm going to die here.* I wipe a hand over my face as panic bubbles close to the surface. It won't help if I go to pieces. Noise and tears make her angrier. I stay quiet, sobbing silently, and return to the surgery wing.

"No. That way." Bethany shoves me down a different corridor, and pain sears my spine as her nails claw my back. I gasp and twist away, miss my footing and stumble into the wall.

"Hopeless. How did you even escape? This way's quicker. Move."

"Okay, okay." If she's angry now, she'll be furious at the sight of the me-sized hole I've made in the wall. The corridor Bethany forces me through contains more sealed doors. Is this my death march? I have to distract her. "Are Maria and Cassandra here? Are they still alive?"

"Why do you care? Be worried about your own fragile life, human."

"You made a mistake, you know? Taking everyone from the same job. The police are on to you. They'll find you."

Bethany slams me into the wall and I gasp. Her face presses so close to mine that my eyes cross just to see her, and that awful smell wafts over me again. "Stupid human world. So many rules. How were we to know?" she demands. "Useless meat sacks break down so fast. We didn't have a choice, we had to move off the streets. Needed bodies. Bacitriet walked right into our offer, a willing body to house my pet. Oh, don't worry, he didn't suffer. Though my pet does find his form rather constricting." She points to her own chest. "He provided this woman and a place to conceal my minions. It was so simple to encourage the signing of the soul extraction contracts and take over his staff recruitment. A permanent supply of bodies you could say."

Oh God.

"But humans *care* about their offspring and mates. We did not know. No matter. Once this is done, we will choose a new place. We understand this world better now. The hunters will not find us this time."

"Once what is done?" *Oh my God, Mig. Stop asking questions. Do you really want to know all the gory details?*

She smirks. "You already know. To stay forever, the spell demands three souls, loved and innocent. It took us a while to understand we needed subservient souls. Three at the heart of the dark, under a full moon."

"It failed the first time, didn't it? What happened? Did you kill Cassandra and Maria? What happened to them? When you killed Annie, something went wrong, didn't it? She ended up in the computer and your plans fell apart. Then the police were sniffing around and—"

Bang!

Bethany rears back, her head snapping to the side, bones cracking sharply as her head twists impossibly around. That noise had come from the floor below. *The police?*

A shout drifts up from beneath our feet. "Margaret!"

Sam.

Bethany snarls. Her neck snaps back to normal and she bellows a hideous animalistic sound that skitters across my mind. I bolt and scream, "Sam!"

"Don't run." Bethany groans. Her nails scrabble and scratch at the linoleum as she lopes after me. The sound makes me scream. I round the corner and run into another reception area, darting round a smaller doorway. I've taken the corner too fast, and hit the wall, bouncing off and stumbling forward on unsteady feet. "Shit!" I keep running for . . . anywhere. Just away, hoping Bethany will lose sight of me and I can find somewhere to hide.

"Margaret!" Bethany's angry shout is echoed by Sam a moment later. Only Sam's voice sounds desperate. Worried. *How did he find me?*

Terrified sobs broken by hiccups mewl out of me, and I bite down on my fist to stop any noise escaping. More corridors—endless corridors. Hopelessly lost and panting hard, I skid to a halt, listening for footsteps, but I can hear nothing over the pounding of my heart. My head screams at me to go back for Elisa, my gut drowns it out, demanding I hide. My gut wins. I tug on the nearest door handle. It doesn't turn. I try the next door. It opens into a windowless room almost identical to my initial prison cell. I can't bear the thought of being trapped again. I continue along the corridor, opening doors, but all the rooms are empty . . . then I jerk and stop. *Why was that first door locked?*

I run back, unthinking, and slam my body into the wooden door. It pops open as a throbbing pain erupts through my shoulder. Argh, they make it look so easy in the movies. A flickering bulb lights the room in spurts of white light. A woman in a tattered gray skirt and torn blouse sits slumped in a chair. Stringy black hair hides her face, her chin is pressed tightly to her chest. Her hands are bound to the chair as mine had been, and a strong scent of urine makes me gag. Her skin is clammy, but I find her pulse when I wrap my fingers around her wrist. I start picking at the silk knots. "Hey, hey can you hear me?" I tap her hand, but there is no response. I reach for her face.

She wakes, lurching back, hissing. Her eyes wild, like those of a frightened beast. I fall on my butt. "It's okay! I'm not her. I'm not Bethany." The Asian woman is like a feral cat, her mind lost in fear. *How long has she been here?* I creep closer and lower my voice. "I'm not *her*. I'm not Bethany. My name is Mig." I'm anxious to get the woman untied and out of this prison cell before we are discovered.

"Not . . . her?" The woman's voice is barely audible, scratched and raw.

"Not her," I promise. I crouch beside the chair and try to catch her unfocused gaze. She lifts her head, staring at me through her hair, and searches my face for the truth. "I need to untie you." I display my hands, so she can see my fingers— no claws.

"Who?" Her voice croaks. I wish I had water but I have nothing to give her. "Who are—?"

"I'm Mig, I want to help you. Please?" I inch closer and reach out with slow-moving fingers for her wrist. Every muscle in my body aches and my bruised shoulder burns like it's on fire. The woman's eyes don't leave my face. Her nostrils flare as I touch her skin. I move slower, not wanting to trigger her again. Dark purple, green and gold marks cover her thin arms. She rocks ever so slightly in her chair. "What's your name?" I ask, keeping my voice friendly.

"What?"

"Your name."

"Cassandra." It's whispered so quietly, I almost don't hear it.

I take her hand. *This could have been me.* It still might be. "Well, hi, Cassandra. Nice to meet you at last, though obviously not under these circumstances." I press a smile onto my face.

"What ha-hap—"

"Let's get you out of that chair and away from this room." My voice strains as I battle with the immovable knots. Blood has stained the cloth and dried like glue. I flake at it with my fingernails, but there is no use. I slip my charm free and press the blade out. This bracelet has certainly come in handy. I'll have to thank Sam once we get out of this. *If we get out of this.*

Cassandra rocks back and forth, her movements growing jagged as her breathing quickens. "She'll know." The warning turns into a high-pitched whine.

I wipe a hand over the sweat on my face. I'm worried anything I say will scare her further. I try for slow and confident, like I did with Elisa's daughter when she broke her arm. Hide my panic and pretend I know what I'm doing. "Cassandra! Listen to me. You need to focus on me, focus on my voice." The silk gives way and I pull it gently from her injured skin, suppressing a gasp as it reveals red, weeping sores.

She blinks. I'm not entirely sure she knows I'm real. I tug her out of the chair and grab her under the arms to stop her from falling. Her body is like jelly that hasn't set right. I can't carry her, but I'm not leaving her behind. "Cassandra?"

If she can't carry her own weight, I don't know what I'm going to do. I shake her arm. I don't want to hurt her, but I might have to scare her to get her adrenalin up. "Cassandra!"

Her knees lock. She holds onto me with trembling hands. "I can't."

"Yes, you can. Come on. I'm *not* leaving you here and I don't want to be here when she comes back. Do you?"

Cassandra's wild eyes, whiter than they are brown, lock onto my face. I make my voice stronger, forcing my lips into a smile. "We'll get out of here together." *What about Elisa?* I swallow back my fear for my friend. Cassandra can't wait. I have to get her out of here now and come back for Elisa.

"She's not human." Cassandra's fingers clamp onto my forearm, her grip is surprisingly strong for her weakened condition.

"I know," I whisper. "I saw her face, her true face."

"She's a monster." Cassandra digs her nails in, her stare darting to the open door. "She killed Maria and Annie." Tears pour down her face, but she doesn't wipe them away. We take a few wobbly steps toward the door. I swallow down my nausea.

Maria's dead. I have to save my breakdown for after we get out of this hell space.

"Go slow," I urge. If Cassandra falls, I won't be able to pull her back up. Though my gut screams at us to go faster, I walk her in small circles to help her find her feet. "What happened?"

Her eyes are becoming more focused. Perhaps she senses escape has finally come. "All three of us were in a long room. I think at work, the boardroom. Everything was covered in plastic, so I'm . . . not sure? Maria was killed right in front of us. Bacitriet stabbed her. Blood soaked everything. Bethany grew bigger, brighter. Annie was screaming. I . . . I was so scared."

Gritting my teeth, knowing I don't want to hear what happened next but also knowing I have to hear it, I urge her to continue. "What then?"

She's too pale and out of breath. How can I get her out of here? "There was a storm, an explosion . . . I don't . . . Annie screamed. Everything lit up, sparking like lightning and I heard a crackle, a loud bang. Annie . . . Annie was . . . gone. Bethany's phone exploded and she lost her mind. They moved us that night. Out of the office, and out of the city. We came here. I don't know where we are. I've been here for such a long time." Her voice breaks. "I'm so tired."

"That's how Annie ended up in Bacitriet's servers," I say. "I guess souls can't just float about, they need somewhere to go. She must have been sucked into Bethany's work phone." I wonder if Bethany messed up the spell. Why didn't Annie return to her own body? Then again, if my soul had been extracted, I wouldn't know what to do or how to get back in either.

"What?" Cassandra blinks at me, her nose crinkling as if she's trying to decipher my ramblings.

"Nothing." Bethany has three souls again: Cassandra, Elisa and me. She will cast her spell soon. I have to get Cassandra out of here right now. Elisa will be safe if we leave, and then the police will rescue her and everything will go back to normal.

Plan in place, I pull Cassandra toward the door, my body protesting every step, but the closer we get, the more she struggles. "Come on!" I urge.

"The moon . . . is it full?"

I freeze. "Yes."

"She has you and me . . . no, it's okay. She needs three. Under a full moon."

"Let's go." I drag Cassandra out into the corridor.

"What? Why? We're okay. She won't hurt us yet." Cassandra's eyes are wide, her nostrils flaring, and her ragged nails dig into my arm.

"She has three and night is falling. We have to go now. Move," I insist. Her face screws up as she understands my meaning.

Somewhere below us, a woman screams, loud and throaty. Metal clashes like knives in a cutlery drawer. I drag Cassandra forward as another scream tears the air. There's a grunting sound, and it grows louder. The only way out takes us directly toward the battle, but an inhuman roar stops us in our tracks.

"What was that?" Cassandra digs her heels in.

"Our rescuer," I tell her. At least, I hope it is. As we pass the surgical suite, Cassandra jerks away from my hold.

"You work for her, don't you? You're bringing me there to kill me. No! Let me go!"

"Hey!" I snap. Cassandra's pupils have shrunk to pinpricks. They roll back in her head and she falls onto me, crashing us both to the floor.

I shove her dead weight off my legs. "Cassandra?" There is no response.

She is out cold.

I struggle to my feet, my side aching where Cassandra's bony limbs have jabbed into me. Tears well in my eyes as I study the broken woman on the dusty floor. I chew the inside of my cheek. I could leave. Go with plan A. Get the hell out on my own. I can call the police and wait for them to rescue Cassandra and Elisa. If Bethany needs three souls, then as long as I'm not here, they'll be safe. That's the logical approach, but guilt gnaws at my conscience. *Ugh.* Nope, I can't do it. I can't leave her now that I've found her.

"I'll just take a look," I whisper, even though Cassandra can't possibly hear me. I creep down the corridor toward the sounds of grunting and shouting, hurled abuse and thumping. A lot of thumping, like people bouncing off walls. The clash of metal too.

Cassandra screams.

I spin around, and I'm horrified to see Bacitriet holding Cassandra around the neck. He hoists her high above the floor, her feet dangling as she kicks weakly. He isn't watching Cassandra; he's staring directly at me. He still looks like a frail old man, but he can't be. Not in reality. How is he lifting her like that?

"I thought you knew better, Ms. Solder."

I back up. Can he chase me while holding Cassandra in the air? Time to find out.

"No!" Cassandra moans. I pray she'll understand my choice and I will her to hear my promise to come back for her.

I run.

In seconds, I find the staircase and pelt down it, two steps at a time. Breath scours my lungs. At some point, I'd stopped crying. I guess even fear has an expiration date. I hit the next floor and run along the corridor. "Sam!" I scream.

For all I know, he's already dead and my scream has alerted Bethany to my location. I keep running, out into an open room. The entrance foyer by the look of it. It's a room the size of a basketball court, with holes cut into the linoleum marking the places where furniture has been forcibly removed. A semi-circular reception bench bisects the hall and beyond that are two large doors, nailed shut with heavy wooden planks. Beside the planks is a smaller glass door, almost hidden in the wall of wood. It's dark outside, and the glass reflects my pale face back at me. If that door doesn't open, I swear I'm going straight through it.

Clashing steel collides, creating sparks like an angle grinder on a construction site. It snaps my attention to the space beside the reception desk. Two figures move out of a dark corridor in a crazy dance of parry and thrust. I blink back spots and squint to make the figures clearer.

They aren't dancing, but their fight has the balletic quality of experts in their field. Two warriors in peak perfection, like a scene from a movie. Sam's raised arms hold long blades of glinting silver. He lunges and twists, inhumanly fast, as he attacks. Bethany counters every move, spitting and slashing with her claws. She leaps impossibly high, flipping over Sam's head to land on all fours behind him, bounding back up to lunge at him again and again. He darts out of reach each time.

"Sam!" I cry.

His movements falter as he glances my way, and I realize my mistake immediately. The split-second distraction is all Bethany needs. She slashes at Sam's face, roaring in triumph.

"No!" I scream.

Too fast for me to see, he twists, catching her claws against his swords. Bethany pushes and slips to the side, breaking through his defenses, and her jagged mouth bites down on his exposed neck. My breath catches. *No!* I almost run forward, but Sam bellows and throws her off. Bethany hits the wall, rattling windows and wood, leaving a full-body dent in the plasterboard. She falls to the ground with a thump. Chalky chunks of wall cascade onto her head from above, and a tube light shatters as it hits the tiled floor beside her legs.

My gaze finds Sam as he staggers, falling to one knee, blood pouring from the wound in his neck. *Your fault. You've killed him.* I step toward him and Sam's dark eyes lock on mine. "Get out of here," he commands.

I run for the doors.

I hit the glass full tilt and bounce back, crashing to the floor. Light flashes before my eyes, leaving me stunned. Even my teeth hurt. "Fuck!" Forcing my aching body up, I stagger to the door again, swearing, and tug at the handle. "No! Come on." I brace and push at the glass. Nothing. Reversing my action, I tug with all my might. My shoulder screams in protest. Trapped. *It's glass, you idiot. Break it.* Red dots fill my vision. I pound against the thick glass, but it's no use. I need something sharp or heavy.

"Margaret!"

I freeze. *Oh no.* Shooting a glance over my shoulder, I see Sam slumped at Bethany's feet. She has her fist in his hair. When she realizes she has my attention, she tilts his head back further than it should be able to go, her other claw held ready to slash open his exposed throat. Blood stains his face and shirt in large patches.

"Friend of yours?"

My mouth is bone-dry. I can't leave him here to die and Bethany knows it.

She shakes Sam's head, eliciting a moan. "Margaret! Come back here," she calls again, her voice all sweetness and light. "I *will* kill him, Margaret."

"No," he groans.

The demon needs three souls. But do the souls all have to be women? I look back through the window. How far off is dawn? Cassandra said Bethany's spell must be done under a full moon. Is that midnight or at any time through the night? Can she perform whatever she's planning once the sun rises?

My heart clenches. Sam came here to save me. I can't let him die.

I drop my hand and turn away from the glass. Bethany releases Sam. He collapses. She peers down at him, teeth bared in an evil smirk. "Where ever did you find him, Margaret? He's *yummy.*"

Tears roll down my face and I don't respond. She pokes his body with a clawed foot. He doesn't make a sound.

Please don't be dead.

"What *is* he?" She bends over, a strange, fixated expression on her face. She sniffs his neck.

"What do you mean?"

"His scent is odd. Makes my eyes itch," she says thoughtfully. She regards my confusion with disdain. "He's not human."

Not human? That's not possible. She's wrong. She has to be. A shiver runs over my skin. My cold neck. I always get it around Bethany, Bacitriet . . . and Sam.

Oh. Shit. Sam's one of them? I force the horror of my sudden knowledge out of my mind. If I dwell on it, I'll freeze entirely. "What are *you*?"

She gestures for me to move away from the window. "It won't save you to know what I am, Margaret."

Sam's fingers twitch. I think of my favorite fictional heroes. Buffy, Doctor Who, Captain Marvel, Veronica Mars. At this point, all of them would stall. *I can do that.* I keep my stare glued to Bethany's face. "Tell me anyway."

She snorts. "I'm Gendruit."

"Bless you."

"This is not a game," she snarls.

As if I don't know that. I'm gonna die here. Sam's gonna die, and Elisa too. I'm scared—totally terrified—but how will that help me? "I'm sorry. I just . . . come on, this is crazy. You're a receptionist. I'm a personal assistant. I don't understand any of this."

A sharp spin sends her back to Sam. She kicks him in the head and his body falls limp once more. *Sam!* I swallow hard. "A Gendruit? What is that? A monster?"

She sneers. "Monster? Please, I'm a demon."

A steady scrape of uneven footsteps come closer. I inch toward to the door as Bacitriet shuffles into view. "Him too?"

Bethany laughs, great huffing breaths between sharp teeth. "Not in the slightest." Turning to Bacitriet, she points at Sam's body. "Get that somewhere secure."

"Very well." Bacitriet gives an obsequious bow and hefts Sam over his shoulder, barely grunting at the dead weight.

She's the boss? She called Bacitriet a pet so she must be. What did she do to him? How could an old man have the strength of a younger one?

Bethany approaches, her smell preceding her. "Whatever your hero is, I will discover it. Come along, Margaret. We have so little time left."

That's what I'm afraid of.

I keep a steady distance between me and those sharp claws as I step over Sam's discarded sword. Bethany's smirk grows wider. Does she think I'll try to snatch it up and attack her? Please. I know she'd be on me in less time than it takes for me to bend over. A second sword glistens with dark gray liquid; Sam drew blood. If someone as strong and as obviously skilled as Sam was unable to defeat her, what hope do I have?

Every step from freedom sounds a death knell in my head. This is it. The end.

I'm going to die.

Chapter 31

Bethany tightens the silk around my wrist, as if cutting off the circulation is punishment for my escape. I grimace, the pain makes my eyes water. From the hospital gurney she's tied me to, I eye Sam over her head, slumped in the chair Bacitriet shoved him into. Blood coats his face, matting his hair, and the wound in his neck looks putrid. Bacitriet has tied him to the chair with plastic zip ties.

Is Sam really a monster? He's certainly imposing, intimidating and exudes confidence usually. Right now, he wouldn't scare a ghost.

Bethany pats my head and steps back. "There, now. It won't be long." Bacitriet stands watching her, unblinking. "Fetch the others," she orders. He bows and limps away, his footsteps scraping the floor.

My hands aren't trembling anymore. For some reason, my heart is beating in its regular rhythm, as if I'm grocery shopping. Maybe it's a natural reaction to death. Perhaps my subconscious has already accepted my imminent demise.

Bethany drags my hospital bed closer. The wheel on the right rear leg is faulty, it keeps locking up, jerking me sideways. There are two other gurneys in the operating theater, making the already cramped room feel even smaller. The handrail on the bed beside mine hangs drunkenly off the side, and the foot of the last bed sags, broken in the middle. Bethany arranges the three beds like the spokes on a wheel, the heads pressed together tightly.

Will it hurt to have my soul stripped from my body? I imagine it will. Sam said it hurt. I need to stall. I replay all the weird things back from the past few days, searching for something to say to extend the delay. I've got so many questions about how everything fits together. If I'm going to die I want to die at least understanding what the heck has been going on. "What was the signed soul contract about?"

Bethany straightens and releases my ankle. "What?"

"The contract signed in blood that Bacitriet had me deliver the other day. Is that how you get the empty bodies for your people, the demons who escaped with you? And what was with the bloody gym bag? Was that your bag? I assume the scarves and the makeup were yours. Was that your house, I mean Bethany's house, that I delivered it to?"

"What are you talking about?" She snaps her misshapen lips, her rot-stinking breath inches from my face. All I can see are her teeth, and I gag on the smell.

"Janquil Nyugen's soul extraction. You didn't know about his contract?"

"There were no others. All have been housed."

Well, that's interesting. "So who is in Janquil? Doesn't Bacitriet work for you?" I hum as various scenarios play out in my head. "You do know all the demons jammed into the human bodies don't you? Your faction or cronies, or what have you? Unless . . . unless Bacitriet is getting more out. Do all of the demons there support you, Bethany? What is Bacitriet doing? Sick of your control, is he? Maybe he's freelancing? If he's not totally loyal to you, then what's his game?"

She hisses and spins away, her hands a blur as she readies a vial. Pink liquid sloshes around inside as she moves toward a tray of sharp implements. I jerk my leg away when she slams a scalpel into the mattress and howls.

Perhaps I can get them to turn on each other, and buy us more time. "You didn't know, did you?" Bethany lowers her head, breathing loudly through her nose. "Bacitriet's up to something. What's he planning? A way to save himself when you get dragged back to hell?" I glance at Sam. "Did he give you up? Report you to the hunters to save himself?"

"Shut up!"

I barely flinch. *Got you.* "Bethany, can you trust him? Who is he working for if it's not you?" Sam's head twitches, but I ignore him and focus on the monster. "Who does Bacitriet need bodies for?"

Bethany snarls and then sweeps from the room, leaving me staring at the door. *Holy crap, that actually worked!*

I drop my head to the thin pillow, breathing in the scent of dust and mothballs. I can't see Sam properly from here. "Sam?"

"Ugh."

"Sam?" I'd seen him fight. If anyone can get us out of this, it's him, provided he isn't over there dying on me. I activate the blade on the cross charm and start sawing the silk around my wrist. No matter what happens, anything is better than just sitting here, waiting for death. "Sam?"

"What happened?" His voice cracks. He clears his throat with a cough, but it remains thick. "I see our situation has not improved."

"You're good." I put as much sarcasm as I can into my words, hissing as I cut myself on the blade. "Damn it."

Sam sniffs. "What happened? Are you hurt?"

"I cut myself. I'm more worried about you. She bit you."

"Poisonous bite. It's affected my strength." He coughs, a wet, phlegmy sound. "And my vision, it seems."

"Are you still bleeding?"

"The wound is closing. Slower than it should, but it is closing. I need time to get my strength back."

Closing? *He's not human, remember.* He's got to be a vampire. No that's not right. I've seen him outside during the day. What the hell is he? "I'm getting us out of here. Trying to, anyway. Thanks for the charm. It works like . . . well, you get the idea." My fingers keep cramping, twisting high to manipulate the tiny razor.

He grunts, straining against his own bindings, and I hope his Incredible Hulk manoeuver will work. It doesn't. He slumps back. "This doesn't look promising."

"Bethany's preparing her spell. We don't have long," I say, sawing away. "And if we get out of this, you're going to tell me everything. Starting with who and what you truly are."

He grunts again. I get one hand free, making quick work of the second scarf. His head twists, catching sight of my movement. "Hurry."

"Do you think I'm taking my time?" I focus on the fraying threads.

"Why didn't you run?" he asks. The legs of his chair scrape the floor as he heaves from side to side, turning slightly. Dried blood coats his neck but, incredibly, the wound does look smaller than it did a little while ago.

"You were hurt. She threatened to kill you."

He leans his head back, eyes closing as if in disbelief.

"What are you?" I demand as my other hand comes loose. I sit up and saw at the bindings on my legs.

"You should have run."

"You're not human," I accuse.

"No."

I'd expected him to lie. "Are you a demon?"

"No."

"*She* beat you," I remind him. "Do the demons you hunt usually beat you?"

He lifts his head, meeting my eyes. "I'm dangerous."

I scoff. "You sure look it." I swing my legs over the side of the bed. A groan escapes me as I put weight onto my feet. Every twist brings my aches flaring back to life. "We're probably going to die here, what does it matter if I know?"

"I cannot," he grits out. "I am sworn against it."

What does that mean? I gape for a moment, then move toward him on wobbly legs and saw at the plastic around his wrist. "No silk for you, I guess."

"I am not a good man, Margaret." His voice is soft. The intensity of his stare burrows into me. He *does* look dangerous, and I should be scared . . . but I'm not afraid of him. He came here to rescue me.

"Are you going to kill me, Sam?" My fingers still on his wrist. His pulse beats fast beneath my fingertips.

"Of course not," he breathes.

My voice is equally soft. "Swear to it."

"I swear." His hand twists to capture mine. "You should not trust me."

But I do. "Are you lying?"

He shakes his head. "Never to you."

I lift an eyebrow. "Better the devil you know, right?"

He smirks, his eyes closing for the briefest of moments. "Indeed."

Footsteps startle me upright. I'd only cut through the plastic tie around Sam's right wrist. "Lie back down," he urges. "When the moment comes, run."

"But—"

"Promise me, Margaret."

"Fine. Yes." I jump onto the trolley bed, my aches screaming. It brings tears to my eyes. I breathe through the pain and wrap the silk around my wrists, holding them still and pray Bethany won't notice the cuts.

How will I know when to run? My gaze falls on Sam's bowed head. *I'll know.*

Bethany stomps back in, dragging Elisa behind her. Cold sweat covers my skin from my fingertips to my hairline. I can't spot any bruises or injuries on my friend. Bacitriet limps through the door, carrying Cassandra. Her vacant expression tells me she's given up the fight.

"Mig!" Elisa cries, catching sight of me.

I rise up onto my elbows, making sure to keep my arms still. "Are you okay?"

"What the heck is going on?" Elisa's eyes widen as she takes in the room, me and then finally Sam. I'd promised Sam I'd run, but there's no way I'm leaving here without Elisa and Cassandra. Hopefully Elisa and I can carry the weakened woman out between us while Sam does his thing. Whatever his thing is. *Not human, remember?*

"Mig, what's happening?" Elisa's wobbly voice betrays her terror. She cries out as Bethany throws her across the empty bed next to mine. I want to leap up and drag her away from the evil creature. I bite my tongue hard enough to taste blood and glare at the back of Sam's head. We have to act now before Elisa and Cassandra are tied down and can no longer help us.

Bacitriet shuffles closer, lowering the practically comatose woman to the last bed. His face is a mass of bruises. Clearly, Bethany advised him of her displeasure over the contract. Part of me is glad. He deserves it and more, but Bethany has kept him alive. *She still needs him.*

I'd only released one of Sam's hands. When he makes his move, precious seconds will be lost while he frees himself. He'll lose the element of surprise. I have to distract Bethany and give him the best chance. "You trust him now, do you?" All eyes snap to me. I catch the tiny shake of Sam's head. Can't he understand I'm trying to help?

"Mig?" Elisa's voice is barely audible.

Bacitriet's focus comes to me, so I keep digging. "Did he tell you he was doing it to help you? Maybe he's the one who stuffed up Annie's extraction? After all, they were his computers. Is this all part of *his* master plan?"

Bacitriet snarls loud enough to shake the walls. His crooked teeth bend and elongate into a snout. Air catches in my throat.

"Control yourself," Bethany orders. Bacitriet straightens, and his face pops back into place.

Cassandra launches upright and lets out a scream that shatters everyone's eardrums. Bacitriet flinches back, hands clapped to his ears, and crouches to escape the unending noise. Bethany reacts the same way, suddenly off-balance, and staggers into the wall. Sam lets out a roar. His back ripples in a way it shouldn't and he stands, snapping the plastic tie around his left wrist. He runs at Bethany, who is unsteady on her feet, still shaking her head. She gnashes her teeth and slashes sharp claws in his face. Sam shoves a shoulder at her chest and pushes her into the wall, his hands wrapped around her throat. I spring from the bed and, without particularly planning to, knee Bacitriet in the head. He falls back, and his body changes. Bones crack as his head elongates, sprouting coarse black hair.

My heart thumps double-time at the sight. "Shit!" I grab Elisa's hand and pull her off the bed. She shouts something in my ear, but I can't hear her over Cassandra's continuous screams. The insides of my ears feel wet and cold. I'm sure they are bleeding.

The transformation seems to take a lot out of Bacitriet. He wavers on his feet, moaning and shaking his head. He'll recover in moments. I snatch something silver and sharp off the trolley and stab it into his shoulder. He growls low in his throat. We have to get out of here *now*.

Furious hand-to-hand fighting between Sam and Bethany sends the trolley next to me flying into the wall. Sam yells over his shoulder. *"Run!"*

"El, help me." Together, we drag Cassandra off the bed, and her scream cuts off as she hits the ground. My muscles are nothing but pain. I force myself forward and loop an arm around Cassandra's waist. "Come on." Elisa presses in on the girl's other side, her hand brushing my shoulder. I look across at her. "Hey."

My best friend's eyes are red, her lips pale in the dim light. "Hey."

Between us, we maneuver Cassandra toward the door, jerking to a halt as Bethany slams into the wall right in front of us. Sam is on her heels, pounding his fists into her body. I tug our three-person conga line around them.

"Mig, what is going on?" Elisa is trembling. Lines of mascara have left long black marks on her cheeks, her skin deathly pale by comparison.

"We have to get downstairs."

"That woman is a . . . a . . ."

"Receptionist."

"Bull dust."

"Yeah."

Between us, Cassandra is a zombie, animated but with no life to her. At least she moves under our direction. I just wish she'd move faster.

"Mig?"

I puff out a laugh. "Short version: Bethany and Bacitriet are literal monsters. They killed Annie and Maria. This is Cassandra. Bethany is planning to use us as . . . fuel for her spell to remain on Earth. Sam came to the rescue."

Our pace slows as we hit the stairs. I tighten my grip on Cassandra's arm and shuffle her forward.

"That's—"

"Nuts? I know. We have to get out of here."

"Where are we?"

"Abandoned hospital, I think."

"F . . . f . . . fuzzballs!"

"Yeah."

Any second now, Bacitriet is going to catch us. Or Bethany will, after she defeats Sam. I'm not going back upstairs for hell or death. If Bacitriet appears, I'll go down fighting.

"The glass door. That's our way out."

A loud howl destroys our taste of freedom. My heart stops —at least it feels that way.

"Go, go, go," I shout, and we run in an awkward, odd gallop.

A monstrous shadow leaps over our heads, skidding across the linoleum. It turns with a screech of claws. Covered in black fur longer than my arm, the creature's teeth drip saliva. Its lips rise exposing more teeth, snarling viciously.

Bacitriet.

"Fuck!" My boss is a giant hound.

My heart gives a heavy thump, kick-starting back into rhythm, and races in a way that makes my body twitch. Adrenalin. Red eyes bore into mine as the creature stalks forward. Our standoff is a joke, and he knows it. Crouching his upper body, he crawls along the cracked floor like a cat playing with a mouse, standing between us and freedom.

Elisa screams and releases Cassandra. I'm forced to drop her too or she'll pull me to the ground with her. One of Sam's blood-stained blades lies beneath the reception desk. I dive on it and hold it up like I know what to do with it. The Bacitriet-hound snuffs and barks.

I firm my grip around the blade hilt. *Here, doggy, doggy . . .*

Behind the Bacitriet-hound, the window explodes into a million pieces, shards large and small spraying across the hospital floor. The Bacitriet-hound springs sideways, crouching low, and growls at the two figures standing in the gaping entrance.

They are dressed in padded army fatigues, dark glasses fastened to their faces with elastic. Two perfectly set perms, one white and one gray, and the scent of lavender drifting in with the light morning breeze.

No freaking way.

"This looks like quite the party. Sorry we're late, Margaret," Rose calls. The giant crossbow in her hand doesn't waver from where it is aimed straight at the Bacitriet-hound's head.

Berry doesn't say a word, only salutes me with her rapier.

What. The. Freaking. Hell?

The Bacitriet-hound roars and springs directly at my grandmothers.

I let out a scream.

Chapter 32

"Mig, duck!"

I hit the ground at Rose's order, landing over Cassandra to protect her too. Elisa drops down beside us.

Thwap thawp.

The Bacitriet-beast lets out a high-pitched howl that shakes the foundations. More glass shatters, spraying the floor. When all is quiet, I lift my head.

"Mig, your—" Elisa's voice wobbles.

My jaw is still metaphorically on the floor. "I know. I don't—" The reality won't sink in. It's impossible. Berry is wielding her rapier like a pro, letting out a war whoop as she runs at the staggering Bacitriet-beast. One of Rose's arrows juts from the monster's jaw. Rose nocks another shaft into her crossbow and ratchets it back with sharp, practiced movements.

"Margaret, you need to move, dear," Berry orders.

The ground shudders, rolling us sideways. The Bacitriet-beast stumbles as Rose's arrow penetrates his thigh.

"Honey, get your friends out. We can't be worrying about you now," Rose shouts, ratcheting her bow again.

The beast growls. He shakes himself and swipes one massive claw at Berry. She darts out of his way, stabbing her rapier into his leg. He lets loose a cry that raises the hairs on the back of my neck. She dives out of his reach.

Attacking my grandmothers? Oh, I don't think so, mate.

I'm still clutching Sam's sword. I race forward and thrust it into Bacitriet's hairy hide. It slides in like butter. Hot black goo spurts out from the wound, speckling my hand.

I don't have time to think. I duck, withdrawing the sword as he turns on me, and slice at whatever I can reach, expecting to hear claws next to my ear the second before he rips my head off.

But he only roars in my face. The stench of raw meat shoots up my nose and embeds into my brain. Strands of my hair blow across my eyes, blinding me as he staggers away. Berry takes off after him. Rose follows, spinning back to shout at me, "Get your friends out of here!"

Silence falls like a curtain.

"What the actual fuck?" I stare at the disaster area that is the hospital's waiting room, and at all the glass, plaster and wood. A black puddle is spreading from my feet to the stairs. The goo covers my hand and the sword I hold. More glass and shards of wood lay scattered where the beast took out a chunk of the reception desk. I firm my grip on Sam's sword. Elisa touches my shoulder, snapping my awareness back to the present. Sound returns in a rush. Cassandra's sobbing. Elisa's rapid breathing. An occasional sniffle—that's me.

"Let's go," I say, and kneel beside Cassandra. Her body is like cooked spaghetti. I fight to get her upright, but it's useless when there's no way I'm going to let go of my weapon to use both hands. "Elisa, help me."

"We need to get out of here."

"Yes. Help me," I repeat. Her blank stare sends a cold shiver down my spine. "Elisa?" I understand she's scared—heck, I'm petrified—but somewhere in this nightmarish building, my grandmothers are fighting a giant hell beast and Sam is battling a demon. We can't just stand here processing what has happened.

"The devil," Cassandra mumbles. She stares straight at me, her hand becoming a vice around my wrist. Steady pressure squeezes until I fear my bones will break.

"What are you talking about?"

Cassandra's eyes roll back. I tumble against the wall and fall onto my butt. Elisa helps push the unconscious woman off me.

"We have to get her up," I say.

"She's out cold."

"Grab her feet." I shove the sword into my belt where it dangles down one leg, soaking my jeans with black blood. I hoist Cassandra's upper body in my arms, and we stagger toward the gaping hole. Upon reaching the path that lines the building outside, I lower Cassandra to the ground and pull the sword from my belt.

"Mig? What are you doing?" Elisa asks. She doesn't move, standing stiff, solid, just staring at me.

"My grandmothers are in there. I'm not leaving until they do." In my head, I'm not thinking of my grandmothers—well, I am—but I'm also thinking of Sam. Sam, who came to rescue me. Sam, who got hurt trying to save me. Sam, my neighbor and who I hope might be my friend. *Maybe more?* Despite being not human. He kept his promise. Protection. He came to save me, so I'm going back for him.

"If Cassandra wakes up, get her out of here," I order. Without a backward glance I return to the hospital.

*

A scream hits the air, but I can't tell who made it. My heart pounds as I creep toward the shouting that follows. Sweat slicks my palms. I clench my fingers tighter around the hilt of the thin-bladed sword, the handle solid and cold in my grip. My shirt sticks to my skin in places that restrict movement.

How is any of this real?

My life changed so much in only a few weeks. All I'd wanted was a new job. Instead, I'd gotten involved in a murder mystery, and now I'm tiptoeing into a supernatural killing ground to help my grandmothers and my new neighbor fight real monsters. My body trembles as every step takes me closer toward doom. I have no plan. This is so unlike me.

Berry shouts something; Rose bellows a reply. I can't wrap my mind around it. My grandmothers are . . . what . . . ? Demon hunters? And Sam? I don't know what he is. I'll only find out if we get out of here alive. My knuckles ache as I grip the sword's hilt tight with both hands.

There is a grunt and a hoarse male cry from somewhere up ahead. *Sam?* I run into the chaos, but before I can make sense of what I'm seeing, a body hits the floor at my feet.

Sam.

His eyes are closed and he's covered in black blood. His chest jerks as if something is forcing him up off the ground by emerging from his back. *What the . . . ?*

"Margaret, get out of here!" Berry shouts. She grapples with the Bacitriet-beast, dodging the staggering monster's claws while keeping her hand pressed tight to his side. Black liquid pours from the rapier buried in his skin. The thwack of another arrow alerts me to where Rose is: hanging up in the rafters, dangling from one hand, aiming her crossbow at Bethany with the other. Bethany spins circles in the middle of the room, clawed fingers flapping at her back, searching for the arrow buried in her shoulder. Her arms aren't long enough. She twists and hisses angrily, fixated on removing the shaft.

Sam grunts and rolls over, pushing to his feet.

"Here." I shove the sword into his hands. He grins, exposing blood-stained teeth. His swollen cheek is like a ping-pong ball, and there are black and blue bruises around each eye.

"Thanks." He runs at the Bacitriet-beast and attacks from the rear while Berry attacks from below, pulling her rapier free to thrust up again and again. Two on one now, the Bacitriet-beast looks on its last legs. It staggers first one way, then the other.

"Go help Rose," Berry bellows at Sam. He changes direction and heads for Bethany. The demon has got the arrow out and is now playing with Rose like a cat with a string. I don't know how to help her. I fear I'll only get in the way. Berry keeps pace with the Bacitriet-beast as he grunts and falls on his face. His heaving sides shudder and, with a final intake of breath, falls still. The Bacitriet-beast—my boss—is dead.

I look for Rose. Bethany leaps up and rips Rose down from her line. They hit the ground together, Bethany tumbling one way, Rose the other.

"No!" I scream. Berry and Sam race to Rose's side.

Before I can move, sharp pain explodes in my hip, leaving me gasping. I slap my hand down and pull away fingers that have turned bloody.

I've been stabbed.

Chapter 33

I turn, wondering at the cause of the sudden and insanely painful hole in my side. I press my hand to the wound, trying to keep hot sticky blood inside my body. *What hit me?* The staircase looms in front of me. At the top of the stairs, there is a shadowy shape of a man. I can't see his face. Blood drips from my side onto the floor and I stare at it, unable to comprehend what is happening. I lose balance and someone catches me.

Sam? A stinky, sweaty shape presses against my back. Bethany hisses into my ear and her arm wraps around my throat, cutting off my scream. She drags me toward the stairs, her clawed hand clamped over my mouth. I struggle wildly, grabbing at Bethany's thick leathery arm and pulling with all my strength, but I can't shift her. We twist and I stare up at the stairs. I can't lift my head so I can't see beyond the feet encased in white snakeskin.

Help me!

The feet turn away. My bracelet flashes, regaining my attention. The angel wings tap-dance against my skin. The cross charm!

I let my hands fall to my sides, slumping as though I'm giving up the fight. It forces Bethany to take more of my weight. I look for Sam or Berry, but they are focused on Rose.

I'm on my own.

With my little fingernail, I press on the cross charm and activate the blade, imagining I can hear it unsheathe with a tiny *ting*. I'll only get one shot at this.

"Can't . . . breathe," I mumble and let my whole body sag, becoming a heavier burden.

The hand across my mouth loosens. Bethany's grip shifts as her other arm takes my weight. I dig the tiny blade deep into her leg and fall between her arms as her grip reflexively opens and she jerks away. I bellow. "Sam! Rose, Berry!"

Bethany claws at my body. I roll away and clamber to my feet, lashing out with an elbow. I connect with something that makes a squishy crack before I run. My side screams in pain at the movement, forcing air from my lungs, but I don't stop. To stop will be to die.

Not today.

I haven't survived all of this to fall at the final barrier.

"Margaret!"

I crash into a hard body, punching anything I can reach, searching the ground for white shoes. All I see are black ones. Hands grab me and I lose my mind, kicking and punching with everything I have, using every inch of the fear and rage in my body to fight back.

"Margaret! Margaret, it's Sam. You are safe." His soft voice is welcome to my ears and it stops my flailing. I peer up into the handsome face marred with dark bruises, his skin splattered with blood. He smiles and I can't help but smile back. "What happened?"

I twist, searching for Bethany. She has collapsed in a heap behind me.

Did I kill her? The stench of blood is overwhelming. I spy the blood pouring from her shoulder and sides, creating a pool around her unmoving form. She'd been fatally wounded well before grabbing me. By the looks of it I'd just stalled long enough for her to bleed out.

"White shoes," I say, my gaze darting around wildly. Where is he? That man—the watcher. I see nothing but Sam's caring stare. My throat hurts with every breath I take. As does my side. Tears blur my vision.

"Margaret?"

I press my hand to my side.

"Margaret, you are injured."

"Yep. Hurts like hell." I reach for the wall. Sam grabs my arm and helps me to the floor. "Where's Bacitriet?"

"Your Grandmother Berry laid the final blow."

I lean into Sam's damp side, inhaling his musky smell. "Where are they?"

"Clearing the scene," he says.

"Is she okay? Rose?"

"Perfectly well. Her fall looked bad but she controlled her descent, and those outfits are well-padded."

I glance up at him. "Wait, my grandmothers are cleaning up Bacitriet's body?" Sam's hands are warm against my skin. "Are they really okay?"

"Yes. Who are they?"

"My grandmothers." Has he lost too much blood? Hit his head? He knows who they are.

Oh.

He means the fighting.

"I thought I knew them but . . ." I stare blankly at the floor, then spear him with a sharp look. "I could ask you the same question." I peer down to find him holding my hand.

"It was very brave of you to come back. Earlier tonight, you stayed to cut me free when you should have run. Before that, you offered yourself to the demon when she would have clawed out my throat. You saved my life several times today." He presses a hot kiss to my cheek. Heat spreads through my body right up to my skull, making me dizzy. I turn my head connecting our lips, and pour pain, desperation and confusion into him. He groans and falls into my kiss as if against his will. I almost pull back but his hands tighten around my sides. I gasp at the sensation of sharp knives digging into my skin. He releases me instantly, whispering apologies.

"You came. You said I was under your protection. You saved me." I tell him. He had come when no one else could. "How did you know I was here?"

"You called for me."

I did? I think back to that moment in the corridor after my initial escape. I *had* called for him, but how had he heard me? "Sam, are you a demon?"

"No. I am a far worse kind of monster."

I shake my head. "No. You saved me."

"Always," he whispers as his eyes soften. His arms tighten around me again and I press up to kiss him.

"Margaret?"

I'm pulled from Sam's lips by soft hands, and surrounded by the smell of cold cream and lavender. Four arms, Berry and Rose, squeeze the life out of me. Berry's flak jacket is hard and a little wet beneath my fingers.

When my grandmothers finally let go, I fix them with my best I'm-pissed-off-at-you-lying-old-biddies stare. "You owe me an explanation."

"We're glad you're okay," Berry says simply.

"Are you hurt?" Rose asks, sliding her crossbow behind her back. My hand falls to my wounded side and Rose gasps at the sight of it. "We must close that immediately."

"I'm fine," I say. I'm determined to get the truth out of them. "What are you even doing here?"

They fall silent. Berry glances at Rose and shrugs. "Margaret—"

"We're demon hunters."

"Rose!" Berry's lips tighten into a straight line.

"We can't hide it now, Berry," Rose tells her. "Come along, Margaret. Let's find your friends."

"Hide what? Rose, I don't . . . Sam, I . . . Sam?" I turn and fall sideways, Rose catches me just in time, setting me on my feet as I search the room.

Sam is gone. My chest tightens at the realization that he's left. But he promised to protect me. "Always," he said. Where did he go? My lips turn cold.

"Best he be on his way," Rose says.

"What? Why?"

"Whoever he is, he has proven himself to be a friend. However, he is still hiding something. With the authorities' imminent arrival, it would be best he not be interviewed. Don't worry too much about it for now," Berry says, and pulls a bandage from her chest pocket. "Come, let's have a look at that wound."

I hiss when her fingers poke my injured side. "I'm so confused."

"All you need to know, dear, is that demons are real. A long time ago, they escaped from hell and we've been putting them back ever since."

Hell. Sam said he let them out, and that it was his punishment to hunt them down and put them back. "But, how . . . ?"

"Family business, dear. I guess it's time for you too, but we'll talk about that later, after we fix this wound," Rose says.

Berry slaps Rose's forearm. "I thought we were keeping her out of it?"

"We were." Rose glances at me. "Your parents don't know. You must not tell them."

A laugh bubbles out of me. "Tell them what? That their moms are monster hunters?"

"Worry about it tomorrow." Rose pushes Berry out of the way and helps me stand. Berry pops up on my right side. "Now, don't look as we walk past, alright? It is not a pleasant sight out there."

I nod. I have no intention of looking. My head feels full of cotton wool, and I sway as we wobble through the room. I see things regardless of my promise. Blood, damaged walls, a hound's paw . . . *Oh God.* I slam my eyes shut and let my grandmothers lead me outside.

Chapter 34

My feet stop on the cobblestone path that leads from the hospital to the gravel carpark. I stare in surprise at Detective Bryce. She's wearing another perfectly fitted charcoal gray suit, with a flak jacket wrapped over the top half. It gives her a strange, bulky appearance. She slams the door of her dark sedan closed and walks toward us.

"What are you doing here?" I gasp as my ankle rolls on the gravel, sending pain ricocheting around my body. I peer around for my friend. "Where's Elisa? Cassandra?" I glance back at the hospital. Three levels of red brick and large stone blocks loom over us. Many of the upper floor windows are boarded up, and broken glass lies outside the window my grandmothers shattered for their dramatic entry.

My shoes crunch over the loose gravel. I can't see any gardens from here. They must be around the back.

"We found your friends outside. My people have taken them to the local hospital. You did a brave thing, Ms. Solder. Those girls did not stop asking about you."

Rose opens the back door of Bryce's car and pushes me to sit down. She climbs in after me and yanks a plastic tub with a cross on it from the footwell. "That's how we got here." Her fingers dig into my side, bringing fresh tears to my eyes.

"You know my grandmothers? Both of them?" I ask Bryce, ignoring what Rose is doing beside me.

The detective squats down in front of me. "Is she okay?" she asks, eyeballing Berry.

My grandma nods. "Crazy kid came back for us."

"Hey, stop talking over me. Ouch, Rose!"

"I'm sorry, dear." Rose pours more of whatever it is in the bottle over my side. It burns and I gasp. "Hold still," she mumbles, holding up a needle.

My stomach surges. I push her off and gag, but thankfully, there is no vomit. Knives and swords I'm apparently fine with, but I draw the line at needles. I glare at the detective. "You know about . . ."

"Demons?" She nods. "I'm sorry I didn't warn you. You wouldn't have believed me anyway."

I grunt and glance at the horror hospital we've just escaped. "How long have you known?"

"It's my task force," she says. Something tiny and very sharp pierces my skin. I flinch, but refuse to look. Berry holds my hand, wincing as I squeeze her fingers. I peer at Bryce through wet eyes.

"My grandmothers are in your task force?" I ask.

Bryce's head tilts as she laughs. "Oh lord, no. Your grandmothers are a menace." The two ladies in question grin broadly at that. "We've crossed paths before. They called for my help when you disappeared. We tracked Bacitriet's phone and they insisted on coming along."

"You couldn't have handled what we found inside, dear. Right person for the right job and all that," Berry says.

I press my palm to my eyes, both incredulous and a bit embarrassed.

"As I said, they're a menace," Bryce laughs. "But Berry is correct. My rental vehicle is not equipped for fighting giant demons. I've discovered the hard way that guns don't stop the beasts, only slow them down for a time. Sometimes not even then."

"But you know about demons? You have a task force?" I can't make sense of it. "My grandmas? I don't . . . what do you do? How does everyone in the world not know about this? The internet. Social media. I've never . . ."

"Strange events, odd circumstances, unexplained deaths. All fall under my jurisdiction," she says. "Unfortunately, that also includes dealing with local monster hunters, and, in this case, that includes your grandmothers." Her lips are pressed together in annoyance, the expression at odds with Berry's beaming smile.

"What happens now?" I ask. "Am I still in trouble for delivering Bacitriet's bag?"

Rose tsks beside me, tugging something through my skin.

"What bag?" Detective Bryce says, her expression too innocent. "We were just lucky you and your friend stumbled upon this abandoned hospital while bushwalking and overheard someone inside screaming. It's condemned, you know. Due to be demolished. That young woman is very lucky you found her. Poor thing ingested some terrible drugs and had a rather nasty reaction. You probably saved her life."

"Oh, come on," I blurt. "No one's going to believe that."

Bryce's grin becomes distinctly shark-like. "I assure you, they will. Especially when you confirm the story." I gape at her. Bryce stands up. "This is not something that can get out, Margaret. You have a decision to make. Protect yourself and your grandmothers, or tell the truth."

"But demons are real." My voice trembles.

"Are they?" She walks away, heading toward the hole in the hospital window.

Rose pats my hand. "All done, dear."

I peer down at my side. There's a clean white patch stuck to my skin. "Rose? Berry?"

Berry sniffs and pushes her glasses up her nose. She holds out a hand and tugs me to my feet. Pain robs me of breath.

More tears spring into my eyes, and I swipe them away angrily. "How can I keep this a secret?" I ask. Rose climbs out of the car and joins us to stare at the hospital. "Demons and monsters are real. People will die if they don't know what's out there. How can we not warn everyone?"

Rose wraps a soft arm around my back. "Honey, it's for the best."

"What about Sam?" I shout after the departing detective.

Bryce turns. "Who?"

"My neighbor, Sam. Is he one of your task force buddies?"

Bryce's stare falls on Rose before flicking to Berry. "No one else came out."

I stare up at the hospital walls. *Sam?*

"Come along, Margaret. Let's go home." Rose takes my arm, holding tight as if to stop me from going back inside. No fear of that. There's no way I'm going back in there. *Where did you go, Sam?*

Berry comes up on my other side. "Don't scare us like that again," she admonishes.

I nod. From now on, all I want is a quiet life.

After I find a new job.

Epilogue

"Are you still having nightmares?" Elisa asks as we walk along the river inside Angels Park. Her makeup is heavier than usual and her eyes are bloodshot and shiny.

"Aren't you?" I grimace, grasping my takeaway coffee with shaky hands. I raise it to my lips and sip the hot liquid, all of my movements occurring at half-speed. At least the coffee is normal. The barista in the Angels Park kiosk does a good cup. I ache all over. Rose's needlework is impeccable, of course, but having her stitch up my side is something I never want to experience again. It's hard to process everything that has happened. Monsters and demons exist, and my grandmothers are demon hunters.

Constant nightmares leave me screaming myself awake most nights. I delay going to bed by staying up and watching romantic comedies until exhaustion overcomes me, only to find Bethany and Bacitriet waiting for me each time I close my eyes.

I'd rather see Sam. Every time I think of him, I feel the passionate touch of his lips against mine.

I lost my job of course. Bryce's task force raided Bacitriet Consulting only to find the floors completely cleared out and the staff missing, presumed dead or demons inhabiting human form. That's not the official story, of course. I have no idea how Bryce was able to suppress the true story, but I've not seen a peep of it in the news. I haven't been to visit Mom and

Dad yet either. Mom will see how much I've changed just by looking at me and will demand to know what has happened. I don't know what to tell her.

My longing for independence resulted in learning I'm a lot more resilient than I'd ever given myself credit for. My panic over Jack firing me is laughable now; I'd held it together quite well in the midst of an impossible drama, and all without a plan.

Jack.

Yeah, I'm still processing that. Those were his shoes on the stairs at the hospital. I'm absolutely positive. I don't know what it means, but I know I have to look into it. He is connected with all of this somehow and it has me questioning how I lost my job in the first place. There is something bigger going on and I'm going to have to find out what.

Elisa, still in recovery herself, drags me out to Angels Park for a coffee every morning. After two weeks, it has become routine for us to walk along the river and talk.

"I'm reading my nonna's books," she tells me today. "There's still so much to learn about my history and abilities. I'm trying to get in contact with a cousin on my mom's side who might know more. I'm hoping she'll be able to teach me."

"You want to explore it?" I ask. "After everything that happened?"

"Are you kidding? I felt so useless, Mig. If I'd known a way to help us escape, maybe we could have gotten out sooner, and without you getting hurt. How can I not look into it? I found Bethany in one of the books, or at least the demon that took Bethany's skin. Bacitriet too. He's a hellhound, Mig, and here's the weird thing. Neither of them have magic or are known to have psychic powers. I can't see how either of them were able to scrub your house of energy. It had to have been someone else."

"Sam? Or maybe it was his horrible brother." I float the ideas. "If Sam is a demon hunter, who's to say his other brothers are not? Or—" My mind returns to the white snakeskin shoes. The name seeps out of me. "Jack." Elisa's head snaps up. We've talked about him before. On long nights, after El's kids have gone to bed, or days while they're at school. Questioning if I had really seen what I'd seen. I'd been pumped full of fear and adrenalin at the time, tired, dehydrated, and hungry. I could have hallucinated the shoes.

"He'd have to have power of some kind," Elisa says.

I'd never seen anything weird in all my time working for Jack. "I don't know. I'm sure he was there. Why was he there?" It was the endless unanswered question.

"We'll find out." El says in her assured Mom voice.

Quacking draws my gaze to the river. I watch a family of six ducks splash and swim around in circles. Breathing deeply, I inhale the scent of my coffee. In my head, I can still smell blood.

"Speaking of, how's your side?"

"Hurts like hell." My hand falls to my waist. It hurts whenever I stand. Or sit. And lying down is an exercise in pain management. "Mom and Dad have no idea I've been hurt. I've been avoiding them—told them I have the flu and don't want them to catch it. I don't know how much longer I can hold them off." A kookaburra laughs in the distance. I let out a wobbly breath.

"You're wound up today," she comments.

I sigh. "I just can't seem to settle."

We listen to the ducks and watch the slow-moving water. It's so peaceful out here. I should be able to relax, but I can't. My shoulders are a tense line of knotted muscle and my neck cracks every time I move my head. I keep flinching at shadows.

Demons exist.

"How are you doing?" I ask.

"Nothing feels normal anymore."

"I know." I keep my distance from the water's edge. We're getting close to where I found Annie's body, and a thick pressure grips my head. I rub a finger over the wrinkled skin between my eyes.

"Sam hasn't come back," I announce, and I know why, though I don't say it out loud. It's me. It must be. He hasn't come back because of me. I wanted to know everything. He'd promised to tell me everything. For all I know, he left because he'd completed his mission and, with the job done, moved straight on to the next one.

Had he used me to get close to Bacitriet and Bethany? Maybe I meant nothing to him at all.

No. I remember the look in his eyes, the touch of his hands. The kiss. It meant something. I know it did.

But I can't help thinking that he has run off. He's not the type of guy to let a human get close. It's funny. I couldn't be more scary than the monsters he fights, surely?

I sip my cooling coffee.

"Have your grandmothers said anything?"

That makes me grumble. "They're avoiding me. El, you saw them. They were dressed as soldiers. Rose carried a crossbow, for crying out loud. And she could use it!" I break off and stare out over the river. A twig bobs and weaves as it floats downstream, and I watch until it disappears from view.

Elisa laughs. The sound is strained, as if she's forcing good humor. "So."

"Monsters are real."

She shudders and wraps her jacket tighter around her chest. We are both avoiding scarves. Hardly surprising.

"At least we helped Cassandra." That's the only good news to come out of our ordeal. "She called yesterday, did I tell you? She's traveling back to her parents' place. Queensland, I think."

"That's good."

"Yeah, but . . . Elisa, she thinks she was drugged."

Her eyes widen. "What do you mean?"

"She doesn't remember a thing or, well . . . she won't admit that she does. She refuses to listen when I try to explain what really happened."

"But . . ."

"I know that's the story we have to give, but I was there. I know the truth. Why would she lie to me?"

"She's afraid." Elisa glances at her phone display. "Oh, shoot, I've got to pick up the kids. It's a half day at school. We'll talk later?"

"Definitely." I wave as Elisa sprints off toward the carpark. I wander around for a while, lost in thought. I need answers. Berry and Rose are avoiding me but I know where they live. They can't hide from me forever. I'll stake out their home if I have to.

Why did Sam leave?

I might never see him again. My chest suddenly aches as I imagine my heart breaking into pieces and falling into my stomach. It hurts. More than the wound in my side. I'm human. I must mean nothing to someone like him. An entertaining dalliance while on a mission, James Bond-style. I feel faintly nauseous, and embarrassed that I thought there was more to that kiss than just happiness at having escaped a monster's clutches.

I find myself standing next to the angel statue that looks like Sam's brother and stare out across the river. Pain radiates from my side, my chest, my heart.

I've been feeding that monstrous cat of his. I'm surprised Sam didn't take his pet with him. None of his house has been packed up either, leaving me to hope that he might one day come back. Mephistopheles let me in—at least I assume he did, blinking up at me with those giant eyes of his. I want to explore Sam's house and learn more about him. I've held off in case he returns, wanting to respect his privacy. But what if he's trapped somewhere, unable to get back home, and I am just sitting around waiting for him to appear like a heroine in a romance novel?

Where did you go?

A glint of black catches my eye through the trees. I hadn't noticed a statue down that way before.

I follow the nearly invisible path and head deeper into the darkness. Everything is so overgrown down here. The cloying smell of rotting leaf matter and damp dirt fills my nostrils as the air grows colder. Very little sunlight kisses the ground, and what does glints like diamonds as the wind shifts the heavy boughs above my head. It feels like no human has ever found their way to this corner of the park.

The black shape looms out of the shadows. I instinctively step back but it doesn't move. I shoot a look over my shoulder. I can't see the river from here. Thick silence surrounds me and I hold my breath, not wanting to disturb it.

This angel is different. Black as night, wings stretched impossibly wide, its solid stance emits a sense of immense power. Sinewy muscles strain against the stone it's cut from, as though it's trying to escape the very bonds that give it life. I'm eye level with its feet, and from this angle I can't see its face. A dirty plaque is pinned to the stone. I spend a moment rubbing the dirt away to expose the inscription.

Angel of the Dark. The Fallen One. Lord of Hell.
Samael, the First Son.

My chest tightens.

Don't look.

I creep back until I can see its face, already knowing deep down what I will find.

Familiar features stare down at me. His face, his body. Eyes that touched my soul.

Samael.

Sam.

What . . . the . . . fuck?

My neighbor is the devil.

I'm in love with the devil.

Shit.

ACKNOWLEDGEMENTS

To anyone who wants to write, it is worth it. There have been times where I have stared at a page and wondered what on earth am I doing. Yet despite my doubts and imposter syndrome I keep writing because I need to tell and share stories. You, my readers, are what keep me going. I wrote this story for several reasons. The main one was to write about the crazy older women in my life. My A-Team. Janet and Margaret. As well as my grandmothers Olive and Shirley. Such amazing women with incredible lives and stories to tell. I hope that wherever you are now I make you laugh as you made me laugh every day.

Linh, you keep me motivated, inspired and working hard. Talking to someone who is also going through their writing journey (though a different journey) helps me to realize we are not alone in our writing bubbles – no matter how isolated and lonely it may feel at times. Writing is what we do, and it is who we are. Your creativity astounds me and humbles me. Thank you for your advice and friendship.

To Cat McCredie and the #authorsforfireys 2020 auction. Thank you!

To the #Auswrites crew. You keep me inspired. You keep me motivated. You keep me writing. #readmoreaussiebooks

To the Australian Book Lovers!! Thank you for your support and for your incredible website and podcast. Veronica and Darren you are amazing. Thank you for everything that you do. Readers, if you don't know about this website – I forgive you, but get onto it immediately! www.australianbooklovers.com. Aussie authors are the best!

To Margo, Carolyn, Edmund (and, of course, Linh), for your CP & Beta-ery goodness! You all help to make my stories better. Thank you for your valuable time. Keep on keeping on. I can't wait to read more of your words soon.

To my incredible editing team: Kate, Libby, Rebecca. Thank you. I could not do any of this without you.

To my amazing cover art designer, Pat. You are incredible. Thank you, Red Tally Studios.

And a big thank you to Mark Furness and Liquorice Light Publishing for your amazing assistance with putting *Boss from Hell* together with me.

To Mum and Dad, who keep reading and bugging me to find out what happens next. *Shhhhhhh spoilers* Wait until you see what happens next. Thank you for all your support! I love you both.

James Gatherum-Goss and the team at Dymocks Knox City in Victoria, Australia. Thank you for all your support. To see my books on your shelves is a dream come true. Thank you for supporting local authors. Readers . . . get out there and support your local bookshops and booksellers! They are truly awesome people.

Gerry. I love you.

Please consider leaving a review on your favorite bookish websites.

WHITE FIRE

Everybody lies. Watch your back.

Sure, Agent Toni Delle has trust issues. Mate, her canine robot partner and Zach, her attitude-enabled shipboard Computer Intelligence Interface constantly tell her that – but as she told them, that was because of The Smuggler.

She would have refused her new mission altogether if it wasn't for the insane amount of money... Oh, who was she kidding – danger, betrayal, secrets, lies – these were all the things she loved about her job. She just didn't expect The Smuggler would be involved. If she'd known that she would have told her boss to jump out of an airlock, in space, without a suit.

So she takes the mission: find and stop a new weapon being manufactured and smuggled into the hands of criminal elements all over the galaxy. And hey, while she's at it, can she also find the missing weapons designer linked to these shipments?

The only problem is she has to rely on information provided by The Smuggler himself. And he may not be the only one capable of betrayal.

THE GOOD, THE BAD AND THE UNDECIDED

Everyone – the good, the bad and the undecided – has a story.

While Toni Delle is crisscrossing the sector, investigating a criminal empire intent on war, other members of the White Fire world are busy with their own endeavors. The businessman closing a treasonous deal that will bring conflict to the galaxy. The politician giving the biggest speech of her career in the shadow of an assassin. The smuggler who can't be trusted, desperate for redemption. The Good, the Bad and the Undecided is a collection of twelve short stories set during the thrilling events of White Fire – A Toni Delle Adventure. A cast of guns-for-hire, undercover agents, revolutionaries and rogues reveal their part in Toni's adventures. Because everyone – the good, the bad and the undecided – has a story.

THE BUTTERFLY STONE
The Stones of Power Book One

"DON'T LET THE SHADOW TOUCH YOU."

Beware! Something is after Tracey Masters, a Mage-kind teen in a mostly non-magical world—a world where people like Tracey are often feared, and oppressed. Add to this stress a crazy family life, the schizo pressures of school, friends, and bullies, and working a boring job as an assistant at her uncle's detective agency for magical types, and life isn't just hard, it's chaos! That is, until a mysterious woman walks through the door with a case about a missing necklace known as the Butterfly Stone.

The case seems to be the big break Tracey is looking for to prove herself and her abilities as Mage-kind. But she unexpectedly finds herself dangerously connected to it when the evidence takes a turn that reveals secrets from Tracey's past, and places her friends and family in mortal danger.

She also discovers that she's being hunted by a shadow that senses her magic is the key to unlocking the power it's after.

The magic within the Butterfly Stone is too powerful to be contained, but if Tracey doesn't learn how to control it, and escape the threat of the shadow that surrounds it, she could lose everything and everyone she cares about ... beginning with her younger sister, Sarah.

VIA WYVERN'S PEAK PUBLISHING

THE TIGER'S EYE
The Stones of Power Book Two

"REMEMBER THE LOST ..."

Tracey Masters is ready to train harder, dig deeper, and get more in touch with the magic that is pulsing inside of her. She has faced the threat of the shadow, and it nearly consumed her. With the help of her family and close friends, Tracey overcame the darkness and now realizes just how hard being a Mage-kind teenager really is. She won't be caught off-guard again.

Clawing at the edges of her mind—of her memories—she senses a new evil encroaching. As Tracey sets off in search of the other Stones of Power, she continues to wrestle with questions about her past. Racing to discover who she really is, Tracey must decide how far she is willing to go to protect her family and friends.

What cost—what sacrifice—is she willing to pay in order to find herself, locate the other stones, and break an ancient curse that is destroying generations of family history?

Painful betrayal, a threat that's too close to home, mind-altering visions, dangerous magic, and a new heartthrob at school all scream for Tracey's attention. But can she trust her own choices, or her memories? What is real, what is fake? Tracey must decide if she can believe in her own magic, and her friends, before everyone she loves is erased from existence.

VIA WYVERN'S PEAK PUBLISHING

THE CROW'S HEART
The Stones of Power Book Three

"I SEE HOW IT ENDS ... I WILL BE ALONE ..."

The Tiger's Eye is secure, and Timothy is trapped inside the Serpent's Kiss. The shadows of the past finally seem to be behind Tracey Masters.

Hot off the heels of victory, Tracey and her friends waste no time in pursuing a lead on the fourth Stone of Power. However, that lead, her uncle's client, takes them across land and sea, to a mansion from an older age ... the very same that the Sect of Six lived in. When they arrive, the client mysteriously cannot be reached.

Working under the guise of actors on the newest Prince Henry film, Tracey has a limited amount of time on this so-called getaway to find the fourth stone, find out what happened to Uncle Donny's client, and to save her crush's sister, all while avoiding the ire of their at-odds chaperones. No pressure!

If that wasn't worrying enough, the group of Mage-kind and Norm teens are attached by a monstrous entity on their way to England. With Timothy silently locked away in his own Stone of Power, suspicions turn inward, with clues pointing toward the very council that oversees Mage-kind.

Shadows may be in the past, but there is a devil in their midst.

VIA WYVERN'S PEAK PUBLISHING

www.ingramcontent.com/pod-product-compliance
Lightning Source LLC
Chambersburg PA
CBHW020329120726
47904CB00002B/337